Once and Forever

Ainsley knew what she was risking when she told Nathan Fairchild of her love for him. For it was not the love of a child for a parent, or of a sister for a brother, or of a friend for a friend. It was the love of a woman for a man—a man whom she would give anything to have. And deep in her heart, even as she gave voice to her desire, she knew what Nathan's response would be.

She knew he would shake his head. He would tenderly tell her that it was impossible. He would gently threaten never to see her again if she persisted in her foolish passion. She knew when he bent to kiss her, it would be on the brow.

"Just this once," she said, unable to hold back her feelings. She grasped his broad shoulders with her hands. "Since I will never speak of this again, I pray you, just once. Kiss me." And she pulled Nathan toward her.

Nathan could not deny her . . . not just this once . . . as his lips came down on hers and she rose up to meet his warmth in a moment of searing truth that nothing either of them could ever do could erase from their minds or their hearts. . . .

Harvest of Dreams

by

Jaroldeen Edwards

AN ONYX BOOK

ONYX
Published by the Penguin Group
Penguin Books USA Inc., 375 Hudson Street
New York, New York 10014, U.S.A.
Penguin Books Ltd, 27 Wrights Lane,
London W8 5TZ, England
Penguin Books Australia Ltd, Ringwood,
Victoria, Australia
Penguin Books Canada Ltd, 10 Alcorn Avenue,
Toronto, Ontario, Canada M4V 3B2
Penguin Books (N.Z.) Ltd, 182–190 Wairau Road,
Auckland 10, New Zealand

Penguin Books Ltd, Registered Offices:
Harmondsworth, Middlesex, England

First published by Onyx, an imprint of Dutton Signet,
a division of Penguin Books USA Inc.

First Printing, November, 1994
10 9 8 7 6 5 4 3 2 1

I have spread my dreams
under your feet;
Tread softly because you tread
upon my dreams.

—W. B. Yeats

Fairchild Family

Nathan Fairchild
1720–1776

Chastity Pembroke Fairchild
1722–1752

Talmadge Fairchild
1739–1821

Ainsley Windsor Fairchild
1738–1816

Nathan Windsor Fairchild
1777–1868

Tricia Brewerton Fairchild
1778–1846

The flyleaf of the Fairchild Family Bible, on display in the
center hall of the Marshfield estate in New Parrish, Connecticut.

Prelude

QUI TRANSTULIT SUSTINET.

He who transplanted still sustains.
　　　　　　　—Motto of the state of Connecticut

The storm began in the dead hours after midnight when even the restless earth ought to sleep. Carrying slivers of ice in its breath, it blasted across the western wilderness of Massachusetts Bay Colony, gathering strength, roaring through the valley of the Connecticut River, thrusting itself over the Pocumtuck Hills and onto the cleared fields and stockaded walls of the small, isolated settlement of Marshfield.

Like driven nails, the icy snow hammered into the unpeeled bark of the fort. The palisades were quickly coated with thick, wet snow, and upon this firmly sticking base each successive blast of wind laid another layer, and another and another.

Silently, relentlessly, through the night the wind dropped its heavy burden against the wall of the fort, and built a snowdrift high and deep.

As dawn approached the storm blew itself out and an uneasy stillness filled the air. Small scurries of wind randomly ruffled the surface of the deep, fresh snow, whisking it up in wispy circles and sifting it back down, as though putting final touches on the night's work.

In the first pale rays of the early sun, the mad architecture of the night was revealed. Against the northwest wall of the fort, an immense ramp of snow sloped from the field below to the top of the stakes. In its windswept, icy perfection, the snowdrift was an entrance crafted by glacial engineers.

The surrounding wilderness was cloaked in eerie silence and the fresh, deceptive innocence of white snow. The drift looked like a cruel prankster's cunning invitation into the very heart of the sleeping, unsuspecting village. Silence, silence everywhere. Silence made more silent by the dying of the wind and the night.

The village of Marshfield was the westernmost settlement of Massachusetts Bay Colony, lying isolated and exposed on the farthest reaches of the Western Reserve. Inside the village, the weary citizens of Marshfield lay sleeping, unaware of Nature's traitorous handiwork. Lulled by a false sense of security, believing the walls of their fort to be unbreachable, they slept on toward an unimaginable dawn.

PART ONE

Nathan

... lips that have smiled, eyes that have shed tears, ...
  children and the begetters of children ...
Born here of parents born here from parents the same,
  and their parents the same ...
All, all for immortality,
Love like the light silently wrapping all.
—Walt Whitman

Chapter One

As the storm had begun in the dark of night, the sound of the wind had disturbed Chastity's restless sleep. She turned heavily in the narrow bed to press closer to Nathan's back, burrowing into the warmth of his broad shoulders and listening to the reassuring comfort of his steady breathing beneath the heavy quilts.

When the icy snow lashed against the leaded glass windows of the room where she and Nathan slept, she winced. She knew a fine dusting of snow would be sifting through chinks under the doors and the house would be freezing cold when they got up in the morning.

A motherly impulse urged Chastity to get up to check on the children and make certain they were warmly covered. But the thought of getting out of the bed's sweet comfort to put her feet on the ice-cold floor made her weary body rebel. She could not force herself to move from the small cocoon of warmth next to her sleeping husband.

"The children will be fine," she reassured herself, fighting a nagging whisper of guilt. "They're likely huddled next to the chimney stones in the loft, and burrowed under their feather ticks like little hibernating hedgehogs." She smiled at the thought.

The sound of the night blizzard had caught Chastity off guard, coming so late in the season—almost April—and with two weeks of springlike weather preceding it. Everyone in Marshfield had assumed winter had played itself out, but if there was one thing living in this wild land had taught Chastity, it was that the weather kept its own counsel and answered to no man. She abhorred Nature's unpredictable ways because of her own innate sense of orderliness.

As she lay in the dark, her mind drew a mental picture of her home, drawing its comfort and security. She huddled closer to Nathan's warmth, glad he was safe and real beside her. She was so thankful he had made it home from Boxford Falls before the storm had hit.

In the darkness, her mind lovingly traced each line of her home, as familiar to her as the faces of her children. She felt like a miser secretly counting her treasure.

The massive fieldstone fireplace took up one wall of the great room. She and Nathan had chosen the rocks from the banks of the river with their own hands. The hearth was banked now and the fire had sunk to a few glowing embers, but the huge chimney passing through the upper floor into the sleeping loft would retain warmth in its stones for several hours.

In the whisper of light from the dying fire, she saw the gleam of copper and pewter on the mantel and the dark shapes of Windsor chairs, tucked closely against the long harvest table. Everything was in order: the heavy, double-thickness doors shut and bolted, windows latched, everything in its right place. Chastity sighed and shifted her position.

She found herself unable to return to sleep. Her mind was as restless and unsettled as the March wind, and the baby she carried in her seventh month had begun to kick and thump against her like a little trapped thing in a cage.

A sudden, sharp pain flashed under her ribs causing her to draw in her breath with a gasp. This confinement had been plagued with these unfamiliar symptoms—so different from when she had carried her three other children. Just this past week, she had noticed her hands and feet beginning to swell. It worried her to think about it.

Her troubled mind began to sort through the events of the day. What a strangely unsettling day it had been! She had spent most of it anxiously waiting for Nathan's return from Boxford Falls. He had left Marshfield three days earlier to ride to the town of Boxford—the nearest community to Marshfield. The journey was a distance of almost thirty miles along the Mill Trace Road.

Boxford was a more frequented and better-supplied settlement than Marshfield because it was located near a series of minor falls on the Connecticut River and was closer to established settlements. The Connecticut River rose far to the north of the Reserve, but by the time it reached Boxford it had become a river of respectable size, and continued to grow in width and depth as it flowed on toward the colony of Connecticut. Boxford Falls was a market town, where the farmers of Marshfield could sell their products and have their wheat ground into flour. It was also the place where Marshfielders could hear news of the government in Boston, and the most recent developments in the continuing struggle between the French and British.

For the past two weeks, the wilderness of the Western Reserve had been in the grip of an extraordinary warm spell. Prevailing and insistent southern winds had melted the winter's accumulated snows rapidly and spring seem determined to make an early and emphatic arrival in Marshfield.

Chastity had not trusted the fickle warmth. It was still March and her fearful instincts told her it was too soon for the earth to be exposed to warm winds and sunny skies. Something was ominous and disquieting about the unseasonable weather. Only in the heavily wooded copses, where the wide trunks of hardwood trees shaded the ground, had a crusting of snow remained.

In the first days of the thaw, the ground had become a quagmire of frozen mud, making even the short walk to the outhouse a trial. For nearly a week the Mill Trace Road to Boxford had been impassable. Marshfield had been completely isolated.

The wind had remained strong and warm, however, and the mud dried up so quickly that the road had become open again. By week's end the cleared fields outside the fort walls had lain so fresh in the sun that they had seemed begging for immediate plowing and planting.

"Only it is too soon," Chastity had fretted. "It is too soon to trust the soil to nourish seeds. What a treacherous month March is!"

The warmth had fooled even Mother Earth, for just that morning, Chastity's older son, Talmadge, had burst into the house holding a nosegay of crocus blossoms—windflowers, as the Indians called them—in his strong young hands, weeks before they should have bloomed.

"Mother! Look what I found growing in the south field!" he had exclaimed, thrusting the gift of flowers toward her with his bright, exuberant smile. His eyes were exactly the color of her own, cobalt blue, with the same thick black lashes. Sometimes when Talmadge met her look directly, Chastity had the sensation she was looking into a mirror.

Without even taking notice of the flowers in her son's hand, she had upbraided him furiously. "And what were you doing in the south field, Master Talmadge Fairchild? Your father has told you never to leave the fort without his permission. He is gone for three days and you deliberatley and wantonly disobey him. Would you be caught in deadly sin? Are you not aware of the constraints of obedience upon covenant children of this congregation? Since your father is gone, it is to me you must answer for such grievous disregard for his orders."

The flash of stubborn anger in her son's eyes had not been lost on her. So like herself! So proud and defiant! But she stifled her sympathy. Talmadge said not a word.

"I will not justify the rules to you, Master Fairchild, although you know full well it is for your very life they are made. Your father will deal with this breach when he returns from Boxford Falls. Now, fetch water from the well if you please. I must scrub the spring mud from these floors."

Later on in the day she had seen the fragile crocus blossoms thrown on the ground by the spring well, and her heart had twisted with regret. Why could she not have accepted the flowers from her son's hand? Why must she always be at odds with him? He was slipping away from her. To see this firstborn on the verge of manhood, almost like a stranger to her, and she, not wise enough to know when to treat him as a child and when to treat him as a man. Not yet twenty-nine and already the mother of a twelve-year-old son.

Through the early part of the day the southern winds had continued to be as balmy as June. Chastity had rejoiced to think Nathan would have fair weather to make his journey home from Boxford Falls. She was eager for his return. Somehow his presence kept her fear in check.

Talmadge had avoided her all day, working in the barn, readying the stall for Zadok, Nathan's gray stallion. Zadok was one of two riding horses left in Marshfield. The only other stock in the small community were four heavy-footed plow ponies, ten milkcows, an aging bull, a herd of sheep and goats which wintered inside the fort, and small flocks of domestic fowl. Much of Marshfield's livestock and its riding horses had been requisitioned by the Colonial regulars for the winter campaigns against the French and Indian raiders.

In the afternoon, Chastity had cleaned and scrubbed the wide plank floors of the great room. The fire in the wide hearth had blazed vigorously and she had opened the door to let in the fresh air. Beyond the fallow yard she had seen Talmadge moving to and fro in the barn, his strong young arms digging out the filthy straw which had accumulated in the stalls. Watching his fierce, quick motions, she'd known instinctively, that he was still hurt and angry from her scolding.

Young Thomas and little Mercy had abandoned their household duties. The confinement of the indoors had become a prison to them in the long days of winter. They and the other children were playing truant from their chores to run in the sunlight. The children turned their winter-pale faces to the rays of the sun as though their skin were thirsting for light, drinking it up and yearning for more.

Chastity listened to the sound of their sweet, thin voices carried on the wind. Mixed with the lightness of their laughter she heard the chilling rasp of winter coughs. Coughs which would never heal. Chastity recognized the sound and hated what it meant. Before summer there would be fewer children to play in the streets of Marshfield.

In sudden anxiety, she ran to the window and called more sharply than she had intended, "Thomas! Mercy! Will you leave me to work unattended? Come in at once."

The children, obedient to her command, returned to the house, seven-year-old Thomas to his spelling and Latin and five-year-old Mercy to her stitchery. The children worked quietly, not wanting to attract their mother's notice or displeasure.

In their childlike way, they were puzzled at the change which had come upon their mother over the winter. They could remember when she had laughed and played. She had not been like the other prim, dried-up mothers. With her dark curls and dimpled smile, Chastity had seemed like their dearest possession.

There always used to be a treat or a surprise in their mother's pocket, and the children could remember summer days tramping with their mother down the road to carry a lunch hamper to their father in the fields. She would swing their hands in hers, and her blue eyes had sparkled with fun.

Whenever they had a bruise, or cut, or hurt of any kind, they were used to her firm, small hands gently touching the

wounded skin, and her sweet voice murmuring until the
greatest hurt seemed soothed away.

Now there was no more laughter, or singing, or stories—
only the Holy Scriptures read in a tight, measured voice
each night, the small frown which never seemed to ease between their mother's eyes, and her quick, anxious gestures.
Watchfulness and fear had become Chastity's constant companions.

Seven-year-old Thomas could even remember exactly
when the change in his mother had begun. It had been last
autumn, when the leaves were gold and red. He had been
romping with friends in the the meeting house yard and
Neighbor Warren had been walking toward them. Thomas
remembered that he and his friends had known they were
caught red-handed. They had stood, looking guilty, trembling, waiting for Neighbor Warren's chastisement.

Suddenly a group of men had thundered down the main
street of Marshfield on horses that were lathered and heaving. The men were dressed in fringed leather jackets and
doeskin breeches. The boys had run to hide behind the fence
of the meetinghouse as the men of the village hurried from
their tasks to come talk to the visitors. Thomas's father, Nathan, had come up and saluted the man at the head of the
company.

"We cannot stay," the stranger told Nathan urgently. "We
have only come to warn you and to refresh our horses."

The horses were taken to be watered and cooled down,
while the men entered the meetinghouse. Thomas and his
friends had hoisted up one of the smallest boys, who peeked
through the window, but he reported only that the men
seemed to be listening hard to the man in leather.

Within the hour the hard-riding visitors had left, but it
seemed to Thomas, that from that day on nothing had been
the same. For one thing, the grown men of Marshfield had
left their harvesting and had begun to work immediately on
felling timbers for the fort walls. Before the first snows,
their pretty village was surrounded by a high, rough fort,
which had only one gate through which no one could pass
except by permission. Each night the gate was secured with
a heavy crossbar.

The men took turns standing in the watchtower. None of
the members of the community were allowed to live outside

the village. Families who had built homes out in the cleared fields were moved inside to live as guests in village homes. Of course, lessons and chores were the same, but the mothers seemed more silent, and the smallest infractions were met with severe scoldings.

One night Thomas had crept over to where Talmadge lay in the sleeping loft and whispered to him, "What is it? What is everyone talking about when they think we can't hear?"

Talmadge had rolled over and whispered back, "It's what the ranger told them when he came. It's the reason for the fort. You're old enough to know."

Thomas's eyes were round in the dark. "What?" he whispered with excitement.

"Quippac," Talmadge replied. "The Indians attacked Quippac, with the help of the French. They burned it to the ground."

"Where's Quippac?" Thomas asked with a shudder.

"To the north and west of us," Talmadge said. "They killed everyone except a few women and children. They took them prisoner and are taking them up to Canada. The rangers said the government may be able to ransom the women and children back."

Thomas threw his arms around Talmadge and began to shake. "I'm frightened, Tal!" he whimpered. "What should we do?"

Talmadge gave his young brother a hard squeeze. "You don't need to be afraid. You don't ever need to be afraid. You're a Fairchild. Fairchilds will not be frightened.

"Look at Father. He knows everything, all the worst, and he never feels fear. Fairchilds act. That's what he told me. When there is danger, we act." Talmadge's young voice was filled with pride and conviction.

"But what could we do," Thomas asked in a small voice . . . "if . . ." He swallowed, not wanting to say the words. " . . . if it should happen here? What could we do?"

"Fight," Talmadge said simply.

"But what if we didn't have any weapons to fight with?" Thomas was close to tears. "What then?"

"If I have no weapons I will fight them with my wits— with my fists" Talmadge whispered fiercely. "I will fight them, and I will win."

Thomas heaved a sigh and snuggled down next to his

brother. "Probably they won't come," he said softly. "Quippac is so far away, I never even heard of it before."

"Probably you're right," Talmadge said, patting his brother's shoulder awkwardly.

Just as Talmadge was falling asleep he had a vivid dream. His father, with his fair hair blowing, was standing on the top of the fort, his tall, lean body astride the entrance. He was dressed in a buckskin uniform, and the rest of the village was loading and handing him rifles as quickly as he could shoot them. In the clearings outside the fort were dead and dying Indians lying in profusion, their war paint bright on their cruel faces. He saw his father's handsome face, proud and valiant and invincible.

For Thomas the long, dark winter of confinement had begun that next day, right after he'd heard the terrible secret whispered to him in the sleeping loft.

The long winter had finally passed, though, and the unexpected early thaw seemed to bring hope. There had been no news of further disturbances. The unseasonable warmth had seemed like a comforting message that all would be well.

However, in the last weeks of the winter, along the Mill Trace Road travelers had brought disquieting rumors. At the end of February a trapper passing through Marshfield had made mention of Indian movement to the north. An itinerant trader bringing goods from Boston had brought tales of rumored French and Indian raiding parties along the northern borders. He spoke of children captured and being ransomed.

Nathan had weighed each of these accounts carefully, but had concluded that the stories were nothing but repetitions of old events. Alarms made good gossip on a long journey, Nathan had told Chastity and these ragamuffins on the fringe of society liked nothing better than to shock and startle the "good folk." Chastity was not so sure, however, that the tales should be ignored. "Something in me feels like a dark cloud is hovering," she whispered to Nathan.

"All is well," Nathan assured her. "The winter is almost over. New settlers, troops, commerce on the Mill Trace Road—all will be well. You are carrying a babe, and your protective heart is overacting.

Had it only been three days since the young British lieutenant had ridden hard into Marshfield? As Chastity had seen him, first his red coat, and then his horse's hooves thundering on the main street, she'd known that the thing she had feared all winter had finally come. She had stared at the soldier's horse. It was covered with white foam, its flanks heaving. She'd known then that she was staring at the white horse of her own personal apocalypse.

The soldier had told Nathan breathlessly, "Two settlements on the northwest border were raided last week. We don't know much more than that. Everyone killed or taken prisoner. The government dispatched our company to locate the raiding party. No trace of the attackers, only the burned-out ruins. Not a living man, woman, or child.

"Our regiment has been billeted at Boxford—that's why they sent us. We returned yesterday. All we found were tracks, abandoned canoes along the upper Connecticut, and a lot of dead and scalped bodies. The Lawton and Singleton settlements were burned out, empty."

Talmadge had stood listening to everything the soldier was saying. That his father did not send him away made the boy very proud, as though somehow in his father's eyes he had at last become a man.

Other men came walking across the yard to where Nathan and the disheveled rider were talking. It gave Talmadge a sense of manliness to be standing in the circle as they heard the sobering news.

Quietly, Nathan bent and said to Talmadge, "Would you take our guest's horse to the barn and give it feed and water? Then rejoin us in our deliberations."

"Yes sir," Talmadge said eagerly. The weary soldier dismounted and Talmadge fed and blanketed the muddied pony. Then Talmadge hastened to rejoin the men, who had moved inside the Fairchilds' house.

They sat, with grave faces, around the harvest table before the fire. Chastity and the younger children had gone to the Warrens' home to allow the men privacy.

"The matter of the moment," the young Boxford courier was saying, "is that it is a possibility that Marshfield is in some danger as you are in the outlying region of Massachusetts, close to the water courses of both the Housatonic and Connecticut River systems, and are exposed and unprotected."

"Well, my good man," growled Abijnah Warren, a short,

stout man with an intelligent and benevolent face, "why don't you tell us something that we do not already know?

"Although," Abijnah continued, turning to Nathan with raised eyebrows, "were you aware there were troops whiling away the winter in Boxford Falls? I must say that is new knowledge to me."

Nathan nodded. "To myself as well. Why is it they have chosen to reenforce Boxford Falls and have given us no assistance?"

"The river," the young officer stated. "Boxford is on the river and they have tried to cover all settlements along the rivers. The demons travel upon water in their canoes, striking swiftly and silently. They would need to approach Marshfield overland, which is likely a deterrent."

"But they can scarcely escape upstream!" Nathan commented. "They must have to go overland."

"Yes, but they seem to melt into the woods and hills," the lieutenant whispered. "It is as though they are smoke or air. One moment they strike, the next they are gone."

Young Talmadge's eyes sparked, and before he realized what he was doing he had spoken aloud. "But that is blind nonsense. They are only men, and men can be found and caught and beaten."

Talmadge expected his father to frown at his audacity, but his father turned to him with a grave look of respect. "That is so, my son," he said, as though he spoke man to man. Talmadge felt his heart almost burst with pride.

"It is the judgment of the British Colonial Command that the savages and their French instigators will not dare come farther south," the soldier continued. "Especially if they are traveling with prisoners. Their winter campaign is probably over.

"However, you should evacuate Marshfield, as you are the most exposed and least fortified of the settlements. We are ready to accommodate all of you in Boxford until safety can be restored or you decide to return to Boston."

"We appreciate your generous offer," Nathan replied, "but if we evacuate and miss our spring planting we will lose everything. Ten years of labor. All our worldly goods, as well as our home, are here. Why will not the soldiers come to Marshfield? Are we not citizens of Massachusetts Bay Colony and entitled to protection? I will ride back to Boxford

with you tomorrow to plead our cause with your commanding officers, for a contingent to come to our aid."

So, it had been decided that Nathan would ride to Boxford
Falls and arrange for military protection. He had begun the
three-day journey with the south wind still blowing hard and
warm, and the muddied narrow track of road to Boxford
dried hard as rock. The hopes of all Marshfield had ridden
with him.

For Chastity, it had been three long and anxious days of
waiting, but now he had returned—long past due—but at
least home again.

In the late afternoon, before Nathan had arrived, as Chastity had finished scrubbing the floor, Talmadge had come in
from the barn. The boy had stood by the door stamping his
feet and Thomas and Mercy, sitting near the door in the
weak sunlight, felt a sudden, cold draught as the wind blew
across the threshold.

As the children had hastened to close the second outer
door, which doubled the protection of the entryway, Chastity
observed that the wind, blowing hard, was coming from a
new direction.

Rapidly the sun had clouded over, and the brilliant blue of
the sky changed to a dark and heavy gray.

Chastity, glancing out the window, noticed mothers running to hurry their children indoors, the shawls they had
hastily thrown over their shoulders flapping violently in the
wind. Within an hour, the outside temperature had dropped
below freezing, and the house, which had seemed so light
and airy early in the day, became as chill and dark as it had
been in the winter.

"Quickly, Talmadge," Chastity had said, "you and
Thomas carry in a large pile of logs. It looks like winter
plans to have one more roar, and your father probably coming home in the face of it on the road with the soldiers. Pray
God they arrive soon or they shall have a miserable ride."

The boys built a crackling fire in the wide fireplace, and
Chastity put on the iron kettle to boil. She filled it with dried
pole beans and a small piece of salted pork. Soon the rich
fragrance of cooking filled the room.

She looked at the diminished provisions in the pantry, and
prayed this would be the last storm of the winter. The sum-

mer harvest could hardly come soon enough if the supplies
were to make it through till it came.

Night came swiftly, and with its coming the freezing wind
had died down. An ominous waiting stillness seemed to fill
the twilight. No stars were visible, only a thick, darkness,
and a cold mantle of air, muffled and heavy, penetrating the
homes of the little community with such pervasive cold that
even the roaring fires could not seem to keep it at bay.

Chastity had paced the floor, her back and legs aching for
rest. "Where is your father?" she murmured aloud. "He
should have been here before dark. What can be keeping
him? He'll catch his death."

Through lowered eyes Talmadge, pretending to read a
book, watched his mother's restless pacing. He wanted to go
to her, to see if he could help or comfort her, but, fearing her
unpredictable moods, he remained in his place, watching and
worrying.

Even though no word had ever been said to him, he knew
she was with child. He had watched the births of foals and
calves, and understood the ways of birth and death, but still
it seemed strange that his pretty, gentle mother, so small and
graceful, scarcely larger than a child herself, should suddenly be changed before his eyes.

He watched her press her hands to the small of her back
and sigh in weariness. He saw the clumsy thickening of her
waist. Was it so hard a thing then to have a child? Had she
looked so exhausted and ill when she was carrying him, her
firstborn?

He was frightened for her. He knew his father was worried too, for he had seen them together through the cracks in
the sleeping loft, after his father thought the children were
all asleep. He had watched his father pick his mother up in
his strong arms, and hold her to him in the wide Windsor
chair, and rock her and stroke her gently as though she were
no older than little Mercy.

"Oh my darling," he had heard his father say, a few nights
ago in a voice so tender he had scarcely recognized it, "I
have done it to you again. But how I love you for bearing
my children. How I have always loved you, since the first
day I saw you laughing as you stepped from your father's
coach in Boston. How I shall always love you. Forever and
always."

Talmadge knew what his father had said was true. In some

strange way which he could not yet understand, he knew that his father loved his mother more than anything else on the earth. He knew his father loved him, his son, as though he were a part of him. His father's love was as sturdy and real as the air they both breathed, but Talmadge also knew, somehow, that his father loved his mother in a different way, with a burning intensity, almost a longing, as though he could never have enough of her.

If Nathan's love for his children was the air he breathed, his love for Chastity, his wife, was his very heart. The young boy did not know how he knew these things, but he did, and, in an odd way, it gave him peace and pride.

It was long after their evening meal, prayers, and the reading of the Holy Scriptures when Nathan had finally stamped into the room. His face was scarlet with cold and his breath blew out like a cloud. The children ran to embrace him, and his clothes were icy to their touch.

"Talmadge, son, bed down Zadok. He is much the worse for this cold journey. See that he is blanketed and fed and close up the barn tight. Mind you bundle yourself before you go out. It is like the very breath of Hell out there. The wind died out about two hours ago, though I feel it is starting to stir again, but the air is iron-heavy with cold. I've never felt anything like it. We are in for a bad piece of weather."

Chastity ran to him. "You're frozen!" she exclaimed. "Come to the fire and let me give you some hot food."

Nathan stamped over to the fire and stood in front of it, holding his gloved hands to the warming flame. Steam rose from his clothes as he stood in the warmth. Chastity sent the children to bed and answered a pounding at the door. Neighbor Warren and two other men of the village hurried in.

"What news, Nathan?" they inquired anxiously.

"The Colonials informed me they were still tired from their march northward and needed another day to rest before they could remove to Marshfield. Try as I would to convince them of our need, they refused to come today. They have promised they will arrive tomorrow or the next day. Not even a small contingent of men would ride with me. They are quite cozy in the warm homes and the arms of the good wives of Boxford." There was an unaccustomed bitterness and resignation in Nathan's voice. The men rose to leave.

"You did all that could be done, Nathan," Neighbor Warren said, placing his hand on his friend's shoulder. "The weather and the stout walls of the fort will be adequate protection tonight, and the troops will arrive tomorrow. Sleep well; you have earned your night's rest."

Lifting his face from his hands and not rising from his chair, Nathan looked up at his old friend. "Did we do the right thing, Abijnah?" he asked. "Are we guilty of the sin of pride to think we could come so far into the wilderness? That we had so little need of others to move this far from their protection and social intercourse? Have we done what was right for our wives and children?"

Abijnah Warren threw back his head and laughed heartily. "Have you forgotten so soon, Nathan? Have you forgotten what it was like in Boston? The British breathing down our necks at every turn. Embargoes on trade, illicit dealings with the French and the Dutch Indies. Hypocrisy and greed masked neatly in brocaded rooms, and every man being measured by his purse and his duplicity. And the evils and temptations of the world arriving with every shipload.

"Have we done right to bring our wives and children to these rich and rolling hills? To plant crops which yield in abundance. To build homes that are spacious and pleasant. To be friends and worship God together, not just in our Sabbath works, but in our hearts as well. To stand on the edge of civilization—civilized and yet free. Of course it was right, my friend. It was right, and well worth it. You have my hand on it."

The stout man put out his muscular, work-hardened hand, and Nathan grasped it in both of his. "And mine as well, good friend."

After tucking the children snugly in the loft, Nathan and Chastity had climbed into bed. As the firelight flickered across the coverlets, he turned and took her in his arms. "Were these past few days hard for you, dear one?" he whispered.

"A little," she replied softly. "I am so short of temper with the children. I reprimanded Talmadge in great anger today. He went out of the fort against your strict order and brought home flowers. He will need to be punished tomorrow." Her voice was tired and penitent.

"Did you forget?" Nathan chided her gently. "He is now

a member of the watch. They must canvass the clearings once a day. He was probably out with his patrol."

Chastity gave a quick gasp. "How could I have forgotten!" she moaned. "He should have reminded me. But oh, he is so proud—so quick to take offense."

Nathan chuckled. "He is becoming a man," he said. "That is all. I will speak to him on the morrow and all will be well."

She could hear Nathan's voice growing faint with sleep and could only imagine the exhaustion that was overcoming him after the hard journey of the past three days. In a moment, she could tell by the feel of his relaxed muscles and his slow, deep breathing, that he had fallen fast asleep. Within minutes she too slept. She had continued to sleep until past midnight when the sound of the blizzard had wakened her.

"Nathan," she murmured, seeking comfort in the darkness, and almost instantly he was awake. He turned toward her and took her in his arms, and in the thick folds of the bed their bodies created a well of warmth.

He kissed her forehead, her cheeks, her neck, and her soft tender mouth. Each kiss was like a lick of flame, and suddenly they were together, man and wife, locked in a passion which engulfed them, erasing the pains, fears, and bitterness of the winter world outside their fragile walls.

He slowly unbuttoned her linsey-woolsey nightgown, and felt her delicate, porcelain skin beneath his fingers. How could she stay so fine and beautiful in this harsh frontier, he whispered. Did she know, he murmured that she was like a miracle to him? Always new and filling him with wonder.

As he began to make love to her, Chastity put her arms around him and smiled in the darkness. In her mind she could see herself as she had been the first time he held her in his arms. They were dancing in her father's drawing room, whirling to the sound of violins, and she was wearing a dress of saffron silk, and her dark curls were threaded with golden lilies and her mother's pearls were gleaming on her white, white bosom.

Chapter Two

Manocq and Pebosquaam stood as silent as the trees in the wooded copse at the edge of the cleared fields of Marshfield. They had been observing the village for several days now, noting the arrival of the harried messenger from Boxford and the departure of the Yellow-haired One. The Indians knew that Marshfield was being alerted, and so it was with great relief that they had observed the villager's solitary return from Boxford.

A hasty scouting party confirmed that no soldiers had followed the Yellow-haired One on his return to Marshfield.

Captain Herve de Bouville stood apart from the Indians, leaning into the shelter of an ancient oak tree. He was the commander of the massive raiding party which had left Montreal in early winter. Through the long months his war party had foraged, trekked, camped, and canoed over more than three hundred miles of terrain, finally reaching the Connecticut River system and following it to the very heart of the Western Reserve colonies.

Like his superiors back in France, de Bouville was determined to continue the harassment of all the colonies of New England, to destroy, demoralize, and terrorize the stubborn Protestants who, at first, had only clung to the coastline of the continent, but who were now moving ever farther westward toward the Mississippi.

The French were fanatic in their belief that this continent was meant to be theirs from sea to sea and from north to south, and they were determined to succeed in driving the British from its shore as surely as they would someday drive l'Anglais from the shores of the mainland of Europe.

As de Bouville stood in the shadows, waiting for first light, he fought off the penetrating cold by meditating deeply on his mission. He reflected on the motley band he had led through the long winter. He had begun the hard campaign with one hundred of his own French troops, and a mixed party of one hundred and forty Abenakis and Christianized Indians of Caughnawaga. In facing the savage hardships of winter, the Indians had fared better than his own troops, and now, from desertion and death, he was down to fifty French regulars and sixty Indians.

A trusted contingent of French soldiers and Indians had departed with the wretched band of prisoners from the successful raids on Lawton and Singleton. They were force-marching their prisoners back to Canada. In this bitter cold weather, few would survive.

Herve hated these stubborn New Englanders with a deep, insular hatred that knew no remorse. He had watched without emotion as the men under his command killed, maimed, and tortured the colonists in their defenseless settlements. Herve considered such death and suffering to be, quite simply, the price of war.

The stupidity of these heretics! Their pride and persistence inspired in him nothing but anger, hatred, and more desire to destroy. War was war, with no place for sympathy or weakness. The English were the enemy, whether in this new land or in the old lands on the other side of the ocean; and, as such, they deserved nothing but the death which awaited them.

The English and their colonials, Herve noted contemptuously, recognized no other people as their equals. This was why the fools made such terrible mistakes in their colonization methods. It was also why the Indians, who at first had greeted the English as friends, had grown to hate the arrogant New Englanders who treated them like ignorant animals rather than as equals and men.

The French, Herve was proud to note, were much more pragmatic in their colonizing. Realizing that the Indians were the aboriginal inhabitants of these lands, they had sought to win them to the French side. They had intermingled with the Indians, played and dallied with their women and even married them; traded and hunted with their men. The priests freely lived among the Indians, teaching them French and converting them to Catholicism, the one true faith.

In the locked battle for this rich frontier the French had found their Indian allies invaluable. The tribal warriors were perfectly suited and trained for the kind of warfare that was

necessary in the wilderness. No prolonged classic battles, no
planned campaigns, only slash, burn, and destroy and then
vanish before reprisals could be mounted. Herve had learned
these methods well.

If only we had not foolishly alienated the Five Nations of
the Iroquois, France would have this land in a stranglehold,
he thought grimly. But it has only slowed the inevitable. He
knew of the plans to fortify the Mississippi, further harass
the frontier. Once they bought the Dutch allegiance in Albany with trade, the land would be theirs in the end.

He felt the lust for battle rising in him. At dawn his force
would attack, even though he knew that he would lose many
men in trying to breach the strong walls of the fortified
town.

Two of his Indian scouts were murmuring to one another,
their voices filled with excitement. Herve moved from behind his tree and joined them in the night shadows.

"Quiet!" he hissed. "you will rouse the watch."

Silently, Manocq raised his hand and pointed toward the
fort. In the graying light of dawn Herve saw, with incredu-
lous wonder, that a ramp of packed snow had created a natural bridge to the top of the fort. The barricade was
breached. It was a miracle! It confirmed, as Herve had always known, that God intended the French and the Holy
Catholic Church to prevail in this new land. Here, before his
very eyes, God had created a stairway to Marshfield. Surely
it was a sign!

For the last several days, as the springlike thaw had continued, Herve had been deliberating over whether to attack,
or to retreat back to Canada, before his raiding party was detected. His numbers were only half of his original force, and
he knew from hard experience that to breach a fort wall
would cost the lives of many good warriors.

However, Marshfield was the largest and most successful
of the western Bay Colony settlements, and if they could
succeed in destroying it, fear would certainly lessen the enthusiasm of any other of the hated colonists who wanted to
settle the Western Reserve. With the French embargo and
privateers bottling up the port of Boston, and the area westward becoming too dangerous for settlement, Massachusetts
would choke to death like a fruit unnourished on the vine.

De Bouville had made the decision to attack, but, as he
had gathered his scattered troops into ambush position, the

storm began. He had thought the blizzard to be a terrible stroke of ill luck.

Now, as he saw the storm's handiwork he knew the storm had been a blessing. This snowdrift! What he had thought of as ill fortune, had become the greatest strategic advantage imaginable. The village was his to take.

He realized the cold weather had also caused the colonists to relax their guard. Scanning the upper ramparts of the fort wall with his spyglass, de Bouville could see no watchmen.

He and his men would be over the walls of Marshfield before the sleeping town even knew it was morning.

With a wave of his arm, Herve silently signaled "Advance," and his travel-hardened, battle-forged warriors moved like flying shadows across the snow-covered fields, running up and over the wall of the fort without a single impediment on the ramp of snow.

Chapter Three

The first rifle shot wakened Nathan and he leaped from his bed. He slipped leather moccasins on his feet and pulled a heavy wool jersey over his head, grabbed his rifle and long knife and sprang to the window. Chastity woke and she, too, could hear the sounds of shots and faint screams. Her blood ran cold. She sprang from the bed, calling to the children.

"Stay where you are! Get to the back wall, away from the windows! Stay low!" She did not recognize her own voice. It was screaming and crying at the same time. "Nathan! Nathan! What shall we do? Where was the alarm?"

"God knows," Nathan groaned. "I should have checked the night watch. They must have slept on duty."

He was standing by the window trying to see what was happening. At the outer rim of the settlement he saw a curl of smoke rising. "I must go, Chastity. Stay in the house and protect the children as best you can."

"No, Nathan, you must stay with us. What will we do!" She was wild with fear and tears were streaming down her face.

"Go to the loft," Nathan ordered sharply. "Pull the ladder up after you. Here, take the rifle and shot. If necessary, defend yourselves. Talmadge knows how. I will return as soon as I can."

Without another word, Nathan grabbed his pistol from the shelf above the door, let himself out, and ran crouching behind the fence toward the Warrens' home.

Nathan was sufficiently schooled in the tactics of French-Indian raids to know that although the Indians had been given rifles by the French, most of them preferred hand-to-hand combat. Speed, fierceness, and their tomahawks were their best weapons, far more useful than the slow, muzzle-loading long rifles. Fear and surprise were also part of the Indians' calculated advantage.

Springing from his cover behind the fence to the side of the Warrens' house, Nathan flattened himself against a wall and peered down the main street that led to the gates of the fort. He felt a jolt of surprise to see the gate still barred. "How did the fiends get in?" he wondered in angry dismay.

The farthest perimeter of the settlement's houses was now engulfed in flames, and he could see warriors running, arms upraised with tomahawks and knives, moving like dark silhouettes against the rim of fire.

He saw men, women, and children, running from the burning houses, being cut down by rifle shot from formations of French soldiers. Dead and wounded bodies were slumped in the snow. A small platoon of French regulars in tattered blue coats, holding their bayonetted rifles before them, swept into the Otises' yard and climbed the smoke house roof. From this elevated vantage point they began a volley of shots, which rained down like hail on the street below. Without even taking aim they made the street an alley of death. The cries of the wounded and dying assailed Nathan's ears.

The din was horrific, with the sounds of rifle fire, the screams of victims, the hideous blood cries of Indian fighters, and the roar of fires devouring homes and barns.

In spite of the rain of bullets, Nathan darted into the street and crossed over to the Otis home. He saw a war-painted Indian with an armload of hay and a torch moving stealthily along the side of the house, tamping hay along the foundation. With knife drawn, Nathan leaped onto the warrior's back and thrust the point, with all his force, under the man's left shoulder blade.

Blood covered Nathan's hand and the warrior's death scream ended in a hideous rattle. Instinctively, Nathan dropped into a low crouch, and, hearing a blood-thirsty cry behind him, whirled with his knife outstretched, not even seeing his target. Nathan had a hunter's natural instinct and his knife slashed into the arm of the unseen attacker who was lunging at his head with a tomahawk. The weapon fell from the brave's useless hand, but he leaped at Nathan with an enraged snarl. Again, Nathan's instincts saved him. Reflexively, he held out his hand to ward off the attack and the

Indian impaled himself on the blade of the outstretched knife.

Dropping the body to the ground, Nathan snatched up the fallen tomahawk and ran toward the backyard of the Otises' home. He could hear sounds of shots and screams within the house. Behind him, down the main street, came the garbled noises of the battle.

As he rounded the rear corner of the house, he saw the Otises' back door thrown open and a huge Indian streaked with war paint, with wild, black hair streaming down his back, dragged Faith Otis into the yard. The warrior was holding Faith's wrists in one hand, her long hair twisted around his fingers and arm, while his other hand was slashing away the bodice of her dress with his knife. Her breasts were exposed, and her face was a mask of terror.

"My children!" she was screaming. "Don't hurt my children!" Her plea was full of a mother's agony and Nathan thought no mortal man, of any color or creed, could remain unmoved, but her attacker continued his furious slashing and her bodice fell from her bosom. Her shoulders and breast were scarlet with blood.

Nathan ran to her rescue with a shout of such horror and anger that he sounded like a madman even to himself. Before he could reach Faith the massive warrior plunged his knife into the woman's heart and then turned to Nathan. Raising his huge bronzed arms like columns of destruction, the blood-streaked Indian hurled himself at the madman who was running toward him.

Nathan saw deathlust in the Indian's eyes, and Nathan was overcome with such feelings of vengeance and hatred that he felt himself to be no longer a man, but rather some primeval beast with no other emotion but the desire to kill. With strength which knew no bounds of fury, Nathan threw the tomahawk in his hand straight at the hated face of the enemy.

The sharpened ax smashed into the Indian's face and the force of Nathan's throw imbedded the blade in the man's head up to its haft. The face of the battle-maddened brave was literally split in two, but the forward impetus of the warrior's attack, even in death, continued its onward lunge and he crashed into Nathan. Nathan was conscious of a sickening stench of blood, sweat, musk, and dead campfires as he fell under the weight of the dying Indian.

Shuddering, Nathan struggled to throw off the heavy body. For several dreadful moments he was locked in the dead man's bloody embrace, but he managed to work himself free.

Nathan hurried to where Faith lay. He saw immediately that he was too late. The Indian's knife was buried in the young woman's chest and she lay naked to the waist, full, tender breasts white against the snow, her blood flowing like a crimson ribbon across them.

Nathan felt bile rising in his throat, and he bent gently to arrange her nightgown to cover her. He knew if the battle was lost, and there was time enough, the Indians would cut the breasts from the bodies of the women. They did this as the ultimate act of humiliation and degradation for the interloping white women. It was not a sexual act—it was an act of contempt and calculated cruelty.

"Mother! Mother!" Nathan looked up and saw the oldest Otis's nine-year-old boy, running out the door. He was chased closely by an Indian whose face was obliterated by grotesque war paint. The boy spied his mother lying in the snow, but before he could get to her, the Abenaki grabbed the child and twisted his arm viciously. Without a trace of fear the boy ignored the pain and fought the warrior, beating at him with his free arm and kicking with the fury of a wildcat.

Reaching into his belt, Nathan snatched his pistol. He had only one shot, and he hesitated a moment, fearing he might hit the boy but suddenly the boy wrestled free from the Indian's grip, and in that instant Nathan aimed and fired. The Abenaki fell in the doorway.

Behind the fallen brave Nathan could see a cloud of smoke filling the Otis house. He was too late. The attackers had set fire to the house from the other side.

The boy ran to his mother's side and pulled the skirt away from her face before Nathan could stop him. As though paralyzed, the child stood gazing in horror at the desecration of his beloved mother.

"Quickly, Ezra," Nathan said, grasping the boy's arm. "Come with me. We must seek shelter."

Unmoving and uncomprehending, the boy continued to stare at his mother's corpse, then suddenly turned aside and vomited. Nathan grabbed the lad's arm, and with Ezra still retching, pulled him across the back of the lot. The boy moved like a mindless scarecrow, and Nathan whispered harshly, "Forget what you saw. You must act as a man!"

Nodding numbly the boy tried to respond, but his feet stumbled as he ran. The two of them crouched behind the icehouse for a moment, and Nathan whispered, "I must cross the street to return to my house. We will make a stand there. Do you understand?"

The boy's eyes were blank with shock. Nathan shook Ezra roughly. "The street is under crossfire; you must run very fast, and low. Do you hear me, Ezra? Fast and low." Nathan took a deep breath as a rattle of shot hit the stones of the ice house beside them.

"Now!" Nathan ordered. "While they reload." He yanked the boy's hand and dragged him into the street. "Faster, Ezra!" he shouted. "Faster!" Another volley of shot scattered around them and Nathan felt something tear at his shoulder, and a feeling like a hot branding iron.

"Faster!" he shouted. The boy seemed to be lagging even more—he was almost a dead weight—so Nathan turned and threw the child over his shoulder and dived behind the hedgerow by the Warrens' yard. "Quickly, Ezra," he hissed. "They are coming this way." The boy said nothing and Nathan lifted him down from his shoulder. Blood was pouring from Ezra's mouth. Nathan turned the lad over and saw where the bullet had entered at the base of the skull.

Shaking his head in pity and anger, Nathan laid the boy gently on the grass and surveyed the Warrens' yard. Indians were gathering, surrounding the barn, rousting out the livestock and preparing to set fire to the outbuildings. Other raiders were bringing stacks of hay to pack around the edges of the house.

Someone in an upper window was firing a rifle and had hit three of the Indians, two of whom looked dead; the other was holding his abdomen and groaning. Five French soldiers were kneeling at the perimeter of the yard methodically loading and shooting at the upper windows.

Two families had been living in the Warren house throughout the long, enclosed winter. Mrs. Warren's sister and her husband had built a small settlement house outside Marshfield on one of the cleared lots, but when the fort was built they had moved into the redoubt, along with all the other outlying families.

The Warrens had kindly taken their relatives in, and, with

children, servants, and spouses, there had been fifteen people living within the walls of the home. Fortunately, the Warrens' home was one of the larger ones in Marshfield, but nonetheless it had been cramped and difficult living, and only the sweet graciousness of the two families had made the situation endurable. Nathan shuddered to think what would happen when the home was in flames; the helpless inhabitants would be forced to run out into the yard where only death awaited.

Torn between his desire to help his neighbors and his awareness of the impossible odds, Nathan recognized his own vulnerability if discovered in the open.

He was without a weapon—his pistol being unloaded and the tomahawk lost. All he had left was his hunting knife. He was desperate to be reunited with his own family before the attacking forces reached his home, but Nathan remained for a moment in indecision, hidden in the bushes, praying to know the right thing to do.

Just then the front door of the Warrens' home slammed open, its cast-iron studs clanging against the side of the house, and Abijnah Warren roared out of the door with a pistol in each hand.

"You blood-drenched fiends of the Devil" he shouted. "How dare you come and lay to waste the places of the Lord!" He charged at the nearest Indian, who was holding a torch to the mounded hay, and shot him.

Then Abijnah turned to the Indian crouching beside the dead warrior and shot him in the eye. There was a sudden blur of bodies. French riflemen came on the run with their bayonets flashing and Nathan saw them lunge and lunge again. He also saw the lift and stroke of flashing tomahawks of a dozen warriors.

The door to the Warrens' home was pulled closed from the inside by unseen hands. Perhaps those within would be able to hold out, if the fire did not start. Nathan prayed they could.

A brave also saw the door closing and with a fearsome shriek rushed to prevent it. French and Indians gathered around the door, beating on it with tomahawks and rifle butts, but a series of shots from the upper windows felled two of the attackers and they moved back, seeking cover.

On the front lawn, alone, lay what was left of Nathan's old friend. In horror, Nathan realized Abijnah was not dead.

His scalp was torn from his head, his dark waistcoat was gashed and bloody, the fingers were missing from one hand, and his legs were broken by blows of rifle butts. Abijnah was blinded by blood running from his open skull, and the bleeding stump of his fingerless hand was raised to a heaven he could not see.

"For God's sake," Abijnah shouted to his unseen enemy, "what manner of men be you? Why will you not strike a final blow, for God's sake! Have mercy and fight me to the last!"

Nathan could bear no more. He could do nothing for Abijnah and his one thought now was to get to his wife and children. Praying he was not too late, he snaked along under the hedgerow. The attackers, intent on the steady rifle fire from the Warrens' home, did not see Nathan as he broke cover, using his house as a shield, and ran to the back door.

A Frenchman next to the Warrens' burning barn saw Nathan as he reached his door and shot at him. The distance was too great for accuracy. Nathan pounded on the door and shouted for his son. A tall French officer called an order to the Indians, and four of the braves began sprinting across the snow-covered rubble of the back gardens toward Nathan's house. They were screaming a high-pitched war cry. Beating on the door, Nathan called to Talmadge, "Open the door, son! Open the door!"

Just as the Indians leaped the hedge and came racing along the orchard path toward the wash yard, Nathan heard the heavy bolt slide free and he sprang inside the room, thrusting his weight against the door to close it. He and Talmadge shoved the heavy bar into place.

Seconds later they heard the crash of bodies against the door, and they blessed the foresight which had made the door thick, set in hardwood jams with heavy iron bolts and plates, and the solid weight of the full slide bar to reinforce it.

"Is the front door double-barred and bolted?" Nathan asked. "Yes sir," Talmadge answered. "What is happening? Are we winning?"

Nathan took a deep breath. "No, son," he answered. "We alone must look to save your mother and the children." Talmadge did not flinch, his eyes on his father were clear and brave. "What shall I do, sir?"

Nathan looked at his son, and his heart filled with love.

He put his hands on the boy's shoulders and looked deeply into his steady blue gaze. "Whatever happens in this next hour, Talmadge, always remember one thing. You are the finest son a man could hope to have. You have been noble, obedient, and strong, and every moment of your life has been precious to me." Drawing a deep breath, he continued, "Whatever happens, know that I will always love you."

Talmadge felt he had somehow grown taller. His father had lifted him into manhood with those words. Willing his voice to remain steady, he returned his father's gaze. "I love you too, Father. And I will never fail you."

"That's my lad," Nathan whispered. "Now, let us get to the loft. How much water is there in the house?"

"The barrels are filled. I did it last night before bed," Talmadge answered.

"Good," Nathan said. "Get buckets and douse everything with water." Chastity and the children came down the ladder and the family ran to and fro pouring water on the floor, curtains, doors, and window ledges. Talmadge carried buckets upstairs and drenched the feather ticks and blankets as well as the loft floor.

Outside the house the din of the battle had grown closer. The children could hear the screams and screeching war chants of the Indians. A clatter of bullets hit the side of the house and a window shattered as a burst of shot whined above their heads.

"Quickly!" Nathan ordered. "To the loft."

Chastity had said nothing. Her eyes were blank and she moved like a puppet. When the family was safely in the loft, Nathan pulled up the ladder and went to the small window by the chimney to look down the street.

There was a pitched battle being fought in front of the Warrens' home. The few colonists offering resistance were bloody and unarmed. Men were throwing themselves at the Indians in hand-to-hand combat. Bodies were strewn and the snow was red with blood.

Near the Otis home Nathan saw a frightened cluster of women and children in their nightclothes. They were roped together, their hands bound; a circle of French soldiers and Indians stood guard. How pathetically few the prisoners seemed. In such a few, short minutes were these the only ones left alive from this large, thriving settlement? It seemed impossible to Nathan, and yet the town had been caught

sleeping, lulled into false security by the supposed safety of
their stout fort walls.

Why had the fort walls failed to protect them? Nathan
wondered. How had those walls been so easily breached? He
could not think of an answer, and yet there had been no
alarm to mount any defense. These settlers were brave men,
hardened by years in the wilderness, and given even a few
moments of warning they would have met the enemy with
orderly and stiff resistance, but, caught, sleeping in their
homes, worried for the safety of their wives and children,
they had been completely vulnerable to the swift, merciless
attack.

The entrance to the fort was still closed and yet enemies
roamed the streets in full force. Nathan's mind tore at the
puzzle. He could scarcely believe the evidence of ruin everywhere before his eyes.

Chastity came to stand beside him, her beautiful face
whiter than the snow. "What will they do to our children?"
she asked in a voice as harsh as though she had already seen
her own death.

"It's all right, Chastity," Nathan said, shielding her from
the view. "The Colonial soldiers will be here soon. Until
then, we will be safe in the loft. Go to the back corner, away
from the window, with the two little ones, and let Talmadge
and me hold back the assault."

Chastity turned silently and did as she was told. She and
the children huddled in the dark corner of the loft, while Nathan gave Talmadge orders on how to load the pistol and rifle alternately. Nathan then broke the glass of the loft
window and began shooting at the soldiers and Indians below. His aim was not very accurate because of the range and
angle of shot, but time and again he watched as an enemy
warrior fell. He knew his bullets were beginning to take a
toll.

"The French and Indians may think they have won," Nathan whispered to Talmadge as the boy labored over the rifle
bore, thrusting the shot and wadding into the front and
tamping it deep. "But this has not been a cheap battle for
them. We have made them pay a heavy price."

"And we shall make them pay to the last farthing, shan't
we, Father?" Talmadge said vehemently, handing his father
the loaded rifle in exchange for the pistol.

Nathan looked down at the horde of French soldiers and

Indians converging on their front door, and he smiled bitterly. "So we shall my son, so we shall."

He shot at random on the massed bodies below, but there was no mistaking the sound of splintering wood as the house trembled under the blows and, with a sudden crash, the door flew open.

Nathan and Talmadge ran to the opening in the loft and began to shoot down on the intruders as they poured into the room. The Indians came to the opening to the loft and tried to leap up to pull themselves through. Talmadge loaded swiftly, and shot after shot kept the raiders from getting a handhold.

The family heard the scrape of heavy furniture and realized the French soldiers were building a platform of tables and chairs to give them access to the loft. Nathan knelt on one knee to get a better angle to shoot at the Frenchmen who were beyond his line of vision. As he knelt, a bullet from a hidden rifle below smashed through the opening and struck Nathan in the temple, tearing a long gash across his head.

Nathan fell like a stone statue, without a sound.

Chastity gave a strangled cry, and sprang to her feet as though she had just come alive. "Bring him to the corner, children," she ordered.

Talmadge grabbed his father's shoulders, and Chastity and the other children grabbed his feet and dragged Nathan's unmoving body to the far, dark corner of the loft. Quickly, Chastity pulled up the damp mattress tick and they shoved Nathan's body underneath, then heaped all the bedding over him. When they were finished it looked like a misshapen mess of wet, ruined bed linens thrown in the corner.

"You shoot now, Talmadge," Chastity said, "and I will load." She gathered the younger children behind her, and they all moved to the opposite corner of the loft far from the heap of bedclothes under which Nathan was hidden.

Chastity and Talmadge stood side by side. She loaded the gun while he shot, without seeing what he was shooting at, through the square opening in the floor. They continued to hear the scrape of furniture being dragged, and they could smell acrid smoke, but they did not know if it was their own house burning, or if it was drifting smoke from the burning village. Suddenly there was an ominous quiet below, and Chastity placed her hand on Talmadge's arm to signal him to stop shooting.

The boy trained his rifle on the opening of the loft and
they both stood back toward the wall, with the children behind them, waiting, their eyes fastened on the opening. With
a sudden scream and a prolonged high wail, the final attack
began.

Two hands with streaks of blood and white and blue paint
on them grasped the edges of the loft entrance, and muscled
arms propelled a hideous apparition of glaring eyes, a white
and blue painted face, a mane of black hair, and battle-
contorted features into the loft. Without flinching, Talmadge
shot the invader, and the warrior fell backward upon the wet
mattresses, with blood pouring from his shattered chest.

Chastity handed Talmadge the loaded pistol and they
waited again, but this time it was only moments. While
Chastity wrestled with the rifle-loading rod, Talmadge fired
the pistol, but the shot went wild, and the second Indian was
in the loft, followed immediately by a third and a fourth.
Talmadge threw himself at the nearest Indian and tried to
wrestle him to the ground, but the warrior was strong as
iron, and he grabbed the boy in an unbreakable hold.
Talmadge's ferocious resistance was meaningless.

Chastity pleaded in French, "Do not hurt my children."

An Indian threw her roughly aside and pulled Thomas and
Mercy from behind her skirts. Thomas, large for his age and
fearless as a bear, sank his teeth deep into the arm of the Indian who had seized him. In a single stroke, the Indian
brought his tomahawk down and smashed the child's skull.
Thomas died instantly.

Chastity gasped, and her face went gray with shock.
Mercy began to scream in hysteria, and Talmadge struggled
against his captor like a bear, but the Indian nodded to another warrior and the Abenaki struck Talmadge with his war
club. The boy lost consciousness.

Swiftly the Indians tied Chastity's and Talmadge's hands
and lifted them down through the loft openings. Next they
picked up the screaming Mercy and carried her down with
them. Chastity felt her whole world had become an unbear-
able nightmare. She was consumed with horror and grief.
Her son and her husband dead and her other son and daughter in the hands of captors of such cruel nature that she almost wished them dead. She stumbled through the shambles
of her home, noting with bitter satisfaction the piles of hay
in the corners which the fiends had attempted to light on

fire, but whose dampness had prevented the flames from catching hold.

"Vengeance is mine saith the Lord," she whispered fiercely, feeling a furious and unwomanly hatred, wanting desperately to destroy these men who had done such savage and hideous things to her family and friends. She shook with the desire to avenge herself. "Yea, though I walk through the valley of the shadow of death," she spoke aloud, as she stumbled down the front walk of her home, stepping over the bleeding bodies of enemies and neighbors.

Passing the Warren home she saw the scalped body of Abinjah where he had finally died, after pulling himself across the crimsoned snow from his front door to his gate.

"I shall be a scourge unto thine enemies, oh Lord!" she shouted as she approached the huddled mass of prisoners standing shivering in the morning light. "Lift up thine eyes, be not afraid. The Lord thy God will take thee by the right hand." Tears were running down her cheeks and she could not even feel the bitter cold or the snow that filled her shoes and chilled her stockingless feet.

Esther Hanford reached out her rope-bound hands and touched Chastity's shoulder. "Come stand by me, dear friend," she whispered. Chastity looked at her with uncomprehending eyes. The Indians dumped Talmadge, bound with rope, still unconscious, into the circle of prisoners.

There was sporadic fighting near the meetinghouse, and as the Indian who was carrying Mercy walked into the street, a shot was fired. The Indian fell in the snow, the bullet passing through his side, and into Mercy's back, finally exiting through her abdomen.

The little girl lay in the snow crying, and another Indian came up from behind and threw the beautiful child over his shoulder like a sack. Chastity could see the blood on Mercy's little nightdress and her golden hair blowing in the early morning wind.

Chapter Four

A French soldier came racing up the street toward the meetinghouse, panting for breath. Herve de Bouville watched him come closer from his vantage point near the churchyard. The commander was moving quickly through the burning settlement with a select cadre of soldiers and scouts, assessing the damage and looting for food and supplies for the return march to Canada. The running soldier spotted de Bouville, and shouted a warning. "Colonial soldiers! A short march down the road. They are headed this way."

With a savage gesture, de Bouville summoned his aide and a bugle call sounded retreat. The Indians and soldiers, snatching what supplies they could, began running toward the still-closed gates. The heavy bars were lifted and the attackers opened the entrance for the first time.

The Indians surrounded their captives and marched them at full run down the main street toward the open gate. Small children who fell behind, and mothers who slowed to help them, were tomahawked without mercy. No delay was allowed, and before the prisoners had reached the gate, ten women and children had been killed.

Talmadge was carried by two women whose children had been murdered in the early fighting. Years of frontier labor had given the women strength, and they carried the boy between them as they moved swiftly with the other captives.

The jolting motion brought Talmadge to consciousness and he glanced around him for a moment, getting his bearings, then placed his feet on the ground and helped support his own weight. With relief the women realized he was going to be able to keep up on his own, because their arms were beginning to tire and they had feared they would need to drop him and leave him to the fate of the others.

In a motley jumble of prisoners, Indians, and French, the

column swept out of the fort's entrance and across the snow-covered fields, hurrying toward the cover of the rolling hills. Some of the Indians mounted ponies, as did many of the French officers. The raiders were riding herd on the fleeing band, like sheep dogs corralling an errant flock.

Chastity saw little Mercy, flung like a lifeless doll over the ragged brown pony of one of the braves. The child was alive, for her mother could see her hands and feet flailing against the animal. The brave picked Mercy up so she was sitting in front of him. Chastity saw tears on the little face, and a last glimpse of the bloody white nightgown.

At that moment a pain streaked through Chastity, from her heart to her bowels. The pain tore her apart, and she fell in the field as she ran. The other prisoners swept on past her, while she lay in the snow engulfed in agony. Without even pausing in his swift, silent run, the next Indian who passed clubbed her with his tomahawk and sped on.

Chastity scarcely felt the deadly blow, so great was the pain within her, and slowly a merciful blackness blotted out the smells of the burning village, the vicious cold of the snow, and the horror of all she had lost.

Talmadge saw his mother fall. He wrenched his arm free from the Indian brave who was running beside him and wheeled toward her crumpled body lying behind the fleeing column. Before he could take another step, two warriors grabbed his wrists and shoulders and forced him to rejoin the fleeing party. He fought against them, but they paid no more attention to him than if he had been a small, annoying dog.

He continued to wrestle to free himself, until one of the Indians struck him a heavy blow on the side of his head, and his ears rang and he almost lost consciousness. By the time he was fully revived he found himself running between the two braves, his feet barely touching the ground, his arms held in their hands like two strong vises.

His heart was sick at the memory of his mother lying in the blowing snow, but by now the war party was well beyond the cleared fields and rushing toward the outlying Pocumtuck Hills.

Seeing that Talmadge had become alert, the Indians released his arms with a grunt and moved on through the crush of the prisoners.

The hostages from Marshfield were being herded like cattle, with the Indians on foot working in and out among the frightened, confused, and disoriented captives, and the mounted soldiers and braves riding the perimeter of the group. A brutal pace was being maintained.

Talmadge stumbled through the frozen stubble of the lowlands. Fortunately, his father had insisted that he pull on his boots before the fighting had begun, and so he was not barefooted as many of the captives were. His heavy homespun nightshirt and the thick woolen undergarment which his mother had insisted that all of her children wear during the cold months of the year, gave him adequate protection from the biting cold of the wind. He saw many of the women, clad only in white linen nightgowns, literally turning blue in the freezing air. Time after time he watched women and children fall to the ground, their limbs unable to respond to their will, shivering, exhausted, and too cold to maintain the fierce and relentless pace of their captors.

Mrs. Lamb, a plump, middle-aged neighbor who had often brought homemade bread and peach preserves to the Fairchild home, was running beside the Bramwell twins. Talmadge could see them out of the corner of his eye in the knot of prisoners on his left. The twins were six years old, and they were running together, holding hands as they had done since the day they were born. The little boys were wearing nightclothes and thin bed slippers. Matthew, the sturdy one, who had always protected and looked after his smaller, frailer brother, was having difficulty running. Talmadge could see blood-stained footprints where Matthew ran, and he knew the boy must have hurt his foot. Luke, the delicate twin, was clinging to his brother's hand, and his face was stark with fear. Tears were running down his face and yet he ran along with his limping brother.

Good Dame Lamb, who had grasped a woolen shawl as the Indians had dragged her from her bed, had taken the shawl from her own shoulders and had placed it around the twins. Her act of generosity had left her defenseless against the icy temperature and bitter wind. Talmadge could see that she was having great difficulty keeping up the pace. Her feet were dragging and her face was the color of white marble. Her mouth opened in a grimace, gasping for air. Still, she watched over the twins, encouraging them on, patting their shoulders, and panting words of comfort.

Horrified, Talmadge watched as Mrs. Lamb, a woman

who had been kind to others—who had never done anything but serve and love her fellowman—clutched at her chest, dropping to the ground. Her collapse was so sudden Talmadge did not even have time to cry out.

An Indian warrior rode swiftly toward the fallen prisoner and prodded her with the sharp end of his lance. Blood flowed from her back, but the exhausted woman could not rise to rejoin the moving column. Without hesitation the mounted brave drove his lance through Mrs. Lamb's heart, and then slung her body over the pommel of the horse until he passed a heavily wooded copse.

Talmadge watched as Mrs. Lamb's body was unceremoniously flung into the thickness of the undergrowth so it would not mark the trail of the retreating raiders. Without pause, the retreat swept on.

After that the hours seemed to melt into one another. Everything had become a blur to Talmadge, but he kept one thought and that was that Mercy was still alive. He was the only one left to protect her. He must do everything possible to remain alive.

The day had become a nightmare. A strange and unending nightmare. Occasionally there would be a piercing cry as yet another woman or child collapsed and the Indians dispassionately killed the one who had fallen, and disposed of the body in the thick woods.

The prisoners had become almost numb to the thought of death, oblivious to the cold and to their lacerated feet. Shock had robbed their minds and emotions of the ability to absorb any more. Almost by reflex the survivors marched to the brutal pace, scarcely noting the passage of time, until the whole of their individual world was the sight of their own feet making one step after another in the endless snowy wastes of the unknown wilderness. Hope, mercy, love, civilization, home, and dear ones—all were gone beyond redemption—and life had become nothing more than the next step.

Toward the end of the day, as the sun began to lower and the air grew even colder, the straggling band of prisoners were rounded up in the center of a wide valley. As soon as the pace slowed the cold began to penetrate their wet clothes and the women and children huddled together, trying to share their warmth and to give one another the illusion of care and protection.

Talmadge moved toward the brave who was carrying Mercy on his horse, but the prisoners were boxed together too tightly for him to maneuver close to her. He realized he was pressed next to the Bramwell twins.

"Matthew! Luke!" he whispered "Stay close to me."

Luke looked up at him, recognizing the big, strong boy he had always admired when they played in the town square. "Talmadge!" the little boy cried. "Where's Mother and Father? I've looked and looked for them.

Talmadge did not have the heart to tell the boy that no men prisoners had been taken. All the men had been killed. Nor had he seen the boys' mother anywhere.

Matthew lifted his head and Talmadge was horrified to see how gray the boy's face was. "I think I have a splinter in my foot," Matthew whispered. Looking down, Talmadge gasped. The boy was running with a sharpened twig protruding from the instep of his foot.

"When we start moving again get on my back," Talmadge urged. "I'll carry you for a way. They may let us stop when it gets dark."

With determination, Talmadge pressed his way to the edge of the prisoners so he could see what had caused the delay. The French officers were forming riders into four parties. The parties, with several runners on foot, moved off swiftly in the direction of three separate entrances to the hills that ringed the valley.

The last group of riders were held in reserve. At a command, the Indians prodded the prisoners to begin running once more. Talmadge looked for young Matthew, but the twins had already been swept up in the moving column.

With loud cries and the sharp points of their lances the Indians pushed the prisoners toward an almost hidden gap in the hills. Talmadge observed the horsemen riding back and forth across the trails that had been left in the snow. The horses' hooves pounded up the snow, mixing it with mud and churning the tracks into confusion.

Now Talmadge understood that the other parties had made false trails to the other passes. Each small company had created a decoy trail. Anyone attempting to follow the Indian tracks would find only confusion and deception in the signs remaining in this valley. Precious time would be lost as rescuers tried to decipher which trail was the right one to follow into the hills.

Suddenly Talmadge had a thought. He remembered when his father had bought his new boots. They had gone together to the bootmaker, and as they compared the size of his small foot to his father's manly last, his father had said with a smile, "This will likely be the final time you shall have your boots made to the size of a boy's last. The day will come, lad, when your boots shall outsize mine!"

"A boy's boot!" Talmadge thought. "The regiment will know that none of the prisoners would be taken on a decoy route. Any route with a child's print would have to be the right trail."

As swiftly as the idea came, Talmadge acted upon it, moving out from the body of the column, and running far out beyond the line marked by the running Indian braves. A warrior saw him veer away, and the dark-faced brave ran over to him and shoved him back into the group with such a rough push that Talmadge almost fell.

As Talmadge returned to the relative protection of the other prisoners, he had the satisfaction of glimpsing a row of perfect boot marks—his boot marks,—a boy's boot marks—unerased in the tableau of the snow. "If only the trackers look hard enough!" Talmadge thought, with the first glimmer of hope he had felt since he had heard the first shots fired in the early dawn.

The passage through which the French officer led the prisoners was narrow and winding, with tall, heavily wooded hills on either side. As the captives came through the defile, Talmadge saw that they had been led into a small bowl of a valley, with no apparent exit. The last rays of the cold sun were highlighting the circle of hills with a pale outline, but the valley itself was in dark shadows. The terrain was little more than a long hallway—a widening of the pass—and at the farther end was a small grove of leafless trees, punctuated with thick evergreens. The valley had an aspect of secretiveness and inhospitality. It was without beauty or grace, and, unbidden, the thought came to Talmadge, that this was a place of death.

No campfires were lit, and, in exhaustion the prisoners fell upon the ground. Darkness was sudden and absolute, and Talmadge had no hope of finding Mercy. The prisoners silently drew together. Scraps of clothing were shared and body was pressed against body in silent generosity, sharing the only thing any of them had left—themselves. Somehow they slept.

In the first rush of darkness, Talmadge had an uncontrollable desire to try to escape, but once again the thought of Mercy restrained him and he lay down with the others. In the dead of night, Talmadge heard the decoy parties return to camp.

"They'll come," he heard a woman's voice whispering close to his ear. "They are on their way right now. The regiment from Boxford Falls. They could be there, out in the night. Just minutes away. I feel it. I know it. At dawn, they'll come. I know they will."

But at dawn the captives were wakened by the grunts and rough commands of their Indian wardens. As the prisoners arose from the frozen ground, Talmadge saw the bodies of those who had lain down in the darkness and would never rise again.

This time the Indians did not even bother to move the bodies of the dead. They left them where they lay.

The French soldiers, working with the Indians, pressed the prisoners forward and made them stand in a long line at the edge of the small woods facing the valley and the way they had come.

The pitiful remnants of the once prosperous and thriving settlement of Marshfield formed a straggling front, from one side of the circle of hills to the other. The warrior Indians and French foot soldiers took up positions in the woods behind the prisoners.

Glancing around, Talmadge saw that the mounted French soldiers were nowhere to be seen. A few horses were tethered in the woods, but the horse warriors and the French cavalry had disappeared.

Suddenly, one of the French foot soldiers stepped out through the line of prisoners and flashed a mirror in the light of the dawning sun. From the surrounding hills came answering flashes of mirrors on every side. Talmadge understood. The perfect spot for an ambush. The perfect plan. The prisoners at the front of the line would serve as bait and protection. Anyone entering the small valley was walking into a suicide trap.

Talmadge was sure, as were all the prisoners, that the Boxford regiment was on its way to rescue them. As soon as the massacre at Marshfield was discovered, the army would have given chase and the footprints of the retreating raiders would be easy to follow in the newly fallen snow.

Talmadge was aware that easy tracking would only last a day or two. Already, with the dawn and the dying down of the cold wind, Talmadge could feel a warming in the air and could hear the trickle of disappearing snow. His one hope lay in the fact that the prisoners had been taken scarcely more than a day's march, and that the regiment could follow more swiftly than the Indians could retreat with prisoners.

Of course, Talmadge knew, the Indians' decoy strategy might have delayed the rescuers, but not for long. Especially if they had seen his boot marks. He was certain rescue must be close at hand, but now, seeing the cleverness of the ambush which had been laid, he raged at his inability to warn the Colonials.

Chapter Five

Talmadge and the other prisoners were right in assuming that the army contingent was hurrying toward them.

The Colonial regiment in Boxford Falls had risen before light on the day of the Marshfield raid. Knowing nothing of the waiting disaster, they had grumbled about the necessity of the trip to Marshfield in the freshly fallen snow. The soldiers had traveled raggedly through the cold dawn, the mounted troops plodding ahead and the foot soldiers following at their own rate, unaware of the tragedy that had already taken place on that bleak morning.

At the head of the column, in his heavy red uniform, rode Captain William Danforth, an aristocratic British officer who resented and disdained the detachment of Colonial troops under his command. Like all true British soldiers, he considered it his duty to fight the French wherever and whenever commanded.

The long winter of bivouac and billeting had worn hard on the troops, and as they approached Marshfield they had felt they were going on another fool's errand as they had done all winter—never finding or engaging the enemy. Danforth was convinced that the French-Indian raiding party that had raided the northward settlements weeks earlier had retreated across the border into Canada.

Close to noon the company's advance officer, Lieutenant Ayres, a native New Englander who had seen much of Indian warfare, had pulled his horse to a sliding stop in the snow, saluted the captain, and pointed to the far western sky. The soldiers, following the direction of his arm, stared in horror at the black column of smoke which stained the crystal blue of the storm-cleared sky above Marshfield.

The cavalry rode at full battle canter but, when they arrived at the charred and smoking town, they saw the trail of bodies across the field. It was the path of the enemy's retreat and immediately they gave chase. A handful of men were left in Marshfield to direct the foot soldiers in the cleanup operation when they arrived.

Talmadge's confidence in the speed of the followers was justified. The Colonial troops were well-mounted, and it took them an afternoon to cover the same distance as the retreating French and Indian raiders and their prisoners had covered in a day.

Still, it was not until early darkness—that the Boxford soldiers entered the region of rolling hills and the valleys where the retreating raiders had laid their decoy trails. Captain Danforth raised his hand and the column slowed. He gestured for his lieutenant, Daniel Ayres. "Halt the regiment," Captain Danforth said. "Keep our horses out of the way so we can see if any of the tracks makes sense."

Before them in the gathering gloom they could see numerous exits and open passageways leading in several directions around the low-lying mountains. The footsteps of the retreating war party had been obliterated by horse tracks running to and fro in the snow. It was an old Indian trick. When tracking was inevitable in snow or mud, mounted warriors let the foot party move ahead, while they took up the rear galloping back and forth, obliterating the tracks.

Horse and foot trails could be seen leading to each of the possible valley escape routes. The Colonial troops knew most of those trails would be decoys. The pursuers realized it would be unwise to split their forces because, from the evidence of the tracks, the raiding party was sizeable, and the rescuing party was already greatly outnumbered.

In the end it was darkness that defeated the rescuers. But in the last glimmer of sunlight, Lieutenant Ayres saw one footprint that had not been obliterated by the horses' hooves, and he stared at it with a blinding flash of insight. It was the imprint of a boy's leather boot. Not a French soldier. Not an Indian. A boy. A prisoner. He knew he had found the right trail.

Perhaps, had they known they were less than a half hour's ride from the prisoners and the raiding party, the rescuers would have continued on through the night. However, knowing they had discovered the correct trail, they bivouacked through the night, and then, as the sky grew gray with morning, they cautiously followed the trail leading into the narrowest of the passes.

* * *

As dawn came, Talmadge kept his eyes focused on the spot where the narrow pass opened into the valley, and waited for the Colonial troops. It was less than an hour. He heard the rescue party before he saw them. The sounds of muffled hoofbeats and the jingle of harnesses, and then the advance officers, resplendent in red coats, suddenly appeared at the far end of the valley floor.

It was a short enough distance that Talmadge could almost see the expressions on the rescuers' faces. As the troops entered the cul de sac, drawing up in tight formation, he could imagine the shock and alarm they felt as they peered across the snowy earth to the unbroken line of prisoners, shivering and frightened, a hostage barrier for the Indian warriors who stood in formation behind the prisoners. The Indians held their bows at the ready, and a line of French riflemen sped into kneeling position among the prisoners, with rifles loaded, aimed at the pass where the English Colonials kept pouring through.

Talmadge realized that no shots had been fired because the Colonials were still out of range.

The red-coated regiment swiftly maneuvered into attack formation, with a forward line, a second wave, and a penetration force.

In the frigid morning air the rap of the officers' voices could be heard, although their exact words could not be distinguished.

If the troop attacked, Talmadge realized, they would bring themselves into rifle range. Not only would the Colonials face the superior fire power of the French and Indian soldiers in the woods, but, once they had advanced into the valley, the mounted forces hidden in the hills would swoop down and finish them off. Prisoners would inevitably be killed in the exchange of gunfire and nothing but doom and destruction lay in wait for that gallant force preparing to rescue them.

Without thinking, Talmadge stepped forward and shouted with all his might, waving his arms and running in a wild path toward them. "It's a trap! Go back! It's a trap!" His voice rang through the frigid morning air, but the distance was too great. The Colonials saw the young dark-haired boy waving and running, but they only thought he was calling for help.

An Indian brave rushed toward Talmadge and aimed a

mighty war club at his head, but just as he swung, Talmadge lost his footing in the snow and fell, so the blow was a glancing one.

The boy lay on the ground, in pain and half-dazed, and watched the slaughter. He saw, almost as if in a dream, the huge, red-coated captain, with his golden braid flashing in the morning sun, raise his hand and signal "Charge!"

The thunder of the first wave roared toward him, followed by the opening salvo of shots from the French and the thrum of a legion of arrows flying through the air. Mountless horses reeled in confusion, galloping with empty saddles. The captain was the first to fall.

He watched another officer, tall, with a quiet, courageous face, continue on toward the line of prisoners, and actually sweep into the Indian camp. He was soon unhorsed and clubbed to death, but not before he had left several Abenakis dead or bleeding from the powerful work of his saber.

The few Colonials who survived the fusillade of bullets aimed at their attacking line, fought valiantly with swords or used their rifles as clubs. Those who did not fall in the vanguard, however, were vanquished by the numbers of French and Indians waiting in the woods.

Soldiers and horses lay dead and wounded in the snow, and the valley was filled with confusion. Few officers were left to direct the remaining troops, and the systematic flight of arrows and hail of bullets was deadly.

Watching, trying to struggle to his feet, Talmadge saw the remaining Colonials gather in a closed formation in the center of the valley. With unbelievable discipline, they knelt, loading and reloading their rifles, shooting in systematic battle formation at their enemy. The prisoners, in the heat of battle, had fled for cover. The rescuers began to make slow progress. Even the mounted soldiers dismounted and joined in the battle formation.

Only Talmadge knew there was no hope. At that moment, the French mounted troops, waiting in ambush, came thundering down from the hills. They surrounded the Colonials on every side.

In the milling confusion, the Colonial soldiers tried to remount their horses and begin an orderly retreat.

Talmadge looked up and saw a young subaltern—the only officer left—riding the blood–stained horse which had belonged to the captain. The officer's face was white with shock and despair and he called to a young soldier who looked like he was scarcely older than Talmadge, "Sound Retreat!"

Through the awful din of the battle, Talmadge heard the words—and the anguish in the man's voice—as clearly as though he were the one to whom it was spoken.

The bugle boy in his oversize red coat raised the shining horn, which he wore slung across his chest, and put it to his lips. The first note sounded loud and clear across the noise of the fighting, but there was no second note; an arrow had torn through the lad's throat, and the final sound the bugle made was a wail.

Talmadge watched, as though through a veil, as the troops retreated under the blistering crossfire like a ragged flock of wounded birds, leaving most of their companions crumpled in the snow. As the last redcoat disappeared through the narrow pass, Talmadge knew the last hope of rescue had disappeared as well.

After the sounds of gunfire and combat ceased, a cold silence filled the valley. Talmadge's head was throbbing violently. He simply wanted to lie down in the snow and rest like the bleeding soldiers—lie down and let the coldness and weariness cover him like a blanket.

As blissful unconsciousness reached out to claim him he thought of his sister. Mercy was alive, and he must stay alive and remain with the Indians until he could free them both. It was what Father would have done. It was what he must do.

Before the ambush, Talmadge had seen the brave who had captured Mercy place her in a small grove of trees, sheltered from the wind. The Indian had laid her on a heap of boughs and covered her with his woolen blanket.

The Abenaki's tenderness toward Mercy was a source of confusion to Talmadge. But his head hurt so badly, he was finding it impossible to think clearly. He pulled himself up to a standing position never taking his eyes from the tiny mound where Mercy lay in the trees during the whole of the battle.

The infantry which had been left behind to search the ruins of Marshfield were sickened by the evidence of the brutality and destruction of the massacre. In their first quick appraisal they had noted the massive snowdrift sloping up the side of the fort and had immediately understood how the attack had occurred.

The swiftness with which the Indians must have been able to scale the walls by using the snow ramp would certainly have enabled them to catch the settlers by complete surprise. It was obvious there had been no time for the villagers of Marshfield to mount any sort of organized resistance.

In home after burned-out home, the soldiers stared at the charred timbers and saw the bodies of fathers, mothers, and children hatcheted, shot, or knifed. Bodies, many of them scalped and mutilated, were lying upon front doorsteps, sidewalks, and yards. Most of the dead were still wearing their nightclothes.

In the meetinghouse the searchers discovered three men who had taken a stand there. One was a lad of fourteen. All three survivors were severely wounded. The two older men were unconscious, but the boy was sitting on one of the pews in the bullet-shattered room, muttering incoherently. "Mother said close the door, but the bar won't slide into place. It won't slide. I've tried and tried. It won't move. Something's wrong. Very wrong. I want to do it. I want to do it, but it won't close. It keeps opening. Open. Open. Open . . ."

The men wrapped him in warm blankets and led him, unprotesting, into one of the houses that was less damaged than the others. They laid him on a bed of cornhusks with the two other survivors.

The infantry had arrived in the late afternoon and, in shock and horror, had begun placing the bodies of the dead in the lot by the burying ground. The most heartbreaking task of all was following the route of the retreating attackers and picking up the bodies of tomahawked infants and toddlers with their murdered mothers clutching them to their breasts.

Each scene was one of such brutality that the soldiers thought they could see nothing worse, but when one young recruit, following the tracks across the ruined fields, came upon Chastity, he fell to his knees with a groan and began to sob in great wrenching gasps of horror and despair.

Chastity lay half covered by drifted snow, a vicious gash opening one side of her head. Her long, dark, curling hair blew like glistening wings in the wind, and by her side she clutched her frozen newborn—the child born as she lay alone and mortally wounded. The frozen bodies looked like exquisite statues of the finest alabaster, and even in death, the face of the mother was filled with tenderness.

Chapter Six

After the pitiful handful of surviving English Colonial troops had completed the disarray of their retreat, the Indians and French soldiers regrouped around their disheartened prisoners. Several Indians, shouting and screaming victory cries, galloped across the valley to scalp and strip the bodies of the dead soldiers.

The ghastly sight of this mutilation made the women prisoners turn away, hiding the faces of their children. Several women fainted, but Talmadge watched it all, his eyes slits of hatred filled with silent revenge. Someday, he told himself, I will make them pay for this.

When the frenzy was over, the prisoners were rounded up and harassed on their way. Indian guards circled the group, prodding with lances, and rifle barrels so that the exhausted women and children stumbled obediently across the rough, cold terrain.

Although no quarter was given, and their Indian captors obviously felt the necessity to put as much distance as possible between themselves and the settlements of Massachusetts, nonetheless, the prisoners sensed a slight lessening in the fierce brutality of their guards. It was obvious that the French and the Indians believed themselves to be safe from pursuit.

Not only Mercy, with her terrible wound, but now, several other of the smaller children had been swept up onto horses to ride in relative comfort in front of an Indian warrior. The Indians now talked freely among themselves. Occasionally there was even the sound of laughter as they made some jest.

The raiders were delighted with the contraband with which they were journeying homeward, and Talmadge could see the boots, warm coats, blankets, sacks of food, and dead chickens and sheep that the attackers had looted from Marshfield being distributed throughout their ranks.

The prisoners were ranked as contraband also. They were the most valuable kind of contraband, since prisoners could be used either as slaves or else for ransom. In either role, prisoners signified wealth to an Indian sagamore. Since most of the Indians spoke French, Talmadge could readily understand them. He silently thanked his mother for her insistence on lessons in Latin and French.

As Talmadge marched, he carefully watched the brave who had captured Mercy. The Abenaki rode his pony with a stiff and haughty stance, but the arm with which he held Mercy was firm and gentle.

During the hours of marching the column of prisoners became less and less orderly, until in the later afternoon, the prisoners were walking commingled with the French-Indian company. In this more flexible arrangement, Talmadge was able to work his way closer to the shaggy chestnut mare on which Mercy was being carried.

Talmadge did not raise his eyes, but out of the corner of his eye he examined his sister intently. Mercy's face was so white that for a moment Talmadge was sure she was dead, but suddenly she gave a gasp and opened her eyes. Looking up at the Indian who held her, she said in a piteous tone. "It hurts."

The Indian said nothing, but pulled clumsily on the woolen blanket in which she was wrapped to cover her more warmly. Mercy whimpered and Talmadge sprang to her side. "Mercy!" he cried. "I'm here. It's me, Talmadge."

She opened her eyes wide. "Tal!" she whispered. The Indian glared at the boy but said nothing and did not push him away.

For the rest of the afternoon, Talmadge remained near the horse. Even though his head continued to throb from the blow of the club and his feet ached with cold, he kept up to the pace of the column, and continued his vigilance over his sister.

That night when camp was made, Manocq, who was the Indian carrying Mercy, took the child with hair like moon clouds and laid her on his blanket near the other prisoners. Manocq knew the girl would not live, but she reminded him of a wounded thing in the forest and he would care for her until the Great Spirit took her. He would have liked to take her to the fire, but knew his brother warriors would make mock of him. Manocq was certain that once he left, the strange boy with the Indian hair and the sky eyes would come watch over the girl. And it was true. Talmadge had watched and as soon as Manocq the warrior left to join the others around the roaring fire, Talmadge crept over in the darkness and knelt near the little bundle on the ground.

"Mercy," he whispered. He placed his hand on her and felt the gentle rise and fall of her breathing, so he knew she was still alive.

The Indians had built a huge fire, and painted their bodies once again. This time they were painted to celebrate victory, not to make war. They roasted the sheep, goats, and chickens they had slaughtered in Marshfield, and circulated bottles of rum and brandy.

The French soldiers drank, ate, and talked, but did not join in the wild dancing, shrieking, and celebrating of the Indians around the fire.

Talmadge watched the wild gyrations of the warriors, bedecked in their trophies of war, and thought he could not bear to witness their savage celebration of the destruction of all he held dear. He wanted to run into their midst, grab any weapon he could find, and fight them to his death. Just as he prepared to spring from the ground, Mercy moaned, and he turned toward her with swift concern.

"Water," she whimpered, "I am so thirsty." He scrambled toward the stream he heard trickling in the darkness behind the grove where the prisoners were corralled. A French guard grabbed his arm and twisted it hard. "Where do you think you are going, little toad?" the man asked roughly.

"For water," Talmadge replied, pulling his arm from the man's hand. "My sister is ill."

"Then feed her snow," the guard growled.

"No," Talmadge answered stubbornly. "It would kill her."

There was a pause in he darkness, and Talmadge knew the man was trying to decide whether to run him through with his bayonet as a lesson in instant obedience, or simply order him back to the picket. Either way, Talmadge knew he was prepared to die because he would not go back to Mercy without water.

The silence lasted a full minute and then the soldier, whose face was masked by the darkness, said, "I will go with you. If you try to escape I will kill you instantly—you and your sister."

Talmadge could not bring himself to say thank you to his

enemy, but he felt the first surge of hope since he'd fallen prisoner. When they reached the small brook, the Frenchman unhooked the canteen cup from his belt and handed it to Talmadge, who took it wordlessly, filled it, and hurried back up the bank to Mercy.

The soldier stood by while Talmadge gently lifted Mercy's little head and held the water to her lips. Talmadge could feel the heat of her body through the blanket, and, as Mercy stirred, he smelled the sickly odor of infection.

"When are you going to feed us?" Talmadge asked boldly.

The French foot soldier put back his head and laughed roughly. "You do not understand, little fool," he said. "The Indians are your owners, not us. They will divide you up among them. We will go our way, and the Indians will break into tribal parties and each will find its own way back to Canada. That is why our raiders are never caught as we retreat. We do not return to Canada together." The man smiled craftily at the cleverness of the strategy.

"But we cannot travel another day without food!" Talmadge exclaimed.

"That is none of our concern," the Frenchman said harshly. "The Indians never feed their slaves. You must forage for yourselves, like dogs." With this the Frenchman chuckled again, then added, his voice was heavy with worldly malaise, "As a matter of fact, the day will come when you will wish you were one of their dogs. At least their dogs get an occasional bone thrown to them."

Talmadge listened with disbelief. He knew the other prisoners must be feeling the same racking pangs of hunger that were tormenting him.

None of the prisoners had eaten since the night before when they had enjoyed supper in the warmth of their comfortable homes. Now, far from the heat of the victory fire, the wretched women and children were huddled in the bitter night, hungry, thirsty, and fearing what the next day might bring.

Talmadge's first feelings were of concern for the misery of his fellow prisoners, but as he squatted on the hard ground next to Mercy, he was overwhelmed with the knowledge that she was going to die soon. With that awareness came the knowledge that he, too, would die.

Burning in him as brightly as flame, he felt a sudden determination to live. The feeling was so strong he could almost taste it. From that feeling a decision exploded. He would do battle with his captors! And he would win! The first thing he would have to do would be to survive.

Survival in itself would be a form of winning. Everything the Indians could do to him would be their way of showing him his life had no value, and he must prove them wrong. He would wrest control of his life from them. Somehow he would find a way to live, and to stay strong.

He watched intently the wild celebration in the light of the campfire, alert to everything. The French had pulled out brandy flasks and were passing them from hand to hand. As the Indians drank, Talmadge noted their wildness seemed to mount in fury. They leaped higher and their shrieks were truly horrifying. The smell of roasting animals, the scent of burned grease and boiling corn nearly drove him crazy with hunger.

Much later, as the fire died down, Talmadge, still watching, saw a huge, black-haired Indian with many scalps on his war lance stagger away from the quieting circle of dancers. The man was holding the charred joint of an animal leg in his hand. He gnawed on the meat as he bungled his way through the darkness of the trees down to the small stream.

There was a sound of splashing and grunting, and then the drunk warrior moved clumsily back up the bank toward the soldiers and Indians who were circling the dimming fire, preparing for sleep. A few yards from the place where Talmadge watched silently, the huge Abenaki fell to the ground, and with a belch, rolled over on his back and began snoring. The stentorian sound of the sleeping Indian was like an animal in deep hibernation.

Talmadge sat listening, marveling that the man did not waken himself with his own noise. The French guardsman had moved off and was threading his way through the prisoners, checking to see that all were accounted for. Holding his breath for fear of making the slightest sound, Talmadge got up and cautiously moved through the woods toward the sleeping Abenaki.

As he neared the clearing, his foot stepped on a branch which snapped loudly. He froze in fear, but the Indian's breathing did not falter.

By a thread of moonlight, Talmadge was able to see the Indian lying on the ground. The man's arms were outflung and his barrel chest moved in a massive rise and fall punctuated with the deep rattle of his snoring. In the warrior's far hand Talmadge saw what he wanted—the joint of meat, now little more than a stripped bone, clasped like a weapon.

With stealth born of fear and desperation, Talmadge moved around the Indian and crept toward the food. As his fingers touched the bone, the brave gave a snort.

Talmadge sprang back into the shadows and waited. Gradually, the Indian's breathing regained its rhythm, and once more Talmadge crept forward. He grasped the bone, and gently, a sliver of distance at a time, pulled it free from the massive hand. At any moment he knew the Indian might waken, and spear him to death, but the hunger and will to live within him were stronger than any fear of danger.

Just as the meat broke free from the Indian's hold, the sleeping man gave another drunken snort. His arms flailed in the air for a few moments, and then he heaved over on his side, and continued to sleep. Talmadge was trembling with weakness and tension as he took his former place beside Mercy.

Gently, he put his hand on his sister's shoulder. "Mercy," he whispered, "I've got something for us to eat." There was no reply. He felt her forehead and discovered it was burning hot. Carefully, he peeled the last few shreds of meat from the bone, wrapped them in a tear of cloth from his shirt, and put them in his pocket to save for Mercy when she wakened. Then he took the bone in his hands and began to gnaw on it. He had never tasted anything more delicious.

He ate the sinews, the gristle, the soft bones in the joint, and then he broke the larger bones open and sucked the marrow. With each morsel he could feel strength returning.

He turned his back to the other prisoners, many of whom were sleeping, for he knew he must guard each meager shred of food. It was his first lesson in survival. He would share when he could, but if it was a matter of life and death, he would put survival first.

As night deepened the camp drew silent and Talmadge saw the French guardsman heading toward him. Again, by instinct, he knew his life would be forfeit if he were identified as one who had stolen the food. Swiftly he took the bone and pushed it under Mercy's blanket.

The guard came near and looked at him suspiciously. "Why are you not sleeping?" he asked.

"My sister," Talmadge said with what he hoped was the

right amount of sullen defiance. He wanted the guard to feel
his manner was no different.

The guard stood over him, as if unsure, then shrugged and
walked over to a nearby tree which he leaned against, crossing his arms. In a few moments another soldier came, gave
a password, saluted, and the two men stood talking quietly.
Talmadge heard a short laugh, and the guard moved away
toward the fire.

The new guard noticed the heap that was the sleeping Indian, and walked over to investigate. While he was diverted,
Talmadge quickly dug a shallow hole, buried the shards of
juiceless bone, and covered the little grave with leaves and
snow. He then sat on the spot, so that in the morning any
disturbance in the snow would simply seem the result of his
restless night.

Still hungry, but with his head injury beginning to throb
less, and the exhaustion of the day's march working like an
opiate, Talmadge finally relaxed his vigil. The little bit of
food had refreshed him and he lay down beside Mercy.
Reaching inside the filthy blanket, he found her tiny, fevered
hand and held it in his. "I'm here, Mercy," he whispered,
and fell asleep.

Chapter Seven

As morning pinked the sky there was a grumbled stir of activity among the awakening revelers. The French troops were filling packs and saddlebags and moving quietly into field formation. The Indians, less organized, were milling around, talking in loud and combative voices.

Guards prodded the prisoners awake, and the French commander, whom Talmadge had heard called Captain de Bouville, mounted his bay stallion and rode through the trees. He spoke to the pathetic prisoners from the back of his restless steed, sitting triumphant in his hated blue uniform.

"You will now be left to the care of your Indian captors," he told the prisoners. "We, the French, have not sought this war, and do not wish you personal ill will. However, you have chosen to inhabit land to which you have no legal or moral right. This is an act of aggression and we hope through the example of the destruction of Marshfield, others will be saved from making the same fatal mistake.

"This imprisonment may prove to be an immortal blessing to those of you who arrive in the villages of Canada. Yes, you will be slaves of the Abenaki and Caughnawagas, but many of them are true Christians, and in their villages priests of the Holy Church will teach you the truth of your evil and spiritually rebellious ways. Through conversion you may find a way out of your soul's slavery.

"I know you cannot see it, but you are merely pawns caught in the press of history—a movement of power is here which no force can resist. This land is meant, by divine decree, to belong to France! *Vive la France!*"

With that the French company moved into swift position, and, at a signal, they threaded through the wooded hills which surrounded the campsite. Faster than Talmadge would have believed, the French soldiers vanished from sight.

From each of the three Indian groups, a spokesman stood

forth. Six remaining Frenchmen stood guard by the prisoners
while the Indians argued beside the burned-out campfire. At
last the chieftains seemed to come to agreement, and they
led their units to the prisoners' compound. The women and
children were separated into two groups, but Talmadge remained quietly beside Mercy, and no one bothered him for
the moment.

As the prisoners were moved aside, six bodies remained
lying on the frozen ground. Four children and two women
had died during the night. The Indian chiefs walked among
the clustered women, poking them with sharp lances and
sending them, almost at random, to one of the three Indian
groups.

Sensing what was happening, the women began to cry,
and one woman, whom Talmadge recognized as Goodwife
Harmon, broke from the ranks to run to the children and
snatch her six-year-old daughter to her breast. "No!" she
screamed. "You must let her come with me! Please take her
too." She turned beseechingly to the chief of her tribal
group. He was a heavy, copper-faced Indian, with deep crevasses of wrinkles that made his eyes like slits in his lined
face.

Without a glimmer of emotion he turned to one of the
warriors and issued a sharp command. The warrior sprang to
the woman and hit her a tremendous blow with his heavy
war club. Her skull split open, and a horrified scream rose
from the other prisoners.

The children were divided next, and mothers wept hyster-
ically as they watched beloved children, weeping and
screaming, being carried to other groups. Occasionally, by
chance, a mother and child would be united and their joy
made the sorrow of the others more devastating.

Talmadge continued to watch, although he was rapidly
learning the ability to watch and see everything without
showing that he was watching. He kept his eyes downcast
and narrowed, but from the corners he noted everything, and
recorded it on his ledger of hatred.

Finally, the prisoners were all divided and assigned to a
tribe. There was still some anger and disputation, but the
French soldiers urged the Indians to hurry. Manocq, the
chief of his tribal group, leading his horse by the bridle,
came over to pick up Mercy. Talmadge instantly stood up to
walk beside them.

Suddenly the heavy chief of the other tribal group stomped over and shouted something at Manocq, then pulled the blanket roughly from Mercy. The little girl looked more dead than alive, and her golden hair glistened in the morning sun.

The angry Caughnawaga chief looked at the child with disdain and spat on the ground. Then he looked at Talmadge and grabbed him. The old chief's hand was like a sharp talon, and his long nails pierced the skin of Talmadge's forearm. Talmadge understood the old warrior was going to allow Manocq to keep Mercy, but he was claiming Talmadge for his tribe.

Suddenly, bile rose in Talmadge's throat, and he began to struggle furiously against the old Indian's iron grip. "No!" he shouted. "No! I will not go!"

The Indian's strength made Talmadge's struggling ridiculous and suddenly all the Indians were laughing at this worm of a slave, who struggled so pointlessly. Talmadge was sure he would be dispatched with a war club as soon as their amusement died. Instead, the huge drunk Indian of the night before, Pebosquaam, came forward and placed an enormous hand on the Chaughnawaga chief's shoulder.

Pebosquaam growled a single word and grabbed Talmadge's other arm. For a moment the two powerful warriors stood glaring at one another, and a waiting silence filled the grove. It was a deadly moment. Finally, the older warrior made a sound of disgust and threw Talmadge to the ground. Turning, he stomped over to his waiting cadre, and, without a single backward glance, his Indians encircled their share of the prisoners, about twenty in all, and melted into the trees. One moment they were there; the next moment they were gone.

Pebosquaam lifted Talmadge roughly from the ground, gave him a powerful blow to the side of the head with his massive fist, and then shoved him into the midst of the other prisoners. The warrior walked back to Manocq, who was now mounted with Mercy in front of him, and growled in French, "The dog will know his master."

Manocq said nothing, but raised his hand as a signal, and the Abenakis, shoving the prisoners into their ranks, trotted toward the northern hills.

With his head reeling from yet another heavy blow, Talmadge staggered forward, the ground blurring beneath his feet. He wondered where he was going, and when, and if, he would eat again. He thought about his mother and father and Thomas, all dead, and little Mercy dying. "I am the last of the Fairchilds," he whispered to himself. "Whatever else happens, I must live."

In the next days the Indian party, traveling swiftly, and living off the land, moved northward, and then turned sharply to the west. Crossing the Housatonic, they made brief camp before traveling the short distance into upper Albany.

It was here, on the western bank of the river, that Mercy, as frail as a shadow, finally died. Her wound was filled with infection, and the miracle was that she had clung to the thread of her existence for so many days of arduous travel.

Manocq wrapped the delicate child in his woolen trade blanket and placed her body high in a tree. Talmadge watched in impotent fury, wanting to give her a true burial, but knowing he could not dig a grave in the frozen earth with his bare hands.

The Indian chieftain stood at the base of the tree after he had deposited Mercy's body in its branches, and sang a low and haunting chant. Talmadge did not know it, but it was the chant of mourning. Manocq's warrior soul felt a strange and heavy sadness at the death of the lovely child who had ridden on his horse through the long retreat.

Talmadge felt Mercy's death like the shutting of the last open door in his heart. He felt all light and warmth extinguished, and his heart became a dark thing, heavy with anger, hate, and bitterness.

As he turned away from the tiny silhouette of his little sister, dark in the trees against the night sky, he renewed his two vows, the one to survive, and the other to gain revenge. Rage would keep him alive, and someday life would bring him the chance to repay their brutality tenfold.

As the raiding party and their captives entered the territories controlled by the Dutch traders of upper New York, the prisoners noticed an even greater relaxation of urgency on the part of their captors. The Indians knew they were now in land occupied by men who were, if not neutral, at least indifferent to political elements. The Albany Dutch were a pragmatic group of settlers, who left New England alone to fight for her territorial imperatives if she chose to do so, while they continued their active fur trade with the Indians and French up and down the Hudson waterways and out the harbors of New York.

The earth was still gripped in the chill of winter, but the days were beginning to grow more moderate, and the cold was more endurable. Talmadge was alert and fiercely determined somehow to beg, steal, and trap enough food to keep himself alive. Several more prisoners had died during the journey before the survivors realized the Indians had no intention of feeding them.

Gradually, the captors began claiming individual prisoners among themselves, and a system of owner and slave was developing. From the beginning it was clear that Pebosquaam, the huge, brutal brave on whose face arrogance and cruelty fought a savage battle for supremacy, considered Talmadge to be his own property. Some of the other Indian masters would throw bones and scraps to their prisoners, but Pebosquaam gave nothing to Talmadge and Talmadge would have scorned such gifts, although, determined as he was to survive, he would have taken them.

Pebosquaam called the boy Shenwah, which was his Indian derivative of Chien Noir—Black Dog. All the Indians thought it greatly amusing that Talmadge had jet-black hair like theirs, but that his eyes were blue like water. His pale skin made him ugly in their eyes, and they laughed at what a joke the Great Spirit had made to give a white boy Indian hair.

The Abenakis also thought Talmadge's sullen hatred and fiery temper were funny. He became the butt of fireside humor. They prodded him with sharp spears and baited him like a young bear cub to watch him growl and rear in defiance. It took a while for Talmadge to be wise enough to hide his feelings, and to stop rising to their bait. He learned the Indian trick of holding his face blank, and not allowing any feeling to show in his eyes.

The other Abenakis went on to other amusements when they found they could no longer taunt him into a rage. But Pebosquaam was infuriated when Talmadge stopped responding to his taunts and he hit Talmadge with one of his huge hands. Talmadge felt his mouth fill with blood, but he was silent.

Enraged, Pebosquaam picked up the young boy and shook him like a terrier killing a shoat. Just as the Indian raised Talmadge above his head to dash him into the fire, a sharp command was issued. The Indians around the fire turned to look at Manocq, who had just returned from a scouting foray and had come upon the scene.

Talmadge's head was ringing and he was scarcely conscious, but he knew Manocq's words had been an order to Pebosquaam to stop. Instead, the tall warrior continued to stand in front of the fire, holding Talmadge high above his head.

Manocq spoke in a harsh, commanding voice. His words were in the Abenaki tongue, but, again, Talmadge was sure the order was for Pebosquaam to desist.

Suddenly, Manocq switched to French. "You fool," he said coldly to Pebosquaam. "The battle is over, and now we return to our villages with little enough spoils for our year of war. You would destroy another of our captives? They die fast enough, these puny white men. We will have little ransom for our village. Put the dog down."

The contempt and superiority in Manocq's voice were not lost on Pebosquaam. He was being made a fool before the entire band of men and slaves. First his slave-dog had stopped amusing the other warriors and would not be baited or do as he should, and then he, Pebosquaam, was corrected by Manocq in front of everyone for doing what was his right to do.

"He is mine," Pebosquaam growled. "And he is dead."

With that Pebosquaam again raised Talmadge to dash him into the fire, but Manocq pulled his rifle into position and aimed it at Pebosquaam's heart. "He is not yours. I claim him by chieftain rights. If you kill him, you are a dead man too," Manocq answered coldly.

Pebosquaam shook with fury. He dropped Talmadge to the ground and leaped across the fire toward Manocq, pulling his hunting knife as he flew through the air. As calmly as though he were shooting a squirrel, Manocq pulled the trigger, and the huge form of Pebosquaam seemed to shudder in midflight; he fell at the feet of Manocq, his drawn knife plunged into the ground.

Pebosquaam lay like a fallen oak. Without so much as a glance at the dead warrior, or at the crumpled form of Talmadge lying at the other side of the campfire, Manocq turned and walked away. There was total silence in the circle of warriors; no one spoke or looked another in the eye. Later that night, the body of Pebosquaam was dragged into the forest by two braves assigned to the task by Manocq.

The next morning, as the Indians prepared to begin the day's march, Manocq rode his horse to the spot where Talmadge, bruised and shaken, had lain to sleep. He did not look at Shenwah, Black Dog, but he remained next to the place until Talmadge got unsteadily to his feet and began to walk. Then the Abenaki chief dug his heels into the sides of his pony and moved ahead of the boy.

Throughout the day, Talmadge walked in the tracks of Manocq's pony. He was wise enough to realize that Manocq had not killed Pebosquaam for love of Shenwah, but rather had used the slave as an excuse to get rid of a troublemaker, a brave who had challenged Manocq's authority time and again, and who would have had no compunctions about taking the chief's life had the opportunity presented itself.

Now that the fighting and raids were over, the Indians had no need for Pebosquaam, and he had begun to represent an ever-present danger to Manocq. Therefore, Talmadge had no sense of gratitude or debt to the chieftain for having saved his life. He knew he had merely been a pawn in an internecine power struggle.

The Indians were moving quickly now, covering ground which was crisscrossed with familiar trails, journeying alongside a stretch of lakes and small rivers, leading northward, ever northward, until they crossed the border into Canada.

At last the weather warmed and a hint of spring was in the air. Field and streams were wet with the run-off of melting snow, but the going seemed easier. Among the corps of prisoners in Talmadge's group the only one he knew was young Luke. It seemed an odd thing that the stronger brother had died, and the frail, timid younger one kept plodding along—alone. Talmadge thought he'd sealed up his heart when Mercy died, but something about the plucky little boy with his reddish hair, and pale, freckle–sprinkled face pierced Talmadge's indifference. He began walking beside the younger child, and when Luke grew too tired to stumble along, Talmadge would hoist him onto his back for a while.

When Talmadge found food—and he was very good at it—he began to share it with Luke, and eventually he found himself talking to the boy, whispering to him as they walked.

"You must stay beside me, and I will do my best to help you. We must talk together so that we do not forget who we are. We must whisper together so that we do not forget how to speak our own language." Instinctively, Talmadge knew that he and Luke would have to fight to keep their identity.

At first Luke cried a lot and spoke only of "going home," but he soon stiffened his little lips and held his fear and homesickness in check. With a wrench of pity, Talmadge put his hand on the younger lad's shoulder. "We *will* get back home," he told the boy fiercely. "They will come for us, or buy us back."

"You think so?" Luke's young eyes flashed with a terrible fierceness of hope.

"Yes, of course," Talmadge said confidently. But his heart smote against his breast as though it knew he was lying.

Finally, after climbing a ridge where the sumac, maples, and oaks were sprouting leaves of shining green, the party came within sight of a sizeable village of lodges and wigwams, hidden in a wooded hollow on the shores of a blue lake.

The Abenakis were more animated than Talmadge had ever seen them. They halted their horses, and brought out their war paints. With eager hands they painted and bedecked themselves, and then, remounting—and shoving the prisoners in front of them—they rode in a loose formation toward their home.

The forerunners galloped down the trail, screaming a high, wild incantation. Behind them, the other warriors rode with slow dignity, their prisoners—their bounty and proof of victory—herded in front of them like cattle. As they neared their village, all of them raised their voices in wild cries of conquest and fierce pride.

The squaws, old men, and children came running from the lodges with answering cries of welcome to greet the proud victors. Talmadge tasted the bile rising in his mouth, knowing that this joyous homecoming of his enemies was the final and most powerful symbol of his own defeat.

The Abenakis were home, and for one long and hopelessly bitter moment, Talmadge wondered if he'd ever again know the joy of a home.

Chapter Eight

Nathan Fairchild regained consciousness two weeks after the Marshfield Massacre. He was in a small bedroom above the tavern in Boxford Falls. He had no memory of how he came to be there.

It had been on the second day of the clean-up operation in Marshfield that Nathan had been discovered by a search party as it went through the houses, looking for bodies. One of the men had heard a slight moan and quickly climbed up into the loft, throwing aside the mound of bedding to find Nathan more dead than alive. The side of Nathan's head was covered with matted blood and he was burning up with fever.

"It's Mr. Fairchild!" the young Boxford Falls recruit exclaimed, recognizing him. He knelt beside the unconscious man. "Mr. Fairchild," he shouted, shaking Nathan's arm, "can you hear me?"

Nathan moaned, but remained unconscious. Soldiers carried him gently to a waiting wagon, and a driver and two guards were dispatched to take him to Boxford Falls for medical attention.

No one who watched the wagon carrying Nathan from the ruin of Marshfield had expected him to live. No ordinary man could have survived the ordeal. But miraculously, the years of frontier living, Nathan's relative youth, and his tough constitution withstood the rigors of the rough road, the springless wagon, and the penetrating cold.

Nathan had arrived in Boxford Falls clinging to life, but only by a tenuous hold. The local midwife washed the filth from him and removed the dried blood and putrefying flesh from the slash which creased his head from temple to crown.

The bullet had made an ugly, festering wound, and she knew from the sound of Nathan's harsh breathing that he al-

most certainly had contracted pneumonia as he'd lain unconscious in the cold house under the damp bedclothes.

When the doctor came, Nathan was out of his head, mumbling incoherently. He seemed extremely agitated, thrashing
back and forth in the bed. "Poor man," the doctor said. "No
matter how terrible his dreams and hallucinations are, he
will have to face a far more dreadful reality when—if—he
awakens. It will be a blessing if he can remain unconscious."

Around the clock, caring townspeople kept vigil on Nathan. The midwife, Goodwife Stowe, supervised the nursing
efforts, and the doctor visited twice daily. After a few days,
Goodwife Stowe was relieved to see the horrible restlessness
and agonized thrashing cease. For most of the second week,
Nathan lay quietly, as though he were already dead.

Toward the end of the week, the midwife voiced her concern to the doctor.

"Will he ever waken?" she asked anxiously. "He does not
respond to anything!"

The doctor looked closely at his patient. Nathan lay completely still on the white pillow. His hair was the color of the
sun, and his face, although pale, showed the fading traces of
a once deep tan. On the coverlet, his hands looked lean and
muscular, as though still capable of great acts of strength,
but the noble features of his face were sharpened, honed by
his fevered illness until they seemed almost otherworldly in
their refinement.

"I think the deepened coma may be a good thing," the
doctor said slowly. "His body has begun to heal itself. He is
coming back from the very rim of death. Coming back," the
doctor added grimly, "to a living hell."

All of Boxford Falls had heard the tragic story of Chasity
Fairchild and her newborn infant. The horrible details of
their deaths had hardened the New Englanders' hatred of the
French and Indians, and had forged in them a need for revenge as strong as a band of steel across their hearts.

Instead of frightening the British colonists, the French, by
their dastardly attack on Marshfield, had only deepened their
determination to fight this vicious enemy and win. With the
help of God, against such godless foes, English supremacy
would span this entire new continent.

The Marshfield Massacre by the French and Indian raiders
proved not only a human abomination but a great tactical error as well, for it created a rallying cry around which the

British colonies would unite. The vision of Chastity and her newborn child, abandoned in the sifting snows, had become a symbol of atrocities which no true Englishman, no New England colonist, would endure.

On the fourteenth day, Nathan's fever finally broke. Late in the evening he murmured a single word, "Water."

Goodwife Stowe lifted his head to give him a sip, and he whispered his second word, "Chastity," and lost consciousness again.

The next morning the nurse was dozing in her chair when she was wakened by a crash. Nathan was struggling to sit up in the bed and his flailing arm had sent the nightstand, and its porcelain pitcher and basin, smashing to the floor.

"Doctor!" Goodwife Stowe shouted into the hall. The doctor, who was sleeping in the next room, ran through the door in his trousers and nightshirt. He rushed to the bedside and grasped Nathan's arms.

Speaking in a firm, reassuring voice, he struggled with his patient. "Calm yourself, Mr. Fairchild! Hear me. I'm your doctor. Calm yourself. You are with friends, Mr. Fairchild."

He repeated the words over and over, and gradually Nathan's struggles lessened.

"Mr. Fairchild," the doctor said again, "can you hear me?"

Nathan nodded his head quietly, gave a great sigh, and closed his eyes. In a moment he was breathing steadily. The doctor bent, listened to his heart, and then stood up with a satisfied smile.

"I think he is sleeping, truly sleeping. We shall see what tomorrow brings."

The day passed without incident, and when Goodwife Stowe's supper tray was brought to her, as she took off the cloth and prepared to eat the succotash and hot biscuits, she heard Nathan's voice, normal for the first time.

"Chastity," Nathan said clearly, "what have we to eat?"

Goodwife Stowe ran to his side. "Mr. Fairchild," she said eagerly, "can you hear me? I am Goodwife Stowe."

He opened his eyes and looked at her with puzzlement. Then his eyes slowly surveyed the tiny, unfamiliar room. "Chastity," he whispered hoarsely. "Where is she?"

"Be calm, Mr. Fairchild," the nurse admonished. "I will get the doctor."

She returned on the run, bringing the doctor, who was still

wearing his napkin tucked under his chin, having been interrupted in the midst of his evening meal. The nurse saw Nathan's eyes, open, clear, and struggling to comprehend.

"I know I must be in Boxford Falls," Nathan stated quietly. "We escaped somehow. But my head hurts, and I am having trouble remembering. The raiders burned and killed. I fought. So much blood. I—I can't remember."

"Don't trouble yourself, Mr. Fairchild. You must rest and regain your strength," the doctor admonished. "All will become clear in time."

Nathan would not be put off. "Chastity and the children," he repeated, his voice growing firmer, with a hard edge of command. "Tell me where they are."

Goodwife Stowe turned her head away with a sob, and the doctor gave her an angry look as he turned back to his patient. "All in due time, Mr. Fairchild. If you are to recover, you must rest now. We will talk tomorrow."

In a sudden paroxysm of strength, Nathan thrust himself up from the bed and grasped the lapels of the doctor's coat. "Tell me now!" he shouted. "Where is my family?"

The effort was more than Nathan could sustain in his weakened condition and he fell back on the bed, his face gray with exertion and pain. "Tell me," he whispered, "please."

In a voice made grave with respect and pity, the doctor told him. "Your wife and young Thomas were killed by tomahawk." The good man could not bring himself to tell Nathan about the baby who had been born to the dying mother as she lay alone in the snow. Time enough for the father to learn of that when he was stronger. "We believe your daughter, Mercy, and Talmadge, your older son, were taken with the other prisoners on the march to Canada."

Nathan was silent. The doctor looked at his patient, wondering if the shock might kill him, but on Nathan's face he saw only strength, anger, and steely determination.

"And how is it I am alive and they are dead?" Nathan asked bitterly. "Could I not even defend them?"

"No," the doctor answered firmly, "you could not. You were wounded, unconscious, and taken for dead yourself. They hid you under the bedding to prevent your body from being mutilated. As it happened, they saved your life."

"I wish they had not," Nathan said quietly.

"That is the statement of a fool or a coward," the doctor

replied hotly. "Your life is a gift given to you by the Lord, your family, and those who have nursed you to health. It seems you should have gratitude for that life and the purpose for which it has been preserved."

Nathan nodded grimly, "Yes. And to that purpose I shall be pledged—to find my son and daughter."

The doctor nodded, satisfied. "So be it," he said. "Now rest."

Nathan's recovery was marked by recurring periods of unconsciousness, and it was three weeks before he was able to walk out of the tavern and mount a horse. The doctor could not believe the man's determination—but Nathan was driven by a desperate need to find his captive children.

When Nathan was told of the defeat of the Colonial soldiers who had pursued the retreating French and Indians, he immediately made arrangements to speak to one of the few survivors of the ambush.

Nathan was directed to a bare room above a stable where he found a young, wounded farmboy who had been one of the volunteers in the campaign. The boy seemed scarcely older than Talmadge, and Nathan looked with pity at the arm that had been amputated at the elbow. An arrow had shattered the young soldier's forearm, and by the time he had returned to Boxford and received medical attention, gangrene had set in.

Nathan knelt beside the boy's bed. "Did you see the prisoners when you entered the valley?" he asked urgently.

The boy nodded.

"Were you close enough to see their faces or what they were wearing?" Nathan continued, his heart beating with hope.

"Some," the young soldier replied hesitantly.

"Did you see a boy about twelve years old, but tall for his age? He was probably wearing a homespun shirt. His hair is black—jet black—like his mother's."

The wounded soldier tried hard to concentrate, but his eyes had a glassy, fevered look, and sweat beaded on his forehead.

"Maybe," the boy said slowly. "Yes, I think maybe. Right at the front of the prisoners. He had blood on the side of his face, I think ... Oh ... I don't know. I'm not sure what I saw."

"Try to think!" Nathan begged. "Try! Picture it in your mind. Was there a little girl with long hair the color of sunshine? You couldn't miss her. She's so pretty and so little. If you saw her you'd remember. Think man, think! For the love of God—try to remember!" Nathan had grabbed the soldier by the shoulders and without realizing what he was doing, was shaking him. "You've got to remember seeing them."

The doctor pulled Nathan away from the wounded boy.

"Fairchild!" he exclaimed. "Control yourself. He's doing his best. This is a very sick young man."

The soldier began mumbling. "I understand. They are savages. Nothing they do is human. Out of the hills they came and killed us like we were a herd of stupid geese, and then they stripped us of our feathers and our skin. Drawn, quartered, roasted." He laughed bitterly. "I pity the living more than the dead. If your son and daughter are alive, pray they do not survive."

He stopped talking and his eyes closed, his head slumping to the side.

Nathan sprang toward him, but the doctor restrained him. Nathan cried in a loud voice, "But you did see them? Tell me. Tell me!"

Without opening his eyes the young soldier whispered, "The boy maybe, but I didn't see the little girl, I'm sure of that."

Nathan groaned, and then the wounded boy spoke in a suddenly clear voice. "But I didn't see a golden-haired scalp! It's certain if she was dead they would have used it for a trophy. So she must be alive, don't you see!" He smiled at his inspired logic. "All those scalps!" He lapsed back into mumbling. "Like a rainbow they were. All those colors—but none as bright as the sun. But I dunno, maybe the hair gets darker when its torn away from the head . . . but the colors was bright, hung from every lance and waving in the breeze, and every color some poor, lost soul lying in the snow with their skull as bare as bone."

The boy laughed feverishly and then moaned. "Better my hair than my arm," and then tears came from under his closed eyelids. The young woman who was nursing him motioned for Nathan and the doctor to leave.

The next day Nathan mounted a borrowed horse to ride to Boston. He thanked the doctor and Goodwife Stowe for their generosity. "I shall send you payment for your services as soon as I am able," he promised.

"It is wise you are going to Boston," the doctor said, "even if I do not think you are well enough to travel yet. It would be a fool's errand for you to ride off into the wilderness with the unfounded hope of tracking down the raiders. They will long since be safely back in Canada and their trail will be brick-cold.

"I have been told the governor has opened ransom negotiations with the French," the doctor continued. "The best information you will receive, and the best help you can get, will be in Boston."

Nathan nodded. "I know you are right. It is the place to start, but I can assure you I am ready to do whatever it takes to restore my children to my arms." His voice broke. "Whatever the cost in time, effort, money, or pain, I will find them."

The doctor nodded. "I believe you will, Nathan Fairchild . . . I believe you will."

Chapter Nine

The anteroom of the office of the Governor of the Commonwealth was filled with smoke. The floor was coated with the stains of tobacco, horse manure, and mud from men's boots.

The few benches and chairs were packed with exhausted men and women, and the entire room was filled with the stir of restless bodies.

Among those waiting for an audience were men dressed in the leather hunting garb of the Colonial Rangers, settlers wearing rough homespun and badly cobbled boots, and successful merchants looking soberly wealthy in broadcloth breeches with long silver-buttoned vests beneath stylish waistcoats. Lawyers wore their hair long, pigtailed, and unpowdered, and there were even a few aristocrats in the assemblage, resplendent in brocade, silk stockings, buckled shoes, and powdered wigs.

Nathan had been waiting since early morning and now he could see the sun setting over the Charles River, staining the water blood-red with the reflection. Pushed beyond the limits of patience, he shoved his way through the waiting throng, and pounded his clenched fist against the office doors. The sound of his blows echoed through the building and silence fell on the waiting crowd.

Startled sentries knocked Nathan away from the door and held him at bay with their bayonets. The governor's doors flew open and an angry man stepped out. "What is the meaning of this noise?" the aide asked the soldiers in a voice as sharp as a knife.

"Sir, it was this man. He must be mad."

"Yes sir," said the second sentry. "He moved so fast we couldn't stop him."

The man at the door of the governor's office was dressed in silk breeches and coat, with a dark satin vest. His hair was pigtailed and powdered, which only enhanced his air of power and authority. His eyes were as hard as gray agates.

"It is your business to stop everyone," he snapped at the sentries.

"Who are you, sir?" the man asked belligerently. He spoke with a crisp English accent, and his distaste at having to deal with Nathan was ill concealed.

"I am Nathan Fairchild," Nathan replied, returning the man's haughty gaze. "I am the father of two of the children taken captive in the Marshfield Massacre, and I insist that I see the governor now." With those bold words, Nathan wrestled free from the soldier's grasp and dashed open the doors with a mighty blow from his booted foot.

The governor, in a blue brocaded coat with ruches at neck and sleeves, looked up from his desk with a stern and unruffled gaze.

"What is it, Junius?" he asked calmly, looking at his secretary.

"This man has created an outrageous disturbance, sir," the aide replied. "I will have him arrested immediately."

"This is not a disturbance," Nathan shouted. "It is a rightful demand."

The governor raised his hand in a gesture for silence, and looked at Nathan piercingly.

"I know you, young man, don't I?" he asked musingly. "I'm trying to remember. I seldom forget a face."

"Your Lordship," Nathan answered, "I was first officer on the ship which brought you to Boston fourteen years ago."

"Of course, I remember. You were the one who took the helm when the captain lay dying. As I recall, I told you at the time that I, and everyone on board, owed you our lives."

The governor turned to his aide, who was glaring at Nathan. "You see, Junius, I told you I never forget a face. You may leave the young man with me. I believe I owe him at least an audience."

Junius Comstock, the governor's appointment secretary, gave Nathan a look of pure hatred and retreated through the door, taking his place at a small appointment desk in the lobby. The crowd surged toward the desk, and Junius shouted at them imperiously, "I do not know when the governor will see you! As you can see, he does exactly as he wishes! Take your seats and wait!"

* * *

The governor indicated a seat across from him and Nathan
sat down.

"My name is Nathan Fairchild," Nathan began.

"Yes, I recall the name now," the governor said. He was
a proud and haughty man, but intelligent and not unkind. "I
recall it was your family who owned the ship on which we
sailed. The Fairchilds were always renowned shipowners
and mariners in England. You follow a proud family tradition."

"My uncle—the captain who died on that voyage fourteen
years ago—was the last of the Fairchilds, except for myself," Nathan explained. "When the estate was settled my
late uncle's gambling debts took the last frigate of our family's proud sailing fleet."

"I am sorry," the governor said.

"No need," Nathan replied. "I had long before decided I
did not want to be a mariner. I and my friend Abijnah Warren organized the settlement of Marshfield together."

The governor looked up at Nathan with startled compre-
hension. "Of course, forgive me. May I offer my sincerest
condolences for the dreadful losses which you have suffered."

"Your Lordship," Nathan said urgently, "I must know what
news you have of the hostage prisoners. Whatever must be
done to obtain the return of my daughter and son, I will do.
Whatever the savages are demanding for ransom, I will pay."

The governor regarded Nathan with a solemn expression.
"Surely, sir, that is an idle boast—you must have lost a good
deal of your worldly goods in the raid."

"Everything," Nathan replied evenly. "I lost everything,
but I will find the means for any ransom—whatever is
asked. What is being done?"

"Very little, actually," the governor answered with a sigh
of regret. "The French claim they have no contact with the
Indians, and no control over the disposition of the prisoners.
One tribe of Caughnawagas has sent a courier message, and
we have ransomed back two women and a child for an impossible sum of gold. That is all we have been able to accomplish." The governor paused, as if regretting the need for
his next words. "Mr. Fairchild, we are at war with the
French and I count it lucky that we have obtained even three
of the hostages."

"Did the returned prisoners know anything about the other captives?" Nathan demanded.

"No," the governor replied. "I assure you, we will continue to do all we can. Now, if you will excuse me, I must continue my scheduled interviews or Junius will never forgive me." The governor nodded his head in dismissal, but Nathan leaped to his feet.

"You mean you're finished?" Nathan shouted. "You've run into obstacles and you're abandoning the hostages!"

The governor frowned and looked up from his papers. "Mr. Fairchild," he said impatiently, "we have not abandoned them. We will do everything in our power. However, it is a hopeless task. If you do not believe me, then speak to the French trappers yourself."

Nathan clenched his fist and pounded it on the governor's desk. "How can you sit here in comfort and not devote every ounce of power, every last cent of this colony's treasury, to the return of those helpless citizens? They are the victims of the games played by men sitting in gilded offices."

The governor's voice was edged with ice. "Because of your emotional duress, Mr. Fairchild, I will excuse your behavior. However, this interview is now concluded." The governor nodded to the guard who began advancing toward him.

"In the name of our Saviour and Lord!" Nathan shouted as the soldier grabbed his arm to lead him out of the office. "What must I do to obtain your help?"

As the guard reached for the gleaming doorknob to open the massive mahogany doors, the governor glanced up one more time and surveyed Nathan with his shrewd eyes.

"Perhaps a large contribution to the ransom fund. In gold," the governor suggested coolly. "These investigations are very expensive, the Indian captors are exceedingly greedy, and our treasury is bare."

Nathan nodded with bitter deference, shook off the guard's grip, and let himself out of the office into the crowded anteroom.

He saw the look of cold fury thrown his way by the governor's aide and knew Junius Comstock would never forget him, or forgive the affront to his authority that Nathan had committed.

The secretary sat at his desk and watched with undisguised contempt as Nathan thrust his way toward him through the crush of petitioners and office-seekers.

"Who is in charge of the ransom funds?" Nathan asked Junius without preamble.

A malevolent smile appeared on Comstock's face. "I am."

Nathan felt a shudder at the thinly veiled menace in the words. "And what is your assessment for the ransom of two child prisoners?" Nathan asked, keeping his voice calm.

The governor's aide glanced haughtily at Nathan's shabby homespun clothing. "Five hundred sovereigns in gold," he said with a sneer. "A sum which must be paid by the family, since one can scarcely expect the colony to beggar itself when we are on the brink of war."

"No," Nathan retorted, "one should not expect a colony that cannot defend its citizens to be able to rescue them."

Comstock smashed his open-palmed hands down on his desk and stood up. "Sir," he hissed. "You insult this colony! You insult this office! You insult the governor and the crown!"

"There is no insult in truth," Nathan replied steadily. "I will obtain the ransom money, and you, my dear sir, and the governor, and the whole of this colony had best put every effort at your disposal into obtaining the release of those defenseless prisoners, or I swear to God, I will . . ."

"You will what?" Junius asked, his eyes glittering with triumph. "You swear you will do what, Mr. Fairchild? Just say one more word. You totter even now on the brink of treason. One more word, one threat to myself or the person of the governor, and we shall have you in irons."

"You shall not have me," Nathan replied coldly. "But I shall have justice." With that Nathan turned on his heels and strode through the milling crowd and onto the streets of Boston.

It was a pleasant spring evening, with the salty tang of the sea blowing across the city on an ocean breeze, but Nathan hurried through the streets like a man possessed.

With heavy heart he turned a corner, and walked into the quiet elegance of Back Bay. Brick mansions. Genteel squares. Hypocrisy and greed. He had never wanted to return to this place, and now he found himself approaching the door of his father-in-law, stripped of family, possessions, and friends—little more than a beggar.

He paused by the door which gleamed with a fresh coating of black paint.

A serving woman in white cap and apron opened the door,

stared at him with disapproval, and directed him to the tradesman's entrance in back.

"I am here to see Mr. Thomas Pembroke," Nathan said, and gave his name. The woman closed the door in his face, but within minutes she returned. She opened the door reluctantly.

"You may see the master," the woman said imperiously. "He is waiting in the library.

Only his compelling need could have forced him to walk over that threshold to beg for help from a man who despised him, and whom he despised in return. Nathan headed across the high-ceilinged central hallway toward the door on the left. To his right he saw a glimpse of gleaming crystal candelabra, and the muted blue and rose silks of the salon. The parquet floor shone with beeswax. Painted portraits and oil landscapes in their gilded frames lined the shadowed hall.

Nothing had changed since the night he and Chastity had been married. He could still see Thomas Pembroke, standing silent and furious by the ballroom door. Pembroke had given his consent to the marriage only under duress, Nathan having threatened to expose Pembroke as the slave-trading hypocrite that he was. Pembroke was not likely, Nathan thought grimly, to welcome him now with open arms.

With an impatient hand, Nathan pushed open the library door. The walls of the room were filled with books from floor to ceiling. It was one of the great private libraries of the New World.

Nathan's father-in-law prided himself on his books. It was an obsession with the man. Thomas Pembroke's greatest aspiration was to become conversant with all the knowledge of his time. Apparently the obsession had grown out of hand, for the library gave the appearance of being a room in which the owner lived. A tray with a half-eaten meal was set on the floor, reading lamps were lit beside each chair; and the day bed, covered with a rumpled throw rug and Persian pillows, suggested that the bed had been recently slept in.

Behind a partner's desk with intricate inlays of gilt leather stood Thomas Pembroke himself. Pembroke's eyes were dark and implacable, made all the more so because of the whiteness of his powdered wig and the paleness of his skin. He looked like a man who lived in closed rooms—whose face never saw the sun. His eyes narrowed and he made no move

move toward Nathan—no outstretched hand, no expression of any emotion except hatred.

"You dare to come here," Pembroke said in a low, furious voice, "after what you have done. You dare to come here."

"It is not a matter of dare, it is a matter of must," Nathan replied.

"No!" The word exploded from Thomas's lips. "It is *dare*! How dare you come into my home! How dare you be alive when my daughter is dead! How dare you stand there living and breathing with my grandchildren gone forever! Is this what you stole my daughter for? To kill her in some savage wilderness? If so, then why did you not have the decency to die with her?"

Nathan's face was black with outrage. "Don't you know I would rather be dead?" he shouted. "If my flesh and blood could save her, I would give every drop, every shred. It is damnation to be alive when everything I love is gone. My punishment is enough. You cannot know what I would give or do to have Chastity back again."

"You will not speak of her," Thomas Pembroke roared. "I will not hear her name from your lips."

For a moment Nathan's hands clenched and unclenched, as though he wanted to reach out and grasp the older man and shake him into submission.

"I have come to you to beg that we put our old differences and hatreds aside. It is as Chastity would have wished. We are the only ones left who can save Talmadge and Mercy. I believe that is why my life was spared I will not rest until I have rescued them."

Thomas Pembroke sat down heavily behind the desk. "I have never even seen my daughter's children. They are all that is left of her now."

"Yes," Nathan agreed. "All that is left. We must do everything in our power to bring them safely back."

"We?" Thomas Pembroke said with heavy sarcasm. "We? I think you must have talked to the governor, as have I. It is not a matter of effort or strength that is needed to return them. As I understand, it is a simple matter of money. Gold sovereigns, to be specific. Many, many gold sovereigns. More, I suspect, than you have ever seen in your life."

Nathan let the gibe go past. "Will you lend the money to me or must I go elsewhere?"

"And where else would you go?" Thomas asked angrily.

"You talk as though you had a choice. We are not playing games here, Nathan. I know you have lost everything. It was all invested in that death trap you called Marshfield.

"Thirteen years ago you left this room with pride. You were so arrogant!" Pembroke growled. "You threw everything I created, everything I owned in my face. You denounced everything that I had and now you come back to me as a beggar, and the things which I have gained, my power and my resources, are your only hope.

"You have nothing, Nathan Fairchild. Not money, not power, not friends, not a wife, not children. It is I and not you who have the upper hand this time."

Nathan groaned aloud and sat down, putting his face in his hands. Shaking his head, he whispered hoarsely, "You are making a game of this, Thomas. These are your grandchildren, but believe me, if I had any place else to go, I would not come to you."

The ghost of a bitter smile flashed across Thomas's face. "You have nowhere else to go. This time you will listen to my terms, as I was forced to listen to yours those many years ago when you blackmailed me into allowing my daughter to marry you. Curse you! Curse the day you first crossed this threshold."

The older man sat down slowly at his desk and folded his long, blue-veined hands in front of him. "I will never forgive you, Nathan Fairchild, for taking my daughter from me. I will never forgive you for the harsh life you gave her. And, I will hate you until the day I die for the manner of her death."

Thomas Pembroke looked up fiercely. "I give you the gold you ask for her—not for you! If it were for you alone, I would not give you a pence, I would watch you suffer with a satisfaction which shames me. No, Nathan, I give you the gold because I believe that if it is possible to find and ransom my grandchildren, you are the only man who will be able to do it."

Pembroke took a deep breath. "However, I give you the gold on one condition. You may keep the boy, but you will give your daughter to me, and you will never, never, as long as you live, attempt to speak to her, or to contact her in any way once she is remanded to my care. Do I make myself clear?"

Nathan had sprung to his feet. "This is madness, Thomas," he shouted.

Pembroke's expression remained unaltered. "The boy would be too much like you. I do not think I could change him, but the girl is young. I will not let you retrieve my granddaughter to take her back into a savage wilderness to be raised as a coarse and vulgar farm girl. Do I make myself clear? If you wish to see either of your children again, you must promise the girl to me."

Nathan started to laugh. His laughter was full of pain and desperation and terrible irony.

"Oh Thomas, you poor foolish man. You want Mercy because you think you can use her to replace Chastity. You will close her up in this fancy tomb of a house, and you will treat her like one of your precious books. You think Mercy will be Chastity reborn. Your little girl come home again. But the joke's on you, Thomas, for you see, it is Talmadge, the boy, who is the image of his mother—Mercy is the image of me."

Pembroke looked discomfited, but his cold face did not change. "I care nothing for images. I will have Mercy or you will have no ransom. It is as simple as that, Nathan."

A long silence stretched out in the room as the men tested one another's will, and at last Nathan sighed. "If that is the price, I have no choice but to pay it."

Thomas indicated a strongbox in the far corner of the library.

"There is the gold, Nathan. You may count what you wish." Nathan counted out the five hundred sovereigns and Pembroke gave him a smaller strongbox in which Nathan placed the money. Nathan bent to lift the heavy box by its leather handles.

"Just a moment, Nathan. For all your faults I know you to be a man of honor. Give me your hand on your promise, and I will let you leave the house with the gold. What you do to secure the return of the children is your affair, but when you find them, you are to bring Mercy to me," Pembroke said coldly.

For a sickening moment Nathan stared at the gold. Then, with a heavy heart and a feeling of deepening anger, he shook Pembroke's hand and hurried from the house before he found himself refusing the one essential resource for the return of his children.

"You shall hear from me," he said shortly as he left.

"Not unless you bring Mercy," Pembroke said. "Otherwise I never want to hear from you again."

Chapter Ten

It was almost midnight before Nathan found the house he was looking for. It was on a narrow side street off the waterfront—trim, tidy, with a gabled roof and poured-glass windows with the telltale bull's-eye circles in the panes.

Nathan knocked on the door and after a long pause a voice from an upper window shouted, "Who is it?"

"Is that you, Daniel?" Nathan called, cupping his hands around his mouth and looking up to the window.

"Aye," said the voice. "And who are you?"

"Nathan. Nathan Fairchild. Will you let me in?"

There was no answer. Nathan waited a minute and then picked up the heavy chest and turned to leave. Just then the front door clanged open, and a man in a linen nightshirt came rushing out.

"Nathan Fairchild! You landlocked, beached, old mariner! I can scarce believe my eyes. 'Tis a happy wind that has blown you my way after all these years. Come in, come in." Captain Daniel Cothran, his sleep-rumpled hair giving him a boyish look, threw a welcoming arm around Nathan's shoulders and led him into a comfortable parlor.

In the lamplight, Nathan could see that the thirteen years since he had last seen his boyhood companion had hardly changed Daniel Cothran at all. Daniel's square, handsome face, with its bold, dark eyebrows, deep brown eyes, and rugged jaw, was a little more weathered by sun and wind, but the lines were those of wisdom, courage, and humor. It was a face a man could trust and depend upon to the very death. Nathan felt blessed to have such a friend.

Before he knew it, Nathan was seated in a wing chair, cup of warmed brandy was placed in his hands and Daniel's kind, intelligent eyes were assessing him with concern and affection.

For the first time in all the weeks since the tragedy, Nathan dropped his defenses. Knowing he had reached safe haven at last, he put his head in his hands and wept. Daniel knew the storm would pass, but he knew, too, that grief can be its own best healer and that Nathan had to release the burden he carried alone. Nathan had to acknowledge his grief before it could begin to heal.

Finally, the sorrow was spent and Nathan regained control. Quietly he told Daniel what had happened at Marshfield—Daniel had heard the story of course, but knew none of the details. Last of all Nathan told Daniel in an anguished voice of the desperate bargain he had been forced to make with his father-in-law.

"Well, now, then," Daniel Cothran said, his voice reflecting both wisdom and sympathy. "I think the evil of this day has been sufficient. Let's get some sleep and think on these things tomorrow when our heads and our hearts are clearer.

Nathan nodded numbly. "Where shall I put this damned gold for safekeeping?" he asked.

"Under the bed in the room where I shall put you," Daniel answered. "It will be safe."

Later, lying in Daniel's neat spare room in a borrowed nightshirt, Nathan stared at the ceiling in the darkness, thinking of the fortune in gold lying underneath him and wondering if he would find the way to use the gold to free Talmadge and Mercy.

"Where are you, my children?" he whispered into the darkness, trying to bring their dear faces into his mind. "Are you cold, or sick, or hungry? Do you wonder where I am, and why I have not come? Are you hurt or . . ."

He could not stand to think anymore, and he turned on his side, determined to sleep, but other memories came tumbling out and would not be stopped. He saw Chastity as he had first seen her, stepping from her father's coach and laughing at the footman. A heart so easily made glad, he thought. Oh Chastity! As he fell into a heavy, dreamless sleep, he was certain he smelled the perfume of her hair. She floated into his arms and they lay together in a field of clover-sweet grass and he kissed her rich, soft lips. Then she was gone, like the wisp of mist when the sun's rays appear. With regret, Nathan slept.

"Well, Daniel," Nathan asked the next morning as the two men sat enjoying hot scones and oranges with their morning coffee, "how fares the *Sea Falcon?*"

"She's a bit of a tub," Daniel laughed, "but she's a sweet enough ship, Nathan, and she runs true and clean from Southampton to Boston, with none of the West Indies triangle. Legal cargo, passengers, no slaves and no contraband."

Nathan nodded, understanding Daniel's words. "I'm glad you found a safe and honorable helm, old friend.

"When I lost the last frigate of the Fairchild line that last summer we were together in Boston and we were stranded in this God-fearing harbor"— Nathan's voice was thick with irony—"I did not think anyone could find a way through the mire of hypocrisy and double-dealing on this waterfront. But you've managed to do it, Daniel. You found an honest ship. You are a good man, and the years sit lightly on you."

Daniel grinned, and his frank brown eyes and genuine smile gave Nathan the first feeling in weeks that goodness still existed somewhere in the world. There was such a wonderful, boyish quality in Daniel, that it made Nathan feel young again. "Aye." Daniel laughed. "Port of secret slavers, impressed crews, and godly privateers—'twas pretty slim pickings."

The two men talked on, remembering the days when as young officers without berths they had plied the wharves of Boston searching for a commission. It had soon become apparent that even the proudest of the merchantships in the Boston harbor were involved somewhere in their voyages with slavery, privateering, contraband, or illegal dealings with the French blockaders.

Of all these questionable practices, it was the transport of slaves and the hypocrisy of the shipowners and captains that had most sickened the two young men those thirteen years ago. The most blatant slaver of all was Captain Esterbridge, who had taken over the Fairfield frigate which Nathan had lost in the probate court. Esterbridge was the most powerful captain on the docks, a fat man with mean slits for eyes. He had tried to hire Daniel and Nathan but they had refused the man's offer, and in so doing had offended the powerful captain. The young men had quickly realized that with Esterbridge as an enemy, they would have great difficulty in finding a berth.

That summer Nathan had met and fallen in love with Chastity Pembroke, but her obsessed and possessive father would not consider Nathan's suit. Pembroke had informed Nathan that he considered him to be a penniless social climber, and had forbidden Nathan to come to his house or to see his daughter. Nathan knew that Thomas Pembroke considered Chastity his possession, as surely as his books and art collection, and would never let her go except to a man of his own choosing.

One evening, in conversation with a drunken ship's agent at the tavern near the harbor, Nathan and Daniel had discovered that the ships under Captain Esterbridge's command were secretly owned by Thomas Pembroke, Chastity's upright and self-righteous father. It seemed that Thomas Pembroke, esteemed as one of the most prominent and puritanical members of Bostonian society, had earned his wealth and power by slave trading and continued, secretly, to do so. When Nathan learned of Pembroke's hypocrisy, he decided nothing would stop him. He would marry Chastity and together, they would leave Boston forever. He would give up the sea, for he could not bear to be apart from her, and they would find a place to be together.

Daniel loved the sea. Nathan had begged his friend to come with him to the Western Reserve, but Daniel couldn't imagine himself as a farmer, and so the boyhood friends had sadly parted company.

Just before Nathan departed, Daniel had accepted the captaincy of a clumsy, undistinguished passenger ship named the *Sea Falcon*. "At least it takes me back to the clean, fresh air of the sea," Daniel had laughed in his carefree, warm-hearted way. "I'm a simple man, and so a simple ship should do me well. I shall miss you, Nathan. Won't be the same without you."

Nathan had clasped Daniel's hand, "You are my oldest friend—the brother I never had. I shall miss you. I will pray that the Lord finds us a way back together someday. May the winds blow fair wherever you go."

As the two friends finished breakfast and Daniel prepared to go to his ship and Nathan to return to the governor's office, they shook hands warmly. "Thirteen years!" Daniel exclaimed, "And still our friendship remains as fresh as the unchanging ocean that I ply."

Nathan laughed. "Yes. And as steady as a rock. A friend such as you is worth more than gold, Daniel. I shall see you later today, after I have visited the governor. I'll come to the *Sea Falcon* and give your riggings an inspection."

"Right–o!" Daniel laughed. "I'll see how much you remember of the Seafarer's Manual—although I have always thought, 'Once a man of the sea, always a man of the sea.' I know you have saltwater in your blood!"

Nathan smiled and shook his head. "No longer, old friend. I am a confirmed farmer—and father."

Suddenly Daniel's face was serious and he walked over and clasped Nathan's shoulder. "Whatever I can do to help, Nathan, I pledge you my hand, my worldly goods, my time. Whatever you need that I have—it is yours."

Nathan nodded, too moved to speak, and the two friends parted.

Chapter Eleven

When Nathan entered the governor's office, the anteroom was surprisingly empty. A single sentry stood at the door. "I must see the governor!" Nathan demanded.

"Not in residence, sir," the soldier told Nathan without relaxing his military stance.

"What do you mean, not in residence?" Nathan demanded. "This is a matter of utmost urgency."

"You will need to see Mr. Comstock."

Seething with impatience, Nathan paced the floor of the deserted room. It was hot and humid and fat black flies were buzzing on the windows. The office doors opened and Junius Comstock came hurrying out.

Nathan leaped in front of him. "Comstock, I am Nathan Fairchild."

"Yes," the man replied. "I remember you."

"It is essential that I speak to the governor," Nathan insisted. "I must know where he is."

"That is completely impossible, Mr. Fairchild," the aide replied haughtily. "He is gone on summer retreat in Cambridge. He will be speaking at Harvard College, and then is going game hunting. He will be unavailable for any kind of audience."

Nathan choked back his fury and disappointment. "And the Marshfield prisoners, and the waging of his precious war—do these things stop for summer retreats?" he retorted. "Lives are at stake here! Weeks have been wasted already. Why isn't the Commonwealth doing something?"

Junius Comstock motioned Nathan to follow him into the governor's office and sat down in the governor's chair. He did not offer Nathan a seat, and Nathan had the distinct feeling that Comstock enjoyed sitting behind the governor's desk, playing God.

Making a tent with his hands, Junius spoke officiously. "I am in charge of this matter while the governor is away. I can assure you I will do everything possible to restore the captives."

"Exactly what are you doing?" Nathan queried, trying to contain his anger.

"You are asking to know things which are state secrets, Mr. Fairchild," Junius Comstock retorted. "I cannot tell you of our clandestine negotiations, or who our secret sources are. As soon as we have news of your children we will be in touch with you."

Comstock was obviously dismissing him, but Nathan refused to budge.

"I have the ransom money you asked for," Nathan growled. "Five hundred gold sovercigns."

Junius looked up at Nathan with a flinty smile. "I did not realize you had such munificent resources, Mr. Fairchild. Since you have already collected the ransom money, this places a slightly different light on your case. Please leave the location of the place where you can be contacted. And now, if you will excuse me, I have very pressing work which must be done."

Nathan grabbed a quill from the inkpot on the governor's desk and quickly wrote down the location of Daniel's home.

"I am staying here," Nathan said. "Any time, day or night, you may reach me. I will wait for five days, and five days only, and then I shall begin my own search."

"As you wish, Mr. Fairchild, but I promise you, our resources are at the highest level."

The docks were noisy, and under the shouting of men's voices and the drag of cargo, Nathan could hear the familiar sound of the heavy ships rubbing against the pilings—the scrape and squeak of the spars with their heavy sails furled.

He was looking for the *Sea Falcon*. As he found the ship and walked up the gangplank toward Daniel, Nathan noticed that the former Fairchild frigate, now secretly owned by Thomas Pembroke, rode at anchor in the next berth.

On the quarterdeck he saw the heavy figure of the slaver, Captain Esterbridge. The man's heavy chin and squinty eyes were unchanged. Looking quickly at its hull and deck, Nathan realized that the ship was in excellent condition in spite of its years. Esterbridge was obviously a demanding master. From the bustle on the deck, he surmised the ship was preparing to leave on a voyage.

Nathan stared with regret at his old ship, remembering what Captain Esterbridge had said to him. "A well-run merchant ship should never need to sail with ballast. Some cargo can always be found, human or otherwise, no matter what the port of call."

Nathan thought of the human cargo that must have crammed the holds of that ship over the years. With a shudder of distaste, he turned away.

Standing on the *Sea Falcon*'s deck, Nathan and Daniel leaned against the railing and looked out to sea. "I wish we could sail straight up the coastline, Daniel, past the Bay of Storms, around Acadia into the St. Lawrence River and right to the heart of Quebec. I'd grab those blue-coated Frenchmen by the throat. I'd make them lead me to the villages of the Abenakis and I would throw aside teepees and tear apart lodges until I found my children."

Daniel nodded, "Just say the word, Nathan, and I'll weigh anchor."

Nathan gave a shuddering breath and looked at his friend; his eyes were terrible to see. "They are up there, Daniel," he whispered, looking northward. "I can feel it in my heart."

"Be patient a day or two longer, Nathan. The government must be in communication with the French. It is the only and best thing you can do for now." Daniel's voice gave Nathan strength. "If we went to Canada, we would have no idea where to begin to look in that vast North. You must get better information, and the government is your only hope." Nathan nodded in resignation.

The two men left the *Sea Falcon* and walked to Haymarket Square. They shared a cut of beef and a cornmeal pudding before striding through the gathering night to Daniel's house.

"Thank you, Daniel, for your help," Nathan said as they prepared to retire for the night.

"I wish I could do more." Daniel sighed. "A bed and a crust of bread seems so very little to give."

"It's not the sleep and the food," Nathan said, "it is your goodness that is sustaining me."

After the fifth day of waiting in Daniel's small rooms, Nathan was in a state of agitation beyond reason. The enforced inactivity was like a prison sentence.

Daniel was seldom at home, since he was preparing to set

sail within the week. The long days of silence were driving Nathan mad, and so it was with inexpressible relief that he responded to a knock on the door to find a messenger in a dark cloak and tricorn hat. The man handed Nathan a sealed letter and left quickly.

Tearing open the envelope, Nathan read the contents in a single glance, and then hurried upstairs. Daniel found his friend that evening in the spare bedroom counting the gold pieces of the ransom money.

"Comstock writes to tell me he has made contact with the French military officer who commanded the raid on Marshfield." Nathan said. "Very secret. He says if we go through official channels it could take months. He tells me this officer is boarded on one of the French blockade ships just outside the harbor. Comstock will get the money to the Frenchman by a small harbor sloop which can slip through to the blockade without being detected. He has promised the return of my children within the month."

Daniel regarded his friend with a thoughtful frown. "Don't you think it might be wise to have some proof of these promises before you turn over the money, Nathan?" he asked quietly.

Jumping to his feet, Nathan glared at Daniel. "This man is the governor's personal aide," Nathan said emphatically. "I don't like him, but he does represent the highest office in the colony. If I can't trust him, then whom can I trust?"

Without answering, Daniel walked to the window and looked down at the busy harbor. "Aye," he whispered, almost to himself, "who indeed?"

"What did you say?" Nathan asked sharply. He was puzzled by his friend's caution and lack of enthusiasm.

"Nothing," Daniel answered. "I'm sorry for my suspicious nature. There is one thing you can trust—and that is our friendship. I have missed it most heartily through the years while you have been in Marshfield." Daniel sighed. "How far we have come in those passing years, old friend, and to what unexpected harbors."

Nathan nodded, rubbing his right hand over his neck to ease the tension there. "It is strange how the currents of life lead us where we have no wish to go. I thought I would spend the rest of my life as a comfortable farmer in Marshfield, growing fat and fatherly. Now, here I am back in a city I had thought never to see again, beholden to a father-

in-law whom I cannot abide, and bereft of all those whom I
have loved—save only you, Daniel. You are that rare thing,
a man without guile."

Daniel smiled, but there was a gently troubled look in his
eyes. "I thank you for those kind words, Nathan. But I do
not deserve them. Surely you know by now that life will not
let any of us live without compromise."

The two friends looked at one another for a long moment,
and Nathan said softly, "You have found out more about
Thomas Pembroke." It was a statement, not a question.

Daniel nodded. "Yes. I have discovered that he is the legal
owner of the *Sea Falcon*—and yet I have not had the courage to give up the helm as I should have. I cannot stand to
work for such a man, but . . . I would die without the sea. It
is all I have.

"The *Sea Falcon* is the only ship available to me. Pembroke has asked me many times to sail the West Indies—the
African triangle—but I have refused. I *will not* be a slaver—
but in working for one, am I not just the same?"

"No," Nathan said quickly. "Sooner or later we all must
yield, whether in order to sustain our profession and livelihood,
or else to protect those we love. Each man has his Achilles'
heel, and the predators know it. They find it and use it."

Nathan continued quietly, "But in a way we win—because
we are using them too. Using them to accomplish our own
ends. Using them to accomplish good in spite of themselves.
So you will captain the *Sea Falcon*, saving one crew from
his evil plans. So I will use my father-in-law's gold to recover my children, and then I shall go as far away from this
corrupted and hypocritical place as I can."

"Where will you go?" Daniel asked. "Where will things
be any different?"

"There is a whole world out there." Nathan waved his
arm. "Somewhere there has to be a place where a man can
live unto himself, by his own measure, without the interference of corrupt governments and misled churches and
wretched commerce. I am going to find such a place, and
live there with my children."

"But not Mercy . . ." Daniel reminded Nathan gently.
"Pembroke has claimed her."

"Let him claim away," Nathan declared. "I will take her
where he cannot touch her."

With that, Nathan picked up the heavy box and staggered

down the stairs. "Midnight at high tide," he said. "That is when I am to meet Comstock."

The hour of twelve struck and the wharves were black as pitch. Nathan stumbled toward the stack of bales near Esterbridge's frigate. He waited, listening to the lap of the ocean against the pilings and the clear sound of Esterbridge's crew calling watch.

The Esterbridge frigate and Daniel's boat were both ready to sail with the morning light.

A figure in a heavy cloak moved through the gloom and approached the bales.

"Fairchild, is that you?" The voice was Comstock's. "Quickly!" Junius ordered when Nathan had identified himself. "I must take the gold immediately and give it to the intermediary. He is leaving at dawn to sail to the French blockade. You've counted the money?"

Nathan assured the governor's aide that the ransom was complete. "Very well," whispered Comstock. "Wait exactly one week and then come to the governor's office. I will have orders and directions on how and where you are to pick up your children."

"Has the French officer seen them?" Nathan asked eagerly. "Are they well? Have they been treated kindly?"

"Yes, yes," Comstock said impatiently. "He says they are living in the chief's lodge and are content, but anxious to be returned to you. The Indians were sure your children would bring a good price, and so they have watched over them carefully."

"That is good news," Nathan exclaimed. "Could I not sail with the emissary tonight, and speak to the Frenchman myself?"

"Don't be a fool, Fairchild!" Junius hissed. "This French officer is committing high treason for you. If you draw attention to him, he will be arrested and you will never see your children again. Be patient, man. That is your part."

The gold was exchanged, and Nathan watched as Junius Comstock disappeared into the blackness of the night, his hope mixed with a nagging sense of unease. Somehow it had seemed too easy, and yet Nathan knew he must continue to believe and be patient. After all, the government had failed once in not providing protection for the Marshfield settlers; surely they now felt the need to rectify their mistake. He had to do as Comstock had told him, and be patient.

Early the next morning Daniel bade Nathan good-bye as the two friends breakfasted in the low-beamed kitchen. The *Sea Falcon* was sailing on the noon tide for its scheduled passenger run to Plymouth. The two men parted with affection and a touch of sorrow. "May your children be restored to you when I return," Daniel said, grasping Nathan's hand in his own.

"And may you find heart's ease and satisfaction in your life, good friend," Nathan replied. "You have helped me much these past days, and I will ever be beholden to you."

After Daniel left, Nathan went upstairs to pack.

It was several hours later when a breathless messenger arrived, a young lad in tattered jersey and cut-off breeches. "Sir," he panted to Nathan, "I have an urgent message for you from Captain Daniel Cothran. Forgive me, sir. He sent the note to me by way of one of his seamen, and the man gave me poor directions to the house. I have been wandering these side streets for an hour."

Nathan grasped the note and read it:

"Friend Nathan: I noted at the last moment that Esterbridge took a passenger on board who was carrying a heavy strongbox. The man was cloaked, but I could swear it was your friend Junius Comstock. Am I mistaken? Was the gold not to be sent by sloop with an emissary to the French embargo fleet? Esterbridge sails far to the south of that route. Something does not seem right. Pray that I am wrong. —Daniel."

With a roar of rage, Nathan burst out of Daniel's house and raced along the streets to the docks. Crashing into pedestrians and dockworkers he dashed along the waterfront until he came to the berth where Esterbridge's frigate had been. The pier was empty.

With a despairing look he cast a glance at the next berth, where Daniel's ship had ridden at anchor. It too was gone. With the practiced eye of a seaman he swiftly looked out across the wide expanse of the harbor and saw both ships, with full sails, running speedily down the horizon upon the morning breeze. In minutes they would be gone from sight.

Moving like a man possessed, Nathan ran to the nearest street and hailed a public hack.

"Swiftly, man!" he exclaimed to the driver. "To the governor's office, and do not spare these horses."

They clattered over the city streets and came to the government buildings. The doors stood open, and inside Nathan could see clerks running back and forth, and a general disarray of papers and open drawers. He also noted a pervading sense of alarm.

"What is it?" Nathan demanded. "What is going on here?"

A clerk came out and addressed him nervously. "We cannot say, sir. The governor is returning this afternoon, but these offices are closed to the public."

"Then Comstock!" Nathan gasped. "Let me meet with Comstock."

"I am sorry, sir, that will not be possible," the clerk said emphatically, his eyes shifting.

"He *is* here, isn't he?" Nathan shouted.

"Sir!" the clerk said. "You must treat this office with dignity."

"Dignity!" Nathan exploded. "This is not an office. It is a den of thieves. I will wait until the governor arrives, and I will speak to him."

Nathan waited all day. Late in the afternoon an entourage of coaches and carriages arrived, and a flood of richly dressed men flowed into the building. A small cadre of soldiers hastily escorted the governor to a side door.

"I demand to see the governor. This is a matter that will not wait." Nathan pushed through the throng.

The guards crossed their bayonets but Nathan stood, unmoving. The governor stopped and turned, and the sentries sprang to attention. Nathan bowed. "Your Excellency, I must see you. I have waited the entire day."

The governor frowned, but, seeing the iron determination on Nathan's face, he said, "One minute, Mister Fairchild. Not one moment longer."

Nathan hurried inside the office doors with the governor. "Where is Junius Comstock?" he demanded. "And my five hundred in ransom gold?"

The governor looked at him coldly. "That is just the question, sir, and had I the answer I would gladly give it."

"What do you mean?" Nathan gasped.

"Not only your ransom money, but also the entire ransom exchequer has been emptied. It seems our friend thought he would enjoy the gold more than the French or the Indians."

"What are you going to do?" Nathan demanded.

"Nothing," the governor said calmly. "Do you have a receipt? Any way of proving you gave the gold to the government?"

"No," Nathan said, and a sense of sick horror filled his mind. "Why should I not trust my own government?"

"Exactly," the governor said. "That is the way a citizen of the colony should feel, and if word of this scandal breaks, that essential trust will be eroded forever. Therefore, my good man, in secret we will try to find Junius Comstock and restore the gold but, there will be no public hue and cry. If you try to make trouble, we will simply discredit you."

Nathan thrust his face into the governor's and said softly, with leaden conviction, "You have no intention of bringing home the hostages, or of returning the ransom money. You will sweep it all under the rug. All you intend to do is to continue to sit here in your beautiful, comfortable office—and leave those helpless women and children at the mercy of our enemies."

"That's enough," the governor said. "Your minute is long finished. But I will tell you we do intend to continue our inquiries through the proper channels, and we will obtain the release of as many of the prisoners as we can."

"Inquiries! The proper channels!" Nathan exploded. "Self-serving phrases! I was a fool to come to you. A fool to think anyone here would care about ordinary people. You don't serve us—you use us."

Nathan turned on his heel to leave the room, but at the door he gave the governor one last, penetrating look. "I have found that savages do not only live in the lodge of the Abenaki." With a bitter glance he studied the governor, now seated in his silk-covered chair. "Some of them live in brocaded rooms."

From a relative of Abijnah Warren's, Nathan borrowed enough money to buy himself a horse and frontier gear. He dressed himself in the soft deerskin of the woodsmen. With care he selected a gun, a knife, and traps, and packed his supplies in oiled sealskin.

Although Nathan had never trapped, he had seen the windfall wealth which came to a good trapper after a successful winter. He would get the gold. He would find his children. He would bring them home.

On a warm spring day, but with a heart as cold and grim as darkest winter, he began his journey westward.

Chapter Twelve

On a sweltering day in mid June, Nathan rode into the charred ruins of Marshfield. He had thought he would avoid the place, but somehow he was drawn to it.

All vestiges of the successful farmer and contented family man were long erased. He had become nothing but bone and muscle and his face was a mask—the lines strong, silent, and unreadable. In his eyes were depths of power, anger, and purpose which made others turn away from his intensity. His leather clothes were stained with sweat and dust and, like a true "frontiersman," he rode his horse alert to every sound and movement.

He was a man hardened physically, intellectually, and emotionally. This was not the Nathan Fairchild who had lived in this town. He had become someone else, forged by the flames of the destruction of Marshfield as surely as though he had walked through them.

All that remained intact of Marshfield's outlying structures were the fort walls. The fortress gate hung open, broken from one of its hinges and lying at a drunken angle. The stake walls were already beginning to fall, with gaps in them like missing teeth.

Why trust in anything which man can build, he wondered, when God and nature can undo our handiwork as though it were nothing?

Sadly, he rode down the main street and stared at the blackened ruins of the homes of his friends. He passed the Warrens' yard. The stone foundation of the beautiful home still stood, with blackened timbers rising like the fruit of an evil harvest. In sorrow he noted the wild roses which Abijnah had found and planted along his fenceline. The roses were blooming in wild profusion, as though the blood which had baptized the ground had given them new vigor.

Nathan's own home had fared a little better, although the

windows were smashed, the doors gone, and the walls stained with soot and smoke. The roof had caved in, and some of the chimney stones had been toppled. He walked into the empty great room. All remnants of furniture and personal articles were gone—pillagers and looters had picked the house clean. He did not care. He had no wish to own anything that reminded him of the past.

The meetinghouse was standing as well. It was damaged and defiled, but it could be reclaimed, should anyone ever have the heart to try again in this hostile land.

Nathan's last stop was the cemetery. He had brought an armload of the wild roses from the Warren property, and he found Chastity's small wooden marker. Next to it, he saw the little graves of Thomas and the unnamed baby.

For hours Nathan worked over the graves, pulling weeds, trimming the wild grasses with his knife, carving their names deeper into the wood so the violence of storms could not erase them.

At last, when the ground looked the way he wanted it, he took the roses and gently lay them over the little plots of earth. When night came, he stretched himself, facedown, on top of Chastity's grave and slept on the quiet mound. In his sleep he was sure he felt the earth breathe underneath him.

When Nathan left Marshfield the next day, he followed the directions he had received from the surviving members of the mounted Colonials who had given chase to the Indians those many months before. Without difficulty, Nathan found the first valley they had described and the narrow pass.

He entered the second valley, the one where the ambush had taken place. He sat on his horse and surveyed the valley with sad eyes. "Were you here, Talmadge? Mercy? Were you here? And where did they take you when you left?"

For days Nathan rode in circles, ever-widening, searching for any sign. Where could they have gone from this spot? Nathan wondered. Someone must have seen them on their journey. He decided to head westward, thinking he must find people who had commerce or connections with the Canadian Indians.

Somewhere, somehow he would hear something, or see something, a scrap of conversation, an article of clothing, a suspicious trail. He would find answers.

After crossing the Housatonic, Nathan rode into the Albany region. He had heard about the Dutch traders, that they were friendly with the Iroquois, but also dealt with French and Indian trappers from Canada. The traders knew little prejudice or allegiance. When it came to commerce they were open-minded and strong-willed. They preferred to keep political matters from complicating the conduct of their trade.

Nathan realized it would be a disadvantage for him to be known as a New Englander in this region. From Indian, Dutch, and French trappers alike he would meet with suspicion and distrust, if not outright hostility.

These people hated New Englanders because they knew the people of the English colonies would not rest until America was secured to the British. Better to be thought a *courier du bois,* Nathan decided, a man with no ties and no allegiance. A man of the wilderness.

Since Nathan spoke fluent French he could easily switch from one language to the other. He roughened his voice, and threw in enough patois that it became hard to tell his origins. By now his trapper's clothes were darkly stained and his skin burned to a leathery cast. Only his golden hair made him stand out from the mysterious trappers who ranged the woods and waterways in search of fur-bearing game. Mixing ashes and grease, Nathan rubbed his hair until the color deepened and became lank and lusterless.

As he traveled through the Albany territory he stopped at trading posts and camps. He talked to Indians and trappers and filthy men whose faces were hidden in bushes of hair and beards. In the corners of flea-ridden ale rooms, he eavesdropped on drunken conversations. With traders, peddlers, half-breed children, and dull-eyed squaws, he made discreet and circuitous inquiries.

As summer turned to autumn, he pieced everything he'd heard together, and thought he could reconstruct what had happened. The raiding parties had split up, each taking some of the prisoners, and had moved separately up the waterways of the rivers and lakes which led northward from Albany to Canada.

"Anyone who travels north this year is a dead man," one trader told him. "The French are fortifying the heads of the lakes, and the Indians have staked the trapping territory for their own. The French run with the Algonquin, Abenaki, and Caughnawaga, but the Iroquois of the Five Nations are determined to keep the territory to themselves. There'll be some nasty deeds in those parts, make no bones about it. If you really want to make your fortune trapping, head farther west where there are new rivers and lakes. There's a world out there so full of beaver, fox, and ermine a man could trap his fill by December, and not be able to carry it all back."

"Thanks, for the advice, *mon ami,*" Nathan said. "I shall think on it."

Nathan traded his horse for supplies and headed for the wilderness on foot.

The land into which Nathan traveled had a wild, magnificent beauty. Low mountains, green with vegetation, rolled one upon the other, and in the valleys between the mountains, crystal lakes dotted the terrain like sapphires dropped from the sky.

Each lake was a tiny inland sea, surrounded by its own emerald bowl of hills. From each lake trickled silver streams which followed secret passages to new lakes and new mountains. It was a land of endless beauty, abundant with water, fish, and game.

Often at night, on a high, open peak Nathan would spot smoke from the fire of a solitary campsite, and he would mark the location carefully in his mind. The next day he would travel as far from the area as possible.

The most direct and easy route to Canada would have been for him to follow the Hudson River system northward through Lake George and Lake Champlain. The French, however, had fortified the large lakes, and the Hudson waterway's trapping rights—although claimed by the Iroquois, who were bitter enemies of the French—had been appropriated now by the Algonquin tribes. The Iroquois tribes were being dispossessed, hounded from their ancestral land. In this place of conflict and hatred, danger lurked behind every leafy tree, behind every shadowed dell, and along each riverbank and lakefront.

Nathan survived each day as it came, living with one blind determination: to replace the gold, find his children, and free them. Nothing else. The slowness of his journey northward, and his despair at being unable to envision a foolproof plan that would ensure his ability to find and free his children, nearly drove him mad.

Autumn had begun to turn the hills to flame. The raging

beauty of the Adirondacks, with maples and burnished oak blazing in a glory of color, turned the mountains into bouquets.

At night a breath of frost silvered the evening breeze, and one morning, he rose to find ice crystals sprinkling the edge of the brook. Under cover of the fiery leaves, winter was approaching with quiet stealth. Nathan knew he had little time to decide where to lay his winter traps; his survival depended on a bountiful harvest of fur.

After a week of searching, he discovered a series of hidden lakes and waterways with valleys too steep and well hidden to invite settlement by Indian or Colonial. He knew he was slightly south and west of the large lakes of the Hudson system, but he had observed no traces of Indian trail. He felt certain he was in a region which was unclaimed, and untrapped.

On the second day of his reconnaissance, as he was moving at twilight down the side of the steep mountain in undergrowth dense with waist-high ferns and sumac, his foot caught in a wild grapevine. Within a second he was tumbling head over heels, crashing down the ravine, and landing in a sprawl at the bottom on a gravel spate by the side of a narrow lake.

Nathan had struck his head on a rock in the headlong fall, and for a moment he was dazed. Hearing a sound above him, he shook his head from side to side and gradually his vision cleared. Standing over him were two Indians armed with rifles. They were wearing deerskin without markings of any kind, and it was impossible to tell their tribe.

"What are you doing here?" the older Indian asked in guttural French. The man's hair was streaked with white and it flowed freely around his shoulders and face. The younger Indian wore his hair in two wrapped braids.

"I come in peace," Nathan answered quietly, speaking in French also, keeping his voice calm and unafraid.

The Indians were puzzled. They did not know if Nathan was a Frenchman, an itinerant trapper, a Dutch trader, or a New Englander. Nothing in his speech or appearance identified him. His large frame and light hair belied the easy conclusion that he was French.

"Get up," the older Indian growled in a rough voice, prodding Nathan with the barrel of his rifle. Nathan got up slowly, his hands extended in front of him in a gesture of nonaggression. The two Indians warily herded him into a grove of trees and he saw their small, hidden fire. The fringed bags and blankets which made up the Indians' traveling gear were heaped beside the fire ring.

While the first Indian stood guard, the smaller one came over and tore Nathan's pack from his shoulder. They had already taken his rifle, which they threw on the pile of their own belongings.

With Nathan standing helplessly, the younger Indian opened the pack and scattered Nathan's possessions on the ground. The braves exclaimed over the beads, mirrors, and tinwear Nathan had brought for trading. The older Indian grabbed one of the mirrors and held it up to look at himself. He laughed aloud, showing a mouth full of worn and rotted teeth.

They also found Nathan's parched corn and venison jerky, and each took a handful, then put the rest back in its kidskin bag, and placed the food bag next to the confiscated rifle. In the bottom of the pack they discovered his metal traps. Nathan had three small underspring traps, four single-spring traps, and one large double-spring trap. The Indians glared at the traps and talked between themselves in an Indian dialect.

Although he did not know their language, he could tell by their gestures and the tone of their voices they were angry at this evidence of his intention to trap fur-bearing animals.

The older, heavier Indian turned to Nathan with narrowed eyes. In French he declared, "We are Algonquin. This is our place to hunt. The Great Spirit has led us here."

Nathan felt such revulsion and hatred for these men he could hardly control himself. These Indians, or men like them, had killed, maimed, and violated the bodies of those whom he held dear. He could not bear to be in their presence—to see their filthy hands on his possessions, to stand unmoving as their guarded prisoner. With iron will he held himself in check, knowing any careless or unplanned move would bring his swift death. He was determined, however, to escape, and, if possible, to destroy these savages in the process.

Nathan's eyes felt hot with hatred. "Surely there is enough game for all," he said quietly.

The large Indian drew in his breath in an enraged hiss and raised his rifle, aiming it straight at Nathan's heart. Just then they heard a raucous honking as a flock of geese settled upon the water.

Fortunately, the distraction defused the immediate situation, and the gun was lowered slightly, as the suspicious and angry Indian continued to glare at his prisoner.

"The animals are ours to hunt," the man muttered, "For us and our people."

"But are not the French your friends?" Nathan asked. "Do you not share with friends?"

The Indian looked at him with squinted eyes. Daylight was fading and the light from the fire was dim. "The true French, *oui*," he grunted. "But you do not look like true French to me."

"You do not look like true Algonquin to me," Nathan retorted in a challenge that could not be ignored.

The Indian's nostrils flared with rage, and he pulled himself up proudly. "Fool! You do not know an Abenaki when you see one? I have come from far in the north. My tribe is like the wind. We are the greatest of the Algonquin! Him!" The proud Indian pointed to the smaller, younger native who was squatting a few yards away, his eyes trained on Nathan and his rifle held in the cradle of his arm.

"Him!" the older man repeated, pointing imperiously again. "He is Naskapi, small, unimportant Algonquin—but my people are royalty in the land of our fathers." The Indian used the French word "*roi*", and stood with truly regal pride. His haughty fierceness told Nathan he had struck a vulnerable spot.

Without replying, Nathan glanced from one of his captors to the other. When the Abenaki had spit out the word *Naskapi* Nathan had watched the younger Indian's face turn into a cold mask. He knew that the older Indian, in boasting about his own tribe, had mortally offended his hunting companion.

Slowly, Nathan turned his face to stare at the Naskapi brave. "Is it true?" he asked the younger man. "The Naskapi are small, unimportant Algonquin? Not like the great Abenaki. Are you also the slave of the Abenaki? His servant? Do you clean his catch and obey his order?"

The Naskapi brave growled in anger, like a cornered animal, and leaped to his feet. "Dog!" he shouted at Nathan. "Dare you speak like this to a Naskapi warrior?"

Nathan saw the man's eyes were red with fury and

wounded pride. "Not I," Nathan replied. "He is the one who has said it." Nathan nodded toward the Abenaki hunter.

Instantly, the older Indian realized what was happening. "Do not listen to him, friend," he called to the young Naskapi loudly. "He is our enemy and he speaks with the tongue of a snake."

"He speaks truth," the Naskapi brave replied with lethal fury. "You have called my people small and unimportant. Friends do not speak so."

The two Indians stood glaring at one another, uncertain of their next step but filled with mounting tension and emotion. The younger Indian still held his gun low, but he was balancing it in his hand as though preparing to bring it into action. The older Abenaki, still training his rifle on Nathan, realized the situation was fraught with dangerous undercurrents, and his experienced eyes darted from the furious Naskapi to his prisoner, trying to keep both men under surveillance.

"My words were careless, friend," the Abenaki placated the younger hunter. "We are Algonquin brothers."

"Then you do not think the Abenaki are greater than the Naskapi?" the Naskapi challenged menacingly. "Royalty?" The brave flung out the last word with a sneer.

To apologize was too much for the Abenaki warrior. He could not stand to be challenged in front of his prisoner, yet he knew the Naskapi must be appeased.

"I will kill this dog who has caused our quarrel," the Abenaki exclaimed. "Or you may kill him. I will give him to you to kill. For he has insulted your people.

Nathan shook his head. "Not I!" he protested loudly. "You!" He pointed dramatically at the Abenaki.

"Answer!" the Naskapi screamed at the Abenaki. "You say your people are kings, and mine are slaves?"

It was too much for the proud old warrior. He turned to the younger man and thundered, "Yes! The Abenaki are kings and warriors, and your people are water-carriers and farmers."

The younger Indian shrieked with infuriated pride and, almost without thinking, aimed his rifle at the older warrior and fired. The shot tore through the Abenaki's shoulder but he did not lose his control. The old Indian realized the truth of the situation, and knew that Nathan had created it, so rather than shooting the younger Indian he turned his gun on

Nathan. Just as the Abenaki prepared to shoot the prisoner, the enraged Naskapi rushed toward him with a madness in his eyes, and at the last minute the Abenaki had no choice but to turn his rifle on the younger Indian. The shot went true to the mark and the young Naskapi hunter fell in a bloodied heap.

Immediately the older warrior drew his knife. Even though his left arm was hanging useless, he swung his weapon at Nathan, who dodged. The blade of the knife tore across Nathan's shoulder and back, the wound burning like a red-hot brand.

Nathan lunged for the Abenaki's legs, throwing the hunter off balance, but the Indian held on to the knife and slashed Nathan again, this time cutting his hand. Nathan grabbed the Indian's arm, grappling for control of the weapon. Both men were bleeding profusely.

They struggled in silence, with the Indian's upraised arm holding the knife and Nathan's two hands pressing it away, preventing the knife from flashing downward. Slowly their locked bodies rolled together, one on top, and then the other.

Perspiration poured down their faces at the force of their eerily quiet combat. Suddenly they rolled again, and this time the Abenaki was on top and Nathan beneath, with the open wound on his back grinding into the ground.

Nathan felt himself growing light-headed from the loss of blood. His sight seemed to waver and for one dreadful moment he stared at the knife poised above him, knowing it was about to plunge into his heart. His eyes were dim, but he could see firelight glinting on the trembling blade.

Without conscious thought, Nathan realized the Abenaki was weakening also. Marshaling the last ounce of his strength, Nathan flung the Indian over and into the fire. The Abenaki screamed with pain, staggering to his feet and beating at the flames in his burning hair and clothes. The Indian fell back to the ground, looking like a human torch.

Nathan climbed to his feet and began beating out the flames in the man's hair and clothes. He rolled the man like a log, and finally the blaze was extinguished.

The Indian was a hideous sight. His face was charred and his mouth stretched in a grimace of unspeakable pain.

"Kill me, you dog," he snarled, "Kill me!" It was a command.

Nathan looked at him without mercy. "I'll show you the

same kindness your brothers showed my friend Abijnah Warren at Marshfield," Nathan rasped.

A grisly chuckle came from the Abenaki's parched throat. "Not my brothers—I. I was at Marshfield." The man's voice was hoarse with pain. "Your people died like spineless worms."

Nathan sprang on top of the man and gripped the front of his charred tunic. The Indian's eyes widened with pain but no cry passed his lips.

"Kill me now," the Indian commanded, and only his eyes looked human.

"Not yet," Nathan growled. "Were you with the retreating party? The hostages? Did you see two children?"

"Many children," the Indian gasped. "Weaklings. Good for slaves or to kill for sport."

"Two children," Nathan shouted, "a boy and a girl—a girl with gold hair like the sun, and a boy, with black hair. Were they there? Where have they gone? Tell me, or I shall not let you die. I will keep you alive and watch you suffer."

Blood was oozing from the burns on the Indian's scalp and the man's breath grated with pain.

"I know the useless children of which you speak." The Abenaki's eyes glittered with hatred, and something more. If Nathan had not believed it so mad, he would have thought the Indian was laughing at him.

"The girl died the first night. She had—no spirit. And the boy . . ." Nathan was sure of it now—the Indian was laughing at him, as though he'd won the battle. "The boy . . ." The Indian's voice was so low it was scarcely audible. "He was a yapping puppy. They called him Black Dog. I myself had the pleasure to kill him . . ."

Nathan's vision turned red and he pulled the Indian into an upright position. The Abenaki took a long, shuddering breath. The pain of his massive burns had turned his world into a solid miasma of agony. His vision was going, but through the gathering darkness he saw with satisfaction that he had wounded his adversary more deeply with a lie than he could have with an arrow.

"Yes," the Abenaki panted, enjoying the lie and the power it gave him over his enemy. With his dying breath, the Abenaki whispered, "I roasted the boy on a spit . . ."

Nathan's roar of rage and anguish rang through the empty forest like the primal cry of the earth. It was the last sound the Abenaki ever heard, and to him seemed the sound of victory. With vengeful satisfaction the Indian knew that, though he had left his adversary alive, the man's life would be a living death. The Abenaki knew that with his cunning lie, he had robbed the white man of all that made life worth living.

"Talmadge!" Nathan shouted the name to the heedless sky. "Mercy!" The names reverberated through the silent trees, across the seamless lake.

He dropped his head in his hands. "I am alone." The words were like an epitaph. His loss of blood and his broken heart overcame him, and he fainted. For Nathan, everything went black.

Chapter Thirteen

Three long years went by. When Nathan Fairchild finally emerged from his self-imposed exile in the woods, his sleds were packed with prime pelts—beaver, white and red fox, marmot, and otter. The furs were thick, soft, expertly prepared, and extremely valuable.

The years of solitude and survival had made Nathan as swift, strong, and sinewy as a deer. He had grown self-sufficient and silent, and had closed down the secret places of his heart. In his mind he had created a sanctuary where Chastity and his children still lived. They belonged to him in some eternal and immutable way, and he was determined to live out the remainder of his years with dignity so as to be worthy of being with them again in some better world, some finer place.

With singleness of heart, he had taught himself the ways of the wilderness—how to set traps, how to call the foxes, how to scrape and soften pelts. Now, with that same determination that had allowed him to survive in the wilderness, he would learn how to live in the world of men once again.

During his forest years, he had brought his furs every few months to the trading post in Bounder's Landing near Lake George, and there he had heard the news of the world. Nothing had changed. The long, dragged-out battle between the French and British continued in Europe, and smoldered on the New Continent.

The furs which Nathan trapped, even with the trader's exorbitant exchange, had yielded a substantial cache of gold coins. Nathan had sewed the gold into the seams of his leather clothes. Though he did not look it, he was a wealthy man.

As he walked from the rim of the forest he was ready to begin again. First, he headed toward the southeast, thinking he would visit Chastity's grave one last time and then push on. He did not know where he was going to settle, but he knew he would recognize the right place when he saw it.

As soon as the muddy spring trails dried enough for travel, Nathan began moving down the Albany Trace, following the Hudson River system. Near Albany, he crossed the river on a ferry boat. He was heading for the Pocumtuck Hills and the Berkshires, which appeared like smoke upon the eastern horizon, across the broad river that was now at full flood.

Nathan was still dressed in his wilderness buckskins, long grown filthy with sweat, smoke, and mud. His hair and beard were ragged and he scarcely looked like a civilized man.

In this condition he boarded the ferry with only three other passengers brave enough to try the crossing. The ferry bucked and fought its way across the flooded river, fighting its rope tether and straining the arms and shoulders of the powerful young ferryman.

As the sun began setting, the ferryman and passengers wearily stepped off the boat onto the muddy bank. The other passengers were met by family and friends and melted into the night.

"Dark soon," the ferryman said. "I'll not make another run until first light. Care to sup with me?"

The two men built a fire in the clearing beyond the riverbank, and then, from a tack box, the younger man pulled a homespun sack and pulled out a rasher of smoked bacon, a pouch of dried peas, and a loaf of thick wheat bread.

Before long, the simple meal was simmering over the campfire. Although Nathan had become indifferent to physical pleasures, he found himself smelling the aroma of the food with the first stirrings of genuine hunger in a long time.

The ferryman, used to the silent ways of wilderness men, did not talk or press questions on Nathan. However, the lad seemed to be studying his silent passenger, and his eyes were filled with a look of interest and kindness.

They ate without speaking, and after the meal, Nathan thanked the boatman. The young man nodded and reached into his sack, pulling out three more things: a twist of tobacco, a clay pipe, and a book.

Deftly, he packed the clay pipe, lit it, and smoked contentedly for a few minutes. Then he broke off the half inch of

stem which had been in his mouth and proferred the short-
ened pipe to Nathan.

With a nod of thanks, Nathan took the pipe and inhaled.
There was an almost magical silence in the night, with
only the sound of the river rushing endlessly to some unknown destination and the white, distant stars. Nathan removed the pipe, broke off the tip in return and handed it
back to the young ferryman, who smiled and placed the pipe
back into his own mouth.

Nathan leaned back with his hands under his head and
stared at the night sky. The ferryman had moved closer to
the fire and, in the dying light of its embers, he was carefully reading.

"Where did you learn to read?" Nathan asked, breaking
the silence.

The younger man looked up. "From my mother," he said
simply. "She read to us each night as we grew up."

"And where was that?" Nathan inquired.

"In Woolstone," the ferryman answered. "A little town in
the sou'east corner of the Bay Colony. Soil gave out. Too
many children. We scattered, and I came to the river like a
magnet. I have always loved the water. Like the book says,
". . . beside still waters He leadeth me."

"Oh, yes," Nathan nodded. "I had almost forgotten—the
Book."

The young man looked at Nathan for a long moment.
"Once the rope broke on my ferry," he began, speaking
softly but with purpose. "The boat drifted wherever the water took it. I couldn't steer it, and, after a while, I just didn't
care anymore. I just lay back and went to sleep—figured it
was pointless to struggle. Then, I figured out that if I was
going to be saved, I'd have to save myself."

Nathan smiled. "Are you talking about the boat?"

The ferryman grinned and his teeth shone white in the
campfire's light. "Maybe not. Maybe you just put me in
mind of how I felt when my boat was drifting without a
tether—without a destination."

For a long moment the camp was quiet except for the
crackle of the logs.

"So, what happened?" Nathan asked.

"Somebody rescued me," the lad said simply. "They
reached out and pulled me ashore and towed me back to the
place I was meant to be."

Nathan nodded, but said nothing, and he heard the cover of the boatman's book as it closed with a soft thud. "Good night."

Nathan slept soundly. When he woke he saw that the ferry had already made its return voyage to the other side of the river, but next to him on the ground was the ferryman's leatherbound book.

The book had been placed with great care next to Nathan's pack, with the homespun sack protecting it from the damp ground.

As Nathan picked up the volume a loose piece of paper fell from the cover. The message was written in a bold, young hand. It read, "This book may be the map you are looking for. It will lead you home." The paper was signed, "A Fellow Sojourner."

A few days later, Nathan stood at the crest of a hill. Beneath him the village of Marshfield lay shimmering under the early summer sun. It was a rebuilt Marshfield, with green, cultivated fields and houses made of fresh-milled timber with wood so new it gleamed like burnished gold. Others had come and taken the place of all those who had died.

The fort walls were gone, and on the wide main street leading up to the restored church, red-coated soldiers marched in formation. Men tilled the fields, women were hanging out laundry, children were herding cows and playing on the village green. He shook his head. The sight of Marshfield's robust rebirth was completely unexpected. Looking at it, Nathan knew this place was no longer his home. The Marshfield he had loved was gone forever. The entire Massachusetts Colony seemed to him nothing but a raw reminder of betrayal and death.

Nathan had sharpened his knife so that he could shave his beard and cut his hair. The warm sun had bronzed his face and streaked his hair until it was gold. He had wanted to look less like a savage so that he could enter the town, but now, as he looked at the unfamiliar bustle, too many ghosts of the past seemed to lurk in those pleasant streets.

He skirted the settlement and, after visiting Chastity's grave, which was well kept, camped in a hidden valley.

That night he prayed. He believed in God, but for a long time he'd believed that God had betrayed him. How could a kind and loving God turn his face from women and children? How could He leave him alive when everyone he loved was dead? The questions were too cruel, and they yielded no answers.

Perhaps it was God and God alone who could reach out a hand and pull him from this pointlessly drifting raft that his life had become.

He knew he would not live in Massachusetts. Never again. From stray travelers he had learned that the strain between France, Britain, and the Colonials was escalating. France was trying to bottle up the British by building a string of forts east of the Alleghany all the way down to Louisiana. War was inevitable.

Nathan was sick of it all. He wanted to live where a man could be left alone to determine his own life, fight his own battles, till his own land, and live by his own light.

There must be such a place, Nathan told himself fiercely. This land is scarce begun, and somewhere out there is a place where I can make a mark. But how?

He picked up the ferryman's Bible and began to read by the firelight. "Man that is born of woman is of few days and full of trouble . . ." Nathan nodded. Job had understood. Nathan read on swiftly. "But where shall be wisdom found?"

"Yes," Nathan whispered. "Where? Where?"

"Gird up your loins like a man." The words of the Lord were strong. "With majesty and dignity. . . . go forth."

Go forth. That was what the Lord had said. It seemed so easy, as if there were still love and light in the world. Go forth. In the warm summer night, Nathan lay down to sleep—the sleep of a newborn child.

PART TWO

Ainsley

. . . they are the swift and majestic men they
are the greatest women. . .
                                    —Walt Whitman

Chapter Fourteen

The great glaciers of the Pleistocene period, thousands of feet thick, blanketed Labrador and the Canadian Shield. Rivers of ice, flowing across the northeastern escarpment of North America, moving relentlessly toward the Atlantic Ocean.

In the massive rake of invading ice; rocks, soil, and vegetation were scoured from the face of the land.

Carrying the till, silt, and detritus of its inexorable journey, the ice flowed into the land that would become New England. Here the lowest level of the glacial ice began to melt and to deposit its burden of stones—even as it continued to scrape away the topsoil of the new, unmarked land, pushing ever toward the sea.

The Labradorial glacier, now hundreds of miles south of its place of birth, gouged like a cruel hand across the newly created fields and mountains of what would become Maine, Massachusetts, and Connecticut. Icy fingers dug valleys and scraped up escarpments, making long ridges which stretched, straight and parallel, toward the Atlantic.

The primeval Hudson valley would drain the vast lakes— the largest on the face of the earth—left by the melting glaciers. Through Massachusetts and Connecticut, the valleys and ridges cut by the ice became an eternal record of the glacial flow. The melting glacier left the Connecticut River flowing in one of those valleys, its waters rich with silt. Everywhere the glacier seeded its harvest of stones as a lasting remembrance.

Finally, pushing in front of it most of the topsoil of Connecticut the glacier flowed into the Atlantic Ocean and out onto the continental shelf. Miles out to sea the glacier began to give itself back to the waters from which it had come. The melting ice deposited its burden of rocks, and debris on the ocean floor, and the dying glacier's frontal moraine created

Long Island out of soil and stones stolen from the ridge-scoured land of Connecticut.

Over the passing millennia, new soil formed in the river valleys of Connecticut, and the long scrape of the ridges and eskers became covered with oak, maple, beech, and birch trees. The land grew beautiful, lush and green, with the ridges softened by time and the elements.

Still, under Connecticut's rolling beauty, much of the land's glacier-stripped soil remained sparse and unyielding to the plow, and the fields were sown with harvests of rocks that seemed to spring from the bowels of the earth—tons of rock left by the melting glaciers, brought from the north in the long winters of the gathering ice.

The first settlers in Connecticut were men who saw the possibilities of its quiet harbors on Long Island Sound. A few fortunate families established farms in the rich Connecticut valley. However, the green and verdant look of much of the colony of Connecticut was, by and large, a sham and a deception. The soil, which voluntarily gave birth to sumac, blackberry vines, wild grapes, poison oak, ivy, walnut, hickory, maple, and pine, was not rich enough to support hungry crops of wheat and corn.

Clearing the land for a plow was a discouraging and endless task. Connecticut farmers prayed for sons, because sons could lift rocks. From the time he was a young lad, every Connecticut farmer's son knew that it would be his task to walk before the plow, lifting the endless, heavy rocks that heaved themselves up through the ground.

Each spring brought its crop of new rocks, which had to be rolled or lifted onto rock sleds and pulled to the boundary wall of the fields. The rocks were stacked into rock fences which lined the roads, pathways, planting fields, and houseyards of Connecticut.

Connecticut was not an easy colony. The men and women who had gone to Connecticut had a reputation for being a contentious and independent lot. "Chanquies," as the Indians called them, were known for their thrift, sharp business practices, and aversion to interference from outsiders.

The Connecticut colonists had little love of British rule and not much more for religious tolerance. They had long resisted William and Mary's Tolerance Act—only complying after the threat of fines, duties, and tariffs. They were a fearless group, those early Connecticut settlers, but they had a healthy respect for anything that affected their pocketbooks.

Nathan knew well the reputation of Connecticut Colony, which had only recently established its boundaries. For many decades, it had been divided into two rival colonies—Connecticut and New Haven—each colony wrangling with the other over boundaries and rights, and scrambling to be the first to buy tracts of land from the sachem of the indigenous Indians.

When, under John Winthrop, by order of King Charles II, the colony was united under royal charter, the two factions had remained so ingrained that the Connecticut Colony maintained two capitals where the colonial government met alternately.

The main thing that commended Connecticut to Nathan was that the Massachusetts Bay Colony had no authority or influence over it, even though it had been Plymouth men who first settled the rich valley of the Connecticut River.

Yale University and New Haven were already well established, as were Hartford and Fairfield. The port cities of Saybrook, New London, Norwalk, and Stamford were almost a century old and thriving, but Nathan had heard there was still much land in the colony that had not, as yet, been sequestered. It remained uninhabited and new.

Something in the raw, independent, challenging reputation of the Connecticut Colony drew Nathan. He knew he must find a place where he could put the past behind him and build a new and different life—Connecticut seemed like it just might be that place.

With a summer breeze blowing fresh in his face, Nathan journeyed with long, purposeful strides and by late evening he had picked up the glint of the Connecticut River. With a lift of his heart, Nathan began to whistle softly, and walked toward the river.

He was facing a land haunted by the ghost of the flow of ancient ice. Without realizing it, Nathan would be following the million-year-old path of the glaciers to the sea.

Chapter Fifteen

It was the sharp, insistent barking of a dog that wakened Nathan. Outside the fieldstone outbuilding in which he had taken refuge the night before, he could still hear the beat of the rain. Dawn was struggling to squeeze some daylight through the heavy grayness of the soggy sky, but the small farm building in which he lay was still in semidarkness.

He could smell the sodden hay, and the ammoniacal odors of the milk cow and dray horse standing patiently in the matted straw. The dog was coming closer, its bark getting louder and more insistent. Nathan kept his eyes on the open end of the small building.

Early the night before, after two weeks of travel, Nathan had topped the rise of the ridge and looked down upon the city of Hartford. In the fading sunlight he had seen the spires of the white-steepled church, and the tree-lined streets of the peaceful community. It was a pleasant sight, even in the veil of the early evening rain, but it was not the thing which Nathan had come to Connecticut to find.

Deciding to bypass the city, he struck out on a road winding past sturdy farmhouses, their lighted windows blinking yellow through the wet dusk. He saw cultivated fields, with wheat ready for harvest, and small herds of sheep and cows grazing.

He was heading toward a distant ridge, but darkness caught up with him, and the rain grew thick and heavy. After losing his bearings, he had been thankful to see a small outbuilding at the edge of a mown hay field, and he had ducked in out of the rain. Exhausted, Nathan had fallen asleep quickly, listening to the quiet rustle of the two farm animals who shared the little barn.

The dog burst through the open end of the building, disrupting his reverie. It was a shaggy black and white cur, with pointed ears and a wide, sensitive muzzle. It was sniffing the straw and the floor, and its intent body was quivering with eagerness at the scent of the prey. With a sudden snarl, the dog sprang toward Nathan, grabbing the leather of his pantleg and growling as he pulled and gnawed at the fringe.

Laughing, Nathan sprang to his feet and snapped his fingers. "Off me, you mangy creature," he ordered, shaking his leg. "Off! Or you'll regret it."

The little dog, startled and confused by the command, backed away, stiff-legged and wary, but still barking noisily. The cow and horse became restless, stamping and snorting, and the barn seemed suddenly small and full of bother.

With a sigh, Nathan bent to pick up his pack, planning to be on his way, but another sound stopped him.

"Jude! Come!"

The dog immediately stopped barking and ran obediently to his master's side. A man had stepped through the opening and was staring through the gloom of the barn, his eyes directly on Nathan. In the man's hands was a long rifle pointed straight and steady.

"Now then, trespasser, what are you doing in my barn? Stealing my horse?"

"No, sirrah," Nathan replied calmly. "I am just a simple traveler caught by the inclement weather, and I sought shelter under this roof. Your hay made a welcome bed, and I am most grateful."

The farmer glanced around uncertainly. The two animals were still comfortably tethered where he had left them the afternoon before, and nothing was missing from the tool pegs.

"To where do you make your journey?" The man's voice was still mistrustful, and the rifle still at the ready, but Nathan felt the tension in the situation had eased.

"I am not sure of that, good sir. I am—perhaps the best way to say it would be that I am on a pilgrimage. I shall know the place when I find it." It was an honest answer, and the only one Nathan could supply.

The man cautiously lowered his rifle. "Come here, into the light. You do not sound like a woodsman, but you surely smell like one."

With a dry chuckle, Nathan walked from the shadowed corner of the barn into the gathering daylight which was filtering through the morning fog.

"I'm afraid I look like one, as well. I have, for some time, been a man of the woods."

"Phew!" the man exclaimed. "Our Indians are better groomed than you. Yet surely you are a Christian man, and well educated as well. I detect an accent of our mother country in your words."

Nathan said nothing. He had no desire to bring up the past, or to identify himself to a total stranger.

"Sir, I thank you for your hospitality, and, although belated, I should be happy to pay for the privilege of using your barn." Nathan reached in his jacket pocket and brought out several silver guineas which he dropped into the other man's hand.

"Coin of the realm!" The man was startled. "If you have such money, why did you not enter the town and stay at a proper inn? Why did you not arrange for a bath, and Christian clothes?"

Suddenly the man's grip on his long rifle tightened, and his face darkened with renewed suspicions. "Are you running from the law?"

Shaking his head, Nathan reassured him. "Not running from the law, but perhaps running from civilization. I prefer to avoid the press of the town."

Fixing Nathan with an intent stare, the farmer gave him a thorough perusal, from the top of his head to his leather-wrapped feet. Satisfied, the farmer nodded almost imperceptibly and extended his hand.

"Hyrum Woodcroft," the man introduced himself. "Farmer, deputy to the General Court, and teacher of religious philosophy."

Although Hyrum's introduction was somewhat pompous, Nathan found himself liking the man—perhaps because he put the profession of farmer first on his list. With a slight smile, Nathan shook Hyrum Woodcroft's hand. "Nathan Fairchild," he said, "wanderer and student of religious philosophy."

For the first time since their meeting, Hyrum smiled, a somewhat small and grudging smile, but a smile nonetheless, and Nathan suddenly remembered how good the company of good men felt.

"I am sorry if I imposed last night. I had no intention of doing so." Nathan was genuinely contrite. "And I am especially sorry that you were wakened so precipitately by your dog. Jude? Is that his name? Well, I'll be on my way." With a rueful smile, he added, "It was comfortable to be dry last night. Perhaps I should return to the woods before I become dependent on hearths and beds and people once more."

A shadow passed over Hyrum's face. "You will need to become dependent upon people again. It is not good to turn your face from your own kind—it is like turning your face from God."

Hyrum gave Nathan a piercing look. "Surely you are a man of God, are you not? Not a follower of the New Englightenment or one of those poor delusioned Quakers who are the fruit of Satan."

Nathan frowned. "I am a man of the covenant, but I believe each man must follow his own conscience. I condemn none."

Hyrum ignored the comment. "I do not know what sorrow has thrown you off the natural course of your life, but, from our brief conversation, I surmise you are a man of learning and some importance.

"Something has hurt you, that is clear. But such things are in God's hands, and we do Him and ourselves a disservice if we turn aside, no matter how great the matter, and do not finish the natural course of our mortal experience.

"You must find the place God is sending you, and, when you find it, you must plant your feet there. Mingle with your fellow men, build a home, plant and subdue the earth."

Through the soft fall of the rain, Nathan heard Hyrum's voice, and in it he recognized truth.

"Yes," Nathan acknowledged, "I know. But I will not live with men who speak the word of the Lord on Sunday, and require it of others, but who, on Monday, live only by the rules of greed and self-aggrandizement. I will not live where innocent people are used as pawns in a war not of our choosing—a ridiculous war, fought on this continent, but with the aim of political supremacy in Europe, an ocean away. Such things I can no longer endure."

In three strides Hyrum was at Nathan's side, grasping the younger man's arm with his powerful hand and leading him into the house.

"*Hush!*" Hyrum's voice hissed into the silence. In an intense whisper he continued "You must not speak so. Such words could be taken as disloyalty—treason. Even in my own home we have servants who may well be in the pay of the British. In times of war, no one is safe."

"You see!" Nathan exclaimed. "You are frightened, even in your own house. Such things should not be. I will not live in such a manner."

"Then you must make a further remove," Hyrum said flatly. "You must continue to the south—bearing east or west either way. There is still much land that has been bought from the Indian shamen and never opened to settlement. Just now the tiers are beginning to be released by the original proprietors."

Nathan's eyes glowed in the room, which had grown as dark as the night outside. "Then I shall travel south and east."

Hyrum told Nathan to wait, and shortly he returned with a bundle of sturdy homespun clothes, proper shoes, and some rations. The two men shook hands warmly. "I was a stranger and ye took me in," Nathan said, "hungry, and ye fed me, naked and ye clothed me . . ."

Nathan reached into his pocket and gave Hyrum another silver coin. "You will not be offended if I offer to pay."

Hyrum smiled, a warm, knowing smile. "Of course not. I may be a preacher and a farmer, but I am also a Yankee."

The two men laughed, and Hyrum said, "I have a friend you should seek. He is a man of some learning who is running a trading store and shipyard on the coast near Norwalk. His establishment is at the mouth of the Five Mill River, but somewhat hidden. You cannot miss Windsor Point if you find the right river and follow it to the sea. John Windsor is a man worth knowing."

"Why do you think this is a man I should seek?"

"I thought you might be a man of the ocean because you chose to head east rather than west," Hyrum said patiently. "John Tryon Windsor is a man of uncommon wisdom, and, besides, he happens to live on a piece of coastline that abuts one of the largest undeveloped tracts of proprietory land in the colony of Connecticut. If anyone knows how to become an owner of a piece of that fine and unused land, it will be my friend John."

Without another word, Hyrum pressed a piece of paper into Nathan's hand and, with a swirl of his heavy, high-necked cape, he was gone. Nathan waved to him one last time, and began to tramp across the field to the thick copse of woods on the other side, and beyond that, to the rolling ridge left by the glacier as it flowed to the sea.

Nathan was wearing his leather woodsman clothes, but the suit and shoes that Hyrum had given him were bundled up in his pack. Now, with a bath and a shave, Nathan could pass for a true Christian colonist.

As daylight filtered through the budding trees they sparkled as though they were sprinkled with diamonds. The fresh green of the earliest leaves, spangled with the rains of the day before, gave the world through which Nathan tramped a look as new as the first day in the Garden of Eden.

In the dappled light of the wooded hills, Nathan opened the paper which Hyrum had thrust into his hand at their farewell. It read:

"To John Tryon Windsor: Hail to you, olde friend. I have long wished to sit at your table and converse as in our former times when we were young and full of wisdom.

"Now, as age makes us see more clearly, we clearly know less than we thought. However, perhaps when we meet again we shall have come full circle and again shall know all. I look forward to such a happy occasion when we shall once again be together.

"In the meantime, in my absence, I commend to you the keeper of this note, one Nathan Fairchild, a man who has been my guest, and whose company I have found most pleasant. He is a man whose past is his beginning—and I know little of either, but I believe him to be a man of worth. Help him if you can. Befriend him if you will.

"For the sake of an old and valued friendship.

"From an old friend who values you and yours, —Hyrum Ballard Woodcroft."

There was a postscript. "P.S. My best greetings to your daughter, Ainsley. She must be quite the grown-up young lady by now."

With a smile, Nathan carefully refolded the heavy paper of Hyrum's note and rolled it in a fold of fine chamois which he then placed in his pack. As he continued on his way there was a new spring in his step, and his face was set resolutely toward the southwest, the ridge beneath his feet pointing the way.

Chapter Sixteen

Blooming berries and twisted grapevines heavy with tiny, burgeoning green grapes smashed beneath Nathan's footsteps in the undergrowth, and their sweet smell was all the promise of summer.

Occasionally, Nathan saw sign of new settlements and towns—but no sign of Indians. An old tinker and peddler with whom Nathan shared an evening's campfire told him that the Indians had been gone from Connecticut for nearly fifty years.

"The Injuns sold the land. Deeded it to the original proprietors, and just seemed to vanish. Oh, I see a few of them now and then. Just a handful. Only stay a month or so, and then they're gone. Every summer, fewer come."

The old peddler's beard was grizzled and he only had one tooth that showed when he smiled, but his eyes were dark and bright as candles, and Nathan could tell the peddler did not miss a thing.

"Wouldn't have anything to trade, perchance?" the man asked, peering intently at Nathan across the campfire.

"No." Nathan's answer was clear and final. "I have nothing."

Nodding, satisfied, the old man had fallen asleep. When Nathan rose in the morning it was to the clanking of the pots and kettles the tinker wore around his neck.

"I'm off to New Haven," the peddler said. "Four towns between here and there."

"I'm close to the ocean, then?" Nathan asked.

The old man nodded. "Aye. Not much more than a day's journey. You could follow the coastline till you find what you are looking for."

Nathan smiled. "Thank you, but no, I do not want to follow the coast. Too populated for my taste. I am a man who avoids too much company—much like yourself."

The old tinker snorted. "I don't avoid company. A peddler can't peddle without folk to peddle to."

With a hearty laugh, Nathan clapped the older man on his shoulder. "Thank you, good sir. I have enjoyed your company, and wish you well. Before we part, might you know anything of a stream called the Five Mill River?"

Frowning, the tinker scratched his beard, and then nodded cautiously. "Aye. But it will cost you."

Nathan put his hand in the small pouch at his waist and pulled out a small silver coin. "One guinea," he said.

Astonished, the tinker growled, "I thought you said you had nothing. I took you for a man of your word. All the while sitting there with a full purse. It's enough to give a man in commerce a sense of failure."

Nathan laughed again. "I said I had nothing to trade—and that was true."

The shrewd peddler gave a resigned shrug. "The river you mentioned rises somewhere west of here, and runs in a valley down to the sound. The river's mouth lies between Norwalk and Stamford, I believe. It is a small, no-account river. You will find nothing there. It does not even nourish the land around it. No farming, just empty land. The only reason I know the place is because I avoid it."

With that, the peddler picked up the last of his ill-packed bundles and headed toward a faint trace which threaded through the trees.

Nathan waved to the departing figure. "Thank you. Thank you very much."

Two days later Nathan discovered the rise of a small river and decided to follow it. On the second day the river grew wider and deeper and Nathan thought he could feel a new freshness in the air.

The next morning, he abandoned the banks of the stream and climbed the low ridge that edged its valley. The top of the ridge was washed with a fresh breeze. The trees growing there were small and sparse, and the ground shrubbery, while tangled and low, did not impede his rapid progress. As the day drew to an end, the pleasant ridge made a sudden rise. The sun was just preparing to set behind him, but Nathan, exhilarated by the ever-stronger scent of the sea, and by the brisk, clear breeze that washed over the hill, hurried up the incline.

Near the top he walked through a stand of oak trees. The new leaves glistened like copper in the red-gold light of the dying sun. As he stepped onto the summit of the ridge, he looked about himself. Away from him, in a gentle slope, wide and smooth, stretched an apron of land that was green and covered with the abundant wild growth of the season.

As his eyes lifted toward the horizon, he squinted with pleasure. He was on the highest point of his surround, and from this vantage he could see the splendid expanse of the sound, and the long, flat, low-lying silhouette of Long Island, like a mirror image of the Connecticut coast. He could smell the salt-sweetness of the distant sea, and could see the clusters of trees marking the ports of Norwalk and Stamford—one to his left, the other far to his right. Behind him the oaks rustled and sighed, and for miles around there was nothing but silence and empty land.

That night, in his journal, Nathan wrote:

At the end of the third day's walk along the small river, I crested a ridge to the east, and there, as the sun behind me made the sky like melted gold, I stood in a stand of faire oakes and saw beyond me the shining ocean. The breeze from its waters came up to me, and it was, altogether, the most pleasant of countenances I have e'er seen upon the face of the land. On either side were no houses or establishments of any kind. No sign of the commerce of man for miles about me. Only an untravel'd road trace which seemed to lead to the distant harbors of the seashore, where afar off I could see clusters of pleasant towns and tidy squares of cultivated fields.

Nathan camped that night in the grove of oaks, and the next morning he walked down the hill to the river, which now was wide and deep and rimmed by marshes and grasslands. He bathed himself in the cold water and scraped his face with his razor and the small hard piece of lye soap which he carried.

He pulled out the clothing which Hyrum Woodcroft had provided. The clothes were ill-fitting, but Nathan did not feel he would attract attention in the simple garb. Prepared, he set out along the rutted road which led toward the bustling town of Norwalk.

Chapter Seventeen

Ah! It felt good to be at a seaport once again. Nathan had forgotten how much he loved the voices of seamen shouting across the water, the flap of sails, and the hearty bustle of loading and unloading, even though he knew the tall-masted trading sloops and packets that carried colonial goods up and down the shore of Long Island Sound were often trading illegally. They were running blockades, carrying forbidden loads, avoiding customs inspectors, French blockades, English duty laws, and pirates.

As he mingled with the men at the waterfront, taking a drink of ale, Nathan realized these men did not think of themselves as Englishmen. They owed little allegiance to the Crown, and even less to officious local authorities. Their exuberant sense of self-determination struck an answering chord in Nathan's mind.

More and more, he was sure that he might find a place in this unusual colony where he might be able to live in quiet, independent peace.

Toward the end of the day, Nathan made inquiries about Five Mill River, and its shipyard and inn.

"You'll be thinking of Jack Windsor's place, I'll warrant," one of the sloop captains answered. "It's about a half day's journey by foot down the Rowayton Trace. Can't miss it; it's where the bridges take you."

That night Nathan slept in filthy waterfront lodgings, and the next morning he was up and on his way by the crack of dawn. By early afternoon, after walking several miles along the marshy coast road that looked out over small islands scattered like green corks in the wide, quiet water of the sound, and watching the endless silhouette of the miles of Long Island he turned inland and rejoined the Norwalk Trace. He crossed a wide bridge that spanned the mouth of a slow-moving river.

Turning and looking upstream, Nathan could see the river disappearing inland toward the pleasant rise of a distant green ridge. "My ridge," Nathan thought to himself. "The water of this river flows down from my ridge."

The establishment that lay downstream from him seemed impressive. A large, sturdy dock jutted out into the waters of the river's mouth. The dock was carefully placed so that ships docking at the pier would be hidden from the view of coastal vessels by a point of land that curved around one side of the small marshy bay that formed the river's confluence with the sound. Windsor Point, Nathan realized.

As Nathan walked toward the dock he saw on a hill overlooking the water a lovely building. The Windsor Inn was traditional colonial style painted fresh white with blue-gray shutters and the front door painted black, with a heavy brass pineapple knocker. A wide porch at the front, and a spacious wing on either side, made the inn look as though it were opening its arms to visitors. Neatly painted outbuildings, lawns, and gardens curled around the sprawling inn.

Next to the dock, on an outcropping of rocks, were a series of sturdy sheds. At the end of the row was a supply store, with a sign which proclaimed, "GOODS AND SUPPLIES, John Windsor, prop."

From somewhere upstream in the warren of small river islands and high marsh grass, Nathan could hear the sound of heavy hammer blows and metal striking metal. Men's voices and the sounds of communal labor wafted faintly on the air. Nathan recognized the sounds from long ago. Somewhere a ship was being built in defiance of English mandate. Somewhere close by.

Nathan walked toward the supply store at the end of the dock. When he was almost to the door of the shop, a man stepped across the threshold onto the wooden walkway and began hurrying toward the pier. Nathan had to jump off the walk in order to avoid a collision.

"Forgive me, sir," the man apologized, realizing he had almost run the stranger down. "My daughter tells me I never look where I am going." The shopkeeper's voice was urgent with genuine concern.

"Nothing to forgive, I assure you," Nathan replied. He found himself studying the man before him. About ten to fifteen years older than himself, Nathan judged, but fit as a fiddle. The gentleman's features were strong and pleasant. His eyes were deep and crinkled at the sides, as if their owner smiled often and spent his days squinting into the sun to search the ocean and the sky.

The man's arms were strong and browned. He was of average height, but his shoulders and girth were broad and powerful.

Nathan noted that the man's clothes, though he was simply clad in a white linen shirt with the cuffs rolled up, and bombazine breeches, over which he wore a heavy canvas apron, nonetheless were made of the finest weave, and the man's shoes and stockings of superb workmanship. This was no ordinary clerk.

"You have not come by ship," the man commented. "It is rare that someone visits us by foot. Oh, occasionally down the White Oak Trace—" he pointed upstream toward Nathan's ridge, "—but seldom from Norwalk. They take a carriage on the inland road. Much faster."

Nathan smiled. He knew this was the gentleman's polite way of asking what he was doing on the docks. Strangers who paid too much attention to the waterfront activities might well be unwelcome, or at least greeted with some caution, Nathan surmised.

"I am looking for one John Tryon Windsor," Nathan answered. "Would you know him?"

"Of course, sir," the man replied with dignity. "I am he."

"Then I have something for you," Nathan responded, and, taking the roll of chamois cloth from his pack he unwrapped the note from Hyrum and placed it into the other man's extended hand.

Quickly, John Windsor scanned the note. His face lighted as he read the warm, amusing words of his old friend, and when he had finished, he raised his eyes and gave Nathan the same long perusal which Hyrum had visited upon him.

"You are very, very welcome, Nathan Fairchild," the older man said.

"Thank you, Master Windsor," Nathan replied.

"Not Master Windsor! It is John! John to you, my new friend, and so it shall be forever!" John Windsor's smile was the most generous and contagious smile Nathan had ever seen.

Laughing, he grasped John's hand. "And I am Nathan to you—and so shall be forever."

"Nay, not Nathan. So formal. So stiff. It is not for new friends who are so well met. No." He paused and thought for a moment. "It shall be Nate. Nate, I shall call you."

He grasped Nathan by the elbow, and directed him toward the house, up the flower-edged path to the prominence over-looking the water. "Now, you must go up and make yourself comfortable on the porch. I have one quick errand to do, and then I shall join you. You will tell me all about my dear friend Hyrum, and then we shall discuss your matters.

John Windsor was gone in a whirl of motion, and Nathan walked up the pleasant path. The sounds of the river and the pleasant inn set in the green bosom of the headland hills gave him a sense of peace he had not known for over three years.

How Chastity would have loved this spot. Remote, peaceful, independent—not torn by the power struggles of old and decaying nations. Still, he looked down at the quiet, hidden harbor, and wondered again about the mysterious sounds of building and industry. Perhaps not as free from the struggle as he thought. However, he would put such worries aside for now. The porch looked inviting, and he had been walking since early morning.

As Nathan walked up the riverstone path toward the benches that flanked the door, he passed under a blossoming apple tree, and all of a sudden a rain of petals showered down upon him.

Startled, he whirled around, and then looked up into the branches. The leaves and flowers were so thick he could see nothing at first, but he could hear laughter and whispering voices. He walked closer to the tree and discerned the sole of a shoe hanging about two feet above his head. Scarcely pausing to think, he reached up and pulled on the foot, and to his astonishment, a billow of pink and green and white lace plummeted down on top of him.

Steadying himself, he reached out to break the fall and found himself standing, reeling, with a young girl lying in disarray in the cradle of his arms. She was laughing uproariously, and he set her on her feet immediately.

"Oh," she said, her face scarlet with heat and unsuppressed amusement, "if you could have seen how solemn you looked walking up that path. You would have known what an absolutely irresistible target you made."

Still laughing, she went over to the tree and called up into the branches, "Do come down, Letty. You must see his face. He is mightily surprised."

With that, another pair of shoes and skirts appeared, dangling from the branches. Nathan walked over awkwardly and helped the second culprit to the ground.

"I am most sorry, madam," he apologized to the first girl. "I had no idea you were a young lady—that is, I was expecting a boy. I did not mean to pull you from the tree. I hope I have not distressed or hurt you."

The young girl flushed from embarrassment. "It is I who should apologize, sir." She laughed softly, less sure of herself now that they were face to face. "I am such a silly goose sometimes, and I know my father is going to scold me mightily. But you did look so dour as you walked up the path, and I couldn't help but think that on such a day no one should be in ill spirits, so I showered you with blossoms to make you look up and see the day."

Nathan threw back his head and laughed at the sky. What an unexpected child! "You made me look up, all right, but what I saw was a foot."

She could not have been much older than his son Talmadge would have been. Oh, perhaps a year or two older—but it was hard to tell with girls. She was rather tall, but very slender and her hair was the color of autumn leaves, all red and gold mixed together.

Her eyes, as wide as the sky, were the color of the ocean, not green, or blue, or gray, but some mysterious color that combined all three. Her nose was small and straight and her skin was flawless, soft and pink as the petals she had showered down from the tree. The other girl had smooth brown hair and a sweet, serious face.

Both girls were dressed in finely woven dresses, with white lace fichus tucked in their open bodices, and dainty caps, now crooked, pinned in their wind-blown hair.

Suddenly, the red-haired young woman reached out and took Nathan's hand and pulled him toward the porch.

"You must not tell Father, you know," she told him. "We shall get you neatly seated on the porch, and I shall bring you something cool and delicious to drink, and you will not whisper a word about us climbing trees—and, oh, especially not a word about how we teased you. Father would never forgive our rudeness. Promise now, or you shall be responsible for us being remanded to some dark dungeon on bread and water for punishment."

Nathan found himself bemused. Never had he encountered such a young woman—more child than woman, really, but so audacious and amusing, he found himself thoroughly enjoying her antics, when he knew, as an adult, he should be scandalized by such behavior in the young.

"Very well," he said slowly. "I see your father coming up the walk now. I will not tell him if you promise to be good and obey him in all things from now on."

The young girl ran over and put hand around her friend's waist. "Oh, Letty and I can manage that quite properly, since we are only home on school break for the summer. Surely we can behave ourselves for that long."

Then Nathan had to laugh again. "Why do I doubt that? But I do. I doubt it very much!"

John Windsor came up the porch steps. "I see you have met my daughter, Ainsley. My only child." The love and pride in John Windsor's eyes was so strong that it almost made Nathan sick with yearning as he thought of his own lost children.

Chagrined by his obvious indulgence, John added laughingly, "She's probably a changling, but since she's my only one, I've decided to keep her."

Ainsley ran across the porch and gave her father a joyful embrace. "And aren't I glad you did!" she exclaimed. "So very, very glad. You are the dearest and best father in the whole world."

"Dear, dear," John shook his head, looking quizzically at Nathan. "She must have done something really dreadful, to be making such a fuss over her old father. Do you know something I should know, Nate?"

The girls stared anxiously into Nathan's face to see if he intended to betray them, but he calmly responded, "Not a thing, John. They have been perfect little ladies. As a matter of fact, they were just on their way to get me something to drink."

"Well then," John said, "hop to it, my dears." After the girls had left, John Windsor explained that the girls would begin their last year at Miss Holbrook's Academy in Edgefield that autumn.

"Ainsley's friend, Letty, is visiting as a houseguest for the week. It's a might lonely here for the child and I'm not sure

I've done right by Ainsley in keeping her here beside me for all these years since her mother died. We are isolated, as you can see. Her growing up has been a bit wild. You can see I am a far too indulgent parent. Ah well, her mother died giving birth to her, and I've loved her mother for giving her to me, and I've loved Ainsley for bringing brightness into my life these seventeen years. Ah! How the years do pass!"

Nathan nodded in assent, but something in the sadness of his eyes made John Windsor pause. "Perhaps I should not be speaking of such matters."

"No," Nathan replied, "I admire a man who is unashamed of his affection for his family. It is a most precious thing, John. Do not hesitate to speak of it to me."

Just then, Ainsley and Letty came gracefully through the door and onto the porch, carrying trays set with glasses of cider, cold meats, cheeses, brandied fruit, and crusty rolls.

With a dimpled and mischievous smile, Ainsley came up to Nathan, proffered him the tray, and said softly, "My offering of thanks."

She could not keep her eyes off this stranger's lean and mysterious face. She knew he was a mature man, not so old as her father, but certainly not young. When she had first spied him walking up the path, thinking himself alone, she had wondered at the grave melancholy which marked his handsome features. She sensed he had been remarkable places and seen things she could not even imagine. Her young heart thrilled at the excitement of such thoughts. He was mature, mysterious, and handsome.

Accustomed as she was to seeing men of every kind—seamen, officers, merchants, and aristocrats—Ainsley was only just now becoming aware of men as beings of personal interest. During her childhood, the men who worked for her father had seemed like surrogate uncles, comfortable, familiar—a strong and noisy background to the happy, carefree days of her girlhood.

Her father had been wise enough to warn her about talking to strangers or to seamen unless he, or a trusted servant, was present. From this and other clues she had suspected that there was something secret and slightly menacing about men and their ways with women. However, well protected and cossetted by her father and the staff at the inn, she had grown up surrounded by rough men but happily innocent of fear or the darker shadows in men's hearts.

She did wonder, sometimes, about the relationships between men and women. Never having known a mother, or
having seen her father with another woman, Ainsley found
the patterns of marriage a mystery. She had observed, on the
rare occasions when married couples or families came to
stay at the inn, that there was a tenderness and security that
seemed to exist between a man and his wife. It made her curious, but it also made her feel lost and lonely. Feelings of
loneliness had simply been a part of her life for as long as
she could remember, always lurking at the edge of her
awareness, like something that would surge up at her from
the shadows if she did not keep watch.

Although she had no close neighbors or friends, when she
and her father attended church in Norwalk each Sabbath she
felt a great yearning as she watched the families attending
the services—mothers and fathers walking arm in arm with
clusters of children gathered around them.

She wondered what it would be like to go home to a dinner table with brothers and sisters and a mother watching
over her, instead of sitting alone at the table in the kitchen
of the inn, while one of a succession of housekeepers hurried
her through her meal and scooted her outdoors.

Always, since the first night she remembered waking in
the dark and calling to her father only to have her call un-
heeded, she had dreaded that the aloneness was going to
claim her forever. She had run into her father's room and
found it empty—and she'd known she'd been abandoned.
Her father was the only thing in her life that stood between
her and that feared exile. There was no one. No one.

Her father had heard her crying and had come running upstairs.

"I was just having a last pipe on the front porch, Ainsley,"
he'd comforted. "I was not gone. Don't be afraid, little one.
I will always be here."

But she was afraid, although she learned to hide the fear,
and sometimes even to forget it. She knew, deep in her
mind, even as a child, that her papa would not always be
there—just like her mama, sometimes people went away and
never came back. No one could be there forever.

Hidden under the happy days of her childhood, hidden
under the joy of her father's indulgent love, always she felt
the fear that someday she would open the door and find herself alone.

What would it be like to have a mother? A mother *and* a father? To be loved like mothers and fathers loved one another? She knew the answer to none of these questions. Now, no longer a child, she had long since stopped being afraid of the dark. But somewhere inside, despite her growing maturity, there was still a shadow of that frightened, motherless little girl, who wanted nothing in the world but to be loved, safe, secure, and never alone.

As she found herself reaching the age of young womanhood—the end of her seventeenth year—she found herself looking at the world through the dreams and fantasies of a developing woman. Her yearnings and curiosity were beginning to focus on the mysteries of the love of men and women.

At school, after lights-out, the older girls in the Senior Form would gather and whisper about boyfriends, and kisses stolen at the cotillion or under the orchard boughs. Such whisperings both fascinated and disturbed her.

She knew that one of the reasons her father had sent her off to boarding school was that the men on the dock had begun to act differently toward her. They would stare at her when she came down to the pier, and they no longer spoke to her in the old, comfortable fashion, showing her how to tie better knots and mend sails, or laughing as she gasped in awe at some exotic treasure they had discovered on their last journey.

Without at first understanding what was happening, she had delighted in the bold sailors who had begun to treat her as a grown-up. They smiled at her, and doffed their hats, and hurried to the counter when she was serving them in the supply house to help her lift the merchandise.

On one such occasion, a bold sailor had grasped her waist and spun her around. For a startled moment her face was so close to his that her eyelashes brushed his cheek. At that moment her father had come into the storeroom, and his face had turned red with anger. She had protested that the man was only helping her reach the nail barrel, but her father threw the man out of the room, and turned to her with cold decision.

"Up to the inn, my girl," John Windsor had ordered her. "You are not to come down to the docks to work anymore. Next week it's off to school with you. I have been selfish in keeping you away from it. Selfish, and foolish."

"Oh, Papa," she had cried, "don't send me off, away from Windsor Point, away from you. I shall die!"

It was as she had feared. Now she was becoming a grown-up woman, and her father would soon see that his job of raising her was over—and then what would be her life? Papa would grow older and someday be gone. Where, and to whom, would she belong? Who would care for her, love her, keep her safe? The old fears clanged in her mind.

"No, you shall not die, my girl," Father had reassured her. "You will find friends, and knowledge, and a life of your own."

"But I have a life of my own! This is where I belong!"

"You will always belong here, that is true, Ainsley. But there will be other places where you will belong even more. It is the time in your life to find those places—those people."

So she had gone to boarding school, and her father was right; she had found a wonderful friend in Letty. She had grown to admire Miss Holbrook, and had learned a great deal, but still she felt she was never fully alive except at Windsor Point.

Through the years Ainsley had grown so used to strangers coming and going—the men at the dock, the men on the ships, the men with whom her father did business—that they had all come to seem rather anonymous and interchangeable to her, and she paid them little attention. But this Nathan Fairchild was somehow different. It had caught her by surprise to find her heart leaping out to this complete stranger as he'd walked up the path with his powerful shoulders, graceful bearing, and manly face full of secrets and hidden pain.

Nathan Fairchild had about him an aura of mystery and tragedy, and Ainsley—young, romantic, and inexperienced— was embarrassed to admit to herself that this handsome stranger had captured her mind and her heart. He was the first tragic and noble man she had met—so like the heroes she was reading about in her Greek classics—and to her impressionable mind, so untrained in human relationships, she imagined that her admiration and fascination were the "love" of which her friends and schoolmates talked so much.

She was hoping her father would let her sit on the porch and listen to Master Fairchild's conversation, but she knew Papa would not allow it. He never thought it proper to have her take part in men's discussions.

Still, she thought to herself, I don't care what Papa says is proper, I will find a way to talk to this Nathan Fairchild. I want to know everything there is to know about him.

Nathan took the tray from Ainsley and placed it on the table between himself and John Windsor. "Run along, girls," John said. "You can gather flowers for the evening meal."

Ainsley knew she was being dismissed. She opened her mouth to protest, but her father gave her an admonishing look, and she controlled herself. The two young women curtsied and left, running across the lawns in their fluttering skirts like two joyous butterflies.

Nathan stretched his legs, looking out across the blue waters of the sound, and with a sigh of satisfaction said, "I want to live here, John. In Connecticut. With the sight of the sound in my morning eyes—but far enough from the seashore that I do not live in the confines or influence of a European government, or hell-bent, mind-bound congregation."

Sipping his amber cider, John Windsor thought for a long moment, trying to guess at the feelings and experiences that would make a man yearn for the place Nathan had described.

"Well, Nate," he said quietly, "that's a tall order. Of course, you aren't the first man to come to Connecticut with such a view in mind, nor will you be the last. But don't expect your neighbors in Connecticut to all be such broad-minded, kindly men—we can be a contentious and difficult lot. We demand the right to think, live, and worship in our own way—but we'd sure like our neighbor to be required to agree with us.

"We do not want England to control our purses, but we seem to keep a mighty tight control on them ourselves, and every man has to watch his own interests in every transaction. But I would say that in this colony, by and large, men are fair, honest, courageous, and determined. A man can be happy here. A man can build something here."

"That's what I want to do," Nathan said, his voice filling with enthusiasm. "I have found the piece of land. Do you think you can help me acquire it?"

The two men walked out to the river, and Nathan pointed up the path of the valley, to the faint trace of the road leading to his ridge.

John Windsor understood. "I have ridden my horse to that very spot," he said. "It is a place of beauty. I must caution you, however. You do know that the ridges are hard to farm. The ground is filled with stones."

In a flash of memory, Nathan thought of the fields around Marshfield where the thick, black soil turned under his plow like folds of velvet. "I will make the land blossom as the rose," Nathan replied. "But what must I do to own it?"

"The proprietors for that land have not opened it for settlement yet," John said. "It has been kept as common land for almost a hundred years—since the first tract purchases were made from the old shamen. The original deeds are kept in the Norwalk church."

Discouraged, Nathan looked up at the hilltop just beginning to darken under the shadow of the late afternoon. "Is there no way?"

John laughed. "You were born under a fortunate star, Nate. I have just heard a rumor that the second tier is about to open up. The land will be divided into lots and it will be assigned by lottery."

Nathan sat very still. He knew the next question he was going to ask could possibly offend John Windsor, but, still, he had to ask.

Very cautiously, Nathan began. "I know the proprietors are all members of the congregation, and fine, upstanding members of the community. Surely they are wise enough not to leave these things entirely to chance." He took a deep breath. How to ask it tactfully?

"Does one's place on the lottery list ever get written in letters of gold?" Nathan let out his breath slowly, watching for John's reaction. Nathan was asking if bribery was expected and he knew the suggestion could be taken as a grave insult to the upright proprietors of Norwalk.

With a hearty laugh, John slapped his knees, "Of course gold tips the scale, my boy. Of course it does. Those men haven't hung onto that land for a hundred years for nothing. They are honorable men—but they are practical, too. If you have gold in cash-hungry Connecticut, you can have almost anything you want."

The days and weeks of the summer began to run into one another like the flow of the river, and somehow Nathan found himself still in residence at Windsor Inn. He had planned originally to stay for only a night or two, but John and his daughter, Ainsley, made him feel both welcomed and needed. The warm affection and feeling of family was almost a narcotic to Nathan, and he enjoyed observing the sweetness of John Windsor's relationship with his remarkable and unpredictable daughter.

John had shown Nathan the layout of the supply store, and with the help of Ainsley, who knew the merchandise better than her father, Nathan found himself lending a hand at the busy dock to outfit the swift trading sloops that slipped in and out from the sound.

Often the loading and unloading was done in the darkness of the mild nights. Nathan was careful not to ask too many questions about the cargoes or the imports—where they had come from or where they were going. He knew these were troubled times, and that many a patriot was pressed to find ways around the conflicting laws of the contested seas.

Not the least of the joys of Windsor Point was Ainsley Windsor. She was a young girl of such vibrant joy that in her smile and face the whole of summer seemed to shine. Nathan found himself listening for the lilt of her voice as she worked in the gardens, or brought hot tea cakes and cold ginger beer to the dock. His empty heart couldn't suppress a pang of envy at seeing John Windsor's delight in his lovely child. Watching the father and daughter together set off bells of memory in Nathan's grief-blasted heart. She seemed to him the embodiment of his own children—grown and flourishing.

To Nathan and to John, Ainsley was still a child, but she knew herself to be a woman. Even though her attempts at womanly airs made John and Nathan smile, she recognized, with an acuteness beyond her years, that something inside of her had changed, and that it would only be a matter of time before her father—and especially Nathan Fairchild—would see that she had left childhood behind forever.

Sometimes, catching a glimpse of Ainsley's growing maturity, Nathan realized with regret that his son Talmadge would have been close to her age. Talmadge, had he lived, would have been showing the first beard of manhood. He would be feeling the first confusions of youth, would have grown tall and swift and manly.

Ainsley gave Nathan a glimpse of the children he would never have again, and she amused and comforted him. In her youthful joy, she eased his yearning for his own dear, dead children, forever gone. His sweet, sweet children.

Chapter Eighteen

The first summer of Talmadge's captivity had been the worst. He and the child, Luke, had survived on an inner flame of hope that would not be extinguished.

Summer in the birch forests by the great lake was hot, and the air hummed with mosquitoes, biting blackflies, and gnats. The two fair-skinned boys were like a feast for the insects, and it was not until the sun had burned their skin black, and their meager diet that had made them nothing but skin and bones, that they found some relief from the scourge of winged marauders.

In the first flush of victory after the raiding, when the Indian warriors had returned to their village, there was much celebrating. Campfires burned long into the night, with dancing and singing and much food for the returning braves. The hostages were paraded around the campfire. There was ominous jeering and laughter, but no real cruelty unless one of the hostages broke down and cried—or showed fear.

A slave who showed fear apparently caused his owner to lose face, and so the Indians would bear down on the offending hostage and beat the abject creature—woman or child— and then thrust them out of the firelight into the darkness.

It soon became clear that Talmadge and Luke were considered too worthless to be given any notice. They were placed with the dogs outside the tent of the warrior Manocq, and were given to his mother, a wizened, gray-braided squaw whose toothless face was so deeply wrinkled that her features were lost in the furrows. Her skin was as tough as leather, and so was her old heart.

The woman screamed at them each morning, signaling that they should fetch water in the woven buckets. Since it was summer, there was no need to gather wood, except for cooking. The two boys were often sent with the girls and women to pick berries and nuts. Whenever they left the camp in the company of the berry-pickers, the Indian youths who saw them go would shout epithets at them. Talmadge soon learned enough of the language to know that they were being called "Boy–women!" and "Girl-slaves!" and worse.

Luke was frightened by the shouting and the rocks and sticks thrown at them, but Talmadge would whisper, "Don't be afraid. I will protect you. Be brave and quiet. Listen and learn. We must learn their language—but never speak it."

With his childish eyes round with wonder Luke would ask, "Why can't we speak it?"

"Because we are not Indians!" Talmadge answered fiercely. "We are Colonial English—and shall always be."

Night followed endless night, and Talmadge, sleepless on the ground, would feel the insects move beneath him, and think, I walked to this place—I can walk back again. Home is just over the hills. I will escape. But in the morning he would look at the drawn, pinched face of little Luke, and he knew the boys was not strong enough for a long journey, and also that if he left him here alone, the boy would surely die. I will wait until Luke is stronger, Talmadge assured himself; then we shall go together.

The Indians did not guard the hostages zealously, but they were aware of where the slaves were, and an alarm was quickly sounded if anyone was unaccounted for. The only exception was a woman who had been taken hostage in an earlier raid, and who had been a slave for three years; she often wandered off into the forest. She was pregnant with the child of one of the young braves, and, as the pregnancy progressed, she seemed to know less and less who and where she was.

Talmadge watched from a distance, with only imperfect understanding, but he saw the young woman each day grow more vague and erratic. Her half-braided hair hanging down, her eyes vacant, her ragged gown unlatched, she wandered through the lodges and tepees, mumbling to herself. There was a vague and permanent smile on her face and she seemed to have no feeling of warmth or chill, pain or comfort. One day, Talmadge saw her step on a hot coal and keep on walking in her bare feet, as though she were walking in a drawing room.

The Indians, having a great awe of those who were possessed by the gods, did nothing to harm or help her. They let her roam through the camp without hindrance or ridicule. They called her Woman With Eyes of Air.

On the morning that Woman With Eyes of Air disappeared into the forest, the Indians, suddenly realizing she'd been gone for some time, lost all of their indifference. A party of braves, the best trackers in the camp, took off in rapid pursuit and the sun had not set before they returned with her, roped hand and foot, blood streaming down one arm where she had been shot with an arrow like a running doe. She was burned at the stake, and in her eyes there was no madness, only pain.

A teen-aged brother and sister tried to escape, and they, too, were tracked down and returned. They were spread-eagled on the ground, and left to die of hunger and exposure. The screams of the burned woman could not be erased from any of the prisoners' memories, but the sight of the slow, agonizing death of the other two prisoners served as a better prison than iron.

Talmadge had a quick mind and a gift for language, and by the end of the first summer he was able to understand most of what was said by the Abenakis. He developed a habit of listening to all that was said in the camp. None of the Indians knew or cared that he spoke their language. It was a secret which Talmadge hugged to himself. It gave him a secret source of strength.

He and Luke had found a honey tree, and, though they brought most of the honey to Manocq's mother, they ate a good deal themselves, and found themselves gaining strength. The old squaw was so pleased with the honey that she began to throw Talmadge and Luke an occasional bone or a handful of corn, and life became a little easier for the boys. Gradually, the continual pangs of hunger were eased.

Nothing could make Talmadge get used to the filth or the smells of the fetid lodges, but as he lived among the women and children of the village, he saw the love the mothers and children had for one another. He saw the fathers leave to go hunting and come home with rejoicing. He listened to the humor and wit, the domestic kindnesses and the training of the young boys as they progressed to manhood, and he found himself understanding the common humanity that bound him to these people.

Still, in his heart, his memories of the horrors of Marshfield were undimmed, and he bound himself to a per-

sonal oath that he would never let them make an Indian of
him. He would die first. He knew that it was only a matter
of time before the French came back to the village, and the
hunters formed a party—not to hunt animals, but to forge
back into the British Colonies, to murder and plunder. They
could keep his body captive, but, Talmadge vowed, they
would never own his mind and heart. He would protect Luke
from that fate as well. Each night he whispered the litany to
Luke. They would feast on hate.

"Our enemies sneaked up the ramp of snow. They killed
Brother Warren by inches. They murdered my parents. They
scalped your mother. They shot your father. They burned our
homes. They stole us away. We hate thc Abenaki. We will
never be like them. We will live with honor."

At the end of the first summer the Abenaki village prepared to go to a powwow for all the Algonquin tribes in the
nearby territory. The hostages were roped together and stumbled along, prodded by the Indians, under heavily loaded
packs that they were forced to carry. Talmadge carried a load
almost equal to his own weight because he had added most
of Luke's pack to his own.

The powwow was held near a shabby French fort. The
tribes had gathered there for trading, to swap stories, to plan
for the winter campaigns, and to quarrel. There were blankets, weapons, trade goods, and prisoners to be bought, bartered, and sold.

Talmadge looked at Luke's dark red hair, which gleamed
in the sunlight. He knew that any unusual feature could be
interpreted by the Indians as a sign of luck, and that anything which drew attention to the either of them would be
dangerous. His own hair was so black, and his skin had
grown so dark, that Talmadge was almost unnoticeable in
the crowd of Indian children.

"Lie low!" he told Luke. "Be quiet and invisible." He
rubbed dirt into the boy's hair until it looked dark and drab.
The two boys stayed quietly in the background, not even attempting to take part in the games and feats of skill which
the other boys were playing—even though their boyish
hearts were sorely tempted.

At the first stage of the bartering, two of the French officers came to the campsite. They were acting as agents to
ransom prisoners back to the Bay Colony government. The

French officials gathered together the hostages from all the tribes and began to look for specific individuals, calling for them by name. It was clear that only those whose families had provided generous ransoms would be making the trip home.

Talmadge watched as one Indian looked at the ransom offered him and shouted that it was too little. He took the woman prisoner by the hair and threw her back in with the other prisoners. "She stays until the ransom gold is as high as her nose!" the Indian shouted.

Watching the process, and listening, Talmadge quickly realized that the government had sent no money for those who had no living relatives left to send for them. Even though he knew his immediate family was dead, Talmadge felt a quick surge of hope that his wealthy grandfather, even though he had never met or seen Talmadge, might have felt family obligation, and sent the ransom money. Talmadge's hope was quickly dashed, however, as the French officers closed the empty ransom coffer and, shrugging their shoulders, walked away from the frantic prisoners, many of whom were calling out in French for mercy in the name of God. The Frenchmen merely walked away. *"Rien de plus!"* they shrugged, pointing to the empty money chest.

Talmadge did not cry out; he bit his lip and accepted the fact that there was no one left in the world who cared if he lived or died. All he had left was he self-imposed responsibility to protect Luke. Returning to his campsite with a heavy heart, he sat with Luke behind the old grandmother who was peddling her woven blankets. She had already made a good trade for an iron pot, and was in rare good humor. "My blankets are worth more than you two useless slaves combined," she taunted them, but her words were not cruel, just gleeful.

The boys remained inconspicuous and escaped being sold or traded, and returned with the Abenakis to the village.

Talmadge's greatest fear was that he and Luke would be separated. He knew Luke would not stand a chance without someone to watch over him. The boy would either be adopted and become a bastard Indian or he would die of neglect. Either alternative was unthinkable, so Talmadge watched as the months passed, and the winter came again. He had given up all thought of escape. After all, there was no place to escape to.

* * *

Two years passed in this fashion. Although Talmadge did not know it, these were the first two years that his father spent in the wilderness, trapping game and avoiding the company of mankind while his heart healed.

Talmadge, who like his father believed himself alone, had the satisfaction of seeing young Luke—his self-appointed little brother—grow stronger, although the child did not seem to grow very fast.

The first winter on the first day of snow and bitter cold, after the braves had left for the forts and the winter campaigns, the old grandmother motioned the boys to enter her teepee. Through that long winter they had slept in the smoke-filled shelter. The fire was the two boys' responsibility. For the first time in many years, the grandmother was warm and comfortable through the cold months without having to beg and hunt wood for herself. Her old arthritic bones did not have to brave the harsh weather, and she shared her pemmican and store of dried nuts and grains with the boys with a surprisingly generous hand.

In the early summer, the braves returned with only a few hostages, but many scalps. Talmadge stared at the scalps on Manocq's lance and was sickened. He went out behind the lodge and threw up. The taste of bile was strong in his mouth for days.

One of the new hostages was a boy of fifteen who had been captured from Newland, a settlement which Talmadge had visited with his father in happier years.

"They've rebuilt Marshfield," the boy told Talmadge in a hurried, whispered conversation after dark. Talmadge and Luke had gone back to sleeping on the bare ground since the braves' return. However, they had managed to find scraps of hide to create a makeshift protection. The new arrivals had nothing to protect them from the elements, and the nights were still cold.

"I've got to get back before my master finds me missing," the lad went on. "He's quick to knock me with his club."

"Do you hope to escape?" Talmadge asked.

"Aye," the young hostage replied, "but I intend to do it wisely—and succeed. Do you want to go with me?"

"Not unless Luke can come too," Talmadge replied.

"That scrawny redhead?" Ben Lacey laughed. "We'd stand about as much chance of escaping with that young'un stumbling along with us as if we simply jumped into the fire of our own free will."

"I don't suppose I need to go anyway," Talmadge whispered back. "There's nought left for me there. Luke and I are a team, you see. I'll have to wait until Luke gets bigger, or until the war ends."

Ben Lacey began to slither back toward his own lodge, but his sardonic reply hung in the air. "Not much hope for either of those events, I'd say."

At the powwow that summer, Ben Lacey was among the first to be bartered away to another tribe. The chief who bought him felt the muscles in Ben's strong, young arms and then slashed across Ben's face from ear to mouth with the sharp tip of his hunting knife, leaving a long, wide gash that bled profusely.

"You wear the mark of the wolf. My mark!" the chief boasted. "I shall make a mighty warrior of the Abenaki out of you. Or you shall die. Those are your choices."

Talmadge had seen the hostages whom the Indians had tortured, pressed, and disciplined into savages. He had seen white boys, grown into men, who were more Indian than the Indians themselves. He shuddered when he thought of Ben Lacey. The chief was right, the boy would either die or become a turncoat. There were no other alternatives once he was marked.

Again Talmadge and Luke managed to remain inconspicuous in the confusion of the late-summer powwow. They returned to their small village, and, as the winter began, they were once again invited into the old woman's teepee as soon as the warrior braves had left with the French.

This was the year that Talmadge turned fifteen, although he had almost lost track of time. Each night he and Luke still whispered to each other in English, and Talmadge kept the secret of his fluent knowledge of the Indians' language.

As the winter progressed, Talmadge saw a discouraging change in Luke. The young boy had begun to cough—a deep, racking cough that shook his entire frame. Little Luke's flaming hair had grown lank and lusterless and had lost its curl, and his eyes were like burning coals in a face as white as the snow.

When Talmadge took the little boy's hand as they tramped through the drifts looking for firewood, it felt hot, and as thin and dry as paper.

One morning, when the first thaw of spring had turned the ground to a quagmire and the water dripping from the trees was like rain, Luke did not have the strength to rise from his pallet.

For days Talmadge cared for his young friend, bringing him water, bathing his hot forehead, and urging him to take a few sips of broth. Talmadge felt the little boy slipping away. A week later, in the dead of night, as Talmadge held Luke's small hand, he heard an owl cry in the forest. Three times the sharp cry split the silence of the darkness, and Talmadge felt Luke's hand go limp.

In the morning, Talmadge carried Luke's wasted body into the woods. A watchful Abenaki brave followed him, but Talmadge stalked deep into the forest until he found a small cave. He refused to bury Luke as the heathens did, in the open. Tenderly, he laid the frail body in the ground, and using the heavy bough of a tree, he ploughed up the soft earth and massed it with his hands over the entrance to the little cave.

At last, satisfied that animals would be unable to penetrate the mound, he stepped back and bowed his head. "The Lord is your shepherd, Luke. You shall never want again. Go back to your brother, your mother, and your father. Be happy."

No tears spilled from Talmadge's eyes. His loneliness was so complete it was beyond tears. He knew he would survive, an alien in an alien land. He would survive, but he would never, ever yield.

What Talmadge did not realize was that during that dark winter, as he watched Luke dying, he had been growing into a man—not just in character and resolve, but physically.

He wore his jet-black hair at shoulder length, cutting it with a knife so that it would not grow long enough to braid. He was determined to reject the Indian ways. Like his father, he had grown tall, and was already almost six feet. His shoulders had broadened and his lean, hardened body was strong and quick. Because of his constant exposure to the elements, his skin was tanned to the color of maple wood, but his eyes blazed bluer than robin's eggs and his boyishness had dropped from him like a cloak. In his firm jaw and the set of his lips, in the sternness of his black brows and the intense, watchful expression of his handsome face, there was the look of a man full-grown and mature. Only deep in his hidden heart were the last faint cries of a young orphaned boy still present.

That summer when the warriors returned, it was inevitable that they would see Talmadge, this useless boy-slave, with new eyes. Suddenly he was a warrior-sized captive, unbroken and unused. They became determined to break him, train him, sell him, or kill him. A man of Talmadge's proportions could be a great danger—or of great value. The Indians were determined to find out which Talmadge would be.

In the brutal months that followed, Manocq, as chief of the village, viciously hounded Talmadge. The braves tried to teach Talmadge to make arrows and war clubs, and when he refused to set his hands to the tasks, they beat him so brutally that for days he was unable to walk.

No matter what they did to him, time and time again, Talmadge would quietly join the women as they left camp to gather food and fetch water. He acted stupid, as though he did not know what the braves were doing. They shouted at him and dragged him from the company of the women.

In the great lodge, where only men could meet, they threw Talmadge into their midst and forced him to drink vile-tasting brews. They built a roaring fire, and, as the other men began to dance and scream, the hallucinogenic herbs bringing them to gyrations of frenzy and ecstasy, Talmadge willed himself to sit through the daze and jumbles of emotion, the sweat pouring from his face. He would not dance or sing.

They prodded him with their lances and stripped him. They hung him from ropes lashed to the lodge poles, and they whipped and scorned and goaded him. The swirling colors and noises, blurring with the inflamed passions of his own mind, almost overcame him, but he was able to hang on to a last scrap of himself. Finally, as the manhood rites came to an exhausted, narcotic sleep, Talmadge leaned against his restraints and lost consciousness.

It was useless, Manocq and the other braves decided, to try to teach this fool of a slave. In all the time he had been captive, he had not learned one word of their language, had not spoken, and had preferred the work of women.

"He is possessed of a woman's spirit," Manocq grunted to his mother. "You may keep the slave for the hot season, and then we'll sell him at the next powwow."

After that Talmadge was left alone, except for constant taunts and ridicule. These came not from the braves—for now the young men acted as though he were beneath their notice—but rather from the women and children, who threw rocks at him, ridiculed him, and made cruel jokes.

Talmadge trained his face to have no reaction, even when the most terrible things were said. Often when he slept, young girls would creep up and pull his loincloth aside. "He has the parts of a man," they would giggle, "only he has no use for them." With iron will, Talmadge pretended to sleep on.

Again the braves had returned to camp with hostages and more scalps. Talmadge was sick of the killing and fighting. He felt he had seen enough of men killing men to last for a lifetime. That summer, as he watched the young braves learning the art of battle, sometimes fighting to the death, he knew that he would never fight.

Rocks were thrown at him, fists raised, he was whipped and cuffed, but he would not raise his hand in response. The tribe gave him a derisive nickname, Man With No Fist, and soon they ceased to note his existence. The summer passed quickly and Manocq forgot his threat to sell Talmadge.

In the third winter Talmadge spent in Manocq's village, as the braves left to go to the French fort, Manocq brought his young daughter, Running Water, from his second wife's tee-pee and gave her to his mother.

"This daughter's mother is Nipwok tribe and she is returning to her own tribe for the season of snow. We wish you to watch over this daughter. When we return I will give her as a gift to my bravest warrior. See you prepare her in how to be a dutiful and pleasuring wife. She must be opened and taught."

The winter went by, each day like the other. Talmadge was formulating a careful plan. He would escape, but where he would go, and what he would do, were still unanswered questions.

A few weeks before the return of the war party, a change took place inside the grandmother's lodge. Although the old woman rarely spoke to Talmadge, believing as did the others that he could not understand, late one night, she thrust the maiden, Running Water, onto the skins that served as Talmadge's sleeping place.

In the dark the old grandmother took Talmadge's hand and placed it on the girl's abdomen. "Open her!" the old woman hissed in her ancient, rusty voice. "She must be opened and trained for the delight of her warrior husband. Teach her. Surely you must be good for something. You are a man. Open her!"

Talmadge trembled in the dark and pulled his hand away as though it had been placed in fire. All winter long he had been fighting his awareness of Running Water in the teepee. She was a quiet, silly girl and was often gone for days at a time, visiting in the teepees of her friends. Talmadge knew she was not a virgin. The young Indians played a game called Hide the Mole in the long, dark winters. They had intimate knowledge of one another.

There was no privacy in the lodges. Men and women made love with only the hide of a deer or a bear to cover the act, and children knew the ways of men and women together from their youngest years. There was little restraint and few limitations to sexuality. Talmadge remembered the teaching of his religion, and the tender, private, relationship of his mother and father. He saw few such relationships here—only wanton sexuality. Still, his loins sometimes ached with a need he could not name, and he feared it, and checked his thoughts and urges with the strength of will his captivity had taught him. He would not let his sexual longings turn him into a savage.

Nonetheless, there was something very fresh and appealing about Running Water. True, she giggled behind her hands like the other girls, and teased Talmadge with unkind barbs which she thought he did not understand. But sometimes, when the fire blazed warm in the teepee and the grandmother dozed, he had seen the girl looking at him with speculative glances. Her eyes were dark and she seemed to regard him with hungry curiosity.

Not only had Talmadge promised himself that the Indians would not turn him into a murderer, he had also promised himself that they could not make him turn from his Christian ways. As he had grown older, he had been teased by the young teen-aged girls in surprisingly bold ways. They would lift their skirts to him, or come and pull up his shirt to see the surprisingly white skin—as white as the tail of a doe—that the shirt concealed.

His hot young blood had burned, and he felt all the lust and passion of his new manhood rising in him like a fire. He had fought the temptations—the breasts, the buttocks, the searching hands and limpid eyes—but now, the grandmother was commanding him to service her granddaughter.

Running Water was plump, with juicy breasts and tiny

feet, and she lay next to him as still as a captive rabbit. He could feel her heat, and as soon as the grandmother left, her small, soft hands began to fondle him.

His body responded in spite of his determination, and he found himself lifted by a force beyond his own. He rose above the girl and poised himself to thrust down upon her. She gave a soft moan and whispered, "Man With No Fist, I have you." With a shudder he came to his senses and rolled away, shaking with the conflict of body and spirit.

"I will not be used!" he whispered to himself fiercely in English. "I will not be their servant, their slave, their whore."

The girl jumped up and began to kick him with her small feet. The grandmother joined her and they heaped abuse upon him. The next day the whole village knew the story, and now his name was cried with derision—Man With No Penis.

The time had come, Talmadge knew. He must escape before the war party returned.

Before he could make good on his plan, a small nomadic tribe came to the Abenaki village to visit.

This band of Indians was unusual, they were the last remnants of an extinct tribe. There were some Abenaki in the clan, but the chief, Passakonawa, was the only son of a woman of the Wampanoag tribe—the tribe of pure royalty—the highest tribe of all the Indian peoples. Passakonawa's mother had been the last of the tribe which had become extinct when it was destroyed in King Philip's War. She had married into Passakonawa's father's tribe, a small and noble clan.

The chief was a man of such stature in the Indian tribal structure that he had almost the eminence of a totem. Although he was a man mighty in hunting, judgment, wisdom, and dignity, he and his people were unique. Before his mother, the princess, had died, she had made her son, and all who followed him, promise that they would give up the practice of war. In solemn ritual, they had destroyed the weapons of war and kept only those weapons they used for hunting and defending themselves from the dangers of the woods.

Passakonawa was a chief of legend, not only for his knowledge, but for the breadth of his travels. He was a welcome guest at every campfire, for his people had no enemies. His was a peaceful and neutral tribe. They were nomads, but their place of Destiny was eastward on the shores of the great waters. They forever returned to that land in the cycle of their wanderings.

On the second night of feasting in the village of Manocq, Passakonawa told the Abenakis that he and his people would leave the next morning. He gave the Abenakis thank-gifts of sea shells, salted fish, and sealskins—rich, luxurious furs.

None of Manocq's tribe had ever been to the sea, and so the gifts seemed more abundant and generous than any the village had ever seen. Manocq's tribe was thrown into a quandary. What gift could they give that would not seem small and unimportant in return for Passakonawa's munificence? It was a matter of pride to them to return gifts of equal value to their visitors.

In a quick tribal conference it was decided that they would give fox pelts, two belts of wampum, and one of the grandmother's finest blankets, and with a last-minute, sudden inspiration, the grandmother also offered the man-slave with the Indian hair and the sky-blue eyes.

The grandmother whispered, "He has the appearance of a fine warrior. It will not be many moons until they discover he is a woman-man—but by then they will be too far away to make complaint."

So the gift was made, and the next morning Talmadge was scrubbed, dressed in new moccasins and leggings, and given to Chief Passakonawa as a parting gift.

The chief stood in his full regalia: beaded headdress and bands, quiver and arrows, and leathern-thonged legs. Passakonawa's white-streaked hair hung loose and unbraided. With his beak of a nose and his penetrating, watchful eyes, he looked like an eagle. Talmadge was taller than the chief, but something in the man's gaze made Talmadge feel smaller—younger. Almost against his will, Talmadge looked into the man's powerful, noble face and felt a sense of respect and admiration, something he hadn't experienced since he had last seen his father almost four years ago.

With infinite dignity, the chief looked his gift up and down, and then stared directly into Talmadge's eyes. There was no hint of a smile in the calm expression of his new owner. "Your eyes are like pieces of fallen sky," the chief said to Talmadge. "I think you will bring us good fortune."

Next to Chief Passakonawa a young man, almost the same height and age as Talmadge, stood gracefully, resting his hand on his long bow.

"You are the one called Man With No Fist? I heard of you in the lodge last night." The young man was speaking in the

Abenaki dialect, and even though Talmadge was supposed to know none of the language, he found himself flushing, wondering what had been said about him.

Without changing expression, the young brave stepped toward Talmadge and said quietly, "I think you understand my words. If so, I tell you this. You are called Man With No Fist, and I, Chief Passakonawa's son, am called Meskapi. I have called myself Man With No Friend. Now I say to you that I will lend you my fist if you will give me your friendship."

It was the first kind thing anyone had said to Talmadge in all his years of captivity, and to his great surprise, he found himself fighting back tears.

Talmadge was sixteen years old the year he was given to the tribe of Passakonawa; he had been fighting a silent and lonely battle against his captivity for almost four years.

In the end, it was not cruelty, or fear, or loneliness, or time that captured Talmadge—it was simple friendship.

In the weeks that followed, Meskapi became the brother Talmadge had lost, and Passakonawa, the noble man of the forests, became a mighty foster father to him.

"I understand you," Chief Passakonawa told him. "Because of my mother's people and their terrible fate, I, too, will fight no one. She watched as all her people ceased to exist, she taught me war can bring good to no one.

"We are all brothers upon the breast of the earth. I and my people do not strive to own land. We live from its bounty as a baby drinks its mother's milk. We learn the land's ways. We follow the land and the sea, and the land and the sea cradle us. We are a tribe of peace."

Passakonawa's tribe was moving east, across the land of the Penobscots, toward the shores of the big sea. It was the place they loved the best.

"Come, brother," Meskapi called to Talmadge. "We shall bait our traps for the muskrat with their own scent bags, and we shall clean their pelts and prepare for the cold of winter."

Meskapi taught Talmadge the lore of the woodlands—which mushrooms were safe to eat, where the grubs and burrowing insects hid, how to spear the wily trout and shoot with true arrow the heart of the quiet deer, who gave their life so The People could live.

At night, by the campfire, the young men of the tribe engaged in wrestling matches and feats of strength. It soon became apparent that Meskapi and Talmadge were closely matched, and that each one was unbeatable. Meskapi was the better wrestler, but no one could outrun Talmadge. His feet were like the wind.

At night, in the firelit shadows of the camp, Chief Passakonawa taught the young braves the ancient thoughts and philosophies of The People. Talmadge learned the arts of silence and observation, of self-reliance and service to the tribe before service to self. He learned of sacrifice and fearlessness, and of the noble heart, purified of self, that made a man a worthy son of the earth and sky. He was also taught the secrets of hand-to-hand combat, archery, tracking, and woodlore. Even a peaceful tribe knew that they must give the appearance of choosing peace, and therefore all must know that they were capable of defending themselves if put to the test. "One can only choose peace when one is capable of war," Meskapi told him.

Two years passed before they finally turned their wandering steps toward the great sea—and their ancestral lands.

"We travel to the great waters in the land the French call Acadia, near the place of the great island of rock called Breton. It is the ancient home of our people. It is also the home of the Algonquin, our friends," Meskapi told Talmadge. "We do not hurry, but we shall get there before another season." It was the way of the peaceful tribe. Stoic, brave, and patient, they would make their way to the remembered shores that were calling them.

It began to rain hard, and Meskapi and Talmadge, who were sleeping outdoors by the communal fire, picked up their skins and hurried inside Passakonawa's tent. The young men had hunted all day, and they were tired.

Meskapi had gone back to sleep, but Talmadge remained wakeful, aware, in the silence of the night, of the sounds coming from the chief's bed of furs. In the years that he had been in the tribe, Talmadge had grown used to the sounds of lovemaking in the chieftain's teepee. Passakonawa loved his wife with a devotion that was manly and powerful. She was a plump, quiet woman, with long silver braids and cheeks as soft and pink as crocus blossoms.

Although Eagle Feather never spoke to her husband in front of others except with the formal deference of a woman speaking to her chieftain, in the privacy of the tent, Passakonawa of-

ten sought his wife's advice. She had the privilege of being
named for the Eagle, because her father had been a mighty
chief of the Algonquins. When Passakonawa had selected her
as his woman, he had brought to her lodge poles of the tallest
pines in the forest of Acadia, and she had built from them the
noble teepee in which Chief Passakonawa lived. The teepee, as
the Chief explained to Talmadge, belonged to Eagle Feather.
No one entered it without her permission—not even her husband. And, if he ever displeased her, she could send him away,
and never let him return.

He did not displease her. In the night he heard them
laughing together, and the soft sounds of their lovemaking,
so sweet and tender, it made Talmadge feel safe and whole
rather than embarrassed.

He could hear Passakonawa whispering to his wife of
many years, "Oh thou lovely one. You feel like the silk of
the milkweed. You taste like the first berries of summer. You
are more beautiful than the sunrise."

Once, as Talmadge and Meskapi hunted with Passakonawa, they had remained in the forest overnight. By their small
campfire, Passakonawa told the young men: "The finest
thing you may do in life is to marry the right woman. See
that she is as pure and clear as a brook. Hold her as a treasure, and she will become a treasure to you. She will prepare
your food, beautify your clothing, have warmth waiting
when it is cold, and coolness in the heat. She will make you
strong when you are weak, and she will make the juices of
your manhood have purpose and nobility. If you are a true
member of the tribe of Passakonawa, there is only one such
woman on the earth for you.

"We believe that when the Mother Earth fell from the Father Sun, she carried in her arms all of her children.
Matched, two and two, man and woman in perfect fit—like
each acorn to its own perfect cup."

Idly, Passakonawa bent down, picked up an acorn, and removed the cap at its top. Then he foraged for another acorn
and removed its cap. "You see," he said, trying to fit the second cap on this first acorn, "it will not fit. Each has only one
that fits perfectly.

"When Mother Earth landed, her children were thrown
from her arms—scattered and broken apart. So we must
spend our lives searching for the one that is our own—our
perfect fit. When we find that one, it is the first time in our

lives that our hearts are complete. Together, we are as
Mother Earth intended."

From that time on, Talmadge found himself looking at the
maidens in the camp in a different way. Before, he had
found himself glancing guiltily at the turn of their ankles,
the roundness of their buttocks under the soft deerskin they
wore—hoping always for a glimpse of breast, or the possibility of catching them bathing in the stream.

Now he found himself looking into their faces, trying to
see the mystery behind their eyes. He found himself listening to their conversations, testing for warmth, intelligence,
and something else—something to catch his heart.

The summer that Talmadge turned nineteen, the tribe
came into the thickly wooded hills that led toward the sea.
They were far enough north that they had experienced an ex-
hausting and demanding winter.

In the long nights when families visited from teepee to
teepee, Talmadge had noticed Meskapi's interest in a beautiful young girl named White Dove. Often Talmadge, blowing
his cheeks with the cold, would leap into the teepee and find
Meskapi and the girl sitting by the fire on a deeply piled
mound of furs, laughing or playing with smooth, polished
stones in a game that reminded Talmadge of checkers.

They would look up, surprised and a little shy to be found
together. Talmadge teased Meskapi, and Meskapi laughed
while White Dove's cheeks burned red with embarrassment.

On a hunting trip together, Meskapi took hold of
Talmadge's arm. "When we arrive at the sea, I have asked
my father, and he has told me that I may cut the lodge poles
to give to White Dove. I have known she is to be mine. It
is a happiness I wish for you, my brother."

Talmadge stood very still. "You have made a mighty and
wise decision, my brother. White Dove is a maiden without
peer."

Meskapi was awkward, but he was also so happy that
even in his controlled and careful face, Talmadge could see
the struggle he was waging not to laugh with happiness.

"You must begin to make such a decision as well,"
Meskapi said, trying to sound wise and solemn. "It is time
that we took on the responsibilities of men."

Both young men had known this time would come, and yet
Talmadge found himself speechless, not knowing how to begin.

Later in the afternoon, they killed a large buck. It would take three days of skinning and smoking the meat before they could return to the camp.

On the second day, Talmadge knew he had to say what must be said. "Meskapi, my brother, I am more happy for you than words can say. But your decision has told me that the time has come in my life, too, for a decision.

"I have always known that someday I would need to leave and return to my own people."

For a long time Meskapi was silent, then he nodded sadly. "Yes, my brother. I know you must do this thing. It makes my heart sad to think so."

"You can come and visit me," Talmadge said hopefully.

"I think you are not right," Meskapi answered. "I think in your world there is no place for someone with my skin. If this long war does not end, there will be such bad blood between the white-eyes and my people—there will be no way to wipe it away."

"You have been so good to me!" Talmadge exclaimed. "You are the only family I have. I must go back. Something pulls me. Unanswered questions. If I am to find myself—my destiny—I must go. Yet, if I go back, I go back to nothing. I have no one left."

Meskapi nodded. "Each man must find where he belongs. It is why we journey back to the sea. The Great Spirit will tell you when you find your place, my brother. Our campfire will mourn your leaving. For myself, I hope it will be many moons before the call comes to you."

Talmadge nodded. He was in no hurry to leave. He would wait to see the sea that they had journeyed so far to visit. He would wait until Meskapi and White Dove married, raised their teepee—perhaps even until they had their first son.

For now the ocean called, and beyond it the dark mass of the island of Cape Breton. He would learn the ways of the seal and the tides, and then, when Meskapi and White Dove married, he would leave for the land he scarcely remembered—Massachusetts—and the villages of the Western Reserve.

Chapter Nineteen

The summer when Talmadge had turned sixteen—that very first summer when Talmadge had joined the tribe of Chief Passakonawa and had found himself at last free from bondage—was the same summer that Nathan had come to Windsor Point, and, in the friendship of John and Ainsley Windsor, had at last found, like Talmadge, a feeling of belonging. Neither father nor son had a single thought that the other still lived.

Early in July of that summer, Nathan had watched as his new friend and employer, John Windsor, came down the path. Behind John he could see Ainsley in her blue gardening skirt, gathering peas. The little harbor was trim and quiet and Nathan thought how good it felt to be part of the world again. It had been three years since the massacre at Marshfield Village, and this was the first time in three years that he felt well and truly alive. He had much to thank the Windsors for.

Nathan was busily loading sacks of grain that had been sold to John by a Fairfield farmer. Nathan's muscled arms were bronzed and the chaff from the tow sacks covered him with a golden glow, as though he were edged in gilt.

"The damn British want to charge such a fee for the favor of selling them my grain that I'll not see a penny of profit," the Fairfield farmer had growled as he took John's payment for the wheat with a sour look. "It looks like this French and Indian War is heating up again. There's trouble with the blockades up at Louisburg, and at Fort McHenry at Lake George.

"The British are placing companies of regulars up and down the coast. I tell you, if they choose to billet their soldiers in Fairfield, we'll charge them a fair penny for feeding them." The man concluded his complaints and put the money in his leather pouch.

John had chuckled. "Yes, we'll make them pay. There's more than one way to skin that cat. They've done a bully number on our poor colony. Between blockades, pirates, and customs officials who are no better than pirates, it is hard, indeed, to find a market for our goods."

After the man had gone, Nathan approached John thoughtfully. "How is it that you can find a market for the grain, John, when others cannot—and make a profit. If you do not wish to answer my question, I will understand and I will respect your silence."

With a hearty clap on Nathan's shoulder, "You need not fear, Nate, I am not athwart the law—although there are some that say I do skirt it. I simply say that I know how to avoid it."

Laughing at some inward joke, John hurried off to inventory the bags of grain.

Nathan continued to load the grain sacks onto a waiting sloop, pausing to wipe his brow as John Windsor approached him. "Come with me, Nate, there's something I want you to see."

Leading the way down to the ladder by the wharf, John beckoned Nathan into a waiting gig, and they shoved off and oared upstream, soon becoming lost amid the marsh reeds and small islands.

"I talked to the men from Norwalk," John said. The proprietors are good men. They have held the land until Norwalk had a good and healthy start. Apparently, Stamford has an adjoining tier they wish to sequester for development, so a nice little community should result."

Nathan leaned forward, "And the rise of white oaks? Is that piece part of the sequestration?"

"Indeed, yes." John smiled. "I ascertained as much in a most subtle way—asking after several choice pieces so they would not determine which one was my real interest."

With a sigh, Nathan stroked his oars, heading in the direction which John pointed, toward a wide stretch of water bounded by a sandy island and a tree-shrouded bank. Half-masked by the trees, he saw men moving busily, saw the gleam of new wood, and heard the sounds of hammer and saw.

"The lottery list must be as long as my arm," Nathan said.

"Not so long as you may think, my friend," John replied with a smile. "Most of the names on it are sons and relatives of the original proprietors. A lot of them will continue to live in Norwalk, and simply farm the land they are assigned. So you see, a lot of the land will not bring in money. They are looking for real buyers. Rich, qualified buyers."

"But the lottery . . ." Nathan frowned, trying to understand.

"Listen to me, dear Nate. You have to stop thinking like a Bay colonist and start thinking like a Yankee. You see, we don't believe in being downright dishonest or breaking the law, but we do think the good Lord gave us brains, and the right to make a living—to build something of worth for ourselves and our families.

"The purpose of the lottery is to see that a solid community is developed, before new land is opened for settling. That way, we can have a congregation for everyone to attend, and a solid parish capable of educating its children, and keeping its roads, and meeting its civic responsibilities honorably.

"Connecticut colonists believe the good Lord keeps track of those who will be the pillars of His congregations. Those who work hard, who know how to husband and earn profits—those are the necessary men, the essential ingredients in any newly settled community. So, the proprietors see only wisdom in providing that, if a man is blessed with gold, he shall have the opportunity of winning the choicest land in the lottery. Because, logic says, he will make the most of the best land, and thus, the whole community will benefit."

Nathan nodded, caught between amazement, dismay, and admiration of such pragmatic ethics.

"We will talk later," John assured him. "For now, I want you to see my newest enterprise."

They pulled the gig in to the shore and tied up on a heavy branch. John Windsor parted the branches and they walked around a slight rise. The sounds of activity rang out across the water. Nathan saw the magnificent rising form of an ocean-worthy schooner. Not large, but with sleek lines and tall spars, the main one set like a sloop, but the foremast and jibs and riggings promising the speed and maneuverability of a many-sailed beauty. The hull was trimmer than anything Nathan had ever seen, and yet it had a solid, sturdy look that made his seaman's heart sing. "What a brave and splendid craft," he whispered, impressed beyond anything he could imagine.

"It is, isn't it?" John Windsor's voice burst with a pride that was only equaled when he spoke of Ainsley. "Another few weeks and she'll be ready for her maiden voyage. If she's all I hope she is, she'll be able to outrun pirates and customs runners and blockade vessels—the lot of them. She'll be able to run in and out of coves and inlets, and sail swift and true."

Nathan frowned in spite of himself.

"Oh, Nate!" John exclaimed, "there you go, thinking like a Bay colonist again. Thinking that the letter of the law is what counts. Surely you know by now that people use the letter of the law to rob men blind. Here, we believe in the law, and when it confronts us, we pay up. But in our heart of hearts we keep the spirit of the law, which is that a man has the right to the bounty of his own labors. A man should be able to take his goods to market and get a fair price. A man should not labor so that those who exercise unrighteous dominion can steal him blind."

"I would agree with all of that," Nathan said.

"Well then, you'll see. If I build this boat in the open I must pay three taxes on the building of her: I must pay customs papers and customs bounty to the British, the French, and the Dutch, if they find me in any of the disputed waters.

"With such corruption, and such blurred jurisdictions on the sound and in the trading waters with the Continent, no ship can pay its own way. I am for law and constituted authority, and I recognize British law and Connecticut authority. But on the sound and in the trading lanes we will meet our destruction not by war, but by corruption, currency fraud, and conflicting demands of fees and taxes. So, if we trade by night, and are not challenged—then no fee is owed. If our ship is unregistered, and cannot be caught, then the customs duty cannot be collected.

"If we are confronted by authority, we pay, but if we can avoid such authority we do so. Our colony will perish if we cannot trade. Our currency is worthless because we are bottled up on every side. We are like our rivers—without outlets, we die."

Nathan nodded, the old anger rising in him. He remembered the corruption he had seen in Boston. Honest men who could not benefit from their own labors because the corrupted system.

With a grim smile, Nathan walked down to inspect the

lovely ship. "I'm calling her *The Ainsley*," John said. "As bright as paint, as lively as the wind, and as lovely as the sky."

"She is all of that," Nathan answered, his eyes drinking in the lines of the hull.

"When she goes on her maiden voyage, I would like you to captain her, Nate," John said. "Not a long voyage. Just up the coast to Montauk and back again. We'll see if she equals in performance what she shows in promise."

Three days later, Nathan went into John's sitting room after the rest of the house had retired. He could smell the pungent smoke of John's pipe, and knew he was smoking his last before heading off to bed.

"Do you think this will be enough gold to ensure my place on the lottery list?" Nathan asked. He was carrying a leather sack, heavy with gold sovereigns.

Astonished, John hefted the bag. "Nate, I had no idea you were a man of such substance. Do you have any idea how this much gold will look to the proprietors? They are hungry for gold. Our paper currency is worthless. Men are being ruined by the crisis, and an infusion of pure, true gold will seem like manna from heaven.

"Leave the matter to me, and I shall do everything in my power. I cannot guarantee to get you the land you desire, but I shall try with all my heart. I have many favors to call in, and I will expend them in your behalf. You are more like a brother to me than any man I have ever known. I want you to be happy, Nate."

Without a qualm, Nathan left the gold in John's care. He thought of the last time he had trusted a man with gold, and of the bitter consequences. Unbidden, the face of Junius Comstock came into his mind. As long as he lived he would never forget the man who had robbed him of the ransom for his children. It did not matter that the children were already dead. No one had known that at the time, and the man had stolen the gold which would have been their only hope.

Remembering that awful time, Nathan felt bile in his throat. He had, he remembered, promised himself he would never trust anyone again, and yet, here he was, leaving a large portion of his fortune with a man whom he had only known for a few weeks.

For a moment Nathan searched his heart, and he realized

that he felt no fear or insecurity for his gold. He trusted John Windsor; in fact, he would trust him with his life. A great feeling of peace swept over Nathan. Deep inside, where the pain and grief lay coiled, something healed and a great weight lifted.

If he were fortunate enough to obtain the property he desired, Nathan felt, for the first time, that he could live through the remainder of his life. Nathan had told John Windsor the brief details of the Indian raid and the deaths of his wife and children. In John's eyes he had seen both compassion and understanding. Ainsley, too, knew that Nathan had lost his wife and children. The terrible story of the Marshfield Massacre was known throughout the Connecticut Colony, and there was a swell of silent sympathy and respect for Nathan Fairchild.

Nathan knew he would miss Windsor Point when he left. All through the last sweet days of that first summer, he was conscious of the presence of Ainsley. She had gradually taken over the running of the inn for her father, treating the gardener, the cook, and the chambermaid with a wonderful combination of friendship and authority that inspired them to work long and well. Both Nathan and John were amazed at how capable and mature she was in the role of manager, and they smiled at her indulgently, like fond parents watching a child perform a difficult task with amazing skill.

The food at the inn was splendid, and each Friday night, families came down the Norwalk Trace in buggies to dine there. Travelers had been known to stay for an extra evening so that they could enjoy a second dinner at the polished round tables in the dining room.

The kitchen garden was Ainsley's special pride. Often in the late afternoon when Nathan returned to the inn to freshen up for dinner, Ainsley would be on her knees in the garden picking the fresh vegetables for dinner, a large straw hat framing her sun-kissed face. Nathan would walk over to help. "Let me pick those carrots, Miss Ainsley," he offered. "I expect we shall see them on our dinner plates."

"So you shall, Mr. Fairchild, in the most delectable carrot mousse you have ever tasted," Ainsley replied, her cheeks dimpling with her teasing smile. "I noted you ate it with considerable glee the last time. Four helpings, if I did not miscount."

With dignity, Nathan inclined his head. "I bow to your memory and to your mathematics, Mistress Ainsley."

In the evenings she sometimes read aloud to her father and Nathan, her sweet voice speaking the words of Shakespeare, of Jonathan Edwards, and of the Bible. She was quick-witted, and conversation with her was as delicious as her menus.

Often John dozed in his chair as he savored his last pipe, and in the humid heat of the evening Ainsley and Nathan would step out onto the front porch, looking down to the glint of the water under the moon, hoping for a whisp of a breeze to lighten the heavy air.

For a young girl, she was remarkably satisfying company. She seemed to know when to be silent, and when to speak, and she had a way of making Nathan laugh when he least expected it. All in all, he thought her one of the most charming young women he had ever met.

As summer progressed, Ainsley's hair had turned copper-bright in the sun, and her face was tanned to a soft sandalwood rose, with a sprinkling of freckles that her father decried. "Ainsley, my dear, have I not told you a hundred times to wear your bonnet, shawl, and gloves? You are going to end up looking like an aboriginal princess, and no self-respecting, well-born man will have anything to do with you. You are graduating from school this year, my girl, and, if I can't marry you off I shall be saddled with you for life."

Both Ainsley and Nathan knew nothing would give John greater joy than to have Ainsley forever by his side.

Running lightly up to her father, she stood on tiptoe and kissed his cheek. "For you I shall endeavor to stay as white as a lily—but next summer. Let me have one more summer before I have to become a lady."

"A lady, is it?" Her father laughed. "I have no such grand hopes. I was just hoping for less of a hoyden."

The schooner *The Ainsley* was almost finished. The final coats of paint and varnish, the caulking of the seams, all this was done and drying. The rigging was completed, the spars steady with the new, white sails neatly furled, and the decking, crew quarters, and cargo holds fresh and ready.

The first journey was to be made with ballast rather than cargo. The ship carried Connecticut papers, and was listed out of Norwalk, with no records kept of where or when she had been built.

"She will carry grain, wool, cattle, horses, troops and armor, passengers, molasses, sugar, and whatever else shall make a market for this great colony. She will trade up and down the sound, from New York to New Haven, on up to Boston, and, if necessary, around the blockades and off to England or the West Indies." John patted the ship's hull as though it were a living thing.

"The one thing she will never carry is human freight. Never, as God is my witness, will she bear the weight of men and women who have been sold as cargo."

Nathan bowed his head in assent. "As God is our witness."

The maiden voyage of *The Ainsley* was to be the last great experience of that memorable summer. It was a brief and splendid interlude and it meant different things to John, to Nathan, and to Ainsley.

For John, it was the culmination of a dream. *The Ainsley* would mean freedom and commerce for the brave men of Connecticut who dared to challenge the trade lanes.

For Nathan, it was the first summer of hope in many years, and the chance to breathe the sea and set the sail once again, before he turned back to the land, to became a man of the soil.

For Ainsley, it was a beginning and an ending. The night of *The Ainsley*'s first voyage was the last night that she was ever a carefree, careless child, the last night that she was still completely her father's daughter—and it was the first night that she began to hope that Nathan might someday see her as a woman, and not as the child she left behind in the moonlit sea.

The brief voyage began on a night late in August, by the light of a full moon, with only a small crew on board. The ship, under Nathan's command, edged out of its hidden harbor and into the full tide of the sound. With the sails trimmed for silent running, the ship moved into the expanse of the sea, cutting the crest of the waters with a whisper of speed.

Ainsley, sitting at the bow, laughed at the grace and wonder of it, and shook her splendid mass of hair into the wind. The moon carved her in silver, and Nathan, looking up, was disconcerted to see, not the child of the summer, but the statue of some mysterious, pagan creature at one with the ocean, the wind, and the shimmering night sky. The perception was so unexpected that he abruptly picked up his eyeglass, turning from the sight of her to scan the horizon for any sign of sail or sloop.

When he and John had discussed the future of the sailing vessel, Nathan had thought of his old friend Daniel Cothran. "If you are looking for an ocean-worthy officer to captain your ship," Nathan had mentioned, "I know of a man who is second to none. He is my oldest friend, and a man as true as dye—and better than any I have ever known."

John Windsor, impressed by what Nathan told him of Daniel, had written a letter to him in Boston. Daniel had written back with delight. Daniel was, according to his letter to John, so sickened by the duplicity and slave trade involved in Thomas Pembroke's shipping enterprises that he would resign his commission forthwith. Nothing could have pleased Daniel more than the thought of working with Nathan again. Sometime in the next few days Daniel was expected to arrive at Windsor Point and take over command of *The Ainsley*.

"Before this Daniel Cothran arrives," John had asked one more time, "are you sure you do not want to return to the sea yourself? I would give you the helm in a minute, and Daniel could be your mate."

"No," Nathan had answered, "never. It is the land that is calling to me. A place to belong. A place to think and remember. Do you think I shall get my land, John? When does the lottery take place?"

"Well, the gold was mighty and pleasing to the proprietors, Nate," John assured him. "We shall get you something, of that I am certain. I am praying it is the parcel you desire. I have made that very clear."

The long wait to hear the results of the lottery was beginning to grind on Nathan. Once he had ridden with John and Ainsley up to the oak grove on the ridge. It was a half day's journey from Windsor Point, but well worth the time, for they stood on the ridge and felt the cool, rushing breezes that dispelled the constant weight of the humid, heated air at the harbor by Five Mill River.

Ainsley had packed picnic lunches and the three of them had eaten hugely, sitting on the brow of the ridge in the freshening wind. Then, with her lawn skirts swirling, Ainsley had run, laughing and leaping, down the long slope of the seaward fields. She loved the spot almost as much as Nathan.

She had returned, breathlessly, and stood next to Nathan on the ridge, looking out toward the sea. "What a place!" she had exclaimed. "It is as though the whole wide world is laid at our feet."

Nathan had laughed, commenting that it was no less than she deserved. And, with a jolt, he realized he'd meant it.

As that night of the maiden voyage continued, Nathan began to forget the long wait of the hot summer. The ship seemed to have wings, and the sweet smell of varnish, tar, new rope, and the warm, salty sea lulled him like a song.

"It's a dream, isn't it, Master Fairchild?" Ainsley whispered. She had come to stand beside him on the foredeck. Her approach had been silent, and he saw now that she was barefoot. "She's really a dream ship on a dream sea. And we are only dreams, too."

"Would you like to have me explain a little about the principles of sailing?" Nathan asked, feeling unexpectedly awkward at the sound of her voice, so close beside him in the dark.

She laughed. "I have been sailing the sound since I was five years old!" she exclaimed. "The sloop *Nell* which carries my father's cargo to Stamford and Norwalk—that was my ship. I cut my teeth sailing her."

"Really," Nathan said indulgently.

"You don't believe me?" Ainsley challenged. "Well, I shall show you. I think you should unfurl the jib and set it. When we come to the end of the sound, we shall be hit by the full ocean breeze. With our jib we can increase our speed. There may be French sniffers crawling around. They often come down this far from Louisburg."

Nathan frowned. He did not like taking orders on his own ship. Particularly not from a woman who was still half child.

John was roaming the ship with the pride of a master, clucking over every detail with delight, and glowing in the pleasure of *The Ainsley*'s smooth handling and swift passage.

"Better listen to the girl, Nate," John suggested. "She'll tease until she gets her way."

Nathan shrugged, and squinted up at the jib. There was no question that the air was freshening, and to port he could see the crash of breakers.

He turned to call a crewman to climb the rigging and release the foresail, but, to his astonishment, Ainsley stood there. She had shed her full skirts, and was wearing, instead, the breeches of a cabin boy.

"Yours to command, Captain sir," she said merrily.

Nathan frowned and looked over at John, whose face was ruddy and beaming in the glow from the bowl of his pipe. "It's her last summer," John shrugged; "let her be a child for a little longer."

"Very well," Nathan concurred. "Unfurl the jib."

With a delighted laugh she was off, and Nathan watched her slender silhouette scrambling up the rigging like an agile boy, her hair glowing like flame against the early dawn sky. With an expertise born of active childhood summers, she set the sail, and returned with a jaunty salute.

For the rest of the voyage, she was like sunlight, flitting from beam to beam, climbing the riggings, laughing at the ballooning sails, and drinking in the wind and sea. Nathan felt he was watching a ritual—a last glorious farewell to youth, to the unbridled joy and physical exuberance of childhood. He was glad he was there to see it.

In the dark hours after the moon set on the second night, *The Ainsley* sailed smoothly back into her berth.

There was an odd sense of regret, and Nathan, Ainsley, and John were silent—each with his own thoughts—as they gathered their gear and disembarked.

Battened down and creaking in the rocking waves, *The Ainsley* rode at anchor, waiting for her good and brave new captain, Daniel Cothran.

John, Ainsley, and Nathan walked quietly up the path, each savoring memories of the short, sweet voyage. They knew nothing would stay the same after this summer— change and the unknown lay waiting with the morning sun.

At the door, as the three parted to go to their separate rooms, Ainsley touched Nathan's arm gently. "I leave next week for school," she said, looking into his eyes with her direct, searching gaze. She wanted to see what he felt, what he was thinking. In the darkness all she could see was the solid, real shape of him—his shoulders, his fine head, and the soft, bright halo of his hair. He was so honorable and so fine—

she yearned for the safety his presence exuded. "Thank you for the memory of this perfect voyage, Captain," she whispered.

He patted her hand where it lay on his arm, and she quickly turned away, feeling suddenly shy and afraid of her own boldness.

As she walked away, Nathan was struck by how much she had changed over the summer. Even the sound of her voice, lingering in the air, was that of an adult. As he watched her turning toward her bedroom door, he realized that she seemed taller, and more slender, and that the curve of her waist was anything but childlike.

"Our Ainsley is becoming a woman," he thought to himself with a bittersweet smile. Another child lost.

Chapter Twenty

L etty!" Ainsley called, running up the Academy stairs two at a time, not even stopping at the landing near the palladian window, but continuing up at the same dizzying speed. The dark blue brocade skirts of her school uniform flapped against her strong young legs, and the lace shawl, neatly pinned at her bosom, bunched between her shoulders.

"Miss Windsor!" Miss Holbrook's voice carried up the stairwell with chilling authority. "Come down at once."

With a sigh, Ainsley stopped, turned, and walked down the stairs, slowly straightening her shawl and gown. Her riotous hair had started the day in a bun, but now it had come unpinned and was curling around the lacy edge of her mob cap in an explosion of color.

Standing on the lowest step, Ainsley presented herself with downcast eyes and a contrite demeanor.

Miss Holbrook had to keep herself from smiling. There was something about Ainsley Windsor that gave the school mistress great joy. Ainsley was a brilliant student, quick, curious, intelligent, with wonderful flashes of creative thought. She was also an iconoclast, always wanting to know the "why" of things—and wanting to change the way things were to the way they ought to be.

Ever since Ainsley had come to her school, Miss Holbrook had taken a special interest in the young girl. Ainsley had been oddly ignorant in matters of social decorum and relationships. It was obvious the girl had grown up without a mother's love and direction. Ainsley's emotions were uncontrolled by any concepts of what was and was not acceptable. Her friendships were immediate, deep, and committed—her enmities the same.

As Ainsley matured, she had become even more vigorous in her opinions and decisions. She held to her promises and loyalties with a maturity and fierceness that could only be admired. But God help her if she forms a loyalty or an alliance with something or someone less than desirable, Miss Holbrook thought, for she'll not be dissuaded.

Miss Holbrook wished only that Ainsley could temper her strong emotions with wisdom and self-knowledge. For all Ainsley's bright vitality and courage, she seemed to mistrust her own happiness.

"Did I or did I not hear you shouting on the stairs just now, Miss Ainsley?" Miss Holbrook's rich contralto voice carried so much disapproval that Ainsley knew it was going to be impossible to charm her way out of chastisement.

"Yes, Miss Holbrook," she answered meekly, still looking down at her toes.

"And is it not clear to you, after four years at this Academy, that young ladies do not shout, do not run, do not leap upstairs, do not forget who and what they are? Have we taught you nothing?"

"Yes, Miss Holbrook. I mean . . . no, Miss Holbrook." Ainsley found herself desperately choking back a giggle. "I mean, I don't know how to answer that question, Miss Holbrook."

With a trace of calm humor, Miss Holbrook looked at the girl before her. "It was a rhetorical question, Ainsley, as you well know, and required no answer. My dear girl, I sometimes despair of you. No matter what I teach you, it just takes a summer back at your father's dock and you seem to return feeling that rules of proper society don't apply to you."

Ainsley drew a deep sigh, and looked up at Miss Holbrook. For years she had been listening to the same lecture, and it still did not make sense to her.

"Miss Holbrook—" Ainsley sighed, and spoke with genuine conviction. "—I can't see that just because I'm a girl, the main thing I must learn is never to be myself. To be quiet, obedient, unassuming, predictable—if those are all the qualities a girl may possess, then I shall renounce being a girl forever and go off and join ship's crews as a cabin boy. I shall leave Connecticut and sail off to the West Indies, and lie in the sun and grow brown as a berry and no one shall ever dare to try to turn me into a parlor-bred lady again!"

Miss Holbrook gave a tired smile, but her forehead creased with concern. "Ainsley, your father raised you alone, and in the company of men. He did the best he could, but even he recognizes that you must learn how to be a lady.

"You are not a man. Like it or not, women have certain obligations to society. We are not supposed to live as men. At Holbrook Academy we do not teach you manners and decorum so that you will feel restrained from being yourself. We teach you so that you can be your true self—a lady, so you can enter into society and take your rightful place. Whether you like it or not, young lady, society has rules."

Pausing, Miss Holbrook fixed Ainsley with a stern eye. "Running and shouting on the stairs, disturbing the other students is certainly not appropriate—ever."

Instantly contrite, Ainsley curtsied. "Forgive me, ma'am, I was not thinking of the others. You are right, I was thoughtless."

"Now that you are a senior girl," Miss Holbrook continued, "please try to set an example for the younger children or I shall surely have to tell your father."

Both Ainsley and Miss Holbrook knew it was an idle threat, for John Windsor loved his daughter so fiercely that no one dared bear ill tidings of her to him.

Miss Holbrook nodded in dismissal, and, with another curtsey, Ainsley turned, and walked slowly and gracefully up the stairs, head held high, and not so much as a glimpse of ankle showing. When she reached the second floor room she shared with Letty, she hastened through the door, closed it firmly behind her, and then burst into a joyous smile.

"Dear Letty, guess what? The post has come and we have letters from home. Two for you and one for me. Oh, how I love to hear from Papa, all about dear old Windsor Inn—who is staying, and what meals Cook is fixing, and what ships have eluded the customs agents and the blockades—oh, it is such delicious gossip.

"I feel that all of life is at Windsor Point, while we are stuck in this quiet, deadly dull country town."

Ainsley tossed two of the letters onto Letty's bed, and then, with a happy bounce, flung herself on her own bed and tore open the thick, creamy envelope. Three pages of finely written script fell into her lap. She began reading as avidly as though she were starving for the words.

"Dearest Ainsley," Letty said softly, sitting primly at the small secretary desk by the window, "you are such a passionate creature. Everything is always the most, the worst, the best to you. Edgefield is not a deadly dull country town; it is quite lovely. And Windsor Inn, although a very nice place, is quite off the beaten path, and has very little feminine company—so it is certainly not the very best place in the world. I should think as we grow older that you would learn to moderate your views."

"Pooh!" said Ainsley, rolling over onto her stomach and glancing up from her letter to look at Letty. As always, Letty looked smoothly groomed, her brown hair neatly parted in the middle and her dark brown eyes, slightly nearsighted, peering at the return address on the envelope in her hand.

"If it were not for me you would die of boredom, Letty Cavendish. Admit it!"

A small smile curved Letty's lips. "Perhaps, Ainsley. But that still doesn't mean that I am not shocked by your behavior."

The two girls had been close friends ever since they'd first come to the Academy as boarding students. Holbrook Academy was situated in the community of Edgefield, in a beautiful valley west of Fairfield. The school was housed in a large, columned building, with old beech trees lining the driveway. The younger girls lived in dormitories on the third floor, beneath the eaves and gables of the house. The final form girls, sixteen and seventeen years old, lived on the second floor in rooms which they shared with a single roommate. Classrooms, dining room, parlors, and offices were on the main floor. The school took day students from wealthy families in the nearby towns in addition to the boarding students.

The curriculum of Holbrook Academy included literature, rhetoric, decorum and etiquette, mathematics, geography, Latin, and painting. On Friday afternoons the girls were given ballroom dancing lessons by a visiting dance master, and on Saturdays they learned needlepoint and pianoforte or singing.

Sundays were strictly observed. The young ladies walked in a neat, modest procession to the Edgefield Congregational Church where, they sat in four rows of stiff, wooden pews in the east gallery balcony overlooking the church. The three-tiered pulpit was raised so high that the minister stood halfway to the balcony, far above the heads of the congregation seated on the main floor of the high-ceilinged meetinghouse. Unfortunately, this also gave him a better view from which to make sure the pupils were paying strict attention to his sermons.

In the winter, foot-warmers were brought in a wagon by the two freed black men who did the manual labor of the school. The young ladies from the Academy sat through the hours of the sermon with their feet comfortably perched on the wrought-iron cases, carefully filled with glowing coals and placed at the foot of the pews before the students arrived for services.

Brosian and Ebenezer were muscular, silent men. They lived in a neat, two-room shed next to the school's large garden. They had come to Boston on a ship that had transported slaves from the West Indies to Virginia, but had been immediately freed by the God-fearing Connecticut woman to whom they'd been given as a gift. The hard-working men had hired themselves out to the Academy as indentured workers, and had become, in the ten years they had been there tending the garden and grounds, maintaining the buildings, and stables, and fetching and carrying the privileged young ladies who studied at the Academy, as much a fixture of the institution as Miss Holbrook herself.

Miss Holbrook had started the school fifteen years earlier, when she had been thirty years old. Like Brosian and Ebenezer, Miss Holbrook had given her best years to the school. Now, at forty-five, Miss Holbrook knew her youth had gone forever, and that her entire life would be invested in other people's children, making attachments only to see her students leave and forget.

"Oh, Letty," Ainsley exclaimed, "I didn't mean to sound like I don't like the Academy. If it weren't for the school we never should have met, and you are the dearest, best, most wonderful friend in the whole world!"

Letty shook her head, and laughed. "There. You are doing it again. Always so . . . passionate."

Ignoring Letty's admiration, Ainsley continued, "Father's letter is full of the most wonderful news. I will share mine if you will share yours."

Letty flushed. "Nothing much to share. A note from Mama telling me that she has finished another sampler. She also has a touch of dyspepsia."

Ainsley made a face. "Is that all the news? What about your other letter?"

Letty turned her soft, brown eyes away from Ainsley, "Oh, it's just a line from Martin Brewerton."

"You sly dog, Letty!" Ainsley squealed. "How could you keep such a thing to yourself! Martin! Writing to you! Tell me everything. Please, please. This is the most exciting thing you've ever done! Still waters do run deep!"

Her face scarlet with pleasure and self-consciousness, Letty ducked her head. "Ainsley, you do exaggerate. It is just a short note wishing me well for fall term."

"Will he come to see you from Yale, do you think? It's so close. Hardly a day's journey away. He is such a quiet, thoughtful young man. I was most impressed when I met him at your home this summer. This is such adventure!"

Letty stood up impatiently. "You make far too much of it, Ainsley. We have known one another since childhood. He is but a friend . . ."

Leaping to her feet Ainsley ran over and embraced Letty. "I did not mean to tease. Only I do think you are such a prize, and I love anyone who sees that in you. Especially a man who will be educated at Yale. You should be the wife of such a man."

"You are incorrigible, Ainsley. You have created a marriage out of a simple, innocent note."

"Very well," Ainsley said. "Just wait and see. I can foretell the future. It is one of my gifts."

"For example, Father writes that Nathan has been awarded his chosen property from the lottery drawings. The proprietors have opened up the new tier of common land to the northwest of Norwalk, and Nathan got the ridge with the white oak grove on it. You know, the high ridge overlooking Five Mill River, with the fields and valleys, and the far view of the sound. It is so beautiful. Do you remember—I wrote you about visiting it."

Ainsley's eyes were misted with memory. "The ocean breeze catches your hair, and the land falls away like rolling green velvet." Ainsley's voice was soft with pleasure, and for a moment silence filled the room. "Nathan loves it, and so do I."

Letty, feeling uncomfortable for some undefined reason, said formally, "I am very happy for Master Fairchild. I know that was his desire." Suddenly Letty paused, startled by a realization.

"You called him Nathan!" she said in an astonished voice.

"Nathan! A man almost old enough to be your father—and you called him Nathan!"

"Of course I did!" Ainsley responded. "That is what I always call him in my mind—oh, not to his face, of course—but in my mind he is always Nathan."

With a rush of concern, Letty walked over and sat beside Ainsley on the edge of the bed. "But Ainsley, dear, whatever are you thinking? Surely you cannot imagine that you and Mr. Fairchild . . . ? He thinks of you as a child, and well he should." Letty's expression was dumbfounded and Ainsley, looking at her, laughed merrily.

"Don't be such a prim and proper prude, Letty. Of course, Mr. Fairchild does not think of me as a woman—yet—but in six more months I shall be out of school forever, and the whole world shall begin to think of me as a grown woman. Nathan shall too.

"At Christmas, Papa shall give me my coming-out ball, and you and Martin Brewerton shall be our guests, and Nathan will see me as I really am." Ainsley's smile was bright with her dream.

"The minute I saw him walking up our pathway, his face so sad and handsome, I knew I was meant to make him smile again. Oh, Letty, have you ever met anyone so wonderful? So tall, strong, and wise? And his splendid eyes that seem to hold the sky. I cannot imagine him not being a part of my life.

"When I saw his land, and stood on the point of the white oak ridge with him, I knew exactly what he was thinking. Exactly what he was feeling." Ainsley's voice was breathless with conviction. "It was like we were one person, and I knew, as surely as he did, that this land would be his—and that it would be mine too. Someday. I know it, Letty. I just know it."

Letty looked at her dear friend. They were closer than two sisters could ever have been, and Letty knew that this was not another one of Ainsley's passing enthusiasms.

For the first time in all of their years of friendship, Letty sensed the deep, unswerving commitment of Ainsley's powerful loyalty and love. Once given, it could never be changed or swayed.

Tears came to Letty's eyes. "Dear Ainsley," she said, putting her arms around her friend's shoulders. "I fear you sow your own ruin with such wild feelings. I cannot bear it. Pray that this will pass. You know so little of love. I do not think you can know if that is what you are feeling. Please, please don't set your heart and mind."

Ainsley said nothing, but Letty could see by the stubborn set of her friend's jaw, that her plea had come too late.

That fall, the big news had been that Miss Holbrook was getting married. It was all very sudden, and the girls at the school had been whispering and giggling since Halloween. Mr. Clay, Miss Holbrook's fiancé, was an itinerant school-teacher, who had been hired to teach the upper-form girls rhetoric and elocution, and the younger girls penmanship and geography. He never smiled.

Ainsley thought Mr. Clay was a nasty, dour man and could not abide him, but Letty felt he was a man of great rectitude and learning. It had been apparent to everyone that Mr. Clay had his eye on Miss Holbrook, although Ainsley, with her usual insight, whispered to Letty after lights-out that she thought Mr. Clay was more interested in the school than in its mistress.

By November, the banns were being read in the Edgefield congregation. Mr. Clay had endeared himself to the minister, and to the upright members of the congregation. He had also made himself known to the parents who visited the school.

"The way Mr. Clay acts, you'd think he already owned the place," Ainsley hissed to Letty. "I hope Miss Holbrook is not being taken advantage of."

Letty was dismayed at Ainsley's words. "Nonsense, Ainsley. You wouldn't want poor Miss Holbrook to be a spinster all of her life, would you? How lovely that she will be married, and to a man of such education and rectitude."

Ainsley giggled. "I don't see how his rectitude would make him much fun to be married to. I wonder if he ever un-ties that absurd cravat, or bends his neck. Wouldn't you hate to hear that pompous voice saying sweet things to you in the morning?'"

With a scarlet blush, Letty turned her face away. "We shouldn't speak of such intimate things, Ainsley."

Ainsley was frustrated by the description of such things as "intimate." It seemed to her that all the important things of life were kept secret. She knew that she was no longer a child, and yet there was no one to go to, no one to tell her about the feelings of men and women, and what it was they shared.

She wondered about marriage. Not just the sex part. She had seen horses, dogs, and cows mating and she knew the biological truth from her own quick and intelligent observations. No. What she needed to know was what it was like for men and women to be together. How did they talk to one another? How did they express the mad, sweet things that shook their hearts—as her heart shook when she thought of Nathan? Why were such things so often silent? Why did no one speak of them?

In spite of everyone's excitement about the betrothal, Ainsley suspected that Miss Holbrook was not marrying because of mad, sweet feelings that shook the heart, and Ainsley wondered if it would be right to marry for any other reason. It seemed to Ainsley a remarkable and splendid thing that Miss Holbrook had not let her unmarried status stand in the way of making something of her life, and it seemed distinctly unfair that Society would say it was better for Miss Holbrook to give up her estate and her accomplishments in order to marry an inferior prig of a man, than to live life according to her own rules.

One evening Miss Holbrook came into Ainsley's room. "I have something I wish to discuss with you, Ainsley. I fear Mr. Clay and I have differing opinions on the status of Brosian and Ebenezer. I think it would be best if I released them from the authority of the school before January given the change of direction that will take place here at the school upon my marriage. Do you suppose your father might have need of their employment at Windsor Point?"

Ainsley felt a ray of joy. "But of course he does! Father should love them to work for us. I shall miss them so much when I leave here, anyway. Papa can send the carriage at Christmas, and they shall drive down to Windsor Point with us."

Miss Holbrook smiled with genuine relief. "What a perfect solution. I shall write your father without delay."

"And I shall do the same," Ainsley laughed. "All will be well."

Ainsley thought of the tensions that must have been behind Miss Holbrook's request. Without a doubt, Ainsley was certain she did not want to attend school the next semester under the odious leadership of Mr. Clay.

How could Miss Holbrook marry such a man? She, Ainsley, would never marry just for the sake of being married. Nothing in the world was more dear to her than her freedom to be herself. She could only marry a man who could understand that right.

If she loved a man, she would gladly bring everything she had to the marriage—possessions, talents, effort, and her heart—but only if it could be given freely. No part of her could be given as chattel.

"I will bring myself to the man I love. I will not be taken or given by another," she vowed silently. "I can only be given by myself."

Chapter Twenty-one

A fine snow hung in the air like a veil against the deepening blue of the early winter evening. Captain Daniel Cothran and John Windsor were walking up the pathway from the docks to the porch of the inn. Through the light flakes of snow they could see the pillars of the porch twined with garlands of holly for Christmas. The great wreath on the front door was twined with cedar greens, nuts, apples, and satin ribbons. All in all, a most pretty and welcome sight after a long day of unloading cargo.

" 'Tis a fine job you have done for me, Daniel," John said heartily to his new captain. "Two score trading voyages up and down the sound, and only one customs boarding. That's quite a record. We've sold the horses, fleece, and grain of Connecticut and brought back tools, china, pewter, sugar, and gold—the things the colony needs to survive and thrive. Ah! It gives me such pleasure!"

Daniel smiled. "It gives me pleasure as well, John. *The Ainsley* is a fine boat. She handles like a seaman's dream."

" 'Tis more than I can say for the daughter for whom she is named." John chuckled. He stopped walking and turned his head, listening to something in the evening air.

"What's that?"

Daniel, too, stopped and listened. Faintly, through the gentle fall of the snow, he heard the sound of jingling harnesses, and the creak of turning wheels.

"I think it is coming from the Norwalk Trace," Daniel said.

"That's a surprise." John frowned. "I expected Ainsley, but she would be coming down the White Oak Trace. It's faster."

"Maybe not," Daniel reasoned. "If the snow is heavier inland, they may have had to travel along the coast. They could have cut over from the Rowayton Trace."

A huge smile broke out on John's face. "Of course. It must be Ainsley!" The two men turned and hurried toward the crossroads where the White Oak Trace and the Norwalk Trace met at the bridge.

The closer they came, the more distinct the sound of harness, hoof, and carriage rang in their ears, and suddenly, through the thickening curtain of the snow, they saw the closed carriage with the four fine grays pulling it. Seated next to the driver, muffled in heavy great coats, with scarves and large tricorn hats covering most of their faces, were two men with dark skin and luminous eyes.

The driver pulled the horses to a halt and saluted the two men standing on the road.

"Mr. Windsor, sir, I bring you precious cargo," the driver said. Scarcely were the words out of his mouth than a fur-framed face poked out of the curtains to see why the coach had stopped. Ainsley, seeing her father, threw open the door and leaped from the high coach to the ground.

"Papa!" she cried, running toward him and embracing him with her strong young arms. "It is so good to be home!" She looked up the road to catch her first sight of Windsor Inn, all aglow now with candles in each window, and bright festive greenery proclaiming the holiday season.

"Oh, it is a wonder! So beautiful! How I have missed this dear, dear spot!"

She was dressed in a cape of white wool trimmed with white fox fur. From under the hood, her unruly auburn hair burst like fire, and framed her sweet face. She seemed to glow in the gathering twilight, as though all the beauty and glory of the day had gathered into her shimmering eyes as pure and bright as the flame of a candle.

Daniel, standing in his heavy seaman's coat, with the collar turned up and snow beginning to gather on his fine, dark hair, stared at this beautiful apparition, and felt his heart tremble. He almost reached his hand out, involuntarily, to see if it would warm against her light.

He thought her the loveliest thing he had ever seen. He was a quiet, steady man. A man who rode his ship at sea with legs firmly planted and his eyes trained on the far horizon. Nothing in his life had prepared him for the deep stirring in his heart that he felt as he looked at the radiant young woman standing in the snow.

"Oh dear!" Ainsley exclaimed. "I am so happy to be

home I have quite forgot my manners. The two of you must
be frozen, as are Letty and Martin—and I can't think how
cold poor Ebenezer and Brosian must be. We had to take the
Post road down the coast. Once we reached the Rowayton
Trace, I just could not wait to be home. I would not let us
stop."

She ran over to the coach. "Dear Mr. Edmund, do drive
the coach up to the inn. Father and I and . . .?" She stopped.
"I'm sorry. We haven't been introduced, but you must be
Captain Cothran."

Daniel smiled, bowing in acknowledgment. Ainsley called
back up to the coach, "Letty! Martin! Go up to the house
and get warm—we'll join you shortly."

The coach rattled away. Ainsley linked her arm in her father's and walked briskly up the path, pausing to exclaim
over and over again at the wonder of being home. The snow
melted on her upturned face.

Walking quietly beside father and daughter, Daniel listened to the joyful, vital voice of Ainsley Windsor, and
thought he had never heard any music as beautiful as the
sound of her speaking. He suddenly felt young and alive, as
though a door had opened into another room in his life, a
room he had never known existed. Until this moment he had
never realized how much a woman—a splendid woman—
could change the very essence, the very texture of a man's
life.

Typically, Daniel said nothing. He was wise and calm
even in the midst of such an epiphany of emotion, and he
simply accepted the reality of the existence of Ainsley as a
gift from some unknown god. Just as he had accepted Nathan's friendship since the day they had met as boys on the
playing field of their grammar school in England.

These feelings and these people—bonded to him in some
uncalculable way—had simply come to his life. Had filled
some great empty spot. He could not explain it—or why he
was so fortunate. They were simply a part of him.

Arrangements were quickly made for the arriving party.
Letty was sharing Ainsley's room, as she always did when
she was a guest of the Windsors', and Martin Brewerton, the
young Yale student, was placed in a room next to Daniel
Cothran. Ebenezer and Brosian were escorted by John Windsor, who had wholeheartedly agreed to employ them in his

establishment, to their assigned quarters in a stoutly built cabin in the cluster of buildings above the dock.

"You'll get the lay of the land soon enough," John assured them. "Lots of work to be done, but it is the kind a man can feel satisfaction in doing. But for today, just rest and get acquainted. Tomorrow will be time enough for you to get started."

Ebenezer and Brosian looked around the main room of the cabin. It was a cheerful place. The table was set, and there was bread, a roasted chicken, and pickled beets laid out. A fire was crackling in the fireplace, and a spray of green boughs over the door gave them welcome.

With dignity, Ebenezer offered John Windsor his hand. John took the taller man's muscled hand and shook it gravely. Then he turned to Brosian, and shook his hand as well. "Welcome to Windsor Point. You have a home with us as long as you wish to stay."

When John returned to the main building, the living room was brimming with laughter and fun. Young Martin Brewerton was playing a lively number on the pianoforte, and Letty and Ainsley were singing the words, something about "the rising of the sun, and the running of the deer . . ."

Letty wore a dress of deep blue merino wool, her chestnut curls smooth and shining in the lamplight. Dancing merrily, and singing breathlessly, Ainsley was flitting about the room between the chairs, tables, and settees, her plaid underskirts fluttering, showing the froth of her lacy petticoats around her dainty ankles.

Daniel Cothran stood by the fireplace, his elbow resting on the mantel. His eyes never left Ainsley's graceful figure. One evening in the Caribbean, he had been alone on the decks and had seen in the clear night sky a glorious mass of clouds. The clouds had been outlined in a brilliant aura of crimson, and from the heart of them came great flashes and bolts of light that dazzled against the smooth sea, and sent shimmers of blue, green, gold, and silver into the night. He'd known it was only a distant storm, but for him it had been like a mighty show—a choreography of brilliance that had filled his heart and mind. Watching, listening, looking at Ainsley filled him with the same wonder and delight.

"Now then, my girl," John said, entering the room, "this group must be fair famished, and if I do not miss my guess, dinner has been waiting for some time now."

"We were waiting for you, Papa dear. We'd rather have your company than a fresh dinner any day!" Ainsley ran over and threw her arms around her father. Embarrassed but pleased, John patted her shoulder and herded the group into the dining room.

Around the table the talk was eager. Ainsley expressed her concerns over Miss Holbrook's coming marriage. "I will not return to that school, Papa! They will be married in January. Right after the first of the year. School will not be the same, and I have no desire to attend under the tutelage of that odious man."

"Now then, Ainsley," her father admonished, "this is an affair of no concern to you. Miss Holbrook is right. If this Mr. Clay is an upstanding man, she is far better off married to him. Marriage is the natural state of woman."

Outraged, Ainsley opened her mouth to argue, but her father forestalled her. "Remember our guests, Ainsley. They do not wish to hear your views on such matters."

She was instantly contrite and turned to Martin. "We are so pleased you are able to come visit us for the holidays, Mr. Brewerton. Letty told me that your parents have been detained in England, along with her own."

"Yes." Martin inclined his head. "My father was called back to England by family matters, and Letty's father, as you know, is negotiating new trade and customs tolerances for the colony. They traveled together, and estate matters have detained them for several more months."

Letty blushed. "I did not want Mr. Brewerton to spend a cheerless holiday alone in New Haven. You were so kind to include him in your house party, dear Master Windsor."

"We are delighted to have you both," John declared. "This old place has been yearning for the sound of young people. Tomorrow night we shall dance away the hours of Christmas Eve. Thanks to Daniel, we have had a very good year, and there is much to celebrate. You, Daniel, shall lead the first cotillion."

"It will be my honor, John." Daniel bowed, and then turned toward Ainsley. "If Mistress Ainsley will give me the privilege of leading it with her."

"Of course she shall!" John roared with good humor. "What a night we shall have."

Ainsley smiled at Daniel and looked at him carefully for the first time. She liked the strong, square face, the direct eyes, and the mouth that seemed formed in a constant smile. This is a man worthy of Nathan's friendship, she thought.

"I should be honored, Captain Cothran, and I promise not to step on your toes. Letty and I have been practicing the new dances."

Daniel laughed. "Pray for me, then, that I do not step on yours, for I fear the sea has left me little time for practicing the niceties of the ballroom."

Laughing, Ainsley rose from her place. "Then we shall both practice together. Come, Martin and Letty, we shall teach Captain Cothran that new minuet that you were playing. Papa, you shall watch, and then perhaps you will decide your dancing days are not over after all. It is such great fun."

With that, Ainsley curtsied before Daniel, and he rose. Martin began to play again, and the two girls each took one of Daniel's hands.

In reality, he was a fine dancer, and had soon mastered the new step. The stately dance was graceful and delicate, and, at the last figure, Ainsley touched the tips of his upraised hand, turned in a slow circle in front of him, and dropped into a deep bow. He wanted to grasp both of her hands in his own.

How could there be a young woman so totally unconscious of how she looked? Of her effect on men? So completely without artifice that her very naturalness became an artifice too powerful to be resisted? Why had not Nathan told him of this young woman? What did Nathan think of her? He had scarcely mentioned Ainsley's name to Daniel. When the two friends conversed, Daniel spoke of *The Ainsley* and his voyages and Nathan spoke of the house he was building on the property he'd bought with a great deal of gold.

Nathan's dream had come true, and now he labored day and night to build something on the land that would last. A monument to his broken dreams and lost loved ones. Something to mark the fact that the Fairchilds had passed through this life and had not gone unnoted and unknown. He was determined to build a place where they would be remembered. A new and better Marshfield—one that would endure.

Nathan had said little of this magnificent Ainsley, this woman who filled Daniel's heart with celebration. So shining, so glorious—so innocent and unaware of the shimmer that she cast on all around her. Even John Windsor seemed brighter, younger, and more robust, as though her very presence was his sustenance and strength.

Later that night, as John was supervising the dousing of the candles, Ainsley crept into the dining room. The silver was polished and gleaming on the sideboard, and the tables had been stacked away so that the broad planks of the floor would be ready for the dancing and festivities of the next day. She touched her father's arm.

"Who is coming to the ball tomorrow?" she asked, looking around the room with hungry eyes, as though to drink in the joy of homecoming.

"Well, as you can see, I've taken no guests in the inn over the holidays, having saved every room for family and house guests. Many of my old friends from Norwalk are coming, all of the captains and officers that are not at sea, the commander of the Colonial regulars stationed in Norwalk and his officers, plus all the young daughters of our friends and neighbors . . ." John sighed; he was weary, and tired of thinking. "All is planned and ready. Now off to bed with you, young mistress, or you shall not have your beauty sleep."

Still, she stood hesitantly. "And the new sequestration? Are there none coming down the White Oak Trace?"

Understanding dawned in John Windsor's eyes. "Nathan? Is all this fuss just to ask if Nathan Fairchild is coming? Of course he is, foolish girl. Would we have a celebration at Windsor Point without my finest friend?" He shook his head and, taking her arm, lit their way up the stairs with the bracket of candles he held in his hand. In the flickering candlelight Ainsley smiled to herself, all the tension and weariness of the day suddenly dispersed.

The musicians were the first to arrive on Christmas Eve. They warmed themselves at the blazing fireplace, and then ate hugely at the groaning buffet table. Never had such a feast been seen by any of them before! Hams, glazed with honey and browned sugar; turkeys, carved into thin slices and rebuilt so that they looked untouched, but would reveal the carved and juicy meat at the slightest touch of a fork; piles of candied fruits, whole and colorful; mounds of breads, cakes, cookies, and tarts; bowls of jellies, compotes, and creams; hot sausages in chafing dishes; holiday pies, and great bowls of punch—both cold and steaming hot.

The air was filled with the scents of cinnamon, spices, evergreen boughs, and sweet wood smoke. The rooms danced with the light of myriad candles and fireplaces. Out on the porch the air sang with the crisp, cold sea breeze, and the world sparkled under a light, white blanket of snow.

As the afternoon wore on, the first guests began to arrive. Some, the closest neighbors, had walked, but most came in crowded carriages, bursting out with a profusion of laughter, bright greetings, and a flurry of whirling skirts in a rainbow of colors.

Among the guests there were some sober, scrupulous Congregationalists, whose clothes were gray, dark blue, and black. They wore their dignity, however, with a benign good humor.

Aware that many of their friends were sensitive to worldliness, and not wishing to offend them, Ainsley had chosen a dress of soft, deep gold rather than the flamboyant crimson she had wanted to wear. The subdued color only served to enhance the brilliance of her hair, which she had declined to powder. The abundant auburn curls, pulled up and piled on top of her head, could not be tamed or subdued. The great puffed sleeves of her dress were caught with bows made from the same netting as her fichu, which was sprinkled with tiny sparkles of gold. When the light caught the flashes of gold, her creamy neck and lovely face looked as though they were floating in stars.

As Ainsley prepared to descend the stairs, she took Letty's hand and led her to the pier glass at the end of the hall. The two friends stood side by side. Letty was dressed in a dress of dark purple brocade. Her lace collar was cream-colored and her dark brown hair, gleaming like mahogany, was pulled into gentle curls about her ears.

"Let us always remember tonight, Letty," Ainsley whispered. "Always. Whatever the New Year brings."

Frowning, Letty looked questioningly at her friend. "What is it you are thinking?" she asked anxiously, thinking Ainsley's comment a bit onerous.

"Oh, nothing," Ainsley answered. "Only that our lives are soon to be at a crossroads. Let us remember tonight."

They went down the stairs arm in arm. The rooms were already filling with guests and laughter. Eating, games, con-

versation, and motion filled the rooms, and Ainsley and her
father walked from group to group with ready, welcoming
hospitality.

Glancing at the buffet, Ainsley saw Daniel Cothran, resplendent in his sea captain's uniform, his unpowdered hair
in a neat queue. He was surrounded by several young
women, fluttering around him like bees at a blossom. Daniel
looked distinctly uncomfortable, and Ainsley, catching his
eye, saw his mute appeal for help. She walked across the
crowded floor dexterously, and placed her gloved hand in
the crook of his arm. "Sorry, dear ladies, but I must steal
Captain Cothran from you for a moment. There is a message
from *The Ainsley*."

Following her lead, Daniel threaded his way across the
packed room, and they burst out onto the empty porch.
"Br–r–r!" Ainsley exclaimed. "It's colder than I thought out
here, but you looked like you could use a little air."

Some younger party guests were out on the lawn riding on
sleds. Their laughter decorated the air, like the plumes of
breath which Ainsley blew from her mouth. "There wasn't
any message, you know," she admitted. "You just looked
like you needed rescuing, and, after all, I am 'the Ainsley,'
so I thought I could get you away."

"I am most grateful." Daniel Cothran nodded rather formally. "I should love to hear a message from this Ainsley."

She smiled. "Well then, you shall have to fetch me a
cloak, for I am near to freezing."

Daniel slipped back into the hallway, to the noise and the
warmth, and grabbed his heavy captain's cloak. As he came
back to the porch he put it around her shoulders, fighting the
urge to let his hands linger on her arms.

With a little sigh, she walked over to the edge of the steps.
Her eyes lifted and she looked into the dark night, far inland,
toward the tall ridge rising many miles away. The ridge was
invisible in the darkness, but her eyes yearned to see it.

"Do you suppose your friend Mr. Fairchild has forgotten
it is Christmas Eve?" she asked wistfully.

The tone of her voice was not lost on Daniel, and he wondered for a moment what it meant. "Perhaps he has," Daniel
replied. "It has been such a cold winter that he has scarce
been able to get the work on his house begun. He is living
in a small, split-slab cabin, with the barest of creature com-
forts. John and I have often begged him to come stay at the

inn until spring, but he is enamored of his land, and seems to feel at home nowhere else."

"Yes," Ainsley breathed, "I knew it would be so. But surely he will come for Christmas."

"Aye," Daniel replied, "if he has not lost track of the days."

Just then, John Windsor came bustling out onto the porch. "The musicians are ready, Daniel. I wondered where you two had gone. It is time for the cotillion to begin."

With a graceful bow, Daniel offered his arm to Ainsley. After handing the captain's heavy cloak to her father, she accompanied Daniel into the dining room, which was now all set for the dances to commence. With a splendid flourish she turned to Captain Cothran, placing her daintily gloved hand over his. The director of the musicians nodded, and the quadrille began.

After four sets of music, both the dancers and the musicians paused for refreshment. The young women went upstairs to freshen themselves. Ainsley found Letty sitting in a window seat at the top of the stairs. "Letty," she exclaimed, "you and Martin have hardly danced at all! Every time I look for you, I find you in a quiet corner talking to one another. This is supposed to be a festive party, but the two of you look mighty serious."

Without looking at Ainsley, Letty blushed. "We have not seen one another for some time. We have much to discuss. Our families have been close friends all of our lives. We have so many mutual concerns—especially now, with our parents across the ocean, so far away."

"Oh, Letty!" Ainsley cried. "How thoughtless of me! Of course you must be worried. But do try to be happy and carefree, just for tonight."

"You do not seem altogether happy yourself," Letty said sympathetically. "I have seen your eyes when no one is watching. What is the matter, Ainsley? It is a lovely party—"

Just then Ainsley glanced down the stairs and saw the front door burst open. A man walked in, splendid in a black great coat, with a full half-cape collar and high, shining boots. The shoulders of the coat were dusted with snow, and the boots were coated as well. It was Nathan.

"Where's the master of this house?" Nathan roared. "I understand there's to be a party here this eve, and I intend to be part of it."

John Windsor gave a great shout of welcome and strode over to clasp Nathan in his arms. "Nate!" he exclaimed, "we thought you had forgotten us!"

"No, never!" Nathan replied. "Such a celebration as this—and with our young Ainsley coming home? What kind of a friend do you take me for? I must apologize for being late, but my horse threw a shoe halfway down the trace, and I have had to walk these past five miles.

"Merry Christmas, John, and gratitude for the joy of your friendship and your hospitality." Nathan handed a wrapped gift to John Windsor, who immediately unwrapped it to discover a magnificently carved pipe.

"Now where is that child? Surely they did not hold her at school for disciplinary detention?" Nathan shouted, looking about the room. Everyone laughed at the suggestion, and Ainsley, stifling the urge to fling herself down the stairs, walked graciously down, her gloved hand lightly touching the banister.

Surely he must see my heart beating, she thought to herself. Surely he can see that I am a woman, grown and ready to live and love. Surely he will see me now—as I really am.

"Dear Master Fairchild," she said, with what she desperately hoped was dignified restraint. "We are delighted you are here. Has your horse been tended to?"

Nathan, caught off-guard by the formality of her welcome, replied with a courteous bow and kissed her hand. "Yes, thank you, Mistress Ainsley. I introduced myself to Brosian—he seems a most capable man—and he took my horse to the barn. We shall have him reshod by tomorrow."

They stood eyeing one another awkwardly, neither quite sure of the other. Ainsley held herself tall, with her head in a regal pose, hoping that Nathan would see her as a mature adult.

Nathan was amused at the pose. She seemed to him like a little girl playing dress-up, and yet, there was something real in her maturity, and in the splendid truth of her womanhood, that made him hesitant to laugh or tease her, and so they both remained uncomfortably silent, uncertain of a way to break the unexpected impasse.

The music began again, and the guests moved off to the

dance floor. "This is for you," Nathan said, handing Ainsley the other wrapped gift which he held in his hands.

Ainsley stood holding Nathan's gift, her eyes fastened on the wrappings. She did not dare to look directly into Nathan's face. If anything, he seemed handsomer and stronger than she had remembered. He must have worked his land through the months until the snows had come. His hands were bronzed and muscled and his new clothes, well tailored and expensive, gave him a look of unaccustomed importance and confidence that, strangely, undermined her own. He no longer seemed the lost and wandering man who had stayed at the inn through the last months of summer.

She was desperately disappointed. In her mind she had written and rewritten this scene a hundred times, and always she had been bright, warm, and witty—and Nathan had been dazzled by the change in her, by her very presence.

Why could she not fit him into the pattern she yearned to have him fit? Why could he not just sweep her off her feet and carry her away? Love her the way she wanted to be loved? Teach her the things she needed to know about how to be with a man—how to be a woman with a man? Why did he always seem so complete all in himself?

There was a part of him as unknown, as mysterious, as separate from her as it had ever been. Her growing up, her love for him, her pity for him—none of these things seemed to change the way he really was. But he must have thought of her sometimes? Else why would he have brought her a Christmas present? Her heart cheered a little.

"Aren't you going to open it?" Nathan asked, his voice mildly mocking. "The old Ainsley would have had the paper torn off in a trice."

She looked up at him with a flash of her old impulsiveness. "The new Ainsley is more restrained," she retorted, "more patient."

With that, Nathan laughed aloud. "Yes, I can see that."

Flushing, she pulled the ribbons from the gift and opened the box. In a mound of red velvet rested an exquisite gold locket. Ainsley gasped.

"It's beautiful, Nathan," she whispered, "too beautiful."

"Open it," Nathan said, scarcely taking note that she had called him Nathan. "It is to be your first piece of grown-up jewelry."

With trembling heart she opened the locket. Inside was a

lovely miniature painting of a house with a high, gabled roof and dormer windows, set in a lovely grove of trees.

She looked up at him, puzzled.

"That's the architect's rendering of my house. I had him do one in miniature for you, since I know what a curious minx you are. And, since you caught the vision of how beautiful my place—my Marshfield—could be, I wanted you to see the dream for yourself."

Nathan moved to stand beside her so that he could see the picture with her, and Ainsley caught her breath at his nearness. She still couldn't speak.

"Marshfield," Nathan said softly, "that's what I am going to call it. The new Marshfield. Where only good things can happen. Where only the happy memories will be allowed." He was silent for a moment, and she knew his thoughts were far, far from her.

"It's a beautiful locket, Nathan," she whispered at last. "Really, really beautiful. What is in it is beautiful, too. I will treasure it for all of my life."

Nathan laughed. "Well, you certainly don't need to keep the picture of the house in it. I expect you to replace it one day with the picture of a fine young man. Now, let me look at you."

He held her hands and stared at her. "Wonder of wonders—you are almost a young lady," he exclaimed, "and a beauty at that. Who would have thought such a thing possible!"

She pulled her hands away, affronted. "Don't tease me," she said. "Help me put this locket on, and then I shall show you how well I can dance."

Chapter Twenty-two

Captain Daniel Cothran stood with a small group of men by the side of the banquet table. The buffet had been almost depleted by the hungry partyers, but the platters were still covered with enough food to satisfy any appetite. With a steaming cup of wassail in one hand, Daniel listened to the conversation around him, his intelligent eyes assessing the information.

"How can we establish trade relationships? As long as France stares down its nose at us from Cape Breton . . . like a cannon trained on the whole of the coastline . . ."

"French privateers, protected by that hellish Fort Louisburg—and to think we had it in our hands a decade ago actually breached the fort—had it surrendered to us and then . . ."

"Damned British. Our good Connecticut boys, the noble Connecticut 4th, risking life and limb, won the fort for 'em, and they gave the place back to the French in that hellish King George War—"

"Yes, and gave Connecticut a decade of misery for our pains. Ten years of our paper money becoming worthless because we had to print so much to pay for the campaign. Inflation, no currency to trade."

"When the British threw our victory back into the French lap like a bone to a dog, it became apparent that the British have no respect for us colonists. How many times do we have to be kicked in the teeth? They don't value anything we do, so why should we back them in this ridiculous war with the French?"

John Windsor and Martin Brewerton were standing with Daniel Cothran, listening to the conversation of the irate townsmen.

"Excuse me, sir," Martin said to the Norwalk merchant, Warren Fletcher, who had just spoken. The older man's red, angry face showed the depth of his aroused emotions as he turned to stare at the young Yale student.

Martin's round, serious face showed no discomfort or apprehension as he spoke with quiet conviction. "I feel we owe loyalty and gratitude to our mother country. This is, after all, a British colony, and we are British colonials. It would behoove us, sir, not to forget that, for, as you know, loyalty is the measure of the man."

Warren Fletcher's face grew redder, and he answered with a snort, "You young popinjay! I thought they taught you how to think at Yale. Here you are spouting aristocratic British pap!"

With a sharp intake of breath, Martin drew himself up. "I will not consider that an insult, sir, since you are old enough to be my father and consider me to be a boy."

Martin continued, "I assure you, I am a man—not a boy. My opinions are those of a man who prizes both citizenship in this great colony, and its ties to England. Should a man—forget his parents? Should we, if we are to wear the title of manhood, forget the nation which is parent of our nation? I think not, sir."

With a slight bow, Martin turned to John Windsor. "If you will excuse me, Master Windsor, I think perhaps this is my dance with Mistress Letty. And might I have the honor of speaking with you privately later this evening?"

"Of course you may, my boy!" John said heartily, trying to ease the group's tension. "Now go dance and leave all of us old men to our complaining. It is the pleasure of age to speak when we can no longer act—to criticize when we cannot produce."

One or two of the men in the group laughed at John's wit; Warren Fletcher frowned. "I must be on my way, John. Such festivities are not really suited to me and mine. This is probably more merrymaking than the Lord would approve, and His day is rapidly coming."

Ever the genial host, John grasped Warren's black-clad arm and guided him toward the cloakroom. "I am right glad that you joined us at all, Warren. Your wife and daughter have added beauty to the occasion, and, although I know you disapprove of dancing and music, still, I hope the food was to your liking."

"Hrmmph," Warren Fletcher answered, motioning to his wife and daughter, had been sitting quietly in their chairs at the side of the room throughout the evening. Dressed in black and gray, with prim, lace–trimmed collars at their throats, mother and daughter looked much alike. Both had long, refined faces, large, dark eyes, and mouths set in permanent lines of disapproval.

Only John Windsor had noted that during the liveliest of tunes, the daughter's toe could be seen tapping, almost imperceptibly, beneath her modest gown.

After the Fletchers left and the knot of men at the side of the table broke away from their conversation, Daniel Cothran turned to see his old friend Nathan whirling Ainsley onto the dance floor. The deep gold of her skirts swayed gracefully as they followed the stately patterns of the dance. As Ainsley pivoted and curtsied, then stepped toward Nathan, Daniel got a clear glimpse of her face and almost gasped at the transparent look of joy and love he saw there. Her green eyes drank in Nathan's face as a child dying of thirst would drink at a pool of water.

A feeling of great sadness overwhelmed Daniel, because it was not until that moment that he realized how indelible his attraction to Ainsley had become. He fought the twist of jealousy and pain in his heart, not wanting to be envious of his best friend. He must hide his feelings for Ainsley, must resign himself to knowing his love for her could never mean more to her than that of a dear brother.

Oh, but what he would give to have her look at him, just once, the way she was looking at Nathan now. And yet, something in Nathan's calm and rather indifferent exterior made Daniel certain that Nathan was completely unaware of the depth and nature Ainsley's feelings for him.

With a sense of premonition, of hurt, pity, and love for them both, Daniel somehow knew that this was a doomed love. He knew, better than anyone in that room, that Nathan's past was filled with so much loss and grief that he was not ready to love again—might never be ready.

The places in Nathan's heart where a woman as brilliant, complex, and full of needs as Ainsley would have to dwell were filled to the brim with memories of lost love and pain. Something essential in Nathan was dead and gone. On the outside he would live a manly life—one of good cheer and kindness, service and rectitude—but his inner life was one of silent loneliness, and Nathan kept it so. His secret heart—the place where the love of man, woman, and family dwelt—was walled up, shored away in a quiet, bittersweet tomb where his lost family was cherished, remembered, and longed for.

"Poor Ainsley," Daniel thought. "Poor Nathan." With a rueful smile, he tossed down his cupful of punch. "And poor me."

Nathan, catching sight of Daniel, grabbed Ainsley's hand and left the dance. "It's Daniel!" he exclaimed, clasping his friend in a fond embrace. "Good to see you, dear friend. How was your last voyage, and are you ashore for a while? If so, come and see me before the snows make travel impossible."

"You're a sight for weary eyes, Nathan!" Daniel answered heartily. "Being a landed gentleman seems to agree with you. Of course I'll come to see you, weather and tide permitting. We are waiting for a shipload of oxen and horses from the Stamford Upper Division. The weather has slowed the arrival of the cargo, so I shall be up to Marshfield sometime next week."

"I'll hold you to that promise, good friend. Now, dance with this pretty butterfly for me, while I get myself something to eat, for I am fairly famished." With a smile, Nathan gave Ainsley's hand to Daniel. She quickly masked her disappointment and graciously walked back to the dance, her fingers light on Daniel's arm.

Not long after the Fletchers' departure the party began to thin out. The guests gathered up their wraps and moved into the crisp night air. Carriages, coaches, and wagons were filled, and foot and muff warmers provided with fresh, glowing coals by Ebenezer and Brosian. The voices and laughter seemed to hang in the air long after the conveyances with their jingling harnesses, were out of sight.

Wearily, John Windsor closed the front door against the frosty air. The musicians had packed up, and the servants were clearing the last remains of the holiday feast. Nathan, Daniel, Letty, Ainsley, and Martin were helping the last guests with their coats and hats.

"Fine party, John." "Good to have you home, Ainsley . . ." "May the Lord bless you." "See you at services tomorrow." The parting words were full of neighborly affection.

Ainsley ran to the porch, so full of the delight of the evening that she did not feel the cold. "Good night," she called, waving her hand till the last group walked out of sight. "Good night, dear friends, good night."

Shaking his head, Nathan grabbed his great coat, walked out to the pillar where she stood, and placed it over her shoulders. "You will catch your death, my dear girl," he said.

She laughed and looked up at him. "I am so happy right now that I don't think I should mind dying."

His face went suddenly blank and he turned away from her. "It is not a matter for joking," he said coldly, walking back into the house.

Devastated, Ainsley followed him. "I'm sorry, Nathan. I—I didn't mean to sound flippant."

He shook his head and smiled, but the glow of the evening was spoiled.

The group stood in the parlor at the foot of the stairs. As though with one accord, each sought a comfortable place to sit and they formed a small semicircle around the hearth. John, by long habit, pulled out his old pipe, and then, thinking better of it, took the pipe Nathan had given him as a gift and filled it from a twist of tobacco.

"Will any of you join me?" he asked the other men. They shook their heads. "Well then," John said, raising the new pipe like a glass in a toast, "here's to a new year. A year, we hope, of prosperous crops for you, Nathan, of prosperous and safe trips for you, Daniel, and of success in your studies to you three young students."

Martin leaped to his feet. "Sir, that is the matter which I wished to discuss with you."

John nodded, "Very well. Shall we go to my office?"

"No, sir. What I have to say may be said in present company."

Martin took a deep breath, and even though the room was beginning to cool, perspiration moistened his brow. Letty reached over and took Ainsley's hand in her own. She held on for dear life, as though Ainsley were a life preserver and she a drowning woman. With a surprised glance, Ainsley stared at her quiet friend, knowing something of import was about to happen.

"Mr. Windsor, it is my understanding that while Letty's

parents are in England you are her appointed guardian. Is that correct?" Martin asked.

John nodded, his eyes never leaving the face of the young man in front of him.

"Sir, I have been recruited to act as aide and secretary to Lord Easton, commander of the British Highlander regulars and the British 5th Infantry Division. Lord Easton has just been commissioned general of the Colonial regiments of Fairfield, Stamford, and Norwalk, and all ancillary communities as well."

There was heavy silence in the room. Suddenly the French and Indian Wars, which had seemed so far away, were a shadow moving before their eyes.

"My father has recently inherited a title in England, and with the title comes the responsibility for the oldest son to receive his commission in the regiment. Lord Easton and my father are old friends. I will be sworn two weeks after New Year's Day."

The three men rose from their chairs and shook Martin's hand. "Well done, my lad," John said. "I know you are a man of conviction, and I admire that. But why such a rush? You have but a few months to complete your degree at the university."

"Without explaining any of the details," Martin replied, "I will not be betraying confidence if I inform you that the British army—we—are about to billet our regular regiments in the coastal communities I have just named. It is here that we will await the word to prepare the final assault on Fort Louisburg. As you know, if we can conquer the fort, we own Canada."

With a short, bitter laugh, Daniel remarked wryly, "Then why did the British give it away when we won it for them the first time?"

Martin turned with a quick flare of anger, but then fought down his defensive reaction and nodded in agreement. "What we must face is our situation today. This dreadful war must come to an end, and we have the will and the means to end it. The French will lose, and, with God's help, we will secure our boundaries and our sea lanes in the name of the crown."

"Here, here," said John Windsor, and the other men nodded in agreement.

Nathan was silent, his eyes dark with unreadable emo-

tions. Ainsley felt his brooding presence and her heart cried
to know what he was thinking and feeling.

"Mister Windsor, sir, I am to be assigned to General
Easton's personal staff at headquarters. He has requisitioned
my home in New Haven as his residence and command post.
We will be wintering there, and, I am assured, except for
campaigns, we will continue to use the estate as headquarters for the Regular and Colonial regiments."

The young man was obviously still nervous, and John
knew that he was coming to the point of his discourse.

"Would you, sir, be willing to allow Miss Cavendish to remain here at Windsor Point, to have the banns read, and to
give her to me in marriage? I have written and obtained permission from both my parents and the parents of Letty—
er—Mistress Cavendish." Martin reached into his waistcoat
and brought out two heavy pieces of paper filled with purposeful handwriting.

After reading the letters, John looked up intently at the
two young people. "Are you sure you do not want to wait?
After all, you are young yet, and there is so much uncertainty."

It was Letty who answered, springing from her place beside Ainsley and standing, small and determined, next to
Martin. "That is why," she declared in her sweet, clear
voice. "We have loved one another since we were children,
and if Martin is to go to war, it is our wish that we will have
this one dear winter as man and wife to remember."

The room was absolutely silent, with only the crackle of
the dying logs to break the stillness. The moment length-
ened, and then John Windsor broke the spell. With a jovial
shout, he pulled the two young people into his embrace.

"I shall give you a wedding, the likes of which you have
never seen!" he exclaimed. "It shall put tonight's party to
shame."

"No," Letty said sweetly, "such a wedding would not sit
well on the brink of war. Let us be married with only the
dear souls in this room to bear witness. It shall be the truest
wedding of all."

"Letty, you shall marry your blessed Martin after all. I am
so pleased for you." Ainsley kissed her dearest friend.

"And now, Papa, with a wedding and the billeting of soldiers in Norwalk, and the accounts of the inn in dreadful
shape, and with no one to take care of such matters, I de-

clare that I, too, am through with schooling. Certainly
through with Miss Holbrook's—soon to be Mr. Clay's—
Academy."

John frowned. "We are too tired to talk over such things
tonight."

"Please, Papa," Ainsley begged. "Who will plan the wedding and help Letty—"

"Tomorrow, Ainsley," her father thundered. "We will
speak of it tomorrow. Today has held enough for any one
day."

Ainsley walked up the stairs pensively, but in her mind
she repeated over and over to herself, I will not go back to
school. I am a woman now. I will not go back to school.
Papa and Nathan need me. I'll make them see it. I will not
go back to school.

Chapter Twenty-three

On Christmas Day, after services, John Windsor spoke to the minister of the Norwalk congregation on behalf of his ward, Letty Cavendish. The minister, aware of the position of the two families involved, declared that he would send word immediately to the New Haven minister, and the six-week banns could be waived.

Without belaboring the point, John mentioned that Lord Easton would be coming to Norwalk at the end of January to make disposition for the billeting of one of his regiments of British regulars, and would be pleased to attend the wedding at that time.

Pastor Bingham, his austere, ministerial countenance seeming unimpressed by Anglican nobility, nonetheless nodded his head in acquiescence. Martin and Letty walked out of the church house together. In the shadow of the tall spire, they moved toward the carriage as if in a dream. Her hand lay on his arm and they maintained a decorous distance, but their eyes could see nothing else but one another.

Behind the betrothed couple, Ainsley walked between Nathan and Daniel. The two men were carrying on a conversation over her head, and she was quiet, watching the consuming joy and passion of the newly engaged couple in front of her. Yesterday they had simply been her friends. She had been a part of their world, comfortable and easy in their presence, but now she sensed they were in a world of their own, one from which she was subtly excluded.

She shivered with a sudden chill of loneliness, and to ward it off she laughed at nothing, and threaded her hands into the arms of the two tall, powerful men on either side of her. They looked down at her, surprised, and then each patted her hand, and walked on, looking down at her with a smiling indulgence that made her want to shout, "I am not a child!"

The holiday week passed quickly. Not a moment went by
that Ainsley did not entreat her father to allow her to remain
at home. The thought of returning to the Academy without
Letty was more than she could bear. Even Miss Holbrook
would be gone in a sense, and in her place would be someone unknown—Mrs. Clay. No, Ainsley would not go back.
Besides, the more she roamed and rooted about the inn, she
could see signs of neglect and mismanagement.

Her father was always so busy at the dock and the shipyard, and with the supply and import stores, he scarcely had
time to sleep at the inn, let alone watch its day-by-day operation.

"Papa, you need me," Ainsley pleaded. "I know I'm
young, but I will be eighteen years old next month. Older
than Letty, and she's going to be a married woman."

"But your education . . ." John protested.

"Papa, I'm not receiving any education at the Academy.
All we learn are useless skills for useless women. I would
learn more in a week of running the inn than I would in
years at the Academy."

John sighed. He knew there was truth in Ainsley's words,
and she was older than most young women who remained at
school. Without Letty she would feel lonely and at loose
ends. Of course, often the Academy used the older girls for
teaching the younger ones, but Ainsley was better suited to
running an inn than to being a schoolmistress. He did not
fancy that role for her in the least.

Still, John vacillated until one evening, when he and Nathan walked across the docks, the winter wind tearing at the
mufflers around their faces. John expressed his dilemma,
and Nathan turned to him quite seriously. "You need her,
John," he said simply. "She has been away at school long
enough. Besides, she knows the inn and how to manage it
better than a woman twice her age—and certainly better than
you do.

"The license of innkeeper is a position of merit—
especially for a woman. Some of the finest innkeepers in
Connecticut are women. Have the town fathers elect her to
the official appointment for Windsor Point. For Ainsley,
such recognition would mean far more than a worthless di-
ploma."

"Sage advice," John conceded. Changing the subject, he
touched Nathan's arm, and they stood in the stiff breeze

coming off the water. "And what are your plans, old friend?"

"I am going to apply for the license of innkeeper on the White Oak Trace. Then I shall send all my custom down the road to spend the next night with you, and you shall do the same for me. I believe the General Court is going to allow us to become our own town within a year."

"So soon?" John exclaimed, surprised.

"Lots of families are fleeing the troubles in upstate New York, and many of the sons of the original proprietors have returned. The land is almost all assigned, and we have over thirty families already. Enough for our own school."

Pleased, John clapped his friend on the back, and the two hurried toward the welcoming sight of the inn's lighted windows, which promised warmth, food, and comfort.

"You see, John," Nathan smiled, gesturing toward the smoke streaming from the chimney, "that's Ainsley's fine hand at work. Already things are running more smoothly. Keep her, John. We can both use her cheerful ways. We are getting a bit dour in our bachelorhood."

The week of holiday was over. Martin had left for New Haven to accept his commission and to arrange for his uniform and orders. Letty, missing him already, had gone to her room for a rest. John and Daniel were holding a final meeting with the crew of *The Ainsley* before Captain Cothran embarked with the load of horses and oxen which had finally arrived. The destination was the West Indies, running through the French blockade and on through the winter seas to the islands of eternal sun.

Ainsley had decided that she liked Daniel Cothran very much. He was like the older brother she had never had. She had sought his company in the days since the party, and there was something warm and restful in his presence. She was surprised to think how much she would miss him when he left on his voyage.

Daniel was always ready to listen to her and to understand. She admired his profound friendship for and loyalty to Nathan, and she sensed the closeness of the two men—like a tough, resilient bond that could be stretched over years and space. When Nathan was with Daniel, he seemed more at ease than with any other person.

It was a morning of good-byes. Nathan was due to leave

for his beloved Marshfield the next morning, and had been packing the supplies which he had purchased at Windsor's store.

Although Ainsley had at last convinced her father to let her stay at home and so knew she would be seeing Nathan frequently, still the thought of his departure depressed her. He had so been so busy with her father and Daniel that she had not had one moment alone with him. Late in the afternoon, bored and lonely, Ainsley glanced through the windows of the parlor, down across the snow-covered lawn to the restless, leaden expanse of water. Striding along the water's edge was a tall figure, wrapped in a greatcoat which flapped like the wings of a restless eagle. She knew at once it was Nathan. Without a thought, she threw on her white cape, pulling the fur hood around her face, and ran across the lawn, mindless of the snow.

The path was familiar to her feet; she had walked it a thousand times in every season of the year. The wind howled across the water, so that Nathan did not hear her approach or notice her presence until she touched him. As he turned with a start, she saw deep sadness and introspection in his eyes. It took him a moment to focus on her face, and in that brief second, he stared at her as though he did not know who she was.

"Ainsley," he said softly, his mind still far away. "How young and pretty you are. So untouched by the world. So safe. May the Lord keep you so . . ." Nathan bent and gently kissed her forehead, a kiss so like those her father had given her as a little child that something within her finally cracked.

"Oh, Nathan," she cried. "Don't you understand? I don't want just to be safe—I want to be loved. I love you so. More than you can ever know.

"I have loved you from the moment I saw you walking up our front path. I have been holding on to that love so hard. Oh, you must feel it! You must have known it. Please, Nathan, look at me. Really look at me. I am not a child. I am not a little girl. I am a woman. Older than Letty—and she is getting married." With a deep breath, she dashed the tears from her eyes.

"I understand you, Nathan. I know that you are lonely— but I am lonely too. I know loneliness. I have known it since I was a little girl and I hate it. I know how to fight it.

"Please, Nathan, love me just a little. I can help you fight the loneliness, too. If you can't love me ... then need me ..."

Her voice was coming in gasps, snatched from her lips by the bitter wind, carried on her frozen tears. Ainsley scarcely knew what she was saying. She only knew that somehow she had to penetrate that awful look of desolate sorrow that she saw on Nathan's face. Somehow she must make him look at her as she really was—see her fiery love, the passion of her heart, and know that he could rest in that love.

"I know you don't love me—not yet. But, oh, Nathan, let me love you. Let me care for you. I have enough love for the two of us—forever, even if you never love me. I will love Marshfield. I will help you build all the things you have ever dreamed of—please, Nathan. Please."

She was standing in front of him, holding the fabric of his coat in her small hands. Her hood had fallen to her shoulders, and the cold, damp breeze swept the coppery tendrils of her hair against the gray sky, the only color in the gray and white world.

As though turned to stone, Nathan stood wordlessly, his hands at his side, his eyes riveted on the passionate young woman before him. He was literally speechless. Her declaration of love was so totally unexpected that his mind could scarcely frame itself around her words, and the dazzling aura of her overwhelming emotion was like a foreign thing to him—a language he had once known but could no longer interpret.

She was right. She was no longer a child, and yet, to him she would always be one—and as such, infinitely dear, something to protect and cherish. It was like a sword in his heart to see her pain. She was suffering—and he was the cause of her suffering, and he could do nothing to help her.

With iron firmness he pried her hands from his coat, and took them gently, covering them with his own. He spoke in a stern, fatherly voice. "Stop it, Ainsley. Stop right now. Do not say another word, my dear, dear girl. Not one more word."

She gasped at the command in his voice, and was silent, but tears streamed down her face, her cheeks scarlet from the cold, whipping wind.

He continued in an intense, low voice, and the force of authority behind his words was so powerful she could hear him distinctly above the wind and the waves.

"You do not know what you are saying." He said the words, slowly, as though speaking to an uncomprehending child. "This is only an infatuation caused by your loneliness and the emotions aroused by the engagement of your best friend."

"No! No!" she protested, struggling to free her hands. "It is you who do not understand. Their love is a whisper compared to what I feel for you."

Nathan shook his head, and his face was so intense that she fell silent again.

"No, Ainsley. Do not say such things. You are spoiling something precious to both of us—to your father, to all of us. I love you, too, but as a friend, a daughter . . ."

Her eyes flashed and she opened her mouth to protest.

For the first time a smile crossed Nathan's face, "Very well, as you wish to be considered a woman I will now love you as a sister. Will that satisfy you?"

Then his face grew serious again. "Dear Ainsley. All of life is waiting for you. Somewhere there is a young man full of hope and promise and ambition. He will give you the life you need and deserve.

"I am past such feelings, Ainsley. I have nothing left to give except the love of a friend. I carry too much else in my heart, and even if I were younger and a match for your fire, I would not burden you with such a man as myself. You are something rare and glorious, Ainsley. In you burns a fire that matches the color of your hair. Some fortunate young man shall be warmed by that fire—but it is not I. I am beyond that kind of warmth."

"Nathan," Ainsley whispered, her heart cold with fear at the finality of his response. "Nathan, I have enough fire to warm both of us a hundred times over."

Again he shook his head. "Speak no more of this," he said, his voice filled with warning and admonition. "We have spoken of this once, and now we can place it behind us, and continue as if nothing had passed between us. But if you continue to pursue such thoughts, to express and feel such emotions, then the only thing I will be able to do as a gentleman is to absent myself from Windsor Point. That would give me sorrow beyond measure. Please, Ainsley, be wise in this. Hear what I am saying and understand it."

She stood silent and broken. His heart was wrung with

pity, but he knew he must not bend. It was crucial that she understand what he was saying.

"This is just an infatuation, Ainsley. It will pass like the mists of morning—and someday, when you have experienced real love, you will see this for the impostor that it is."

She heard the determination in his voice, and again she began to weep.

"I could not bear to lose you, Nathan. Not to see you! I would die rather than have that happen. If you say I must never speak of these things, then I shall not, if to do so would cost me your presence and your affection."

"Then dry your eyes, dear Ainsley, and speak no more of such impulsive and irrational thoughts. Wc shall bc as wc were before—cherished friends—and, when the right young man comes along, we shall laugh together at this day."

Nathan reached into his pocket for a handkerchief, and tenderly took her chin in his hand, wiping the freezing tears from her cheeks. Carefully, he lifted the fur hood from her shoulders and placed it around her face. She looked up at him, a mixture of joy and misery on her beautiful face, her eyes shining like emeralds with unshed tears. Just to be close to him seemed like safe haven and happiness to her.

"Oh, my darling, darling Nathan, if you say I must, I shall never speak of this again. Never by word or deed. But I shall never change or forget what I have said and what I feel. Never, never, never."

"You are very dear to me," Nathan answered quietly. "As much love and tenderness as is left in me, I feel for you and your father. I know you will keep your promise and so we shall always be dear and precious friends."

He bent to kiss her once again on the brow, but she pulled back from him slightly.

"Just this once . . ." She grasped his shoulders with her small hands. "Since I shall never speak of this again, I pray you, just once, kiss me." With an almost shy and tentative hesitancy, which was all the more endearing because it was so unlike her normal boldness, Ainsley pulled Nathan toward her.

Bending to her trembling entreaty, Nathan took her lightly in his arms and placed his lips upon hers. Their faces close in the shadow and warmth of her hood, Nathan felt a strange silence and peace, as though the wind and water held their breath, and suddenly the sweetness of her full and tender lips overwhelmed him. Instead of the quick, fatherly kiss he had intended, he involuntarily clasped Ainsley against his chest, lifting her from her feet, and pressed his mouth against hers with a hunger that no longer had a name for him.

It was only for an instant. He heard her muffled gasp, and came to his senses instantly, pulling away from her.

Knowing that what he said next would determine the whole future of his relationship with the Windsors—whether that friendship would continue or be forced to an abrupt end—Nathan took a deep breath and carefully released Ainsley from his embrace.

Smiling, willing his eyes and face to show no trace of anything but brotherly kindness and friendship, Nathan said lightly, "There now, my girl, you have been thoroughly kissed, and I expect that to last you until the right man comes along."

Ainsley said nothing, but Nathan noted that her tears had ceased, and she looked at him with deep, perceptive eyes, as green as glass. There was about her an unnerving calm, as though she understood exactly what had happened. "It shall last me until the right man comes again," she whispered.

He shook his head. "Do not be deceived by what you think happened, Ainsley," Nathan warned her. "Nothing happened. Remember my words. They were true. This was your first kiss. Nothing more."

As they walked together toward the inn, they both began speaking carefully of impersonal things—his journey on the morrow, Letty's wedding, the voyage of *The Ainsley,* and her joy at not being sent back to school. They were searching for the new ground on which to build their future relationship.

Nathan felt the crisis had passed, and all would be well but Ainsley's mind was whirling. None of her feelings had changed, she was certain of that, but she wondered how she could feel such a jumbled mixture of emotions. Wild, uncontrollable joy—because, young and inexperienced as she was, she was certain she had interpreted Nathan's kiss correctly— but also hopelessness, because she also understood the implacable truth of Nathan's words, his absolute determination never to love or marry again.

How, she questioned, could she feel such absolute passion, love, and delight on the one hand, and such misery and hopelessness on the other? But, at least he had confirmed that he cared for her, that her friendship and company were dear to him. For now, that would have to be enough. She knew he had made no idle threat. If she insisted on expressing her love and need for him by openly pursuing him, he would feel it necessary to leave and never return.

It was like walking on a delicate bridge of ice, slippery, hazardous, and heart-catching—but her love waited on the other side, and however long it took, however careful she had to be, she would cross that bridge. This one kiss would have to last her until, one day, he would kiss her again, and the next time it would be for always. Of that she was determined.

She never once stopped to think that perhaps Nathan was right. Perhaps her love for him was simply her first infatuation, and her desperate need to have him love her in return stemmed from her fear of loneliness and abandonment as her only friend prepared for marriage. It never dawned on her to ask herself if perhaps her determination to have Nathan love her came from her childhood habit of wanting what she feared to lose—and believing that by patience, cajoling, and determination, sooner or later she would find a way to have it.

She feared to rethink her conviction that she had found her true love, for, if she were wrong, she would be alone again. It was a comfortable thing to love Nathan. He was steady, strong, and unchanging. If she loved him—even if he did not love her in return—she could feel safe.

She had fastened her dreams on the conviction that she loved Nathan, and it would become a small, hot, secret fire which she tended in her heart and would not let go.

Chapter Twenty-four

Connecticut had suffered for almost a decade from the devaluation of its paper currency. When the Connecticut Colonials had outfitted the expedition to destroy the French fort of Louisburg on Cape Breton Island in Acadia in 1745 in order to free the New England coast from the grip of French privateers, Connecticut had printed large runs of paper notes to cover the enormous cost.

Three years later, when inflation, lack of trade, and a dearth of negotiable currency had brought the struggling colony into a deep financial depression, the bitter colonists had watched in disbelief as England ceded Louisburg back to the French. The colonists believed their sacrifice and victory had been thrown back into their faces by the English, and they felt angry and betrayed. The scars would never heal.

For a long ten years, Connecticut had barely survived, struggling to bring in industry, trade, prosperity, and sound banknotes from New York, England, and Rhode Island.

Now the British were preparing to mount a final assault on the French, hoping to recapture Louisburg, and to attack both Quebec and Montreal. If the strategy succeeded, England would bottle up the French in Canada, and then force them to surrender their rights to every part of the New World. In spite of discouraging news from Lake Champlain, Fort Ticonderoga, and Fort McHenry, the English and Colonial governments were determined that this time they would succeed once and for all.

Norwalk, Stamford, and Fairfield all were being used as staging areas for British regular troops. With considerable satisfaction the town elders watched as the sum to be billed the crown for the billeting of soldiers grew and grew. Soldiers were housed and fed and supplied—and careful Yankee accounts were kept of every penny due. The final bill would be presented to England, and it would be paid in hard English currency. For the first time in many years, hope seemed to flood the streets of the villages and towns of Connecticut.

Windsor Inn was thriving, and Ainsley, its mistress now for more than a year, ran the business with such efficiency and decorum that guests marveled. A few young officers, resplendent in their red-coated uniforms, had come to call, but Ainsley, with a sureness born of the absolute knowledge that her heart was already given, turned them away with merry banter and an adroitness which offered no offense—and no hope.

Spring was lying upon the land like a green and golden patchwork quilt. The raspberry canes were already in bloom, and the bees filled the air with a pleasant hum.

Daniel Cothran came running up the path toward Ainsley, who, in an old straw bonnet and deep-pocketed apron, was standing in the kitchen garden with Ebenezer and Brosian. She and the two men worked so well together; they understood her every wish, and she need only smile and nod to send them rushing to accomplish the task at hand.

Today they were transplanting the seedlings which had sprouted in the cold frame: cucumbers, tomatoes, petunias, and marigolds. It was Ainsley's belief that mixing rows of flowers in the vegetables confused the bugs and thus protected the plants. Besides, she contended, with her own brand of impetuous logic, the vegetables tasted better when grown in the same soil as the richly perfumed flowers. "Color has its own taste," she had laughingly told Nathan.

"Daniel!" she cried, seeing the captain. In the time that Daniel had been master of *The Ainsley* and living at the inn between voyages, she and Daniel had become fast friends. She found his companionship comforting and honest. There never was a better, kinder man. He brought her news of the greater world, and gifts from England, the West Indies, New York, and Rhode Island—and sometimes from China, India, and Europe—received in trade. The inn was filled with shawls, decorative bowls and plates, blue willow china, and other treasures he had brought from his travels.

She liked to know that he thought of her when he was away. It made her feel she had an unchanging friend. Nathan, too, was steadfast in his friendship, but, since that fateful day over a year ago when she had poured out her love to him, they had never made mention of the subject again.

"I saw the sails of *The Ainsley* as you made harbor today, Daniel," she called. "I came to the dock to welcome you, but you sailed into the shipyard instead. Is anything wrong?"

"No," Daniel replied. "Just being cautious. I tell you, my girl, you are a sight for weary eyes. You look more like spring than spring itself." She raised her cheek and he kissed it formally, fighting down the urge to sweep her into his arms. Daniel had grown used to his love for her, and most of the time it stayed in the comfortable place he had made for it in his heart. But sometimes he thought he would go mad with the sight and sound of her so close, knowing she must never suspect the depth of his feelings.

Ever since that first Christmas, when he had noticed an unexpected distance between Ainsley and Nathan, Daniel had felt there was a sad, lonely look behind the natural brightness of Ainsley's beautiful face. He wished he could talk to her about it, but he understood that in human relationships there are many things which are better left unspoken.

He sensed her loneliness, and that she needed a friend. Someone to help her understand herself, what she felt—what was real and what was imagined. However, he could find no words to help her speak of such intimate things. So many secrets in so many proud hearts, Daniel thought.

Ainsley linked her arm in Daniel's and they walked companionably toward the porch. "So, if nothing is wrong, why didn't you come to the dock?" she persisted.

"The sound is growing thick with ships, and the British customs agents are everywhere. I have just brought back a load of pewter and English silver for your father's store—got it in trade for the wool and leather sent down from Litchfield. Found a fine small dock in Rhode Island, and a most helpful merchant—but the trip was a close one, and I think until the British presence sets off for the north, we shall put *The Ainsley* in dry dock, scrape her scuppers, repair her, and get her ship-shape. No hurry to be off to sea."

Ainsley smiled, only guessing at the incredible daring and adventures which had to accompany every voyage Daniel had made since coming to Windsor Point. Each journey was fraught with danger and the unknown—not only the sea, but also the privateers, pirates, and warships.

"What a remarkable man you are, Daniel Cothran," she said softly, with genuine admiration.

He was caught by the affection in her tone, and turned to her with a half-hopeful smile. She caught his eye and, with a happy toss of her head, laughed. "If you are indeed going to take a bit of a recess from your incessant travels, then I have a task for you . . ." Daniel raised his eyebrows in query. "To harness up the rig and drive the two of us up for a good visit to Marshfield. "The Seeleys will be there to chaperone," Ainsley said. Neither of us have seen Nathan for weeks, and work on his inn must almost be completed. Aren't you dying to see it?"

Daniel took a deep, disappointed breath. It was Nathan, always Nathan, and yet, he had to admit, he longed to see Nathan too. Daniel smiled with genuine anticipation. "What a capital idea! Yes, of course. I should enjoy seeing Nathan and the new Marshfield very much. Perhaps your father will come too?"

"Papa?" Ainsley sighed. "He's been very busy. Keeping the army supplied is running him ragged, but he does love to watch the accounts mount up. When do you think we shall actually see all this lovely money that is owed us by the Crown?"

"Soon enough, my dear," Daniel answered, "if the British win the war—and they must win it! If not, I fear this is their last chance, and it may be the British who have to turn tail and run. I feel their interest in the colony is waning anyway. They have all the complexities at home and on the Continent that they can handle. We are becoming a most fractious and unprofitable child."

Ainsley laughed. "That's what Papa says I have been since the day I was born."

The new Marshfield was perched on the edge of the high ridge, overlooking the hills rolling down to the far marshlands and the sound. The road, winding and circuitous because of the valley of the river and the convolution of the ridges, created a journey of over ten miles. Nathan's architect had created a spacious Georgian colonial, with a broad gabled roof and four heavy columns which ran two stories high and supported the overhang beneath the gables. The massive front door, with its heavy brass knocker, was just two short steps above the bricked pathway that led to the entryway. There was something infinitely welcoming about the door, protected by the high overhang, and yet immediate to the traveler.

Because of its size and beautiful setting, the house had a glorious presence. Ancient oak trees lifted their branches above the roof and, in the summer, dappled the house with their shade.

Nathan had designed the building so that one side could be used as an inn and the other, almost a mirror image, his own private home. The front door opened into a wide center hall, with a large central staircase which divided into two stairways at the landing, one going to the left, one to the right. Above the landing was a large, multipaned window that filled the hallway with light and air.

The center hall went through the entire house and ended in French glass doors which led to the back gardens, the stables, barns, and grape arbor.

Ainsley had helped Nathan select color and fabrics for the large house. On either side of the hallway was a parlor. The right parlor was furnished as a common room for an inn. The left parlor was for Nathan's own use and the door to that part of the house was kept closed. At the back of the inn was a cozy, window-banked dining room overlooking the gardens and grape arbor. Under Ainsley's direction the walls had been painted a deep raspberry and draperies of white linen, woven with an intricate scroll in the same raspberry hue, had been hung. The ceiling was white, with two wide beams stretching across it from which hung nosegays of drying herbs, and the fireplace mantel matched the dark walnut stain of the beams.

Under Ainsley's expert tutelage, Nathan had learned how to staff and run the inn. His chambermaids were young girls from nearby farms whom Ainsley hired and trained. His cook and man-of-all-work were a Mr. and Mrs. Seeley, who had run a small waterfront eatery but were anxious to move inland away from the noise and the clutter of the Norwalk harbor.

Once, when John Windsor had been persuaded to take some time off and accompany her to Marshfield, he had asked Nathan why he wanted to run an inn, and Nathan had answered, "Three reasons, John. The first reason is that if our new township is to grow and thrive, we must bring in commerce—and commerce needs a place to rest its head.

My second reason is that, with no family of my own, I sometimes enjoy company."

The two men had been smoking pipes under the lattice of the grape arbor overlooking the beautiful vista.

"The third reason, John my friend, is that I have spent the last of my gold on this establishment, and now must earn my way like any other honest man. I had hoped to raise wheat in my lower fields, since they're covered with the thickest, richest topsoil on all of my acreage. However, I am pained to discover that we are unable to raise wheat in the sequestration. Why, no one knows, but all wheat that is planted is destroyed by the wheat blast. The kernels do not fill up. The plants sprout, but do not mature. No amount of fertilizer, water, light, or warmth seems to make a difference."

"Aye," John had said. "I had heard something of that, but the proprietors kept it mighty quiet until all the land was lotteried off and sold."

Nathan had nodded ruefully. "Don't feel bad, John. Even if I had known, I would still have bought this land. I knew it must be mine from the moment I first laid eyes on it."

"And I knew it too," Ainsley had said, coming up from behind and hearing the last of the conversation. "Marshfield—your personal estate—your home." She had breathed the word *home*. "It just grows more beautiful. You have created something wonderful here, Nathan. It will last you as you dreamed, and be a blessing to many."

Nathan saw the carriage coming up the trace and recognized it at once. He could see Daniel at the reins, and Ainsley, wearing a yellow straw bonnet, sitting at his side. Nathan ran down the brick walk and out onto the road. Grabbing the harnesses, he pulled the horses to a halt and greeted his two friends with whole-hearted welcome.

"How good to see you!" he exclaimed. "Daniel, you've been so busy you haven't even seen the finished place." Nathan waved a proud, proprietory hand toward the lovely edifice, its spacious facade and windows shining in the setting sun. "You are just in time for dinner. Let us hope Mrs. Seeley has outdone herself."

In fact, Mrs. Seeley had outdone herself. They were served in Nathan's personal dining room, a stunning room dominated by a huge fireplace and a high, white-plastered ceiling with moldings and paneling painted a soft gray-blue.

The candles were lit, and a small round table, set with pewter and blue and white dishware was placed on the deep-blue carpet in the center of the room in front of the fire.

They dined on roasted pheasant that Nathan had bagged earlier in the day. With the tender meat, they had candied sweet potatoes, and new peas picked from the garden, as well as pear preserve and large crusty loaves of freshly baked bread. For dessert there was a honey cake topped with chopped nuts and clotted cream.

"Do you always feed your guests so?" Ainsley asked, "You will never make a penny if you do."

Nathan laughed. "Everything you have eaten has come from my own lands—or been traded for. Not one morsel cost me true coinage. As rare as real money is, we in the sequestration do not waste it on one another."

"But surely you charge your guests at the inn real money!" Ainsley exclaimed, alarmed at Nathan's apparent disregard of wise business practice.

"My dear Ainsley, never fear. You have taught me well. No one sleeps in my inn until their coin is in my hand."

Ainsley sat back, relieved. "You love this place too much to lose it," she said a little testily, annoyed that he still teased her when he knew she was giving him sound advice.

After a while Ainsley went into the kitchen to confer with the Seeleys. She checked through Nathan's books and receipts and saw that everything was in order, then she went upstairs to the rooms of the inn and conferred with the chambermaids who were just preparing to leave for home, having turned down the guests' beds.

The inn's common room was filled and she knew there was at least one family staying in the large adjoining rooms. As best she could tell, the inn was doing a lively trade.

While Ainsley made her rounds, Nathan and Daniel talked as the night deepened. Daniel explained the increasing traffic in the sound, and the rumors of imminent war. Nathan was silent for a moment.

"The sequestration has formed a Train Band, and I have been asked to be the commander. We have been drilling and preparing for muster for over six months." Nathan watched closely to see his friend's reaction.

Daniel was astonished. "How many men?"

"Thirty," Nathan answered. "Thirty good men—all willing to do their duty wherever they are called. We are fit and ready. I am proud of my boys, and tomorrow morning you shall see us drill on the lower pasture."

"Whose idea was this?" Daniel asked.

"Lord Easton has commanded Train Bands in every community, and since we hope to be granted a charter, we felt that mounting our own Train Band of irregulars would be the best way to prove we are strong enough to stand on our own." Nathan smiled. "Perhaps it was my own idea, although so many agreed with it I could scarce claim it—but I am so anxious that we be a self-governing community. I do not like being under the direction of Norwalk and Stamford congregations."

"Going to battle is a costly way to gain your freedom," Daniel observed dryly, "but then you know that full well."

Nathan nodded. "It may be that I and my neighbors are too impatient. But it will be worth the cost.

"There is another reason I bring up the matter, Daniel," Nathan continued. "I have already discussed the matter with John and he is agreeable to the request; now I wish to ask it of you.

"If, as I have been given reason to suppose, our Train Band is remanded to the Connecticut regiments under General Amherst, then we shall almost certainly be asked to participate in the final assault on Louisburg. We will need to requisition a ship, and I have asked John if he would let us outfit *The Ainsley*. He has agreed, if you will agree to remain as her captain. Will you, Daniel?"

Pausing in thought, Daniel looked at the floor for a long moment, and then met Nathan's eyes. "Frankly, Nathan, it surprises me that you are so eager to be part of this war. I thought you had no liking for political conflict."

Nathan stood up and began to pace. "For politics and empire-building and the corruption of power—no, not one scrap of liking. But this is a cause I believe in. This continent should be rid of the scourge of the French and their Indian allies. Nathan's voice faltered for a moment, but then he continued in an even stronger voice.

"We deserve the right to be safe in our homes, and in the privacy of our own lives. This damned war must come to an end. Not one more child should be sacrificed on the altar of empire-building! The French must be conquered."

"But you have no love for the British . . ." Daniel pointed

out. "If you volunteer to fight at Louisburg, you will be fighting for them."

"No. Nor for any government of corruption, unrighteous dominion, or misused power. No, I fight not for them, but for my own land—for this new Marshfield, and the men and women who are my neighbors.

"It is hard to forget how bitterly I was deceived by that secretary to the Bay Colony governor, who should have used the power of his office to help rather than to exploit."

Daniel nodded. "Aye, that man—Junius Comstock—what a wicked piece of work he was. I've heard of him once or twice in the West Indies, and then rumor placed him in Rhode Island. If it makes you feel any better, he is a man shunned by all decent society. He will never show his face in the Bay Colony again."

Just then, Ainsley walked into the room. She had changed her traveling clothes for a forest-green gown of linsey woolsey. It was a simple frock, tight at the waist with a high fichu of lace at the throat. Her hair was caught in a simple knot at the crown of her head, but, as always, the unruly curls pulled away and danced around her face.

As she walked into the room, both men looked up and felt the impact of her beauty. Nathan could not believe that he had once thought of this self-confident, accomplished woman as a heedless little girl. It had been a long time since she had seemed like a child to him.

Daniel simply felt his heart lift as it always did at the sight of her, and, in silence, he enjoyed the wonder of just being in the same room with her.

"What serious faces you two are wearing!" Ainsley exclaimed. "I can see it is time I joined you and regaled you with a little lighthearted gossip. You are about to become two old and melancholic bachelors."

She sat down on the little side chair which she had needle-pointed as a housewarming gift for Nathan, and motioned for Mr. Seeley to serve the small tray with its sweet biscuits and decanter of Madeira wine, which he was carrying through the door.

Nathan pulled his chair closer to her, and Daniel completed the circle by standing and leaning against the mantelpiece where he could observe both of their faces as they talked.

With vivid humor, Ainsley described the antics of Martin

and Letty's baby girl, Lucinda, who had been born scarcely a year after the marriage. Letty had come for an extended visit to Windsor Point and Ainsley told how the little girl had learned to walk, tottering between Ebenezer and Brosian, who held their arms to her; she had moved between them like a tiny metronome, as though she could not decide which one she preferred.

"Who could imagine that little sprig is walking. Letty is to have another child in three months. I swear, I don't know where the years are going!" Ainsley concluded.

As Ainsley chatted on, Nathan glanced up at his friend, Daniel, who was strangely silent. In the glow of the firelight he saw an expression on Daniel's face which astonished and moved him. Not realizing he was being observed, Daniel was watching Ainsley, listening to her every word, and on his face was a look of such naked love that Nathan had to look away.

In a moment, Daniel moved from his position, and stretched his arms, making a humorous and off-hand statement that dispelled the strong impression. Nonetheless, Nathan could not shake his strange perception. Daniel had been his friend and a bachelor for so long, that Nathan had ceased to think of him as a man who might wish to marry. The two of them had discussed thoughts of marriage when they were young, but in these past years it was a subject that never came up. Somehow Nathan had assumed that Daniel was one of those men who was wed to the sea.

Now, looking at his friend, Nathan realized that Daniel was simply the kind of man who fell in love once in a lifetime, and what a pity for him that it had happened now—and with a young woman who did not know or recognize a man's love. Ainsley, so passionate and headstrong, and yet so incapable of reflecting on her own feelings. So wise and knowledgeable about some things, and yet so innocent and unteachable about others.

"You two probably have business to talk about," Daniel said. "I think I'll take a quick turn around the garden and head for bed. I'll see the two of you in the morning at regimental drill."

"Whatever is he talking about?" Ainsley asked.

"Our Train Band. You'll see us in the morning. We are quite smart, and ready for war if we must be," Nathan answered.

"You're not serious!" Ainsley expostulated.

"Come in the morning—eight o'clock sharp in the south pasture—and you shall see how serious we are. These are serious times. Surely Sir William Pitt's determination to settle matters on this continent once and for all cannot have missed your notice." Nathan smiled indulgently.

"Of course not. The Windsor Inn is full of soldiers and government officials. I hear all the gossip, I just didn't think how close it might come . . ." Her voice trailed off as she contemplated what might be the outcome of all the talk she had overheard.

For a moment the two sat in silence. Ainsley gazed at Nathan, every line of his long, muscled body familiar to her. He sat low in the Windsor chair, with his long, booted legs extended toward the fire and his arms folded across his chest. His head was bowed, and his eyes were staring at the fire, but she could tell he was contemplating other thoughts.

Watching him, she felt her love like a physical weight inside her body, heavy, real, and constant. Oh Nathan, she wanted to cry, look at me. Really look at me. You've gotten so used to me, you don't even see me anymore.

Out of the silence, Nathan spoke, almost as though he were speaking to himself. "Why haven't you ever married, Ainsley? So many young men. Young men of good family. Officers. Friends of Martin's. Friends of your father's. You must have had many who wanted to court you. If Daniel and I and your father go off to war—who will watch over you?"

Ainsley stiffened. "No one watches over me, Nathan. I watch over others and I watch over myself—you need not be concerned for me."

He turned to look at her. The dying fire bathed her in a soft, rosy hue. "I do worry about you. I want you to be happy and cared for. That's one of the things that matters to me. You have done so much to help my dream come true. I would like to help you make your dreams come true. You are a very beautiful, gifted young woman. You deserve the best life has to offer."

Ainsley could scarcely control herself. She wanted to throw herself at his feet, but, with an effort, she spoke—more sharply than she had intended. "Why do you bring up this subject now?"

With an effort Nathan tore his gaze from her face, the skin so warm and transluscent in the firelight. He looked down at his hands and sighed. "Daniel is in love with you, you know. He would make a fine husband. He loves you as only a man who has saved his love all of his life for one woman can. Such a love is worthy of you, Ainsley. It is the kind of love you deserve. He is the finest man I have ever known."

With a gesture of impatience, Ainsley stood. "We are both tired, Nathan. I do not choose to continue this conversation. I am not a chattel to be assigned to an owner, I am not a pet to be given to a master, I am not a helpless infant to be placed in the care of a coddler—I am my own woman. I love Daniel Cothran, too. I love him as a friend and a brother. That is all. He is very dear to me—but that is all!" Whirling away from Nathan's penetrating eyes, she turned in a swirl of skirts and sped toward the door. "I am going to bed now. We will speak no more of this and tomorrow I shall watch you and your Train soldiers."

Suddenly Nathan laughed. Threw his head back and laughed with total abandon. "Oh, Ainsley! Just when I was thinking you had become such a sober and mature young dame in full control of yourself and everything else! Here is the Ainsley I remember! Full of spit and fire and a little touch of vinegar!"

Ainsley turned at the door. Frustrated by his laughter, she gave him an exasperated look. "Oh—men!" she exclaimed, and ran from the room. He heard her swift, light steps as she sped up the stairs, and then, distinctly, he heard the muffled thud as she slammed the door of her bedroom. Still smiling, he stood up, stretched, blew out the lamp, and walked into his own bedroom, thinking how much more alive Marshfield seemed when Ainsley came to visit.

Chapter Twenty-five

Like the Gibraltar of the St. Lawrence, Cape Breton Island stood at the gate of the New World. Its rocky, craggy eminence jealously guarded the sea-lanes of the northeastern coast for the French.

Situated north of the wide peninsula of Acadia, the oddly shaped island, with its irregular coastline making countless inlets and cliff-ringed bays, seemed a natural fortress. France had furthered the island's forbidding strength by building a fortress manned and armed with four hundred cannon, near the port of Louisburg. Two batteries guarded the seaward approach—the Royal Battery to the left and the Island Battery to the right. In between, the fortress itself stared boldly down the throat of the Atlantic coastline.

The French behind their cannons thought the fortress impregnable.

Bitter news had come to the English and Colonial forces that the Marquis de Montcalm had led a successful foray against Fort William Henry at Lake George, and had captured the fort and burned it to the ground. The English desperately needed a victory.

Daniel Cothran sat huddled in his cloak. The fog seemed to penetrate even the closed hatch of his small captain's quarters, and the dampness and cold had seeped into his bones. Nathan sat but inches away in the cramped cabin, but he seemed scarcely aware of the discomfort.

As Daniel and Nathan had foreseen almost a year before, when they had first talked that evening at Marshfield Inn of the Train Band and the coming assault on Cape Breton, Nathan's band of irregulars had been called up for the campaign. The Windsors' ship, *The Ainsley,* under the command of Daniel Cothran and the volunteer soldiers, under the command of Nathan Fairchild, were sailing north up the coast of New England as part of the British invading force.

A fleet containing over four thousand soldiers under the command of an unknown general, Jeffrey Amherst, who had brought, as his chief lieutenant, an equally unknown officer named Wolfe, was rocking back and forth in the stormy waves, at anchor off Cape Breton for more than a week in the hope the weather might clear.

"Wretched passage," Daniel Cothran said. "Who would think such a thing in June? It seems more like February. Half your soldiers are so seasick they'll be of no use if we ever do get the chance to attack."

Nathan looked at his old friend. "Sorry for getting you into this," he said. "The ship would have been requisitioned no matter what—but you didn't need to come."

"Nonsense," Daniel retorted. "It is my battle as much as anyone's. I can't let you have all the fun. Besides, now that I have a Colonial commission, maybe I'll be allowed to be a member of your new community—once you get the charter to form it, and once I get old enough to retire."

The ship shuddered under the impact of a wind-driven wave and they heard the call of the watchman. "Eight bells."

"Eight fathoms is more like it," Nathan muttered. "Tethered here like cropped seagulls waiting out a storm."

"You've seen the charts of this coastline," Daniel said. "Rocks, cliffs, treacherous shoals—not a place one would be eager to enter without the advantage of smooth seas and cooperative winds."

"I say, let's sail in under cover of the fog," Nathan growled impatiently. "This Amherst is like an old woman. Everything has to be so carefully planned."

"Wolfe's a firebrand, though," Daniel pointed out. "Between them they make a good combination."

Four days later the weather cleared, and a watery sun could be seen in the pale blue sky. The command came. The larger portion of the fleet would enter the harbor of Louisburg directly and draw fire. A smaller contingent would sail in secret around to Gabarus Bay at the unprotected back of Louisburg. Then this splinter force would proceed in longboats into Freshwater Cove, where they would mount a surprise attack from the rear.

The Ainsley, as one of the swifter and more maneuverable ships, sailed with the smaller force. It had been boarded now

by British regulars, but Daniel and Nathan remained on
board. The rest of Nathan's company had been remanded to
other units.

Armed and wearing the uniforms of irregulars, the two
friends boarded a longboat, sitting among the red–coated
regiment. Ahead of them they could see the first boats approaching the shoreline of the cove. In the distance lay
Louisburg, seemingly complacent, quiet and unsuspecting.
Two yards away they saw the young commander, Wolfe, his
sharp, thin face and angular body leaning toward the beach
as though by sheer will he could make his vessel move more
rapidly.

Suddenly, the pale, quiet peace of the early summer morning was shattered by a fusillade of gunfire. Rising like phan-
toms from the gray rocks that lined the shore were hundreds
of French troops, rifles on their shoulders, firing at the advancing long boats.

Confusion erupted. Boats overturned. In minutes the shore
was red with blood and the slate-gray waves awash with
red–coated bodies. Still the longboats glided forward, and
the sound of gunfire and the smell of saltpeter floated over
the cove.

Wolfe cried retreat, but, by some miracle, the cold, sodden
soldiers of the first boats to land—those who had survived
the ambush—waded into the waiting French troops, driven
by anger and battle-lust. Their bayonets were as fierce as
lightning, and the astonished French faltered, their confident
line beginning to break and fall back.

Seeing the bravery of the few stalwart redcoats on the
shore, Wolfe leaped from his boat and struggled to the shore,
waving his weapon above his head and roaring a great cry of
battle. Daniel and Nathan jumped from their boats as well,
and pounded their way to shore, moving with anger and horror through the floating dead.

The battle raged but a few short hours. The French, aghast
at the fierce, terrifying fury of the British, who seemed immune to fear or death, beat a full retreat. Racing from their
rocky hideouts, they stormed back toward the safety of the
fortress. Their bodies littered the barren landscape like a ma-
cabre path of death to the door of the fortress.

The British surrounded the fortress, and, although Wolfe
and many others, including Daniel and Nathan, chafed at the
long wait, General Amherst lay siege calmly and methodi-

cally. For over a month the British battered the fort, moving closer inch by inch until at last the siege guns were trained full on the ramparts, and the walls came tumbling down.

With the rage and joy of uncaged lions, the British roared into the fortress to find the weary, hungry, defeated French complete in their surrender.

Nathan was assigned to the processing of prisoners, and Daniel was sent back to *The Ainsley* to prepare her for her return voyage. The scenes inside the fort were like a window into hell. The bodies of the wounded and the dead lay everywhere. Smoke from uncontained fires polluted the air and mingled with the smell of death. Water was stale and full of filth and fungus. Even the weak summer sun seemed unable to penetrate the cloud of destruction.

When it was learned that Nathan spoke some Algonquian, it was decided he would act as translator for the officers in charge of the disposition of the Indian prisoners. Reluctantly, Nathan followed the young ensign who guided him through the rubble of shattered beams and collapsed walls to an inner courtyard of the Island Battery where the Indian prisoners had been rounded up.

The Indians stood in groups, some defiant, glaring at their British captors, others sullen, standing with their eyes to the ground. The warriors had been disarmed, but their hatred and anger was like a battering ram, and the redcoats surrounding them kept eagle eyes trained on the silent, ill-clad braves, whose ragged clothes, filthy blankets, and worn deerskins bespoke less than generous treatment from their allies, the French.

"We must first break up their tribal ties," Nathan told the weary captain who sat at the staging table. "If we wish to render them as harmless as possible, we should organize them into groups which have nothing to do with their own lodge.

"Have them identify themselves to you by name, tribe, and chief, if possible. Then I will assign them to a specific guard. Once you break up their tribe, you will have the benefit of their confusion. Right now, they are standing by others who speak and think as one."

The captain agreed, and the process began. Each Indian was escorted to the table and Nathan explained what was wanted. With resentment filling their eyes, but under the close threat of the English rifles, they growled the required

information. Finally, most of the Indians had been allotted to
a guarded contingent. Already the captain could see the wisdom of the plan, for the small groups of prisoners seemed
more subdued and less sure of themselves than when they
had been standing with their own kind.

Nathan threaded his way through the mass of prisoners,
noting with satisfaction that the task of ennumerating, iden-
tifying, and organizing was almost completed. As he gestured for a final cluster of braves to approach the table, he
noted a single young Indian standing by the ramparts. A
British soldier, too, had noted the solitary warrior and was
standing at alert, his rifle trained directly at the dark figure.

Impatient to have the job finished, Nathan strode toward
the last prisoner. He had not realized how it would affect
him to see Indians again. All day long as he had listened to
their voices, smelled the odor of ancient campfires in their
hair and their deerskin shirts, and watched their strong faces,
he had felt surrounded by ghosts—the ghosts of old
Marshfield, the burning and dying; the ghosts of his wife
and children. He wanted to be free of the memories, away
from these painful reminders.

"You!" he said, yelling at the solitary brave. *"Dépêchez-
vous! Ecoutez-moi? Venez! Venez!"* During the afternoon it
had become clear that the one language all of the Indians
had in common was a smattering of French.

The young man did not move. His jet-black hair had come
out of its braids and hung on either side of his face, hiding
it from view. He was uncommonly tall, and he stood with a
lean and easy grace, one leg crossed over the other. Had Nathan thought it possible he would have believed that the warrior was actually sleeping on his feet, he was so still.

Without thought, Nathan reached out and grasped the
man's arm, and, as swift as the talons of a hawk, the Indian's
hand hissed out, clamped on Nathan's hand, and threw it
from his arm.

"Your tribe?" Nathan snapped, anxious to be out of this
hellhole.

"Rien," replied the Indian in a voice as harsh and proud
as the sound of the sea.

"Rien!" Nathan roared, his patience snapping. "You disre-
spectful son of Satan, answer the question."

Furious, as though all the frustrations of the long siege
had somehow culminated in this one defiant prisoner, Na-

than again grabbed the man, this time by the front of his filthy deerskin shirt.

"You will look at me and answer the question!" he shouted. Then, realizing he had spoken in English, Nathan opened his mouth to translate.

The young Indian was suddenly very still in Nathan's grasp. For the first time, his head came up and the heavy black hair fell away from his face. Speaking very slowly, in halting English, the brave said, "I have no tribe. I have no family. I have no chief and no people. I have nothing. I had a friend, but he was killed today. And so, I say the truth when I say my tribe is *rien*."

Nathan stared into the face that was so close to his own. The two men were of identical height, now that the other was standing upright. Something—some great and dreadful emotion—tore at the pit of Nathan's stomach. He continued to stare, like a man in a nightmare or a dream, and the young brave stared back.

Just then, the weary sun, too weak to warm or do its task, dipped to the restless horizon of the bay and, with one last ounce of strength, sent a ray of pure light flashing across the ramparts of the dying fortress. The brightness flashed across the Indian's face, and with devastating, horrified, glorious disbelief, Nathan saw the youthful eyes of the young warrior flash like blue sapphires.

"Talmadge . . . ?" Nathan trembled with an emotion beyond words. "My son. Is it really you?"

As steady as stone, but in a voice that seemed to cry from a deep well of the past, the Indian answered, "Yes, my father."

Chapter Twenty-six

"Put the butter and the cream in the spring house to cool, Ebenezer," Ainsley directed, drying her hands on a blue and white striped linen towel. She was standing at the long, pine bakery table where she had just finished dusting the last of her blackberry pies with a cloud of sugar and cinnamon.

"I'll get these into the beehive oven directly and be finished before the heat of the day." She gave a sigh and pushed away a stray tendril of hair that had fallen from her white mob cap. "It's going to be another day that will feel like an oven. Yesterday I could have baked potatoes on the front brick path."

Ebenezer laughed and picked up the butter crock and cream can. "I'll have these in the cool directly, Miss Ainsley. Maybe you need to put yourself in the spring house alongside them."

Smiling, Ainsley watched as Ebenezer strode down the path to the shady glen beside the little stream, and into the small stone house which spanned it. There, in the dampness, the milk and butter remained fresh and cool.

Ainsley had been eager to accept Nathan's request that she come to Marshfield and manage the inn while he and Daniel went to fight the battle of Louisburg at Cape Breton. John Windsor thought it was an excellent plan and he had sent Ebenezer to Marshfield with Ainsley. Brosian had remained at Windsor Point to manage the inn there in Ainsley's absence.

The long weeks since Daniel, Nathan, and the troop from New Parrish had sailed from Windsor Point had been difficult for Ainsley. She feared desperately and constantly for the safety of all of the men—particularly Nathan and Daniel. There was little news of the campaign, and no one knew if the battle had begun at Cape Breton, and, if it had, who was winning.

Both Brosian and Ebenezer had been anxious to go with the other men on the military campaign, but, with the astonishing build-up of billeted troops and the staggering increase in trade and traffic along Long Island Sound, the inland roads, as well as the coastal highways, were all heavily traveled. Both Windsor Inn and Marshfield Inn were busier than anyone had ever dreamed possible. Innkeeping had become a patriotic necessity.

Ainsley had increased the staff at both establishments. Still, Ebenezer and Brosian were like her left and right hands. They knew almost as much about running the inns as Ainsley did—and they were capable of doing many tasks that were beyond her strength.

She had spoken to the men earnestly. "You see," she said, "if you go, I may not be able to run the inns adequately. I could lose the license, both for Windsor and for Marshfield. What good would it do to win the battle, and lose what we are fighting for?"

So the two loyal men had stayed with her. Their devotion to Ainsley Windsor was deep and true, born in her school days when they had watched over her as a young girl.

Ainsley's prediction about the competitive growth of inns proved true. In the sudden dramatic rise in the demand for overnight lodging, many people saw innkeeping as an opportunity to become rich, and unlicensed establishments began to spring up. Opportunities and profit-mongers brought pressure to bear on the town officials who granted the innkeeping licenses; outrageous bribes were dangled, and it was only because of the excellence with which Ainsley ran her inns that she was able to rebuff these efforts to discredit and dislodge her from her accredited status.

Time and again, in her heart and out loud, she had thanked Ebenezer and Brosian for staying and making it possible for her to retain her official licenses.

As Ainsley continued her morning chores, she reflected on the fact that every nook and cranny of the inn was full of travelers.

The White Oak Trace, at an intersection just a few hundred yards from the inn, was busily traveled, with men on horseback, soldiers—both British regulars and Colonial troops—carriages, and pony carts, as well as foot travelers, moving along in a steady stream.

The evening before, as she had listened to conversations in the dining room, she had gathered news of the Louisburg rout. The word had spread throughout the Colonies. There no longer seemed any doubt that the French had been thrown from the Fortress of Louisburg and that the sea-lanes to the Atlantic Ocean were at last open to New England.

For the first time in weeks, Ainsley could feel the iron band of worry loosen around her heart. She had gone to bed and slept without fear of what news the morrow might bring. It felt good to be alive again. Surely, news of the return of the troops would not be long in coming; they would do their utmost to speed their return.

With a new vigor, Ainsley supervised the washing in the laundry yard which overlooked the grape arbor and the lower fields. It won't be long now, she told herself. Nathan and Daniel will be home before the leaves begin to turn gold.

She finished her task and walked over to the edge of the kitchen gardens. Far down the slope below her, she saw the river glinting in the sun. Heat was beginning to shimmer up from the lowland where the barley crop lay green as bottle glass.

The slate roof reflected the sun and the tall chimneys, five of them altogether, were empty of smoke. Not a single fire still blazed. Even the wash fire had been extinguished, and the pies had been removed from the oven. Baked to a perfect, crispy, golden-brown they were now cooling on the sideboard.

Once Brosian had remarked, his voice filled with affectionate-teasing. "Miss Ainsley, there isn't a pie that would dare be burned under your hand. Why, it knows for sure that in your disappointment you'd talk it to death."

What a difference in so few years, Ainsley thought. Such a contrast to the empty, unused land which Nathan had seen, understood, valued, and bought. Perhaps he had had a vision of what was to come. Ainsley believed anything of Nathan. That he was somehow wiser, better, nobler, greater than a mere man.

To her, it seemed there was nothing he could not do—and do it better than any other. She had seen the band of volunteers he had mustered and trained for the war when they had come to Windsor Point to board *The Ainsley.* The men, both young and old, were strong and weathered.

Nathan had reviewed them one last time before embarking for battle. They had marched in their simple homespun clothes, but the rhythm of their step, the beauty of their formations, and the sweep of their lines were an absolute wonder to Ainsley.

"Oh Nathan!" she had exclaimed. "I do not admire war. But I do admire such discipline and strength. What a mighty accomplishment, that you could take humble farmers and transform them into a company . . . a battalion . . ." She struggled for the right words to express her feeling at this wonderful thing he had created through his leadership.

Nathan had smiled indulgently. "It's not my leadership, Ainsley dear. It is men motivated by a common goal."

"And what is it you—all of these men—want in common? To win the war?" Ainsley asked.

"No. To win our own town. To be our own men. Odd that it is only through working together that we can earn the right to be individuals," Nathan had reflected.

Now the men had joined the battle and had won! News took so long to reach Marshfield. She wondered how long ago the battle had taken place. Where were the men now? Where was *The Ainsley*?

On some level she had been waiting all summer, waiting for news, waiting for one footstep, one voice, one hallowed sound. Now, at least, there was hope.

It was midafternoon. The heat continued like an anvil over the earth. Even the traffic on the road had slowed. The humidity was so high that the dampness on Ainsley's brow and upper lip would not evaporate, and she dabbed at her forehead with a dainty lace handkerchief.

Once again Ainsley looked out across the fields to where the river tumbled between the shaded banks. Impulsively, she grasped a large towel from the clothesline and ran with it down the back slope, through the oak grove, along the rock walls that rimmed the fields, and into the ferns and shrubs that lined the river.

When she was too far from the house to be seen, she stepped into a clump of shrub oak and removed the rose-pink frock, with its white pinafore, that she had worn at her chores. With impatient hands she tore off the white cap, stockings, and shoes, and, then, somewhat more cautiously, she removed her pantaloons, shift, and laced waist girdle.

Glancing around, she quickly slipped into the river, her feet sliding on the moss-covered stones. The shock of the cold water was as pleasant as wine. The land for several miles on both sides of the river was Marshfield land, and was as yet untouched by plow or ax. She felt safe, sure that no one was about.

As a girl, Ainsley had been taught to swim by her father. Since they lived so near the docks, he felt it a matter of safety that his daughter, who was such a daring and eager child, should know how to swim. Many a time John Windsor had been grateful for that decision, since she had been fished from the waters of the sound more than once after falling from the dock or her boat.

Now, as she paddled to a deep pool where the river eddied under the deep boughs of an ancient willow, she thanked her father for her knowledge of water.

Knowing she must not stay long—there was still much work to be done before the day was ended—she made one last dive, deep below the surface, and then, with the heavy current of the river tugging at her limbs, she returned to the bank. Crouching in the safety of the overhanging leaves, she checked to make sure she was alone, and then she pulled herself from the river and back into the copse where her clothes hung on the bushes.

Dressed, with her thick, wet hair brushed and pulled to the top of her head in a knot, she began the climb back to the house. Even though the day remained hot, her skin felt cool and clean, and she closed her eyes to drink in the sweet smells of summer. The clover, the ripening bayberry, the moss by the river, the flowering honeysuckle, the sounds of insects and birds, and the whisper of the summer wind in the fields—it was all so beautiful and peaceful that it was hard to think that somewhere men were fighting and dying.

With a shudder, she opened her eyes and walked purposefully toward Marshfield. The sun was beginning to drop lower, and soon travelers would be thinking of food and rest. The inn would be full within the hour.

Crossing the backyard, Ainsley saw with satisfaction that the linens had been taken in, which meant the beds would be freshly made. In the kitchen all was under control, and Mrs.

Seeley informed her that Mr. Seeley was signing in the guests and taking payment.

With a nod of approval, Ainsley turned and walked quickly across the hallway to the guest dining room.

In late afternoon as Ainsley crossed the central hallway to the guest dining room, she saw two men standing near Nathan's carriage house in the shade of the huge elm tree, holding the bridles of their horses as they talked.

The inn had one large barn and coach house in which the guests stabled their horses and kept their conveyances—if there was room. Nathan, on his private, residential side of the building, had built a smaller carriage house in which he kept his own riding horse and his private carriage and team. Guests were not permitted the use of Nathan's private quarters.

Irritated, Ainsley ran out the French doors at the end of the central hallway, intending to direct the two men to the proper location, but as she approached them her heart leaped. She couldn't see their faces clearly, but something in the line of the shoulders, the manner in which the nearer man stood—his hand absentmindedly brushing the mane of his mount, his other hand gesturing toward the rolling slopes of Marshfield—made her heart sing.

"Nathan," she whispered, her voice as rusty on the word as an unused hinge. "Nathan!" The second time she shouted, and then a third time, the name carried on a sob. "Nathan!"

He turned, and with him turned the other man. It was almost like seeing a mirrored reflection, a double image—Nathan with hair as bright as the sun, the other man with hair as dark as night, and yet both with the same blue eyes, the same strong and noble face, the same tall, lean build.

It was only an illusion. The two were identical in height and the breadth of their shoulders, but Nathan's chest, arms, and legs were more heavily muscled.

The younger man also had wide shoulders, but he was leaner, as though his body were made of fine hammered steel. There was in him a watchful quiet, a stillness that seemed so much a part of him it appeared knitted into the fabric of his bones. His face, tanned by the sun to a deep brown, made a startling contrast to the brilliance of his eyes and the whiteness of his teeth. When the strange man moved, it was with swiftness and economy of motion—a grace that was almost imperceptible. In his face was deep

calm, and a sense of unreadabe wisdom. She had thought
Nathan was handsome, but this man, with his black hair and
powerful face, was the most handsome man she had ever
seen. "But Nathan's face is kinder," she instantly assured
herself, dismayed at her disloyal thought.

"Ainsley!" Nathan exclaimed with pleasure. "We were
just coming to look for you. You can never guess! Oh, the
wonder of it!"

With eyes brimming with uncontainable joy, Nathan indicated the other man. "This is my son Talmadge, Ainsley. It
is a miracle. My son. My son—alive, free, and safe at
home." Taking a deep breath to control himself, Nathan
smiled, and turned to Ainsley. "Talmadge, this is Ainsley,
my dearest friend."

At his father's introduction, Talmadge directed his quiet
gaze at Ainsley. For a full minute he continued to study her
and his careful silence stretched across the gathering blue
evening like a fine silver thread. Talmadge's look and his
deep remarkable silence were like a gift. Ainsley, unaccount-
ably, stood and absorbed his perusal with the most peculiar
feelings. She felt self-conscious and shy—almost like a child
again—but she also felt a warm, satisfying feeling of value
and importance. He made her feel as though she were worth
time and thought. His eyes seemed to penetrate to her very
core, as though, in an instant, he knew everything about
her—more than she knew herself.

With a disconcerting feeling of pleasure and puzzlement,
she quickly broke the gaze, glancing away with flaming
cheeks but not before she saw the slow, surprised smile of
recognition that touched his lips.

"We shall be friends, Talmadge—I am sure of it," Ainsley
said, "just as Nathan and I are."

Talmadge shook his head, almost imperceptibly. "No, not
the same," he said softly. He spoke no further words, but his
eyes did not leave hers until she blushed again and broke the
spell by turning to Nathan.

"What news, Nathan!" she cried joyfully. "I must hear all
the details of this wondrous thing.

"But first I shall call someone to bed down your horses.
You shall go to your rooms and wash off the stains of travel, and then I shall serve you a feast and hear all of your
news. *All* of it. I have a million questions."

Chapter Twenty-seven

O ver a dinner of cold roast beef with horseradish, braised potatoes, carrots, batter bread, and blackberry pie, accompanied by cool buttermilk and cheese, Nathan gave Ainsley a brief outline of the events leading to his miraculous reunion with the son he had thought long dead, stopping every now and then to gaze at Talmadge's handsome face. Ainsley listened in silence, enthralled.

On the voyage home from Louisburg, Nathan told Ainsley, he and Talmadge had sat in Daniel Cothran's cabin, hour after hour, day after day, while Talmadge had shared the events of his life since his captivity.

Nathan recounted how Talmadge had eventually become a member of Passakonawa's tribe and had journeyed to the Atlantic coast of Canada.

When the final assault on Cape Breton began, the French began rounding up Indian warriors.

At gunpoint, Talmadge and his friend Meskapi had been hastily armed, along with the other conscripted Indians, and the French had shipped the bewildered braves across the channel to Cape Breton and Louisburg. When the French fortress had fallen two months later, the Indians, many of whom had never fired a shot, had been taken prisoner by the British forces. In the prison compound Nathan had discovered Talmadge.

When Nathan had finished, Ainsley—bursting with the joy of it—cried, "Let us celebrate!"

Raising her glass of golden, homemade wine, she continued, "To joy and happiness! Welcome home, Nathan." Her face shone with such an abundance of delight that it seemed incandescent. Turning to Talmadge, she raised her glass again, and, with tears in her eyes whispered, "Welcome home, Talmadge. Such a long, long homecoming. Such a miraculous homecoming. Welcome home forever."

Nathan rose to his feet, slowly raised his glass, touched hers with an almost inaudible clink, then drank the amber liquid to the last drop. Talmadge rose as well, and, raising his glass to Ainsley and then to his father, drank until he had drained the goblet.

With a sudden burst of feeling, Nathan flung his glass into the empty fireplace. "On such a momentous occasion, one should drink from a glass that will never be used again," Nathan said.

With a joyful laugh, Ainsley threw her goblet into the hearth, and Talmadge, with that graceful swiftness which characterized each motion, threw his almost simultaneously so that the two goblets broke against one another before falling into the unlit logs.

"What a shot you must be!" Ainsley exclaimed. "You must have the eyes of a hawk!"

"And the speed of an arrow," Nathan added, smiling proudly at his son. "You have become a great man. I wish I could thank the chief who became your second father."

Talmadge nodded. "Chief Passakonawa. My brother, Meskapi, was his true son. They taught me much."

A moment of silence followed, and then Talmadge moved on his quiet feet toward the door. "I will go to rest now, Father. Tomorrow we will speak more. I wish to be of help to you here, but I have much to learn. I must learn the ways of my own people once again."

He was gone from the room almost as though he had vanished with scarcely a motion to mark his leaving. Ainsley almost wondered if she had dreamed this dark, enigmatic stranger, so like Nathan and yet so unlike him.

"Your son!" Ainsley breathed, the wonder and unexpectedness of the day overwhelming her. "Tell me more, Nathan. You have spoken so little about your past. Tell me all you can."

Haltingly, Nathan recounted the details of the raid on the first Marshfield and the destruction of his family. With bitterness still in his voice, he recounted the theft of the ransom money and his despair. He told her more about his years of trapping, and of the Indian renegade who had tried to kill him and had lied about Talmadge's death. She could scarcely imagine the miracle that had reunited father and son, when both thought the other dead. She begged Nathan to tell her everything concerning Talmadge's lost years—and how they had found one another.

Long into the night she and Nathan talked, as old friends, she silent, only asking questions when she did not understand; he speaking as a man who has borne a burden for far too long.

The story of his family had, for the first time in years, become a possible thing to share. His life had been resurrected with the resurrection of his lost son.

He told her how, during their long nights of conversation on the voyage back to Connecticut, he and Talmadge had pieced together one another's story—each one asking a hundred questions, and still having a hundred more to ask.

Time after time as they sailed toward Connecticut, Nathan would think of the years when Talmadge had been a young hostage struggling to survive in an alien land. Nathan would reach over to touch Talmadge, as though to reassure himself that his son was real.

Over and over Nathan would say, "Talmadge, if I had known you were alive, nothing would have stopped me from coming to find you, to save you, to bring you home to me. Nothing."

And Talmadge would reply with equal earnestness, "And had I known you were alive, Father, nothing would have stopped me from escaping to come find you. We just did not know."

Thus reassured and understanding one another, they would sit, suddenly silent in the glorious wonder and miracle of their reunion.

Tears had filled Ainsley's eyes as Nathan shared the story. When he finished the night was far gone. Placing her hand on Nathan's arm, she whispered, "Now, you can be whole again."

Nathan patted her hand. "Talmadge will be like a brother, a friend, for you—the companion of your own age you have never had."

Ainsley jumped to her feet. "I think I have quite enough of these surrogate brothers, dear Nathan—you, Daniel, and now Talmadge. However, Talmadge, I sense, is a man quite unlike others. I shall be honored to have such a brother, but I think he will make up his own mind about such matters."

Nathan rose and stretched. "Well, I'll be off to bed. I have grown too old for such late nights, Mistress Windsor, and high time I let you go as well." Nathan picked up the lamp and held it. "Shall I light your way to your room?"

"No," Ainsley replied. "I am much too filled with marvels and excitement to rest. Besides, I think I must check the kitchen before retiring and make sure all is in order for early breakfast."

Although Nathan was obviously exhausted, she could see his reluctance to leave her alone, and yet she knew that if they remained much longer in the pool of soft lamplight the walls she'd built around her emotions would give way. As she had studied Nathan's dear face this night, and listened to the cadence of his beloved voice, her heart had been wracked by overwhelming feelings of tenderness and love. How could she not throw herself on his breast, at his feet, and cry out her love? But she knew she must not, and, seeing his weariness, her love transformed into deep concern. "To bed, dear friend," she ordered. "You are tired beyond wisdom. Tomorrow you shall begin to take over the reins once again, but tonight I am still in charge."

He smiled, but with relief and gratitude mounted the stairs. Sighing, Ainsley walked to the back door, pulling at the chatelaine of keys she wore at her waist preparing to lock up.

Seeing the light of the full moon glowing through the trellises of the rose arbor, she stepped out into the silver-trimmed night and breathed the cool night air.

No sound announced a change, but suddenly she knew she was no longer alone. Without turning she whispered, "Talmadge?" It was he. He had come into the garden behind her in his calm and silent way and was standing to her left, watching her as she watched the moon.

"You are as beautiful as the night," Talmadge said in a quiet voice. Everything he said was spoken with such an economy of words and emotion—and yet its very economy made it seem the more powerful.

At first she was taken aback by his words—much as she had been by his long gaze when they had first met. Still, the words hung in the night air like a banner and her heart fluttered at their sound, something she had never felt before. It made her feel awkward, young, and unsure of herself. In her fear and discomfort at the unexpected feelings, she wanted to flee indoors, but she knew that would seem rude. After all, it was his first night at Marshfield—his home. And even in the short hours she had known him, she sensed he brought something deep, strong, and powerful with him.

She turned to him. "And you are as wise and all-seeing as the night. It is as though you have kept all the wisdom of your first life, and of your second—and you are twice the person for it."

"Perhaps," Talmadge said, in his low, measured voice, the English words still seeming a little rusty and awkward on his tongue, "but this Twice the Person is going to have to learn how to sleep in a bed again. I cannot close my eyes with four walls and a ceiling shutting me in. I am too used to the canopy of the sky.

"I have forgotten how to act when my food is placed before me on a table—and I do not have to hunt and cure it myself. I fear civilization is a distant memory for me. The woods and forests have been my home."

"Then we shall build you a summer bowery tomorrow, and you shall sleep there until you can train yourself to a house once more. Winter will certainly help in the training. The house becomes much more appealing when the snow falls."

Ainsley's heart was reaching out to this vastly mysterious man. Would any of them ever really understand what his life had been? Know what he knew? Perceive his thoughts and feelings?

Talmadge turned and looked up at the silhouette of Marshfield against the night-dark sky. "Such a mighty house," he said softly. "I shall grow to feel it as part of me, I know. How wise my father was to call this place Marshfield. It is a name branded on the heart of the only two remaining Fairchilds."

But there will be more! Ainsley thought to herself. Oh, please, dear God, pray let there be more, some day— Fairchilds that are born from a Windsor heart. With longing and pain, she looked up to the darkened window of Nathan's room. The years were passing, and there was no hint of change in Nathan's feelings toward her.

Perhaps now that Talmadge has returned, Ainsley thought, Nathan's heart will heal and he'll see that I am here, waiting—as I have always been.

Talmadge stood in silence, wondering at the thoughts of this glorious red-golden woman. He hoped that she was not afraid of him, alarmed by his past and his odd ways. For she was the spirit of the sunwoman of when he'd dreamt—and her fire and warmth had burst into the quiet reaches of his long-captive soul. He knew that she was not ready to know this, for her heart was a coiled thing. He had not missed the look of longing on her face as she stared at Nathan's window.

He, Talmadge, had tamed a peregrine hawk once, giving it his patience and love until the hawk had loved him in return and had given up her wild gyrations to come rest on Talmadge's leather-bound arm. So too, would he give Ainsley his patience and love; he could wait until she turned to him, for he knew that she was meant to be his. Mother Earth had at last brought him to the stardaughter who had been joined to him before the world began.

Chapter Twenty-eight

Nathan wakened from a peaceful sleep. The sun was pouring through the windows, and outside in the trees he could hear the chatter of a thousand birds. Through the night, lying on his bed, he had felt the swell and roll of the ocean waves, as though his blood had relearned the motion of the tides in the weeks of his sea voyage.

For a moment he lay in bed, savoring the luxury of fresh linen sheets and the softness of the feather tick. Then with a shout of delight he leaped out of bed, threw on clean clothes, and dashed water on his face and hands.

Smoothing his hair into a neat queue, he sped out of the bedroom and down the hall. "Talmadge!" he roared, savoring the name—a name he had never thought to have the joy of calling again. "Talmadge!" he shouted again, just for the sheer pleasure of feeling his son's name on his tongue.

There was no answer, and Talmadge's room was empty, the bed made and looking as though it had not been slept in. An unreasoned fear clutched Nathan's heart—surely he hadn't dreamed his return?—and he ran down the stairs two at a time, almost colliding with Ainsley who stood in the central hall bidding farewell to two of the overnight guests.

"Have you seen Talmadge this morning?" he asked urgently, without preamble.

Ainsley, sensing his concern and knowing it was a reflex after the years of loss, answered soothingly, "He is out in the west pasture looking at the blood stock. Already he loves Marshfield as much as you. He was up at dawn, has eaten breakfast, and is already at work—you, I might hasten to point out, have done none of those things."

Nathan laughed, as did the departing guests, and Ainsley led him into the family dining room, where a small buffet was set. "Now eat. You have a long day ahead of you."

Ainsley sat opposite Nathan, and began to give him an

overview of the condition of the estate and the financial success of the season. Nathan listened with quiet admiration. She was an extraordinary businesswoman.

"Besides the proceeds from the inn, I have arranged to trade linen and wool, barley, and logs with an agent in Rhode Island. I have been promised we will be paid in either Rhode Island currency, or New York banknotes. We have only been waiting for the return of the sloop to make the voyage," Ainsely told Nathan, hoping he would be pleased.

"You have a great deal of land at Marshfield, but much of it is not very productive. I planted a small field of wheat, just to see for myself. It is ruined. I feel, as you, that it is something in the soil. But wheat is not a possiblity." Her face was creased with concern. "I do not know if the inn can support so much unproductive land. Buisness will not contine to be so robust when the war is over . . . Perhaps you should consider selling some of it."

"No," Nathan said firmly, "the land is its own reason for being. In this place it is the land itself that has value—not what the land can produce."

Nathan made his point gently, then reached over and took her hand warmly into his own. "You have done so well, my dear friend. How can I ever thank you?"

She smiled softly, and let her small hand rest in the nest of his strong brown fingers.

Rising from the table in unison, they continued to look at one another and a palpable tension filled the air. Awkwardly, Nathan let go of her hand. Her eyes dropped, and the spell was broken. Reaching for a last plump strawberry, Nathan stretched and walked toward the door. "I guess it's time I started to work myself. I'll go find Talmadge and give him a tour of the place. Would you care to join us?"

"Oh, yes!" Ainsley exclaimed. "Let me just run and take off my apron and find a bonnet." With skirts flying she left the room. One moment a mature businesswoman, and the next a carefree young girl. It was the thing about her which never ceased to amaze and delight him. She was always so unexpected. What a delightful child!

Standing by the front door, waiting for Ainsley to reappear, Nathan glanced up and saw Ebenezer coming up the coach path, leading Ainsley's gray carriage horse hitched to her small landau.

"What is this, Ebenezer?" Nathan asked. "Are you going on an errand?"

With a solemn face, Ebenezer tied the horse to the hitching post and approached Nathan.

"Mr. Fairchild, sir, could I speak to you in private?"

Surprised, Nathan motioned for the faithful servant to follow him into the small office of the inn. Closing the door he turned to face Ebenezer, who stood, in obvious discomfort, hat in hand.

"Sir, it is not my place to instruct you. It is only that you have been gone so long, perhaps it has made you forget— perhaps you do not remember what a small community this is." Ebenezer's words were soft and uttered with obvious reluctance.

With the ease of long acquaintanceship, Nathan placed his hand on Ebenezer's shoulder. "Old friend, whatever it is you have to say, say it. I will not be disturbed, I promise you."

Without looking into Nathan's eyes, Ebenezer continued to speak, and there was determination as well as reluctance in his voice.

"Mister Nathan, sir, I plan to take Miss Ainsley home today. I know your neighbors. I've overheard their talk. If she stays here with you and your son at home, under the same roof, her reputation will be smirched. I don't plan to let such a thing happen to her." For the first time Ebenezer looked up into Nathan's eyes. "We've got to protect her from any stain on her reputation. You know how narrow–minded people can be. Gossip can ruin lives."

With an astonished gasp, Nathan realized that Ebenezer was completely right, and he was disgusted with himself for not having thought of it. Without her father in attendance or the presence of a suitable chaperone, Ainsley should not be living in an unmarried man's home while he was in residence.

Everyone knew Ainsley was a competent innkeeper, and although there had probably been talk at first, most people now accepted her in that role. But Nathan could not believe that he had become so used to having Ainsley in his life that he had forgotten how fragile a thing a young woman's reputation could be.

He smiled. "I would be flattered to think that anyone would imagine there could be something between a tired, middle-aged man like me and such a beautiful young

woman. However, now that Talmadge is in residence, we
must be doubly cautious. Can't give the idle tongues anything to wag about. Right you are, Ebenezer, and thank you
for being wise."

The two men walked out of the office just as Ainsley
swept down the stairs into the hall. She was wearing a dress
of yellow lawn, as light and airy as sunshine itself. In her
hand was a wide-brimmed yellow straw bonnet trimmed
with lilacs and roses. As she stood in the light from the
high-paned windows, the front door opened. Talmadge,
dressed in a simple, full-sleeved white linen shirt, dark
breeches, and a pair of his father's old riding boots, stood
against the backdrop of the gold and green world outside.
His image filled the doorway, and his strong young shadow
leaped across the marble of the floor.

He stood immobile, staring at Ainsley, bathed in the
streaming sun. She was like all of the colors of summer
caught in a single beam of light. He had not known, could
not have imagined, that such a woman existed. There was
something that connected him to her—something deep inside him—and he knew that if she could only overcome her
fears, concerns, and all the high walls she had built to protect her heart, that she would feel it too.

"Good!" Nathan exclaimed, seeing Talmadge in the doorway and walking toward him. "We're all here, and I have an
announcement to make. Ainsley is leaving for Windsor
Point."

Ainsley whirled, surprise and anger on her face, and
Talmadge fixed his father with an intense stare.

"Whatever do you mean?" Ainsley exclaimed, her eyes
hot. "You just told me to get ready for a tour of the estate
with you and Tal—"

Nathan walked over to her. "I know, Ainsley. Will you
forgive my carelessness and thoughtlessness? Ebenezer has
been wise enough to point out that people will gossip if you
remain in the house now that Talmadge and I are in residence. Your father would never forgive me if there were
even a whisper of a stain on your reputation."

"Hang my reputation!" Ainsley retorted. "I am not a
child. At my age I am close to a spinster, and no one thinks
of convention with spinsters."

Nathan burst out laughing. "A spinster, are you? Well, I'll
be the devil if you are not the youngest, prettiest spinster in

all of the Colonies. No, my dear girl, I am afraid you shall still have to bow to convention, like it or not."

"I will not be sent away like a schoolgirl."

Nathan shook his head. "Ainsley, you know human nature. You know Ebenezer is right. People would have a gossip feast if you remained under my roof without proper chaperonage."

Throughout the argument, Ebenezer stood to one side, but his unrelenting gaze was fixed on Ainsley. At last she sighed, and nodded her head. "You are right," she said, "I cannot remain in residence here, it would be inappropriate."

"That is the case," Nathan said regretfully. "I shall miss your help and your company. I would have liked you to help teach Talmadge in the running of Marshfield—we can't do it without you."

Nathan continued to weigh the problem. "Let me give this some thought," he said. "I will find a solution. Until then, off you go. Talmadge and I shall come down to visit you at Windsor Point next week. I want Talmadge and your father to become acquainted."

Throughout the exchange, Talmadge stood silently looking at Ainsley. She was intensely aware of his eyes, and she felt her cheeks flushing with emotions which she could not have named it she had been asked to. She turned and went back upstairs to pack her bags for the long ride home.

A week later, in the early dusk, John Windsor welcomed Nathan and Talmadge as his guests at Windsor Point.

"I have closed the inn for the next three days," John declared. "This shall be a time to become acquainted with your son, and for you and Daniel to rest from the labors of the long campaign."

For Ainsley, it was three days of heaven. She saw that the finest meals were prepared for the four men. Their rooms were bedecked with fresh flowers daily, and at night she played cards with them, read to them, and listened to their talk.

As always, she noticed what a natural leader Nathan was. When he spoke, all faces turned to him as sunflowers turn to follow the course of the sun.

In Talmadge, so like his father, and yet so unlike, there was a profound difference. In Talmadge's ability to listen and observe, one felt strength. Although Ainsley had known this enigmatic young man only a few days, she felt she could tell him anything and he would have the wisdom to know what it meant. Ainsley found talking to Talmadge one of the most satisfying and comforting experiences of her life.

His face, thin and muscular, with a powerful jaw, and a serious brow, was as handsome as his father's, but pared down, spare, as though refined in a fire until only the steel remained. His eyes seemed more startling even than his father's, perhaps because his face was so dark.

When they sat or walked together she would chatter on, not bothering to weigh anything she said, as she usually felt she needed to do. Something in the way Talmadge listened told her that he would sift away the chaff, and hold on to her real thoughts and words.

People listened to Nathan, and looked to him for leadership, but people believed in Talmadge. Something about his calm and quiet confidence made others feel a deep trust. Whatever Talmadge said seemed right and true. Whatever he said he would do, would be done. It was as though he knew the secrets of the earth—and of the human heart.

"Talmadge," Ainsley asked late one afternoon as they sat on the edge of a small, unused dock which had become overgrown with rushes and marsh grass. Talmadge had wanted to go fishing, and, on impulse, Ainsley had grabbed two poles and walked with him to the quiet spot. Their lines dangled, untaken, in the quiet swirl of the water. "What do you think about your father? Is he changed from the way you remember him? Is he happy? Is he lonely?"

"My father," Talmadge said slowly, choosing his words carefully as he always did, "is a man who simply does what must be done. In that way he is unchanged. He has always been such a man."

Ainsley nodded. "And is he happy? Now, that you are back, is that all he needs? Is he content? Has your return freed him from the past?"

Talmadge was quiet for so long that Ainsley began to wonder if he had heard her question. "He does not think of such things," Talmadge said after careful consideration. "Happiness. Contentment. He does not believe in them. He does not trust them. Therefore he does not let such things matter."

"That is so very sad," Ainsley whispered. Then she

brightened. "But you ... you ... I know you have brought him happiness."

Talmadge nodded. "Yes," he said simply. "And you. You give him happiness, too. We give him as much happiness as he can feel with a heart which has trained itself not to feel."

Ainsley sighed. "Then, if that is all there is, that shall have to be enough."

"No," Talmadge said calmly, casting his line out and almost instantly snagging a large sea bass which had ventured into the brackish water. "No, Ainsley, that should not be enough—not for you. Your hungry heart could not feast on such crumbs."

"How dare you say such things?" Ainsley flared. "What do you know? You have been living with savages. You know nothing of love."

"Those savages, as you call them, know a great deal about love. It is the fire that sustains them through the dark curtains of the years. It is you who know nothing of love, Ainsley.

"My father is a man who gave his whole heart to love many years ago—a love that has not changed through all the lonely years. He carries it inside himself like a treasure and a burden—but it is already given away, and he will not betray that memory. You misread him, Ainsley. You are like the man who stands and reads the sky, and thinks the clouds of morning carry thunder, lightning, and rain when they are in reality, only the cooling mist of the dawn."

Her eyes flashing, Ainsley jumped up from the dock. "Oh, cut that fish loose and let's get back to the inn. I don't wish to speak anymore of these matters.

"No matter what they say is right or wrong, I cannot bear to be banished from Marshfield. There is not enough for me to do at Windsor Point, and I will miss Nathan and the Seeleys ... and, yes, even you." She stamped her foot.

"What is to be done, Talmadge?" Ainsley cried. "Am I to be barred from Marshfield except when Papa can come with me? Then I will just become a visitor—nothing more. I can't bear it!"

Talmadge laughed and shook his head. "No," he said. "No, you are not to be banished. There is a fine secret, and your father and mine are discussing it right now."

"Tell me!" Ainsley exclaimed, picking up a worm from

the bait basket. "Tell me what it is, or I shall put this worm down your back."

With swift adeptness, Talmadge eluded her grasp and said, "If you do, I shall too."

"You wouldn't dare!" Ainsley challenged. "I, sir, am a lady, and no gentleman—"

"I, madam, am not a gentleman." They stood eyeing one another warily, and then she broke past him, pulled out the open collar of his shirt, and flung in the worm.

Laughing, she began to run back along the water to the inn. "I told you to tell me!" she cried.

Talmadge delayed pursuit for a moment while he removed the worm and picked a particularly large worm from the bait box. Then he was after her, swiftly and silently, and before she knew it, he had his arms around her waist and had tackled her to the grass. Holding his worm high above her he said, "You have taken on more than you bargained for."

"No! No!" she screamed, laughing and pleading at the same time. "Please don't. I hate worms. Please! Please!"

Without so much as a hint of a smile Talmadge stared down at her. She thought suddenly, with a little thrill of understanding, that this was not a man you'd want for an enemy. His eyes were like pools of mystery and she stared into them like someone thirsting, yearning to be taken deeper. She was suddenly very still beneath him.

"Do you promise not to try to pry out the secret until you are told?" Talmadge demanded.

He held her small hands in his own strong clasp, and for a fleeting moment she returned its gentle pressure. Then, quickly, she pulled her hands away.

"I promise, I promise," she said breathlessly.

"Very well." Talmadge let her go, and stood up, reaching to help her to her feet. She brushed off her skirts, and the two of them, faces flushed with amusement and exertion, walked together toward the porch.

She felt young, carefree, and a little foolish, but it had been fun for a moment to shed the weight of the serious months that had passed. Her heart was pounding from the exertion, but it was beating, too, from the mysterious emotions that had shaken her as she'd looked up into Talmadge's dark face above her. She could still feel the imprint of his hands upon her waist and wrists. She felt warm and tingling, as though her body in the shadow of his had been lighted by a spark of electricity.

She rubbed her wrist gently, and looked sideways at Talmadge. She was surprised to see him looking at her, as though he had known she would turn.

When they got back to the inn, John and Nathan were sitting on the porch. "What have you two been up to?" Nathan asked.

"You should teach this son of yours respect for his elders," Ainsley replied, laughing.

John looked at his daughter disapprovingly. "Maybe I should have taught you how to behave as a grown woman, and then Talmadge would not mistake you for a child."

Talmadge bowed slightly to John. "Sir, I do not mistake her."

Everybody laughed heartily, and Ainsley flushed and hurried into the house to repair her appearance.

"It's time that man learned some manners," she muttered to herself. "It is disconcerting being around someone who is so unpredictible and mysterious."

An hour later she returned to the porch. Daniel Cothran had joined the other men, and Brosian was serving cool lemonade and walnut cookies. It was the lazy, quiet time of the afternoon, when the sound lay as still as glass and a slow, warm miasma seemed to hover over the harbor.

With self-conscious decorum, Ainsley pulled out a piece of needlework and sat stitching while the men rocked.

"Ainsley," he father said, "Nate has made a proposition that I think you should know about since all of my business will some day be yours—or your husband's, if you ever marry."

"Yes?" Ainsley responded quietly, ignoring the barb about marriage since her father knew her feelings on the subject full well.

She had told her father that she would marry for love— and for love only. The one thing he did not know was that there was only one man on the face of the earth whom she thought she could love, and because she wished to be near him, she could never speak of that love. She knew it was hopeless to expect Nathan would someday love her in return, and had decided she would settle for being his friend. So, she and her father argued about marriage, and she could never explain to him why she would not marry.

"It seems," John continued, "that Nate would like to become my business partner. He wishes to buy *The Ainsley,* and in return will give me partnership in the Marshfield Inn. We will not become owners of the place itself, only the business of the inn, as long as Nathan choses to use Marshfield for that purpose."

"What is the purpose for this partnership, Papa?" Ainsley asked.

"It will give me another source of cash income, which I desperately need in order to keep my supply business running," John answered. "The shortage of usable currency grows worse by the month. Connecticut paper is valueless outside of the Colony, and, unless I have Rhode Island notes, New York notes, gold, or British currency, I cannot buy anything manufactured outside of Connecticut—tools, fabric, weapons, wheat, sugar, spices, all the things we need."

"Nate is selling half ownership of the sloop to Daniel, and with the two of them determining the most profitable way to make use of *The Ainsley,* I will have more time to manage the wharfside business.

"And finally, my dear, if we make these arrangements, we intend to place you in charge of both inns. Nate will build you a house of your own on the Marshfield property, and, with a proper companion, you may be in residence at Marshfield with full propriety whenever you choose."

Suddenly, Ainsley's heart was dazzled. "Oh, Nathan! You have done this for me?"

"No," Nathan said, calmly amused, "for all of us, dear Ainsley. It is a perfect solution. Talmadge thought of it."

The rest of that summer flew by. Nathan, as good as his word, set about remodeling the carriage house into a charming two-bedroom cottage for Ainsley. She chose some of the dearest things from the rooms at Windsor Point and from her father's warehouses to decorate the small, lovely rooms.

A mature widow named Tilden whose husband had bought through the lottery a small tract of land east of Marshfield, sold her property to Nathan, and he invited her to come work at the inn. She became housekeeper to Ainsley, and slept in the smaller of the two bedrooms in the cottage. Mistress Tilden also became the laundress for the inn, and proved herself adept in the kitchen garden as well.

She was a tidy, hard-working, quiet woman, and the arrangement worked perfectly.

More and more, Ainsley left the workings of Windsor Point Inn to Brosian, who knew every detail of the place and kept it with meticulous care.

Marshfield Inn had become busier with each passing season. As the war in the north moved relentlessly to its conclusion, more and more settlers were moving into Connecticut, hoping to take advantage of the depressed money and buy land cheaply. With each new family moving in and settling, Nathan knew he was closer to having his petition for an independent town accepted.

"Ainsley," Nathan said one day, walking into the office of the inn where Ainsley was going over the account books, "I have a request."

"Yes, Nathan." She lighted up whenever he needed her. "Anything I can do."

"I would like to have a harvest fete here at Marshfield. I want everyone within the perambulation line to be invited. We are going to have the greatest celebration ever known, and then we are going to have a meeting.

"If all goes well, next year at this time we will be our own town 'New Parrish'—beholden to no one."

Harvesttime came and the barley was reaped, milled, and sacked. The carded fleece and skeins of wool and linen, as well as the logs for ballast and for sale—all the bounty of the working estate of Marshfield—were prepared for shipment, and all was sent, by wagon to the docks of Windsor Point. Talmadge was to drive the final load, and travel with Daniel on the sloop to Rhode Island.

Two days before the last load was due at the docks, John and Daniel left Windsor Point early in the morning. In their absence the crew would continue stowing the cargo. Riding hard, and on strong mounts, the two men arrived at Marshfield just before noon. They reined their horses in awe at the sight that confronted them—a great festival.

The front lawns of Marshfield were strung with lanterns and gay banners that fluttered in the early autumn breeze. The day was warm and brilliantly clear. Men, women, and children, in clusters and pairs, roamed through the gardens and fields, or relaxed in the pleasant sun. Fiddlers scraped merry folk tunes while the children played games on the lawns.

Across the gracious width of the house, on either side of the wide open front door, were long tables groaning with food. The smell of fresh-pressed cider was intoxicating, and it mingled with the fragrance of pumpkin pie and a great pig roasting on a spit.

The harvest party, filled with the buzz of merriment, laughed its way through the afternoon. As the women began to put away the food, and the children began to sink in exhaustion, quietly napping against a tree or in their mother's arms, the men gathered under a huge oak tree, where they commanded a view of the distant sound.

"Now then, men," Nathan began, "by my reckoning, counting men, women, and children, we have had nearly one hundred and fifty souls here today. It seems to me the time has come, good brothers, to declare ourselves an independent township and our own congregation. Let us look for our own minister, one who will preach to us as we wish to hear. Let us levy our own taxes, run our own school, our own property, our own lives."

"Here! Here!" rose a shout from many voices.

There was some argument. Those living close to Norwalk and Stamford saw advantages in those ties, but they were in a great minority.

"Very well, then," Nathan continued. "We must sign these petitions and present them to the General Court. It will only be a matter of time."

Nathan was chosen to head the committee that would hire the new minister, select the site for the school, appoint the school teacher, and generally oversee the myriad other tasks involved. The name for the new town, by unanimous decision, was to remain as New Parrish—it was one of the last unanimous decisions ever made by the strong, individualistic, and opinionated founding fathers.

Nathan's dreams were at last about to come true. He had established his estate, the new Marshfield, and now was creating a new town, one which would be free of ties and responsibilities to old, established, and corrupt governments. Best of all, wonder of wonders, his son was returned to him, and the Fairchild name could be continued into the next generation. It was the finest day of Nathan's second life.

Chapter Twenty-nine

The heavily loaded wagon, carrying the last of the goods from Marshfield, bumped along the White Oak Trace. Talmadge rode his father's chestnut gelding, a powerful horse of gentle heart, and somehow, between his own calm command and the horse's good sense, the two of them were able to keep the half-wild young horses in check. More and more Talmadge was taking over the operations of the farms of Marshfield. At last, Windsor Point came into view, and Daniel Cothran, catching sight of the incoming load, hurried up from the docks to greet Talmadge.

Brosian and Ebenezer rounded up the horses and led them down to the holding pens where they would be loaded into the hold of *The Ainsley*. Daniel grasped Talmadge's hand and shook it warmly. He liked Nathan's remarkable son very much, even though Daniel suspected that Talmadge, like himself, was hopelessly smitten with the beautiful and unsuspecting Ainsley, who treated them both as well-loved brothers: Daniel, an older, wiser brother, and Talmadge, a younger brother to tease and confide in.

Daniel's love for Ainsley had been carefully banked to a soft and comfortable glow. Knowing his love was hopeless, he had simply learned to keep it within the bounds she had set. He suspected that would never be a possible solution for Talmadge.

Behind those remarkable eyes, Talmadge was a man of total conviction and intensity. Daniel suspected his calm, watchful exterior concealed a man capable of tremendous depths of conviction. If he loved Ainsley, it would be with a passion few men could know or experience. God help them both, Daniel thought.

The two men set to the task of checking, inventorying, and securing the final cargo. When they had finished, Daniel watched Talmadge come out onto the deck and stand facing toward the sea. Something in the young man's face touched Daniel. "You love the sea, don't you, Talmadge?" he asked wonderingly. "Your father was born to it, and, although he was a master seaman, it never really spoke to him. Not to his deepest self. But you—I see in your face the look of a true mariner."

Talmadge regarded Daniel. "I sense that you, Daniel, are truly at home nowhere else but on the water," he said, not asking a question but stating a fact.

Ruefully, Daniel shook his head. "Perhaps. I have loved other things—I have loved—but the sea has taught me the most honest answer, and that is that often the things you love do not love you back. You must learn to love for the joy of the loving—and not for the return."

Talmadge saw the sadness and loneliness in Daniel's eyes. "But it is not a bad life?" Talmadge asked, waiting for confirmation. He liked this friend of his father's. This was a man of truth like Passakonawa.

"Loving anything is the best life of all," Daniel replied. "It is only the loving that makes anything worthwhile. It is its own reward."

Both men stared out at the restless sound. The first cold wind of the season pounded at the waves and whipped them into a frothy spray. "We shall have some seasick horses before this sail is through," Daniel predicted.

"I shall teach you of the sea and ships, Talmadge. You will be a great student and a fine mariner. Let us hoist the sails for Rhode Island, and wish ourselves fair winds and good trading."

Providence's docks were a scene of mass confusion. Talmadge unloaded the horses. Turbulent, frightened, and exhausted from their journey, they were handed over to the ferrier, and receipts were exchanged. In the noise and jumble of a hundred voices, a thousand bodies, ropes, creaking ships, cracking sails, and the shout of bargains offered, denied, and accepted, Daniel, Talmadge, and the crew of *The Ainsley,* unloaded the goods from the bounteous harvest of Marshfield, and placed them in the warehouse of the agent who had purchased them sight unseen from Ainsley's agent.

Opening sacks, tasting, testing for vermin, for quality, for accurate count, the man inspected every inch of the cargo, and pronounced it satisfactory. Farming tools and coal were the cargo which was to be taken back as ballast, but most of the shipment was to be paid for in currency.

As the agent counted out the crisp Rhode Island notes into Talmadge's hand, Daniel breathed a sigh. "It is good to see real money," Daniel said. "The British owe Norwalk and Fairfield huge sums of war debts, for billeting troops, for commandeered shipping, for volunteer colonist troops. I trust they will pay all of their debts, but perhaps not until the war is over, and that may take a number more years."

"Aye," the agent said absently, running down the meticulous list of the inventory. " 'Tis said they are rounding on Fort Ticonderoga, Quebec, and Montreal—but who's to know. News is slow arriving. The British will win, no doubt about it, but when and how—that's the question."

"In the meantime, no one will touch our inflated Connecticut banknotes, and so we are beholden to you for paying us in currency we can use," Daniel said, placing the notes carefully in the strongbox he was carrying and snapping the lock.

" 'Tis all the same to me," said the agent, "if I pay you in money or in trade. Even if I wanted to, I could not pay you in Connecticut money. I, for one, would as soon have a piece of dung as a Connecticut banknote—I could at least use the dung to fertilize my garden; the Connecticut banknotes would be useless."

As Talmadge and Daniel walked back to the ship together through the crowded wharf, Talmadge said gravely, "The day must come when this confusion of currency is stopped. There should be only one currency so that all colonies can trade equally."

"You are thinking like an Indian—logically. A single currency would make too much sense," Daniel said. "Colonials don't like to do such logical things."

The Ainsley was due to sail back to Windsor Point with the first tide of morning. The trip, downwind most of the way, would take but a few days if the weather held. Daniel and Talmadge sat in the cool darkness, huddled in heavy seacoats against the night wind. The stars above were as bright and shining as spear thrusts.

A sudden sound by the mooring line caused Daniel to get to his feet and walk to the gunnels to check the watch. Below him on the wharf stood two men.

"Ho," cried the one, "it is I, Agent Draper."

"Ahoy," Daniel called back, "It is I, Captain Cothran. What do you wish?"

"May we come aboard?" the agent called back.

Daniel nodded to the crew member on watch and a plank was lowered, and the two men boarded *The Ainsley.* The second man was in a heavy cloak with a high collar and a deeply brimmed hat. It was hard to see his face in the shadows.

"This gentleman, who wishes to be known as Smith, is in need of passage to Connecticut. He wondered if you would be willing to accept him as a passenger. He will pay anything you ask within reason, in New York banknotes," the agent said.

Uncomfortable with the mysterious nature of the circumstances, Daniel prepared to say a preemptory no, but just then the man called Smith began to speak. His voice was low and cultured, with just a touch of an English accent.

"Forgive me, good captain, for this most urgent and unorthodox request. You see, I am on secret business for our government, and we have received dispatches that must, in full haste, be sent on to our commanders in Connecticut. I can say no more, but if you are a patriot and a gentleman, you will agree to give me—and your country—aid." Mr. Smith ceased to speak, but the restrained dignity of his words had touched Daniel.

"I shall ask my partner," Daniel stated, and walked through the darkness to the spot where he had left Talmadge. Talmadge was no longer there. Glancing around in puzzlement, Daniel saw Talmadge's shadow. He had moved to stand noiselessly beside the main spar, within easy listening distance of the conversation. Daniel understood that Talmadge was always prepared, always ready to protect those he cared for.

Daniel motioned and Talmadge moved silently to his side. "You heard?" Daniel whispered. Talmadge nodded, and replied, "Let him come. What harm could one man do, even if he is not what he claims to be—which I suspect."

The return voyage was without incident. Smith, the mysterious passenger, kept much to himself, and was no trouble. His luggage, consisting of several leather-strapped canvas bags, was surprisingly heavy, and Mr. Smith himself had overseen its stowage. The only insistence he had made was that he be quartered with his baggage.

Making no excuse or explanation for the request, Mr. Smith gave the impression that the importance of the bags ought to be self-explanatory. In an odd way, his failure to explain his reasons for caution seemed to give Daniel more confidence that the man was what he claimed to be.

As the voyage continued, the wind was brisk and the waves demanding, and Daniel found himself completely occupied with the sailing of the sloop. At his shoulder Talmadge observed, responded, and learned.

"You have a natural way with the sails and the sea, Talmadge," Daniel told him. "No time at all and you'll be a master mariner."

"I would like that," he replied quietly. "I could not learn from a better teacher. I think perhaps your life has been given in quiet ways to the needs of my father. I think he is blessed in such a friend. You are, to him, as Meskapi was to me—a second soul."

Daniel smiled, "I like that thought. A second soul to Nathan Fairchild. Yes, I could accept that as my epitaph."

On the few occasions when Mr. Smith came on deck to take the air, Daniel made an effort to speak with him. The man was courteous, dignified, and interested in the boat, and the details of Windsor Point Landing and the man who owned it.

"I have need of a safe harbor in Connecticut," Mr. Smith said. "I need to have contacts among men of integrity and loyalty."

"John Windsor is all of that and more," Daniel responded.

The man had paid for his passage in crisp New York banknotes, the most coveted currency on the seacoast. His demeanor was above reproach, and Daniel felt Talmadge had been right in accepting the passenger aboard. Only once did Daniel feel a wisp of discomfort, as though a shadow passed over his mind. He had to quell the uneasy feeling that he knew Mr. Smith from somewhere, had met him before. Yet, there was no conscious recognition and he shook off the feelings.

As Daniel and Talmadge disembarked, John Windsor was waiting for them at the wharfside. He spread his arms wide in welcome.

Daniel carried the strongbox from his cabin and placed it in John's hands.

"Ho!" cried John, "a veritable windfall of usable currency. Marshfield shall thrive for another year, and so shall we!" He shook the heavy cash box close to his ear. "Ah! stuffed to the very gills. How I love the rustle of sound paper money."

Mr. Smith was standing close by, supervising the unloading of his luggage. With a subtle shake of his head, Daniel indicated that John should say no more about the contents of the strongbox. Although it was apparent Mr. Smith must have overheard the conversation, he gave no indication of listening, but continued his self-appointed task, ordering Brosian to carry the bags up to the inn where he would engage a room.

Daniel took John's arm and led him over to Mr. Smith, introducing the two men. John greeted the newcomer with his usual warmth and invited him into the supply store for a cup of something restorative.

With a smile, Mr. Smith declined the offer.

"I must be off to Norwalk immediately to begin my mission. If you will forgive me, Master Windsor, I shall join you for a repast another time."

Unloading the coal and heavy farm implements took most of the day, and by nightfall Daniel and Talmadge were almost too tired to walk up the path to the inn. Ainsley was at Marshfield, and so the brightness of their welcome seemed dimmed.

After washing and changing for dinner, the two men walked into the dining room to see Mr. Smith, returned from his Norwalk excursion, sitting at the table with John Windsor. John was laughing with open pleasure, and the two men were conversing like old friends.

Seeing Mr. Smith without his hat and cloak, Daniel again had the uneasy feeling that he knew the man.

"Sir," Daniel said, seating himself across from Smith, "I keep having the presentiment that we have met somewhere before, though deuce will have me if I can remember where."

Smith glanced up from his plate of mutton pie and looked steadily at Daniel. "I have no such recollection, Captain Cothran, although I am told by the good Master Windsor that you are a veteran of the battle of Louisburg, and I was a courier to the commanders of that battle more than once. It is possible you saw my face in some such setting."

"Perhaps," Daniel conceded, "that might explain it. So many faces. So many men whom I saw, but had no introduction to . . ."

"Indeed, sir," Mr. Smith agreed, smiling, "though I must believe that had I seen you I would have remembered. You are a truly remarkable sailor. I, and your country, thank you for my safe passage."

Turning to John, Mr. Smith continued, "My assignment here has been expanded. If it is acceptable to you, I would like to make the inn my headquarters for a few days. There will be messengers coming and going at all hours."

John willingly agreed, and in the next few days the sound of a man, or men, on horseback disturbed the sleep of those at the inn. There were late conferences in Mr. Smith's room, where the lamplight could be seen shining out from under the door, and low voices whispered into the hours of dawn.

At the end of the week, Mr. Smith came to John Windsor in his office by the docks.

"John," he called, stepping across the threshold, "I come bearing news, and asking an important request."

Looking up from his desk, John indicated a comfortable armchair, and Smith sat down.

"It seems I have been given new orders. Rather than proceeding on to New York, I am to take passage on a packet leaving Norwalk with the midnight tide tonight to return to Providence."

With genuine regret, John answered, "We shall miss you, Smith. You are a fine card player and a most witty dinner companion. But, I have observed your dedication to your duty—whatever that may be—and I am certain we are in your debt."

"No, no, John," Smith disclaimed modestly. "I but do my part, and a small one it is. However, it is imperative that my trail in Rhode Island be difficult to trace, and, since I was originally given only New York banknotes, I am somewhat at an impass. New York notes are rather conspicuous in Rhode Island."

John agreed. "Oh, the wretched confusion of these currencies. We are all hostage to this monetary stew!"

"I would not ask," Smith continued, "but it is my understanding that New York currency is most readily usable in

Connecticut. Perhaps we could do one another a favor. I could trade my New York notes for your Rhode Island ones. Thus, I will be able to move undetected through Providence, and you will have made yourself a slight profit. What say you?"

"Well . . ." John hesitated. He had a natural businessman's reluctance against making quick, pressured decisions, and yet, this was a time of war, and a man on a mission of importance was in need.

For several minutes John turned the request over in his mind. "Only part of the money is mine," he said cautiously. "It would be best if I could speak to my partner."

"Who might that be?" Smith asked, "Daniel? Surely he would have no objection."

"My other partner. Nathan. Nathan Fairchild."

For the briefest flick of a moment, Smith seemed to be turned to stone. "He is not here?" Smith asked, his lips still smiling but his eyes as piercing and intense as steel blades. "Is he in Norwalk, perhaps? Can you reach him quickly?"

"No," John replied, "he lives at some distance."

Smith turned away. "Well, I have no time to wait for you to contact him. I must be off tonight. I shall just have to take my chances in Rhode Island."

With sudden decision, John stood up. "I cannot send you off with such a liability. Of course we can exchange your currency. You are right; it will be an action of mutual benefit."

John went to the heavy oak door which protected his closet safe. With three separate keys he unlocked the complex padlock and removed the heavy cash box. The two men spent the afternoon counting out the crisp banknotes and making the exchange.

At last John placed the strongbox back into the safe, keeping out several sheafs of bills to make change at the inn and the store for the remainder of the day, and to give to Daniel Cothran, who was preparing another trading voyage with a second cargo of harvest from three neighboring farms close to Marshfield.

Mr. Smith thanked John royally, and returned to the inn to prepare for his departure.

During the days of Mr. Smith's stay, he had used Brosian as a man-of-all-work. Through the years with the Windsors, both Brosian and Ebenezer had grown to feel themselves respected, loved, and equal members of the Windsor household. No one spoke to the two men as servants. They managed many of the affairs of the inns and the dock. They were valued for their talents and their accomplishments, and were full members both of the community and the congregation.

It was thus shocking and bitterly distasteful to Brosian to be treated by Mr. Smith as a servant, with contempt and casual disregard. Mr. Smith ordered Brosian to fetch and carry, and spoke no words of thanks nor even deigned to look at him when he ordered him about. It was as though Smith regarded Brosian as though he were no man at all.

Without saying a word to anyone, but with a feeling of hatred and distrust toward the stranger who was so charming and gracious in public, and yet, in private, so curt and cold, Brosian put up with the man's rudeness, watching with extra care, hoping to find some scrap of the truth about who this man really was.

Through the passing nights Brosian had observed firsthand the horsemen who came calling on Smith. These men were not soldiers, or men who looked like they had any military training, of that Brosian was certain. These nightly visitors were men of furtive looks, who seemed to need the cover of darkness.

Brosian had stood by Smith's door, listening, while the whispered conferences continued into the dawn hours. He could hear little of what was said, but much of the discussion seemed to revolve around currency. Brosian heard many times the names of various inns in Connecticut. The men seemed to think that was where the most money was circulated in the colony.

One evening Brosian had heard a laugh, and a man said, "Marshfield, it's called. Twice the size of this place. Twice the people to pay and be paid."

"A half day's journey. Less. That's all," another voice added.

"Good," Smith's voice had whispered. "It sounds perfect. Time is of the essence."

Why, Brosian now wondered, if Smith was leaving to return to Rhode Island, had he been so curious about the inns of Connecticut?

Later that afternoon, when John told Daniel about the money exchange, Daniel felt a return of the old uneasiness he had felt about Smith from the start.

He confided his uneasy feelings to Talmadge, and Talmadge acknowledged that the circumstances of the currency exchange were strange, but still, John had seen the notes—had counted them. What harm could there be? The New York notes were worth more on the exchange than the Rhode Island notes, and so they should come out fine, financially. Nonetheless, the two men continued to feel uncomfortable. Something seemed wrong—something they could not put their finger on.

Darkness fell swiftly, and with it a blanket of cold that seemed to promise winter and frost were hovering near. Smith had packed swiftly, and had ordered Brosian to prepare the horse he had rented from John. The horse would be returned on the morrow by a lad from Norwalk, Smith had promised.

By mid-evening the wind was cutting like a knife. Smith whirled down the stairs in his heavy cloak, with his hat pulled tightly down over his forehead.

"It will be a cruel ride to town, and a hard blow up to Rhode Island, John, but I know God goes with me," Smith said, shaking John Windsor's hand vigorously. He looked around a moment, then turned back to John.

"Where in damnation is that black servant of yours?" John Smith snapped impatiently. "He was to have packed my saddlebags. I can't be late."

For the first time a look of disapproval and discomfort crossed John's face. "Brosian is not a servant, Smith. He is a friend and a valued member of this establishment—of this family."

"Sorry," Smith said, but the apology was perfunctory. "I am anxious, and my temper is uncertain. Please forgive me."

Just then Brosian walked down the steps, and, without a word, fastened two heavy bags across the back of Smith's saddle. With a quick salute, Smith mounted his horse, dug his heels into its flanks, and pounded off into the dark.

John turned to speak to Brosian, but Brosian had vanished into the night.

An hour later, Brosian knocked on Daniel Cothran's door. "Daniel," he called urgently.

In his stocking feet, with his waistcoat unbuttoned, Daniel was going over the ship's manifests for the coming voyage across the sound to Long Island.

"Yes, what is it Brosian?" Daniel asked, opening the door. Upon seeing his friend's mud-splattered clothes and face streaming with perspiration, Daniel pulled him into the room. "What's happened, Brosian? Where have you been?"

Gasping for breath, Brosian explained. "I followed Smith. I took a shortcut across the bridge to catch him on the other side, but he never came. He never crossed the river toward Norwalk."

"What are you saying?" Daniel's mind was whirling. "Maybe he took another road."

Brosian shook his head. "I don't think so. I don't think there is any packet leaving Norwalk tonight for Rhode Island. I asked around. The regular packet leaves Saturday night."

"Then where . . .?" Daniel left the question dangling.

"I think I know," Brosian said. "I ran back across the river, planning to come back to the inn, but I heard horses and followed the sound. Three men were riding up to the crossroads. I ran behind the trees and saw them meeting two others. They headed up the White Oak Trace. I swear one of them was Smith. I ran back here to tell you."

Daniel began to pace the small room. "It sounds strange, but still, he has never made any bones about the secret nature of his work."

Brosian shook his head. "I don't think he has anything to do with the army. Whatever he does has something to do with money. When I packed his saddlebags I felt something hard and heavy. Under all those notes John traded him, I found silver banknotes."

Raising his head with a snap, Daniel stared at Brosian, "What do you mean, silver banknotes? There is no such thing."

"Like this," Brosian asserted, pointing to the heavy back of one of Daniel's silver brushes, "a heavy square of silvery metal, with the picture of a banknote carved on it."

"Counterfeiters!" Daniel breathed the word like a curse. "We are ruined! He has passed his counterfeit money on to us! Where did you say they were going? It may not be too late."

"Marshfield, I think," Brosian said. "I heard them talking of Marshfield."

"Of course," Daniel answered. "They'll go from inn to inn, exchanging their notes and disappearing the next day.

They'll destroy the colony. If word gets around that our New York banknotes are worthless we will be dead. No other colony—no other country will do business with us."

"Shall I call Mr. Windsor?" Brosain asked.

"No, this will kill him. He will feel he is to blame. Of course, the one to blame is that snake Smith!" Daniel exclaimed. "Call Talmadge, and meet us with saddled horses in front of the inn."

At the last moment, Daniel had seized the pistol underneath his bed and placed it deep in the traveling pocket of his greatcoat.

The men were silent as they rode through the night, pounding up the White Oak Trace as the full moon strained through the bare, black limbs of the trees. Before dawn they arrived at Marshfield. They tethered their horses in a copse of woods, and approached with silent footsteps. Talmadge melted into the night but a few moments later rejoined his two companions.

"They are here, all right," he whispered. "There are five lathered horses in the barn."

Fortunately, Talmadge carried a key to the back door of Marshfield. The men entered without an alarm.

Swiftly the three men crossed Nathan's private parlor to the door of Nathan's bedroom. Talmadge knocked softly on the door, and then entered as Nathan rose up in bed preparing to shout. Talmadge placed a hand over his father's mouth and whispered in his ear, "It is Talmadge and Daniel."

In total shock, Nathan stared through the moonlit room at his son and his friend. Brosian slipped into the room behind them.

"We have Brosian to thank. Hopefully, because of his alertness we are not too late," Daniel explained. Then he quickly told Nathan what had happened.

"If we cannot catch these felons tonight, we will be financially ruined and our businesses will be quarantined. Worse, they could flood the entire colony with counterfeit notes and even a whiff of such news would be disastrous. John will never forgive himself. We must get the money back, if only for his sake."

Nathan understood immediately. "The men you describe must be in the west wing—the other rooms are full. One of the staff checked them in. They will probably have a guard posted since they must know there is some risk."

With a small smile, Talmadge whispered, "The guard will not be a problem. I will see to it. Give me two minutes and then follow. If there is a guard, he will be silenced."

Before the other men could react, Talmadge had vanished from the room like smoke. Absolute silence. They waited for two minutes and moved out quickly.

Up the central stairs, through the sleeping corridors of the building, they moved like shadows, turning into the hall where the men were staying. Two doors stood side by side. "Which room?" Daniel mouthed.

Nathan shook his head. He had no idea who the ringleader might be, or which room he would be in.

Suddenly Talmadge was at their side. "One down, four to go." Talmadge pointed to a slumped figure in the far corner of the hall. "I think it is this room we want. This is the door he was guarding."

Without hesitation, Nathan stepped forward and threw open the door which Talmadge had indicated. It smashed against the inside wall, and four pairs of eyes looked up in astonishment.

Four men were seated at a small round table next to the bed. On the table were bundles of banknotes which were being divided up among the four. Next to the notes, gleaming in the muffled light of the lantern, were four engraver's plates.

Everyone else's eyes were on the money and the plates, but not Nathan's. He was staring with fixed and horrified intensity at the man whose face was directly across from the door. The light of the lantern emphasized the shadows and lines of the hated face, but Nathan would have recognized it in the flames of hell itself.

"Junius Comstock!" Nathan roared, "first you steal my gold, and now you would steal the very lifeblood of my new colony. You will never destroy again!" Nathan lunged at the table, grabbing at the engraver's plates and throwing them into the fire that blazed at the side of the room.

Junius Comstock, as shocked to see Nathan as Nathan had been to see him, rose from the table laughing. "You fool, you've just destroyed your own evidence."

Realizing the man was right, Brosian grabbed the poker and knocked the plates out of the flames onto the carpet.

While he stamped on the sparks that showered the rug, Comstock, alias Smith, reached under the banknotes on the table and pulled a pistol out, aiming it at the helpless Brosian.

"Comstock!" Daniel shouted, aiming the firearm which he had pulled out of his coat pocket. "You are a dead man!"

In the confusion, Daniel had not noticed that one of the other counterfeiters also held a pistol. This man took aim and shot, as Talmadge, seeing the hazard of the second gun, leaped across the table and wrestled the shooter to the floor.

Daniel fell as the bullet struck him. Comstock whirled to locate Nathan, but Nathan, running swift and low, tackled his knees and threw him back, hard, against the wall. Comstock's pistol discharged into the air and flew from his unconscious hand. Brosian caught the fourth man as he headed for the door and knocked him to the floor.

The noise of the melee roused the sleeping inn, and, within minutes, the counterfeiters were bound and gagged by the guests and servants who had run to the aid of Nathan and his friends.

Nathan rushed to Daniel's side. "My God, are you hurt?"

Daniel's face was gray, but he mustered a smile. "I think it is but a slight wound. But"—he paused, catching his breath— "whatever comes, I want you to know it has given me great pride to fight by your side, to call you friend."

"Hush now," Nathan replied. "It is *I* who thank the Lord daily for your friendship." Gently, Nathan carried Daniel to the bed and carefully lowered him onto the covers. "Rest now, Daniel, your job is to get well. If you need anything, I shall be here by your side."

After hearing and seeing the evidence against the five counterfeiters, the court adjudged them guilty. The Rhode Island notes which had been dishonestly exchanged were returned to John Windsor and Nathan Fairchild, and the entire incident was handled with quiet discretion in the hope of avoiding a currency panic.

Since the colonial jails were an insecure and temporary means of dealing with criminals, and the justice system was impoverished and ineffective, no prison term was assigned. The counterfeiters were instead sentenced to cropping— disfigurement and branding—so that, if at any other time they chose to participate in illegal activities, everyone would know they were convicted felons and be forewarned. It was terrible but effective justice.

As much as Nathan hated Junius Comstock, he did not choose to wait and see the man's fearful punishment. Comstock's cheeks were to be branded with the letter C for counterfeiter, and his ears and nose were to be cropped off.

Junius Comstock, a man of overweaning pride, would become a thing too ghastly to look upon. Perhaps, Nathan thought with rare bitterness, it will make his appearance match the ugliness of his soul.

The night before the cropping, Nathan went to the jail cell where the counterfeiters waited in horrible anticipation of the morrow. "I am not staying to observe the sentencing," Nathan told Junius as they spoke through the bars. "I want you to know I would not wish this on anyone, and yet, you must know that through your duplicity, countless children who were hostage to the Indians, died or remained unransomed and enslaved. Perhaps there is justice after all. You deserve punishment for your fearsome wrongs."

"The gold could not have saved everyone, and I needed it to gamble," Junius answered with a cold laugh. "Gambling is more than mother, wife, or country to me—certainly more than someone else's brat. It is the most costly whore—and, even though it destroys me, I am still enamored. When I lost all of the gold," Junius continued bitterly, "I needed more. It is as simple, and as complex, as that."

Suddenly, Comstock's face jerked up, and he looked at Nathan with blazing hatred. "But how would you know of such things? You are everything I despise. You play by the rules. You gain the whole world and keep your own soul. You even lose the whole world and keep it. I hate men such as you.

"But I promise you this, Nathan Fairchild, you and I are not through. You may have won this round, but I shall find a way. I shall find a way to rob you of the thing you prize most, just as you have robbed me of my face, which was the last thing I owned that was of any value. I promise you, you shall pay."

Chapter Thirty

Daniel seemed to be recovering nicely.

The doctor from Norwalk had been summoned after the counterfeiters had been subdued and had determined that the bullet had passed through Daniel's body. After probing the wound and deciding that the damage was fairly minor, he bandaged the area, which had bled very little, and informed Daniel's concerned friends that he would be fine.

Daniel had attended the trial, giving testimony and seeming to feel only a slight discomfort. Nathan arranged for a sea captain who was at liberty to take *The Ainsley* across to Long Island, exchange the cargo, and then, upon its return to Windsor Point, put the ship in dry dock for winter repairs.

"Now, you shall simply stay quietly at Marshfield until you are completely healed, old friend," Nathan told Daniel. "You shall be cosseted and coddled to your heart's content. All of us owe you so much—and now we shall have a chance to serve you."

Daniel laughed, but Ainsley saw a whiteness around the corners of his mouth and a cloud behind his eyes that worried her. The three were sitting in the sun-drenched front bedroom. Daniel was wearing a claret-colored dressing gown over his white shirt and breeches, and he was shivering.

Ainsley rose to her feet and picked up a pillow from the bed. "Are you in pain, Daniel? Speak the truth to me. You men are so busy being brave that you give those who nurse you no help at all."

With a slight effort, Daniel shifted in the chair. "A little discomfort, perhaps. Odd, after so many days."

"Perhaps this pillow to rest against?" Ainsley suggested gently lifting his shoulders to position the pillow. Daniel winced, and Ainsley was immediately alert.

"Into bed with you Daniel. I want to have a look at that wound right now. No more of this secrecy—I *will* see it."

At the sharp sound of concern in Ainsley's voice, Nathan, too, was aroused. "Is it getting worse then, Daniel? Why have you not told us?"

Too sick to argue, Daniel allowed himself to be helped onto the bed. Ainsley raised his linen shirt and gently removed the bandages, which were soaked with yellow fluids. The site of the wound was puckered, the edges puffed with infection, and an ugly blue and red discoloration stained a large area around the bullet hole. The smell rising from the wound was sweet and foul. With grim eyes, Nathan and Ainsley looked at the festering mass. Daniel tried to smile up at their faces. "Not a pretty sight. I should have warned you."

"The bullet," Nathan whispered. "Damn that doctor. The bullet must still be in you. It is poisoning you."

By nightfall Daniel was writhing in pain. He was running a raging fever, and most of the time he was out of his mind, scarcely knowing who or where he was. Ainsley stayed by his side, placing poultices on the wound, giving him sips of soothing syrups, and holding his dry, hot hand.

The doctor had come, looked at the gangrenous wound and shook his head. "His body is filled with infection. All you can do is try to make him comfortable and pray for a miracle." "I could bleed him . . ."

"No! Damn you!" Nathan growled, "You've done enough damage. Get out and leave him in peace." In the morning Daniel began to vomit. Nothing would stay down, not even the few sips of water he'd managed to swallow. Snow had begun to fall, and overnight the world had become white and beautiful.

"Snow," Daniel whispered, through his fever-parched lips, "Snow. How I would like to taste it once more." Nathan hurried outside and brought in a pan of snow, and Ainsley rubbed it on Daniel's lips. For a moment Daniel felt a little relief from the burning thirst.

"I could almost think myself at sea . . ." Daniel's voice was so faint she had to bend to hear him speak. " . . . the cold spray in my face, and the horizon lighted with the coming sun."

Later that afternoon, Nathan came in and stayed with Daniel while Ainsley slept. She had been with Daniel through the night, changing his bandages and draining the infection from the wound.

Toward evening, Daniel's restless tossing ceased, and he gave a shuddering sigh. "The pain," he whispered in wonder, "it has stopped."

In the lamplight of the early winter evening, Daniel's face was as white as the pillow on which he rested. There was about him an awful stillness.

"Good," Nathan answered, but his heart shuddered at the meaning of that awful stillness. "You must be past the crisis. Christmas will soon be upon us, and we shall dance again, dear friend. Do you remember that first Christmas at Windsor Inn? You looked so handsome and fine dancing with Ainsley. What a splendid pair you made."

Daniel nodded. "I remember. I have remembered it every day of my life since." Daniel's eyes were closed, but he was seeing the memory in his mind.

Through the night, Nathan kept vigil by the bedside. Toward morning Ainsley came in and touched Nathan's arm. "You go rest now, I will keep watch," she whispered. Nathan reluctantly went off to his room, so sleepy he could no longer resist the need to close his eyes.

Ainsley came close to the silent Daniel. Daniel looked as though he were sleeping, but in the sharp light of the dawn reflected from the thousand diamond edges of the snow, she could see that his face had a gray pallor she had never seen before. His breathing was ragged and labored and the bed linen over his wound was stained with dark red blood.

"Daniel," she murmured, bending over the bed, "I am going to change your dressing. The doctor has sent a new ointment that he says will stay the infection."

Carefully, she lifted the cotton bandages from his side. By now she was used to the awful stench, but its heaviness always seemed to shock her. With horror she stared at his wound, black now, like some rotted thing and covering all of his side and abdomen. Gently she applied clean bandages and replaced the covers.

Without opening his eyes Daniel croaked through dry lips, "It doesn't hurt anymore. Is it looking better?"

"Oh yes, Daniel dear," she replied, forcing the tears back from her eyes. "Now you will be able to sleep and get well."

"I don't want to sleep, Ainsley." Daniel's voice was soft, but clear. She bent toward him. "Having you here, feeling your sweet hands care for me, holding me, touching me—this has been the finest time of my life. I have loved the sea, Ainsley. I have loved my ship. I have loved my life—but I would not trade them all for more of these past days with you. I love you, Ainsley. I have loved you like a man loves the moon, or the stars always out of reach, but worshipped nonetheless. It was enough to be with you—to see you—to know that you cared for me. It was enough. But these last few days—they have been, for me, a time of wonder. Thank you, dear, dear Ainsley. My sweet, sweet love."

The tears would not stay. She leaned over him, her auburn hair like the wing of a gentle mother bird shielding her loved fledglings. With a great effort Daniel opened his eyes and looked at her, so close that he could see her spiky black eyelashes and the tears trembling there.

"Hush," she whispered, "you must rest and get well."

"Darling Ainsley, if I am to die now, I thank dear God that the last sight my eyes shall behold is the wonder of you. My last sight is all—all of you." Daniel's eyes seemed to glaze over and he closed them with a gentle smile.

"No, Daniel," Ainsley cried, "wait, wait for a moment."

She laid her head on the pillow next to his. "Oh, dear, dear Daniel. I love you too. You are so precious, so necessary to all of us. We need you more than any of us have ever realized. You bind us together. What shall we do when you are gone? We all love you. We all need you."

His hand groped for hers, and he held it weakly in his own. "It is not I who binds us all together, Ainsley. I have known that. For many years I thought it was Nathan who held us by some common bond, but now I know differently. Oh yes, he is our head—the one we look to for leadership and form—but it is you, Ainsley, you whom we all love. Each in our own particular way. You are our heart, Ainsley. You."

She was crying now. "You have broken that heart, Daniel. How can I bear this?"

"Do not weep, Ainsley. Know that living was more difficult, knowing I could never have you. Now . . . now, I have had these days and I am content. It is poor Talmadge who must bear the coming years. If you must weep, weep for him."

"I don't know what you mean, Daniel," she said gently stroking his forehead. "You have known, always, because you are so wise, that it is Nathan only. I can give myself to

no other man. Talmadge is young. Surely he does not care
for me other than as a friend."

"Hush, Ainsley. You will not see what you do not wish to
see. You think you have an unchangeable heart—but you do
not even know your heart," Daniel whispered. "Talmadge
knows his. This is his burden and his strength. It is the wonder
of Talmadge. Almost as though he were given wiser eyes, a
wiser heart. He sees things clearly—more clearly than any man
I have ever known. And he feels truly. His heart is stronger
than the sun. You have buried your heart, Ainsley. In a childish
dream. Look for it. Find your true heart. Do not fear what you
feel for Talmadge. Do not go on looking for happiness where
it does not dwell." Daniel was exhausted.

Ainsley took a damp cloth from the side table and began
to gently wipe Daniel's face. "We shall not talk of this," she
said sternly. "You are going to get well and we shall scoff
at this foolish talk, and regret what has been said."

Daniel slowly shook his head. "Not the fever talking,
Ainsley. Your truest friend." He took a long, shallow breath.
"Call Nathan and Talmadge now, Ainsley. I would say good-
bye."

She ran weeping from the room, but when she returned with
the two men, she saw, the moment she entered the room, that
Daniel's body held an awful stillness. Nathan, too, understood
its portent. He moved to his friend's side, raised Daniel's arm,
and felt for the pulse that no longer beat there.

With infinite tenderness, Nathan grasped Daniel's strong, cal-
lused hand, which had held the tiller and the lines of many a
journey, following strong and true to the wind and the stars.

"Safe and happy journey, Daniel, dear friend. May you
reach the harbor of Paradise that you have so richly earned."

"Daniel gone," Ainsley wept. "I shall never feel young
again."

Talmadge stepped forward and wrapped the body gently
in the bedclothes, picking Daniel up as though he were a
child. "We shall take him back to the sea," he announced.
"He shall sleep in the arms of the waves he loved."

Daniel's death was hard for everyone. It seemed that a
quiet light had gone from the lives of those at Windsor Point
and at Marshfield. Ainsley thought often of that last talk she
and Daniel had had, and of his allusion to Talmadge.

For the next several months, as the winter dragged

through its long and dreary rounds, she watched Talmadge warily to see if she could detect any of the feelings at which Daniel had hinted. Talmadge was an enigma to her. He always seemed to throw her emotions off-kilter, and had a teasing, ironic way with her that made her think he never took her seriously.

It was a busy winter, Nathan was away from Marshfield setting up the arrangements for the new town, and Talmadge worked long, hard days with the wintering stock, trading, preparing *The Ainsley* for the spring voyages, and overseeing the new properties which Nathan had purchased. When Talmadge came in at night, his clothes crackled with cold and his face was red from the wind and stinging snow. But even then his presence was electric and Ainsley felt it shaking against the comfortable, shuttered walls of her heart.

She pushed the feelings aside, and in her discomfort, she developed a habit of avoiding Talmadge's company.

She kept herself busy running the inn and the household. Only after weeks of careful watching were her fears relieved, enabling her to resume her pleasant friendship with Nathan's son. Still, the sadness of Daniel's passing hung like a pall over the winter days.

In the spring, Nathan and Talmadge went down to Windsor Point to oversee the refitted sloop and to take her on several shakedown runs. Nathan arranged for Talmadge to do extensive sailing under the tutelage of some of the finest masters in Norwalk harbor.

Talmadge was adept and quick, and soon could handle *The Ainsley* as well as any seaman.

When the time came for planting, Nathan returned to Marshfield. John Windsor complained that he seldom saw his daughter, but Brosian ran Windsor Inn without a hitch, and Ainsley found that business at Marshfield was increasing, while business at Windsor Point grew less and less. Ebenezer usually accompanied Ainsley in her stays at Marshfield. As Norwalk and Stamford began to thrive, the inland road through New Parrish was more direct and better kept than the marshy, twisting coastal road. The war with the French had begun to wind down with the capture of Quebec, and all indications were that the British would be the victors. The need for secret harbors had lessened. Norwalk, Stamford, Southport, and Rowayton all offered more services than Windsor Point. The trading dock was doing less and less business.

The changes in the press of business suited John Windsor who was beginning to slow down a little. His knees ached with arthritis, and his teeth were giving him trouble so that his digestion and appetite were not what they had been.

"Getting old," he said to Nathan. "I don't know, ever since we lost Daniel, it's like everyone seems older. Not you, though, Nate. Have you a secret you are not sharing with the rest of us? Except for the silver in your hair, I swear you look younger and fitter than when I first met you."

Nathan laughed. "It's peace of mind, John. Losing Daniel was a terrible blow, but every time I look at Talmadge, and think on that, I feel life evens itself out, and I am content."

"Content!" John snorted. "You are far too young to settle for that, Nate. Far too young. That's a word for old men like me."

"I've good news, John," Nathan said, changing the subject. "We have been granted our town charter and are allowed to form a congregation. The town of New Parrish is about to be born. We walk the perambulation line this month, mark the maps, make the titles, and employ our first minister. We have already begun work on the parsonage. I have donated the land."

"Splendid!" John congratulated Nathan. "Splendid! Let's hope you find a minister who is wise and enlightened and helps you build a community—a congregation—of friendship and harmony."

With a great shout of laughter, Nathan replied, "Highly unlikely, John. We are already struggling like bulls with locked horns over whether we should have a minister who teaches the New Enlightenment or one of true orthodoxy. We cannot decide where to put the first school. Of the three candidates for schoolmaster, not one meets with majority approval, and although we have donated the property for God's acre in the center of the common ground, where the church will be located, no one can agree on which corner the church should be placed."

John began laughing. "Ah, you are a town of true Yankees."

The two sat laughing as the sun set over the waters of the sound, and the spirit of Daniel, which seemed to shimmer in the gentle waves, laughed with them.

HARVEST OF DREAMS 249

"What is this, Ebenezer?" Nathan asked. "Are you going

Chapter Thirty-one

Ainsley opened the windows of the dayroom next to Nathan's massive bedroom. She had fallen into the routine of sleeping in this small room when Talmadge and Nathan were away, as it was easier to respond to the needs of the inn when she was on the premises.

A lot had changed in the six years since Daniel's death. Nathan was off to Norwalk and New Haven seeing to the myriad responsibilities of the newly chartered town of New Parrish. Talmadge often took command of *The Ainsley* and, in all weathers and conditions, was sailing the sound, the ocean, and, since the signing of the Treaty of Paris, had even made a voyage to the West Indies. He was gone so much that Ainsley sometimes wondered if he were avoiding her. Marshfield was a lonely place when the men were gone.

Ainsley rarely knew when to expect either one of them, and so she was often sleeping in residence at the inn when the men arrived home unannounced. Whatever whispers of gossip there might have been over these unusual arrangements had long since quieted, since Ainsley, approaching thirty, was now considered a true spinster, and Nathan—well into his forties—was considered far too old to be capable of lewd conduct.

Even Talmadge's presence was unquestioned. He was at sea so much of the time—and was considered such a mysterious and silent man—that the townsfolk simply trusted him. So any hint of gossip, inflammatory as it might have been, had simply died away.

After much argument and contention, the Reverend Adam Witherspoon had been engaged by the congregation as the minister of the newly formed New Parrish. He lived on the acreage donated by Nathan. A comfortable, two-story clapboard house had been built by the town for the new minister, and the town committee had levied a special tax that had

been used to frame the church at the top of Chapel Hill at
the very center of the budding town.

There were sixty-five covenanted adult members of the
congregation, and over one hundred who attended meetings.
All those living within the sequestration line were required
to pay taxes to support the Congregational church, even
though a small assembly of Anglican Episcopalians met in a
one-room chapel on the far side of God's acre.

The one religion which was absolutely forbidden by law,
written into the town constitution by the founding fathers,
was the hated Quaker religion. No true Congregationalists
could abide the apostasy represented by that faith—if it
could be called such. Not even the Act of Toleration passed
by command of English Royalty could influence them.

New families seemed to move into the township every
week. There was little available land left on the eastern seaboard. The proprietory land of Connecticut was fairly inex-
pensive, and now that the French and Indian Wars were over
and the British had paid their war debts to Connecticut, the
colony was experiencing something of a land boom.

Nonetheless, as the original landowners were all too aware,
disappointment often followed the purchase of land on the
ridges of the colony. In New Parrish, the land, so deceptively
green, was thinly soiled. Wheat refused to thrive, and it would
be more than a century before scientists determined it was the
bayberry plant, which grew in such profusion, that caused the
strange destruction of the grain.

The rocks continued to thwart the most determined farmers. Rock fences lined every field and road—and still more
rocks appeared each spring, as though from some inexhaustible source beneath the ground. No one in New Parrish could
thrive on farming alone. But new families kept coming to
Connecticut, because the lands to the west were still closed
to settlement.

Tales were told of land in the Ohio valley where the topsoil was as deep as a man's arm. Such tales hung heavily on
the hearts of men who had spent everything they owned to
buy a few acres of the common land still available in New
Parrish, only to break their plows, their backs, and their will
on the rocky soil.

Nathan, however, had been blessed. His fields lay at the
far end of the ridge, where the glaciers had begun to melt,
and so, although his fields, too, were rock-strewn, they were

also covered with a layer of rich soil, thick enough to support healthy and abundant crops.

Another source of income had come to Nathan now that trade with the West Indies had opened up. One day when both Nathan and Talmadge were home and saw a rare stretch of leisure time before them, the two men had gone for a tramp. Packing knapsacks, they had set off on foot, deciding they would travel as whim took them for a few days and explore the countryside.

As they journeyed inland through the thick woods, following shallow streams, more than once they came upon clusters of wild horses. The animals, shaggy and skittish, wheeled and thundered away at the approach of the men.

"They are a nuisance," Nathan said. "Sometimes when the foraging is low at the end of a dry summer, they seek out the fields and eat and trample the crop. Damned shame. Some of them are fine-looking steeds; if they could be put to the harness they would make excellent stock."

"And why not?" Talmadge exclaimed. "They are capturable. I have seen the Indians round them up—sometimes one at a time—sometimes in herds. It can be done."

With a frown of deep concentration Nathan said, "Horses are at a premium. So many were killed in the wars. Travel between the colonies is more extensive—everyone wishes to own a horse. People in the Indies are desperate for horses." Nathan sat thinking.

"I could do it, Father," Talmadge said quietly. "Gather a herd and drive it to Rhode Island. In Providence they are filling cargo ships with horses and oxen for the Indies. They have a lively trading yard for the whole of New England. We could turn a fine profit."

The two men returned at the end of the week with unbridled zest. Talmadge gathered a crew and began to train them in the art of roping and driving horses. The young men were all excellent riders, with strong, muscular legs. None rode more magnificently than Talmadge. He and his horse were an entity of sinew, muscle, and heart. Ainsley's eyes were filled with the sight of him, and she flushed with anger and impatience at herself.

Nathan wanted to go on the roundup and horse drive, but town business was sending him to New Haven instead. It seemed having one's own town was more of a chore than he could have imagined. Quarrels and disagreements were a way of life in New Parrish.

The Reverend Witherspoon was unhappy with the schoolmaster, Stephen Dobbs. A firm believer in the Old Testament, Reverend Witherspoon had no question about the validity of the encouragement "Spare the rod and spoil the child."

A young boy in play at recess had inadvertently broken the window of the schoolhouse in throwing a ball. The matter had been brought up before the town committee, since the authorization to spend the money for a new window had to pass through the town tax lists.

Sternly, Reverend Witherspoon had asked what punishment had been given the young culprit. When he was told by the schoolmaster that the boy had apologized abjectly for the accident, and had eagerly agreed to clean the schoolhouse every Saturday in order to repay the cost of the window, the minister had been livid with anger.

"The boy should be publicly whipped," Reverend Witherspoon had insisted. "Such wanton disregard of public property, such vandalism and rowdiness, must be curbed or we shall see a wave of pernicious ungodliness among our youth such as can scarcely be reckoned!"

Stephen Dobbs had not been cowed, and had retorted that the boy in question was one of the most obedient, courteous young lads he had ever known in his twenty years of teaching.

The battle lines were drawn, and suddenly the town was shaken with grievances. Two distinct parties formed, one group that felt the Reverend Witherspoon was a harsh, backward, conservative Congregationalist who could in no way meet the needs of this progressive new town, and another group that felt the world was going to hell and that it was new ideas and permissive ways which would cause the downfall of the community.

Town meetings, held in the church, were more like shouting matches, and Nathan, as the chairman of the town committee, battled to bring some semblance of order. The one thing that seemed clear was that a new minister would need to be found—a minister who would not polarize the feelings of the citizens, but rather would encourage a feeling of community and oneness. It was inevitable that Nathan would need to travel to New Haven to discuss this matter and seek advice from the Congregational committee.

Ainsley stood at the gate of Marshfield waving good-bye to the father and son. Nathan and four of the other founding fathers were off to New Haven, and Talmadge and his crew of young, exuberant horsemen were off to the woods and vales to capture a herd of wild horses. Suddenly, as Ainsley looked at the men before her on their high-blooded, prancing steeds, their faces filled with eagerness and sense of purpose, she wished she could ride with them.

She thought of herself as set in her life, and yet, as she saw Talmadge, magnificent on his horse, surrounded by the thundering of hooves and the hearty sounds of voices in the air, she wanted to leap onto the saddle with him. For a brief and terrible moment she stared into his splendid eyes, and she felt as though she were being pulled toward him. She gasped. How could she think such indecorous thoughts?

Her confusion and shame turned into anger. Talmadge went off to sea for weeks at a time, and then reentered her life as though he had never been gone, teasing her and staring at her and disturbing her hard-won decorum. It wasn't proper. He had lived among the savages too long.

Deliberately, she turned her eyes from his searching gaze and looked at Nathan. The years had been kind to him. His face was a little fuller, but still strong and resolute, and his eyes, which had grown a softer blue, were kinder than Talmadge's could ever be. "Dear, dear Nathan," Ainsley thought, her mind comforted by the familiar, sweet feelings.

What Ainsley could not know was that Talmadge had seen the flash of passion and desire in her eyes before she had deliberately extinguished it, and had smiled to himself.

Oh, Ainsley, Talmadge thought, as he looked at her standing under the archway woven with wisteria, dearest Ainsley, when will you unbind your heart?

She was more a part of him than his own skin. In some mystical way, she lived within him like the shadow of his soul.

Until Ainsley's feelings toward Nathan were resolved, Talmadge could do nothing. How he wanted to show her that the infatuation she had experienced as a young woman, which had now become the comfortable emotional crutch of her life, was just that—a crutch; a dream that allowed her to feel she was not alone, not afraid. It was a love without consequence, a love without risk, a love without responsibility.

He knew his father was unaware of how deep her fixation was. Blind to the subtleties of romantic love, his father thought of Ainsley as a cherished friend and business partner. It had probably been years since he'd even noticed her beauty.

Talmadge lived with the pain and frustration of knowing a tragedy was playing before his eyes, and that he held a significant part. For though he loved Ainsley with all of his steadfast heart, he loved his father too much to disturb or reveal the situation.

Yet neither could he accept the passive role Daniel had played for so many years. As much as he yearned to be in her presence—to hear her voice, to see her face and form—his manly desires shook him and he was forced to leave before his will grew weak. He could not be near her without expressing the depths of his love. In desperation—fighting the urge to clasp her in his arms and carry her away to the highest mountain where he would show her to the sky, the wind, and the night—he would rush from Marshfield and take to the sea. At such times, in the whisper of the sails and the rush of the wind, he could almost feel Daniel's presence and hear him murmur, "All may yet be well."

Now, willing his face to remain carefree, though his heart cried out to claim her, Talmadge doffed his hat to Ainsley, and made a deep, bow of farewell. "When we return we shall bring the fatted pocketbook," he declared. "Farewell, my pretty dame."

With an equally elaborate curtsy, Ainsley returned his gesture. "And to you, oh dashing knight, may your quest be successful." The young men thundered off. Unbidden, Ainsley's eyes lingered on Talmadge's departing figure.

Nathan turned to bid Ainsley a final farewell, then joined the other members of his party, who had started slowly up the road, their horses disappearing in the dappled shadows of the oaks.

The weeks that the men were away passed slowly. Ainsley received a dispatch from Nathan saying that the Congregational committee could reach no decision. Several commissions and legations were sent down to hear the arguments of the community, but no consensus could be reached.

A message was brought by Ebenezer from Windsor Point. Apparently Talmadge had succeeded in rounding up an excellent herd of wild horses that had then been driven to Rhode Island and sold to a trader in the livestock exchange at Providence. The message from Talmadge had come on the packet boat. John Windsor was sending cargo up to Providence on *The Ainsley* and Talmadge would sail back with his friends and arrive within the week. So Ainsley continued at Marshfield, hoping nothing would change, but feeling lonely and unsettled, as though the air were heavy with a promised thunderstorm.

It was an autumn day aglow with burnished rusts and scarlet. The pumpkins lay in the fields, among the sheaves of dried corn stalks. In the smoky haze of the unreasonably warm day, they seemed like pots of gold in the rainbowed air.

The apple harvest was in and apple butter was being made in the inn's kitchen. The rich, fragrant smell of cooking apples and cinnamon wafted across the courtyard.

Somehow Ainsley could not seem to set herself to a task. She had started the day by binding herb sprays in the kitchen garden shed, to hang them for drying. Soon her interest flagged, and she turned the task over to young Alice, the newest kitchen maid.

Then, escaping to the stables, she started grooming her chestnut mare. Halfway through that task, she dropped the currying brush and walked away from the stall. The thought of a long ride in the heat of the afternoon seemed suddenly without attraction.

She ought to be looking over her wardrobe for winter, she knew. Her cape was becoming threadbare, and she needed new boots and hose. Still, nothing caught her attention, and, at last, she wandered back into the kitchen, attracted by the fragrance, only to find the room empty and the jars neatly labeled and cooling.

Her glance fell upon an unused basket of apples. Such pretty ones. Round, red, and perfect. With sudden enthusiasm, she decided she would make apple dumplings for the evening meal. Swiftly, with accustomed practice, she rolled out the rich dough, cut it into squares, and began wrapping the apples, cored and stuffed with raisins, nuts, and spices.

It felt good to have her hands busy. She had taken one of Mrs. Seeley's large white aprons to cover her afternoon frock, and had rolled up the lace ruffles that bordered her sleeves.

Finally, pleased to have accomplished one task for the day, Ainsley cleaned up the dishes and cupboards as the dumplings baked in the oven. The scent of the browning pastry warned her that she needed to check the oven and so she opened the door beside the hearth, and bent, placing the long-handled bakery paddle into the deep oven cavity to pull the bake pan out to view.

As she bent over the pan, checking the pastries, she felt her apron sliding loose. Reaching behind her she grabbed at the ties, and discovered a hand in her own.

Startled, she whirled around to find Talmadge standing smiling behind her. She had to catch her breath her joy was so unexpected and poignant. Embarrassed by the intensity of her emotions, she turned back to the stove.

Clanging the oven door closed, she snatched up the apron. "Talmadge!" she scolded. "Weeks away, and you come home more uncivilized than ever!"

"Is that the welcome I get?" Talmadge laughed.

"It's the welcome you deserve!" Ainsley countered. "Sneaking up on me like that. I nearly dropped the dumplings!"

"From the smell of them, that would have been a pity," Talmadge acknowledged.

Ainsley retied the apron, and reached to check the dumplings in the upper oven. The apron fell to the ground again.

"Talmadge!" she cried, exasperated. "Stop! I'm busy."

"Don't be busy, Ainsley," Talmadge said quietly. "Leave the apron, and the dumplings to burn to a crisp if they must, and come welcome me home."

Something in his voice made Ainsley's hand stop, frozen as it reached for the fallen apron. She straightened slowly, and turned to look at him.

"Yes," she said simply, letting her eyes rest on him for the first time, like an undeserved reward, "that is what I will do."

They walked together out of the kitchen, and down the back path toward the river. He told her of the adventures and the uncertainties of his trip.

"The horses are hard to capture," he said. "They love the freedom of the open fields, the silence of the woods. I don't blame them. It would be an easy life to love. But we found them by the water and where they feed, and we gathered a fine herd."

Talmadge's eyes were full of the memories of the roundup, and she longed to see what he was seeing.

"It seems so sad," she said, "somehow so wrong to take them from the wild. Often I wonder what it would be like to be free to do whatever you wished to do. Free to say and do and think and be . . .

"Is that how it was for you, Talmadge, when you lived with Passakonawa in the woods? Has it been hard for you to come back and be restrained by walls and customs and people?"

"No," Talmadge answered. "I was happy with Passakonawa and Meskapi, but I was never free. Memory always held me hostage. And now, now that I have returned, I am still a hostage."

She did not want to ask him to explain what he meant.

"Oh to be free," she repeated, "truly free . . ."

Talmadge had turned and was looking at her intensely. "Are you unhappy here, Ainsley?" he asked, "Do you feel trapped?"

"No! Not in the way you mean." Ainsley answered sharply. "No. But there is no freedom once you love something." She blushed in confusion. "I mean Marshfield. I love it. If I left, I would not be free. Marshfield would always be calling to me. Do you know what I mean, Talmadge? Once you love, there is no freedom."

"Is it Marshfield, Ainsley?" Talmadge asked, "or is it the man who owns Marshfield that you think you love?"

Angrily, Ainsley turned away from Talmadge and began hurrying back up the path toward the house. "Perhaps I should attend to my baking after all!" she said, hurt and embarrassment making her voice harsh. "You are home less than an hour and already you are baiting me. I want no part of this conversation."

Talmadge caught up with her and touched her arm. "No, Ainsley. You cannot walk away from this conversation. There are things that must be said between us. I am not able to pretend any longer—I don't want to pretend. I will not be like Daniel and live my life a starving man just out of arm's reach of food."

He pulled her toward the shelter of an oak tree, leaning her against its wide trunk, and placed his hands on either side of her. He stood over her, his face filled with an intensity she had never seen. It was as though his presence reached out like a cloak and enveloped her body and soul. She found herself trembling with fear and yet at the same time yearning for something she couldn't define. Somehow, the yearning was more frightening than the fear.

"I love you, Ainsley!" he said, his deep voice ringing with the echoes of his mighty and unchangeable heart.

"No!" she cried, her face strained with anguish and distress. "Don't say this. These are words that will change everything. You can't mean it! I am almost two years older than you in time, and a hundred years older than you in cares and responsibilities. You only feel these things because you are in such proximity with me. There will be other women. Beautiful, young women whose hearts and minds are free.

"Please, Talmadge, please! Don't say any more, or you will change things. Just when everything was getting so comfortable—so safe and easy to live with. I can't bear to lose any more.

"We are happy as we are, Talmadge. Don't ruin it all!"

"We are not happy, Ainsley," Talmadge answered in his firm, reasoned voice. "Denying what we feel. Lying to ourselves. Pretending these feelings do not exist—this may work for you, but it is impossible for me. I cannot stay at Marshfield, Ainsley. I cannot see you every day. Cannot hear you, and feel you near me. I cannot remain if there is no hope for me."

Ainsley was sobbing. "No, Talmadge. Do not say such things. You are so young. You will find a woman, and then you will know what it is to really love. You mistake love. What you feel for me is the great affection of a friend—of a brother and sister. It is powerful, yes, but different than true love."

"No, dearest Ainsley." Talmadge's voice was deep and strong. "I know true love. It is here." He touched his breast with his closed fist in the Indian sign of love.

He stood quietly for a moment. "Look at me, Ainsley. Look at me for the first time. I am a man—of your own years. I know my own mind, and I am not afraid of anything that life has to show. If our love is not to be, I can accept that. I will have to find my own way to live with it. But I will not remain here, to let it eat my heart away."

He grabbed her arms, and pulled her closer. Her hair had tumbled down onto her shoulders, and she had a smudge of flour on her cheek.

Ainsley stared into the clear blue eyes, the tanned, lean face, and felt a terrifying emotion. It was so powerful she could hardly breathe. She wanted to touch him—his hair, his shoulders, his chest. She wanted to kiss his straight lips, compressed in pain. She wanted him to move his hands from where they pressed against the tree and press them against her breast. A great wave of desire and heat rose in her throat, and she turned her face to hide it from him.

With a firm hand he took her chin and forced her to look at him again. "You will not evade this truth," he told her. "You cannot deny that you feel something—something frightening, yes, but also wonderful. You are afraid. But it is nothing to fear, Ainsley. This is love. This is what the love between a man and a woman creates. This is what it feels like."

He grasped her hand and placed it on his wide, smooth chest. Beneath the linen of his shirt she could feel the wild beating of his heart.

"It is that rhythm," he told her. "When two love as we would love, the rhythm of their bodies, their minds, and their hearts is like the great dance of the earth and the tide. It pulls the blood into ecstasy. It is something beyond careful, safe experience. It cannot be controlled or predicted. Love is not comfortable—it is made of fire and flame."

She was breathing quickly now, her eyes bright with emotion, and her mouth dry.

"No. No," she whispered. "It is respect, and familiarity, and admiration. It is security—and the promise of being together. It is loving the way a person looks and walks and talks. It is safe and constant."

His hands found her shoulders and held her so that her face was within inches of his own. She felt the heat of his body, the flame of his great spirit, and it reached to engulf her.

"You are wrong, Ainsley. Great love is not safe and predictable. It is pain, fear, hunger. It is the ability to risk ourselves to find another. It is daring to leave our safe places and give our naked souls into the glorious hands of another—a person so like ourselves and yet so different, that the difference itself will take an eternity of exploring.

"I want to know your secrets Ainsley—the secret wonders of your body, the secret folds and crevasses of your mind— and I will love them all. But love means that you must take the risk of letting me—a man with passions and desires you cannot even imagine—letting me break down the old comfortable habits, lay waste your safe places.

"But in return, my dear, dear, beloved, I will build you a place of such safety and joy that you could not even comprehend in the small little world you have created for yourself. But to get there you must have the courage to leave the old places behind."

He bent his head then, and kissed her. His kiss devoured her lips, and she felt herself sinking into some great oblivion. She stretched toward him, her soft lips seeking more, and she pressed against the full length of his hard, tensile body until she could have sworn that their hearts had melted into one, as though she had drowned in the feel of him.

It was the sense of drowning, of losing herself, that alarmed her, and at the last moment fear washed over her like a cold dash of water.

"I love you too much, Talmadge, to listen to this," she whispered. "You deserve something far, far better. Far more than I am able to give. My heart is given. It is too used to the love I have chosen. I have only the love of a friend left to give. Nothing more." She pushed him away with shaking hands.

"You are lying to yourself and to me. You have it to give—only you are afraid to give it," Talmadge replied simply.

She shook her head and tears rolled down her cheeks. "I cannot help it, Talmadge. I do not choose to love him. I try with all that is in me to stop. I recount his faults, I refuse to think of him. I practice independence, and yet, still, still no matter what I do, I would rather be here in his presence— even though he scarcely notices me—than to be anywhere on earth."

She bent her head in misery. "A crumb of his time is like a feast to me. And, even though it seems absurd, in some strange way I am happy and content because I am a part of his life. A part of Marshfield. For me, that will have to be enough."

Talmadge shook his head. "Ainsley," he whispered, with a sadness that sounded like doom, "you have settled for shadows. You cannot imagine the happiness you turn away from. But I have heard your words, and I believe them. I will not beg. I cannot watch you do this year after year. I will not destroy my father's illusions that all is well, and so I must go."

Horrified, Ainsley grasped Talmadge's arm. She had never felt more devastated. "No, you cannot leave. Just let things stay as they are. You will break Nathan's heart."

With a pained smile, Talmadge released his arm from her grip. "I am a man, with a man's desires. I cannot stay," he said sadly. "I could teach you to love, but I cannot teach you to be wise. Do not fear. I will not tell him why I am leaving. I will only tell him it is my desire to be the permanent captain of *The Ainsley,* and he will be pleased.

"My voyages will be long. I am going to begin the West Indies run. We will take the horses to the Windward Islands and bring back tea and sugar. Between times, I will stay at Marshfield and I will see you, my dear one, for a few days at a time—but that will be all that I can endure."

Chapter Thirty-two

As the white sails carried the ship skimming across the sapphire sea, Talmadge stood at the prow, reflecting again how different the water of the Caribbean was from the waters of the Atlantic. The one so gray and fierce, the other so brilliant and unpredictable.

For over four years now he had been sailing down the coast of the continent, through the windward channel into the Greater Antilles and on to Kingston Harbor.

Through hurricane and gale, through becalmed seas, evading pirates and customs agents, he had steered the fleet and sturdy sloop between Connecticut and Jamaica, bringing his cargo of horses, oxen, and linen, returning with a hold filled with sugar, tea, coffee, and molasses.

Talmadge loved the waterfront, its smells and sounds. Voices of many countries, as rich and decorative as the men and women themselves, rolled around him as he walked the wharf.

In his second year of trading, on a hot Caribbean night, he had met a soft mulatto woman. She was the daughter of a French planter and a slave, and had been raised in the household of her father, educated and loved, but with no legal status. When her father had died she had been thrown out onto the street by his jealous son, who had inherited the estate.

Talmadge had heard her singing in the garden of the home where she worked as a laundress. In his bitter loneliness and manly need, he took her as his mistress. Every year Talmadge spent more time at harbor in Jamaica, spinning out the time when he must purchase his return cargo and sail back north to Nathan, Marshfield, and Ainsley, where nothing seemed to change. He could only endure a few weeks of Ainsley's proximity. His passion for her remained as strong as when he had first known her. The years had not changed Ainsley—except to make her lovelier.

Clothilde's skin was as soft as doeskin, and her eyes like chocolate. On evenings when Talmadge was sad or bored, she played the pianoforte for him and sang in her clear, true voice. He heard the cry of all humankind in the springing sadness and beauty of her music.

"You do not love me, I know, Talmadge," Clothilde told him as they lay together with the warm Caribbean breezes coming into the room on the moonlight. "You love another, and she has all of your heart. Someday she will love you in return, and then you will leave me forever. But I will not be sad. I will be happy for you—because you have been kind to me.

"I will say a prayer and make a charm so that your cold northern girl will grow warm and love you."

But each time he returned from his voyages and entered the house at Marshfield, he felt Ainsley's presence smite him like a blow and every other memory was swept away. Clothilde, as lovely as she was, was like a summer flower, gone from his heart, and only Ainsley remained, like the splendor of a great tree, unmovable and unshakable.

He told himself, cruelly, that Ainsley was growing older. But the ruse did not work because her face became more beautiful to him with the passing years. All the years she had spent caring for the needs of others showed in the gracious intelligence of her glorious smile.

Still, he could see in her eyes the vivid vitality, the daring impulsiveness that made her full of delightful unexpectedness.

"You will never age," Talmadge told her one night as they sat talking over the supper table upon his return. He could not keep himself from staring at her face.

"That is the truth," Nathan agreed, laughing. "As you can see, my hair has turned to silver, and, although Ainsley is but a girl compared to me, still, look at her hair. I swear, 'tis more full of fire today than it was when she fell on me from the apple tree!"

Ainsley raised a self-conscious hand to her head and smoothed her hair down carefully. "You ought not to tease me about my hair. I cannot help its color, and it has been a mighty trial to me through the years. I ought to have worn it powdered, and you, sir, are fortunate in that you will no longer need to powder yours at all."

Talmadge laughed out loud. "She has you there, Father. I

would not trade barbs with this one, if I were you. She is altogether too adept a swordswoman."

There was pain in Talmadge's laughter. How could he sit across the table looking at her, knowing she would be but a few steps away as he went to bed. Knowing she slept alone, and would sleep alone forever unless some mad and unthinkable thing should make his father wake up and see her as she really was—see the passion she had stored up through the years for him alone.

Looking over at his father, Talmadge realized the likelihood of that happening was very small. Over the years Nathan had changed very little. His shoulders were unbowed and he still walked with the spring of a young man. His face, still strong but lined and heavier, seemed even more handsome and powerful framed by the white hair.

However, the years of responsibility and heavy, unshared concerns had placed their mark on his father's features. They held a steely determination, a heavy awareness of duty and reliance that made his father think little of himself or his personal life. This was not a man who was open to passion, or a new assessment of old feelings. Poor Ainsley, Talmadge thought, he will never look closely enough to really see her.

"Now you must tell me the news of Marshfield and New Parrish," Talmadge encouraged.

"I wish there were news," his father growled. "We are still saddled with Reverend Witherspoon. Each time we try to unseat him the wily minister goes about the parish preaching such damnation that he strikes the fear of God into all who would stand against him. The man causes more discord and distress than can be measured. His sermons are like a cane beating."

Ainsley laughed. "The townsfolk of New Parrish take their sins to heart on Sundays. They are most conscious of their neighbors' trespasses, feeling it their duty to bring their neighbors' sins to the attention of the body as a whole, but they somehow have the happy facility of overlooking their own.

"I do somewhat feel that Reverend Witherspoon warms particularly to this task of uncloaking sinners. I am not sure if it is the fact that, as minister, he is not required to pay any taxes, or the fact that he can verbally and emotionally flog the wrongdoer, which makes him cling to his calling with such incredible tenacity."

"Either way," Nathan sighed, "the man retains considerable power and I am beginning to despair that we shall ever unseat him."

Later in the evening, Nathan took Talmadge into his office and Talmadge reported on the profitability of his latest voyage. "We have made good money each year on our West Indies trade," Talmadge remarked. "I visited John Windsor and he is not looking well. The establishment at Windsor Point is becoming run down. Have you talked to John recently?"

Nathan shook his head. "I have been so busy with other matters. You make me aware that I have been neglectful. I shall send Ainsley to bring him to Marshfield for a long visit."

"Father," Talmadge said carefully, "why do you continue to run the inn? Surely the produce of Marshfield and the profits of our trade supply more than enough money for our wants. You could simplify your life considerably if you closed the inn and made Marshfield your home—nothing more."

Nathan looked up at his son. "I have very little money, Talmadge, very little currency. I need the inn for my cash needs."

"But the money from our exports! The passage money! The sale of harvest goods, the returns on the horses—how could you not have money, more than enough to spare?" Talmadge exclaimed.

"Land," Nathan said. "Land. I am buying every piece of New Parrish that comes on the market. All these small landholders who have wasted every worldly farthing to buy unproductive land—land that never should have been sold as farm land—I am buying it from them, giving them enough to start again."

"But I don't understand, Father," Talmadge protested. "Why would you buy unproductive land?"

"Because it is the land that matters," Nathan explained. "This township is located in the crossroads of a dozen different hubs—it will find its own reasons for being. People will come here. They will live here for the convenience, for the beauty, for the air, for the place itself. And the land will be coveted. I know this, Talmadge. Now is the time to gather it in."

"Even if it leaves us impoverished?" Talmadge challenged.

"It will make your children giants," Nathan said, looking out of the window across the night-filled world. "It is my gift to them. The children—my grandchildren—which you will have."

Talmadge stood up abruptly and walked to the door. He did not understand all the reasons for his anger and distress; he only knew he had to leave the room. As he opened the door, he turned and looked at his father with stern and angry eyes.

"Have your own children," Talmadge said, his eyes stormy with conflicting emotions.

The next week Talmadge left on another extended voyage.

Three years passed with little to mark their passing except that John Windsor died. He died at Marshfield where he had lived the last year of his life while Ebenezer and Brosian managed the shrinking business at Windsor Point.

Ainsley cared for her father tenderly. In his last years he took great pleasure in sitting at the end of the front path of Marshfield where the road crossed, and talking to the neighbors, travelers, peddlers, and children who passed by.

To the end, he remained as cheerful and caring of others as though he were still the warm and gracious proprietor of his once-thriving establishment.

"I've loved my life, you know, Ainsley child," he told her one day as she sat beside him. He was wrapped in a warm woolen shawl, his white, sparse hair hidden by a pointed cap with a silken tassle hanging over his shoulder. "The only thing I have not liked was being alone all of these years, and, now, I have the hope of being with your mother again. Death comes to me as a friend. My next great adventure."

He saw the tears flowing down Ainsley's cheeks into the basket of peas she cradled in her lap.

"Here now, dear daughter, no one wants that much salt in their vegetables. Dry your eyes. You shall miss me, yes, but you are not to mourn for me. I will be happy and waiting for you." John's eyes seemed to have become larger and brighter as the sickness which was consuming him made him smaller.

"No, dear one, it is you for whom I mourn. To have spent so many years of your youth alone. So sad. When so many have yearned to give you love, and a home and a family. How can I go and leave you thus? It is my one sorrow." John bowed his head, wearied from talking.

Ainsley leaped up and knelt before her father, putting her arms around him, "Oh, dear Father, do not think I am alone. I have Marshfield. It is like a living thing to me. I care for Marshfield because, in some comforting and wonderful way, I feel like I am caring for Nathan. He has closed himself away from every other personal feeling, Father, and yet I cannot walk away from him. I cannot stop loving him."

"But my dear, dear girl," John whispered, "I hear in your voice that you have given up hope. Perhaps you do not love him after all. I have always thought that Talmadge loved you, my dear."

"The years have passed, Papa," Ainsley said, weeping. "Too many things have been said and unsaid. Even if he did love me once, I do not think he could forgive or forget. No, Papa, I think I will end up as I always feared—alone."

She nodded her head, and together they wept. That night as the pain kept John Windsor awake, he determined to himself that he would speak to Nathan the next day. All the years of silence seemed pointless and foolish to him now.

When Ainsley came in with his light breakfast he pushed the tray away. "I can eat nothing," he whispered. "It causes too much pain. Will you call Nathan for me, and leave the two of us alone?" he asked.

Reaching for her father's hand, Ainsley sat by the bedside. "Nathan has gone to Stamford to fetch another doctor. We are hoping . . ."

John smiled fondly. "The time for hope is long away. What a pity that I should miss my chance to say farewell to Nathan. The good Lord must care for both of you. I will see to it that He does when I meet Him. If it be His will. And . . . if your mother agrees . . ." John's voice vanished into the air like a puff of morning mist, and with it his great, warm, loving soul. He died with a sweet smile lighting his face, as though he had just caught a glimpse of someone very dear to him.

After the year of mourning, Nathan helped Ainsley sell the property at Windsor Point—except for the inn and the dock. She emptied the inn of all the most beautiful furniture, linens, clocks, and dishes, and carefully packed away her mother's things.

The dock and the dwindling supply business, and the inn were given to Brosian and Ebenezer in John's will. The two men were enough to run the business in its diminished size, and it provided a comfortable and steady trade for them. Ainsley inherited John's share of Marshfield Inn, so she and Nathan were now partners.

The inn at Marshfield continued to thrive, and the more Nathan was involved in the business of the community, the more the details of running the estate—the farms, the cottage industries, the inn, and the accounts—fell on Ainsley's shoulders. Nathan had accepted her as a full and established partner; when they were discussing business problems she sometimes had the feeling that he had forgotten she was a woman.

One night, after a long day of dealing with threshing crews and kitchen-supply problems, Ainsley walked into her cottage. Widow Tilden, who had lived there with her had long since gone her own way, and, since gossip was no longer a concern, Ainsley had simply not replaced her.

Walking into her bedroom, Ainsley began to undress wearily. The hand mirror on her dressing table caught the reflection of her candle, and she glanced over at the unexpected flash of light. As she did so, she saw her face and naked shoulders framed in the oval of the glass.

Without thinking, she picked up the mirror and held it so that she could see herself. The face that stared back at her looked surprisingly fresh and young, as though it did not belong to the tired, woman who stood in the room.

Since the death of Daniel, the departure of Talmadge, the death of her dear father, and the long strain of Nathan's indifference, she had stopped thinking of herself as a woman. But here, in the gentle night, she saw that she was still a young *woman,* only in her thirties, with skin that bore no marks of her years, and hair the color of autumn leaves, and a body as lithe, untouched, and smooth as a young birch, its branches peeled and white.

She ran her hands over her hips and her rounded breasts. "Oh the waste of it!" she wept. "The waste of it all. The long, long years. Will this body, this heart, remain forever empty? I think I have been old since the day I was born—but I am young—still young—and bedeviled by my errant heart. Oh, what am I to do?"

Chapter Thirty-three

Alice!" Ainsley's voice was sharper than she had intended. "I asked you to finish the upstairs rooms before noon. Why are you here in the kitchen lolligagging? We are going to be unprepared for the evening's guests."

Without a word, Alice rose from the edge of the table where she was nibbling on a piece of bread and sipping a small glass of milk. "Yes, ma'am," she said, moving toward the door. Suddenly the young woman clutched her hand to her mouth and ran out into the yard. Ainsley followed to find her retching into the slop pail.

"Why on earth didn't you tell me you were sick!" Ainsley exclaimed. "I'll have one of the men take you home. Just stay in bed for a few days until you feel better."

"Oh, no, ma'am!" the girl exclaimed, her face white with alarm and illness. "Please don't send me home. My papa will be angry."

"Why should he be angry with you for being ill?" Ainsley asked. "It is certainly not your fault."

At this the girl's face turned a deep scarlet, and she averted her eyes. "I shall be all right, ma'am," Alice whispered. "Just give me a few minutes and I will be back to my work."

"Very well," Ainsley agreed. She walked away, puzzled and disturbed by the conversation.

In the next weeks Ainsley noted Alice's struggle to continue her normal schedule. Several times she noticed the girl turn white and dash from the room. Once she saw her faint in the backyard as she was hanging out the linens. Mrs. Seeley helped the girl to her feet and gave her a glass of water, but said nothing. There was a sense of quiet strain among all of the help at the inn, and Alice became more and more quiet, trying to be almost invisible as she shrank from everyone's sight and avoided human contact.

Although her loose pinafore smock hid most of her body, Alice was of such a slight build that it soon came to the point that no one could deny the telltale bulge under her apron. One morning Alice came to work with her face bruised and swollen. She was limping, and her one arm dangled uselessly at her side.

Ainsley was horrified, she drew the girl into her office and asked what had happened. "I was thrown from a horse," the girl whispered.

"Trampled by a horse is more likely," Ainsley said angrily. "A horse with a human hand, since I can see the mark of fingers in the bruises on your wrist."

The girl began to weep. "What shall I do? What shall I do? My papa has told me I may never enter his doorway again. I am the child of the devil, and bring evil and curses to all I touch. He has tried to beat the evil out of me. He has hit me with canes and rods and kicked my stomach, but the evil remains."

Ainsley shuddered, and closed her eyes. "Even if your father changed his mind, I would not let you return to such a home."

"But he is a good father," Alice protested. "When my father first . . . came upon me"— the girl flushed—"he hurt me something fierce. I spoke to the Reverend Witherspoon, and he told me it is the duty of every righteous and God-fearing child to honor and obey her father—whatever he requires. The Reverend told me if I did not submit to my father's will, I would be a sinner and doomed to Satan's eternal fire."

Alice rolled into a heap on the floor. "I have tried so hard. I have not cried out when he comes to me in the dark, or argued, or crossed him in any way. Even when he has hurt me I remembered God and Reverend Witherspoon and I held my tongue.

"Then it began to get worse, Miss Ainsley. I began to feel sick, and father was angrier than ever. He told me the curse had come upon me because I am an evil child. He said I have tempted him with my evilness and that is why I am sick.

"He hates me. He says I am a godless child, and the imp of Satan. Today he told me I was a witch, and that is why my body is beginning to change. It is so ugly. He says evil is growing within me and he must beat it out of me. Evil.

Satan is growing inside of me!" The girl began to cry with terror and pain.

Ainsley was shaking with fury. "There is no evil in you, Alice. No evil in you at all. Whatever evil is in your house is in your father."

"Oh, ma'am, you must not say such things!" Alice pulled away, her eyes huge with fear. "You will be damned—and I will be damned for eternity for listening."

"Mrs. Seeley," Ainsley called, "come and bind Alice's wounds and put her to bed. See that she has everything she needs or wants. Take good care of her. I am going to find Mr. Fairchild."

Nathan was out in the south fields, supervising the shearing of the sheep. Ainsley rode up on her mare at trumpet speed. He turned at the sound of the horse's thudding feet and was amazed to see Ainsley, who had become a quiet and sedate woman, riding hell-bent for leather, with her bonnet fallen to her back and her skirts flapping around her knees.

"Nathan!" she called, "I must speak to you at once."

Alarmed by her peremptory voice, Nathan mounted his horse rapidly and joined her as they galloped back up the ridge track. She reined her horse fiercely by the stile near the lower fence, and jumped off.

"We may talk here in privacy," she declared.

Nathan dismounted beside her, and tied their horses to the stile post. Ainsley began to pace, telling him, as straightforwardly as possible, the plight of the young Alice.

"The poor girl does not even realize she is with child. Her father's. He has abused and mistreated her in every way. Surely there must be some way to protect her. And Reverend Witherspoon, with his angry God and his law-before-mercy religion, is as much to blame as anyone." Ainsley was wringing her hands.

"Who is to protect this young girl if her parents will not. Who would dare to say that the rights of such a father should be honored over the rights of an innocent child? The town does not know yet, but it is only a matter of time. Everyone at the inn suspects. When she is found out, will someone bring that man to account for what he has done to this poor girl?"

Nathan's head was hung low. "No," he said. "A few may have compassion for her in the privacy of their homes, but the church, and the town will not. She will be condemned.

She will be excommunicated and publicly denounced. Her child will be given no name. They both will be deprived of the right to own property, and the child will not be allowed to attend the school.

"Her father will have the right take her back into the house and mete out whatever punishment he chooses, both to her and to the child. He can beat them, starve them, or disown them."

Ainsley was horrified. "Surely not. Surely God's law would not allow an innocent child to suffer for the hideous, evil actions of a vicious sin-ridden father! Surely the sin is his! What will the church do to *him*?"

Nathan shook his head sadly. "Nothing. Oh, if he admitted to the sin he might bear some penance—but he will never admit to it, and there will be no proof. The rights of the parents are immutable in the scriptures, as is the requirement of the obedience of children."

"But the girl could tell people what has happened. She could name the father . . ." Ainsley protested.

"Alice will already have been condemned as a sinner. She will not be allowed as a witness," Nathan replied.

Seeing Ainsley's horror and distress, Nathan put out his arm to steady her. "If I could do anything I would, but it will be an ecclesiastical matter, and the Reverend Witherspoon will brook no interference."

In a fit of fury, Ainsley balled up her fists and beat on Nathan's broad chest. "Do something!" she cried. "Do something! Do something!" Then she broke down in tears and sat on the steps of the stile, weeping in despair.

"The only thing we can do," Nathan said, "is spirit Alice away. But where could we send her? Where could we find someone willing to care for her through this ordeal? Nowhere in Connecticut. The church is everywhere; they would find her out. Perhaps in New York, but I have few contacts there."

He was frowning, trying to think through a solution. "Of course, you know, if we aid her in escaping, her father could bring charges against us, and we could be excommunicated as well."

"I don't care!" Ainsley said fiercely.

"Perhaps not now," Nathan said, "but in a small community such as ours it is a kind of death."

"And not to help someone as helpless and mistreated as Alice," Ainsley retorted, "is also a kind of death."

"Let me think on it further," Nathan said quietly.

With heavy hearts they remounted their horses and rode toward the house. Ainsley, her head drooping in thought, rode close to Nathan, and her leg brushed against his as their horses walked side by side on the narrow bridal path.

She was suddenly reminded of Talmadge and the night he's held her in his arms under the oak tree. Her heart shook with unfulfilled desires, and she felt herself empty and unloved.

Her green eyes were wide with her desperate and unexpected feelings. She had imagined herself quieted and under control, and yet, at the most innocent touch, her heart was racing.

To her relief, Nathan continued riding, his face remote and unchanged, seemingly unaware of the contact, or even of her presence.

When they arrived at the inn, Mrs. Seeley came rushing toward them through the kitchen garden, her apron flapping and her mob cap askew. "Enos Huck has come and taken Alice home. Dragged her out of her sick bed and threw her into his pony cart. We tried to stop him, but she wouldn't stay. She kept talking about being damned if she didn't honor her father . . ."

Mr. Seeley, the inn's stablemaster, was standing by the road, his heavy, muscular hands balled in two impotent fists. "The man hit her twice, hard, against the face. Her own father. Said she was not fit to be with God-fearing folk, and he would denounce the devil within her. Calvin's face contorted with anger. "Huck is a huge man. She looked like a little child by the side of him."

Nathan did not even dismount. "I will go at once," he said. "Perhaps Enos will listen to me."

Mrs. Seeley was weeping into her apron. "Such a sweet little thing, Alice was. Hard working and cheerful. She loved the inn, and was so proud to be taking home her little wage. Hoped it would make life easier for her mother and the younger children—and she scarce more than a child herself, and innocent as they come."

"A child," Ainsley murmured, her heart full of pain. "How old do you think Alice is, Mrs. Seeley?"

"I know for a fact how old, Mistress Ainsley. She was

twelve year old when she came to work for us as a kitchen maid, and that was going on three years ago." Mrs. Seeley nodded her head in confirmation of what she was saying.

"Fifteen, or thereabouts, then," Ainsley said.

"Aye, in years," Mrs. Seeley answered, "but younger than that in most ways." Mrs. Seeley blushed. "She knows little of the ways of a man with a woman. She is quiet and shy as a dormouse, and I tell you, I believe she does not have any idea what is wrong with her."

Mrs. Seeley's eyes darkened to an angry steel. "But that evil father knows, and that's for sure. Knows it's his babe, and is afraid the world will know too."

Shuddering, Mrs. Seeley turned away. "He wishes he could make the girl invisible so that his dastardly sin could be invisible as well."

At Mrs. Seeley's words, a shaft of alarm went through Ainsley's heart. "He could hide her. He could imprison her in that awful house of theirs. He could send her away—and no one could stop him. No one. He could even . . ." Ainsley took a deep shuddering breath. ". . . kill her." The words came out as a horrified whisper, and Mrs. Seeley merely nodded her head in assent.

Slapping her mare with the reins, Ainsley took off from the Marshfield gate at a thundering gallop. She had to catch Nathan and demand that, whatever Enos Huck said, the girl would be given over into their custody.

She found herself thinking about the baby. They could hide Alice at the inn. By the look of her, it would be only a few months until the baby would be born, and then, oh, they would care for the infant. They could say it was a foundling, and she could help raise it.

At the thought of the unborn baby, Ainsley began to cry. As she galloped the wind caught her tears and flung them into the air like sparks struck from shod hooves. A baby at Marshfield. A baby to love and raise.

Chapter Thirty-four

Ainsley had never been to the Hucks' farm, although she knew where it was located. The track to the farmhouse was hidden in a scrag of unruly trees and undergrowth which had never been properly cleared.

Although the Huck family attended services regularly, aside from the Sabbath day they were seldom seen in the community. Enos Huck did any shopping that needed to be done at the supply store in the center of the emerging town of New Parrish.

He was a surly man and did not speak to anyone unless there was a specific matter to be discussed. Often he was embroiled in arguments with his neighbors over disputed animals or land rights.

His acreage was on a low rise called Arrowhead Ridge because of the abundance of arrowheads found in the soil. It was believed that a hundred years before, when the great Cronus, sachem of the indigenous tribes, had been the leader of the Indians in this area, Arrowhead Ridge had been a summer campground.

Certainly the ridge was aptly named, because it was little more than a garden of stones, with only the thinnest layer of topsoil covering the granite beneath. Shrub trees, barberries, wild grape and sumac gave the land the illusion of fertility, but in reality the meager, rocky soil could barely be scraped into a subsistence.

Brother Enos Huck wore on his face the same stoniness as his soil. He was quick to judge and accuse others, and he held himself with rigid pride. His family dressed in the humblest of homespun, their shoes home-cobbled and heavy and their faces as joyless as fog.

Ainsley had noticed that Mistress Huck was pale and silent, and as she rode toward the Huck farm, Ainsley realized she had never heard the woman speak a word. The wife

seemed nothing more than a shadow at the side of the huge
and bitter presence of her husband.

Somehow, with flattery and prudery, Enos Huck had won
the confidence of the Reverend Witherspoon, and Enos's unbending propriety and proud appearance of devotion to the
commandments, the family's poverty and their demeaning
humility, were often used by the Reverend as examples to
the congregation.

Who would think, Ainsley thought with disgust, that
under such burning rectitude there lay such unbelieveable
evil. What kind of a father, using the words of Scripture,
would force a young daughter to lie with him, and when a
child was conceived, use the Scripture to justify beatings
and accusations against the innocent girl?

In despair, Ainsley realized that even if they were able to
rescue Alice from her family, her mind and spirit, damaged
by so many years of abuse, might well be beyond repair.

The baby might be damaged as well. Ainsley urged her
mare to run faster. The overhanging trees snatched at her
hair, and the sun had begun to fade. It was almost evening.

Ahead of her she could see the pitiful one-story structure
that served as home to Enos Huck and his family of seven.
It had a forlorn, unkempt look. The garden was straggly, the
plants barely alive, and no flowers or shrubs softened the
walk or doorway.

Although the air was chilly, no smoke came from the central chimney and the small windows were uncurtained. It
was, thought Ainsley, the most unwelcoming home she had
ever seen.

As she rounded the bend, Nathan exited the house, slamming the door behind him, and leaped up onto his horse. The
anger and distress in his face was thunderous, and Ainsley
hurried to meet him.

They reined their horses on the pathway and Ainsley
called across the sound of the impatient, prancing hoofs.

"What says Enos? Will he let Alice come to us?" Ainsley
asked anxiously.

"No," Nathan answered, rapping out the word in fury.
"The man is impossible! You cannot reason with him, or
even reach him. He is furious that we have interfered, and I
fear if we do any more Alice will simply be made to suffer
for our actions.

"She is confined to the loft, and I was not permitted to see her. I don't even know if she is still alive."

Horrified, Ainsley groped for words. "Did you accuse him? Did you tell him we know the truth? That it is his child? Did you tell him we would bring the law . . ."

Nathan shook his head. "What law?" he asked bitterly. "He knows we have no legal rights in this matter. She is his daughter, and this is a moral trangression. Only the church may judge—and he is more than willing to turn her over to the judgment of Reverend Witherspoon."

"What do you mean?" Ainsley gasped, fearing the fury in his tone.

"I mean that if she is still alive, she will be brought before the congregation on Sunday. I have no doubt her father will accuse her, and Reverend Witherspoon will read her out of her covenants, and she will be publicly shamed and destroyed. Oh, her body may live on, but she will be a nonperson, with no rights or regard. Her father can then, literally, do whatever he wishes."

Nathan's voice was filled with bitterness and disgust. "The evil that men do in the name of religion and government should be branded on their foreheads like the scar on humanity that it is."

"And you will do nothing?" Ainsley asked furiously. "You will let this happen?"

"No," Nathan said. "But I cannot fly in the face of church law. Even if we attacked the Hucks' farm with the Train Band and spirited Alice away, we have no place to protect or hide her. Her father would insist on his legal as well as his ecclesiastical rights and we would be arrested and perhaps imprisoned. We would be kidnappers, and she, when he found her, would be a runaway, a fornicator, and an unconvenanted child. Her life would be hell."

Ainsley knew that Nathan spoke the truth. Impulsiveness would only create more tragedy. She hung her head and, once again, they rode together toward the inn, each deep in thought.

Finally Nathan raised his head. "On Sunday, when they accuse her, I shall rise and accuse Enos Huck publicly. The charges will not stick, for there is no proof except Alice's word, and she may be too frightened to repeat the charge.

"You know, of course, Ainsley, that the congregation will not—cannot—accept the word of a flagrant sinner as evidence. Her father, of course, will deny the accusations and say she is a wanton fornicator who is adding dishonor and lies against her father to her list of sins."

Ainsley shook her head wearily, anxious to be home in her own quiet cottage, to pray for the blessing of sleep to wipe out the sorrow of this day. "I do not wish to be in the church on this Sabbath. We shall surely see things which would make Our Lord weep."

The Congregational meetinghouse was packed on Sunday. Reverend Witherspoon delivered an hour and a half of sermon on the wickedness of the human heart. He spoke passionately of the temptations of the flesh. In the midst of his sermon he discussed the fleshpots of New Parrish. Ainsley was horrified to realize that he was including the inns of the community on the list of places that harbored evil and sin.

"Strange men who travel our roads, lie on fresh linens laid out for them by our tender young maidens who in their hearts carry the coiled serpent of Eden. These men, who see the lust in the maidens' eyes, who, as in the Songs of Solomon, lust after the golden goblets of their breasts, and like the deer upon the mountains, take their pleasure at forbidden streams, leaving the fruit of their evil behind.

"Oh, ye men and women, sinners all, you who prosper in our midst and think the Lord does not see behind your silks and satins, behind your fine tables and rich trappings, know this, and know it well—he sees all, and I, as His servant, see all, too. I know you, and I condemn your secret sins.

"Yea, the Lord seeth your secret ways, and He shall make them known to all. Your whited sepulchres shall be opened and the filth of your lives shall be shown to the light of day." Reverend Witherspoon's voice thundered into the vaulted ceiling from the high pulpit, to the very last pews on the back galleries. The congregation had heard whispers of Alice Huck's awful condition. Knowing her father's righteous rigidity, the parishoners knew there would be no understanding or forgiveness for the girl in her own home.

There were also rumors of Enos Huck being the father of the unborn baby, but few, knowing his reputation for meticulous and vociferous morality, gave the rumors any credence. Still, there was a heavy sense of ghastly anticipation in the meeting hall as the sermon came to an end.

With a voice like the wrath of God, the minister called Alice Huck to stand before the congregation. Throughout the services Ainsley kept glancing at the young girl. She seemed to have shrunk in the three days since Ainsley had last seen her.

For a shocked moment, Ainsley thought this could not be the same girl as the sweet, kind-hearted, golden-haired child who had begun working at the inn three years ago. She remembered Alice's pink, smiling face, the clear blue eyes, the quiet, gentle manner. On occasion Ainsley recalled having looked out the window to see the young girl hanging the sheets, her face as rosy as the sun as she drank in the wind, the air, and the freedom of her outdoor task.

Now Alice sat shrinking against her mother, whose face remained expressionless. Alice's face bore a livid bruise, and one eye was almost shut. The girl's skin was so pale that the bruise was the only color on it, and she was so thin that her bones seemed as transparent as her skin.

Haltingly, Alice tore herself away from her mother's side, and, shrinking from the eyes fixed on her with curiosity, scorn, and kindness, she moved slowly down the aisle, pulling the brown fabric of her homespun cloak around her body until she was completely concealed from the prying eyes.

Tiny and terrified, with her head sunk to her chest, she stood in front of the church. Alice was trembling so hard that Ainsley wondered that she could remain on her feet. How dare they? Ainsley raged to herself. No man would ever be treated thusly. Where was the justice? Where was the compassion and love of the Savior? Certainly not in the hearts of anyone in that room.

She wanted to leap to her feet and shout in defense of the young girl, but caution told her that that would only make matters worse. No woman was given to speak in the meetinghouse, and she would seal the hatred of the men against the young girl if she championed her cause.

"Who accuses this woman?" the minister intoned.

Enos Huck leaped to his feet. "I do. I, her father. She has defiled my home with her sins. She has tempted and lain with men, and now she bears the seed of the devil within her. Though I have taught her the word of the Lord, and have taught her by the rod, still she has become a spoiled vessel to the Lord and a shame and an example of unrighteousness to our parrish."

At this, Nathan rose to his feet. "I speak in her defense,

Reverend Witherspoon. This young and innocent girl has not sinned, but has been sinned against by the very man who accuses her."

A great gasp went up from the congregation, and suddenly the meeting was alive with voices. Ainsley sat listening as the men accused and counteraccused—as men shouted for a hearing and for proof of the dastardly accusation.

Finally, the Reverend Witherspoon roared in a commanding voice for order. Ainsley had been watching Alice. The girl stood as though she were asleep, unmoving except for the trembling, never lifting her voice or changing her stance.

"Brother Fairchild has made a most dastardly and vicious accusation," Reverend Witherspoon declared. "Do you have proof?" Nathan shook his head. The Reverend frowned. "Were the accusation against anyone other than our most righteous and upstanding brother, Enos Huck, we might pursue it further. But, as it is, Brother Huck has suffered enough through the evil transgressions of this child.

"Since it is only her lies which accuse him, and she is motivated by unholy anger against her father for his loving desire to restrain her into the paths of righteousness, we will not give any credence to such vile accusations, Master Fairchild, and would caution you that they not be repeated until you have some measure of proof."

There was a long pause, and then the Reverend Witherspoon said in a menacing tone, "There are those who might want to look at the doings at Marshfield more closely, since the inn is the place where this young sinner, this evil Magdalene, has been employed."

The vicious implication in the minister's voice ran like a shock through Ainsley, and she leaped to her feet, but Nathan grabbed her hand and pulled her down. "Let it pass," he whispered. "Tempers are too high, and emotions too inflated. No good may be accomplished here today. We will find a way."

Reverend Witherspoon turned to Alice. Her shoulders bespoke her exhaustion and pain. She would not raise her eyes to meet any gaze, but stood, beaten and humiliated. "Will you speak the name of the real father of your child?" Reverend Witherspoon thundered. "Lay to rest this vicious rumor you have started and speak the truth."

Alice raised her head, her eyes as blank as slate, and

Ainsley thought she would never see a face of more tragedy in her life.

With a pathetic attempt to show pride and courage, Alice stood straight and looked at the congregation. With a gasp, Ainsley saw that the girl was missing three teeth. They must have been knocked out when her father struck the blow that had bruised her face.

"Thou sayest," the girl said clearly. Ainsley began to weep. Those were the words the Savior had used before His accusors.

Unable to restrain herself any longer, Ainsley stood. "Reverend Witherspoon, would it be acceptable, since Alice has been accused and denounced by her father, if I took her in as a ward? Surely her family would be well rid of the matter. The congregation need concern itself no more."

Enos Huck leaped to his feet. "And what of punishment?" he shouted. "If she is coddled, pitied, and cared for, will not all of our young people think that sinful behavior brings rewards? No. Ours is the shame. Ours is the responsibility. We alone shall cleanse and purify this daughter of the evil which is within her. It is our godly duty. We do not shrink from the task. May this be a lesson to all."

Beaming his approval, Reverend Witherspoon nodded to Enos Huck. "Such is the will of God and of this congregation." He turned to Alice.

"Go!" thundered the minister, his great, robed arm rising like the black wing of a menacing bird of prey. "Go! daughter of sin. You may never step through the door of this sacred house of the Lord again. You may never enjoy sweet communion with those of the elect. You have made for yourself a bed of silken revelry, and it shall wrap around you like the winding sheet of hell, and pull you to the depths of damnation."

The shudder that passed through Alice's small body was hideous to see, and Ainsley, Nathan, and the whole congregation watched in morbid, wrenching silence as the young girl stumbled, unseeing, down the long aisle and out the doors.

Her father immediately rose and, with a peremptory wave of his hand, beckoned his family to follow. He walked from the meetinghouse with a look of such sanctimonious suffering on his harsh face that Ainsley wanted to throw herself at him and scratch his eyes out.

Everything in her cried for justice. She leaped to her feet and pushed herself through the crush of people now heading for the doors. When she burst through into the churchyard, she saw the Hucks alone, apart from the rest of the departing members, as isolated as though they were surrounded by an invisible circle.

Ainsley ran to the cluster of the family and pushed herself in front of Enos Huck. "You don't want her," Ainsley said desperately. "She is a source of shame and discomfort to your whole family. Let me take care of her. I shall see that she is sent away. You will never have to see her or the child . . ."

In fury, Enos Huck placed his face close to Ainsley's and spoke with malice and menace. "This is none of your affair. None. It is my family. My daughter. I will do as I please, and no high-prancing, uppity, foolish, covenant-scoffing woman, who does not know—and never will know—her rightful place, is going to speak to me of this matter.

"I am within my rights, and if you, or that Nathan Fairchild, make one more move to touch my Alice, I will tell the world a thing or two—and it will be you who stand before the congregation."

Ainsley stepped back from the unconcealed viciousness of the man's fanatic eyes. "You can't frighten or threaten me, Enos Huck," she replied. "Something can be done."

With rage, Enos began striding down the street and his family flew after him like frightened chicks. Alice would not meet Ainsley's eyes, but followed after the others, trailing their steps.

"We'll do something, Alice!" Ainsley called after her. "Don't despair!" The girl turned at the last moment, and pulling the hood from her face, she gave Ainsley a smile of such sweet friendship and gratitude that Ainsley thought her heart would break.

Ainsley rode home in the brougham with the Seeleys. When she arrived at the inn, the simple, cold Sabbath meal was laid out but she had no appetite. Nathan came in much later, his face dark with anger.

"I have spent an hour with the Reverend Witherspoon, but cannot get the man to bend or listen. Enos Huck has him completely convinced—and he will not even weigh my arguments. He used the Bible against me like a battering ram." Nathan was frustrated beyond control.

"Then I visited with each of the town committee, and the venerable founding fathers have declared the situation a matter of church discipline and ecclesiastical court and will not have anything to do with it.

"They are terrified lest Alice's moral turpitude invade their own families. Truth to tell, many feel real sympathy for the girl—and more than a few are suspicious of the father—but none of them know how to do battle against the moral law of the church any more than do we." Nathan sighed. "Would that we had a more compassionate minister. This matter will divide the congregation and the town. Mark my words."

"I do not care about the congregation or the town," Ainsley exclaimed. "It is that poor, mistreated girl for whom my heart is broken. We must help her, Nathan. If you could have seen the last look she gave me. I will never forget it. She sees us as her only hope."

"Yes, we must try. However, tomorrow I ride to New Haven," Nathan said. "There is much unrest. The British have imposed new taxes, and French privateers are still stinging the coastal shipping. Tariffs and taxes are getting so stiff that Talmadge is once again having to evade the customs collectors as well as the hazards of the open sea.

"The General Court sustains our independent Connecticut constitution and still maintains loyalty to the crown, but the cause of the colonies and the cause of the mother country are becoming separate—and the conflict is almost insupportable. I smell rebellion in the air."

"Surely not!" Ainsley exclaimed. "Surely there is a way of compromise and mutual support. We have fought for the British. We are English as well as colonists."

"But the English think not," Nathan said bitterly. "We have never been considered as equals. We are governed without representation, we are taxed without the benefit of the use of those taxes, and we are ignored and slighted at every turn. No, men will not live thus for long."

A chill ran through Ainsley. "So, Nathan, you suspect another war. That is why you have kept the Train Band active through all these years."

Nathan nodded. "That, and the fact that marching is the only thing this town has ever learned to do in step with one another."

They both laughed, but there was a touch of bitter sorrow in their laughter.

"I promise you, Ainsley, that the first day when I get home next week, I shall go to Enos Huck and have this matter out. Whatever it takes—threats, money, promises—I will give him in order to free Alice to our care. While I am gone, do nothing to aggravate the situation. Promise me." Nathan gave her a firm look, knowing her vigorous and decisive nature. "Nothing," he reiterated.

Reluctantly, Ainsley assented.

The week passed slowly. Ainsley had hoped that Alice would drop by. There was a sense of unease in the town. When Ainsley and Mrs. Seeley went to the milliner's to pick up some morning caps and aprons that had been made for the staff at the inn, they could feel the stiffness in their friends and neighbors.

An odd hush seemed to have fallen on the community, as though they were waiting for some sound, some signal, some resolution to the tragic events of the Sabbath. Groups of women stood whispering on the corners and men rode their wagons or strode down the roads with grim and silent expressions on their faces.

Few young people or children were outside playing in the yards or on the thoroughfares. It was as though their parents feared some foul contamination, like a moral smallpox, had spread from the sorrows of Alice's sin, and they did not want their children infected.

As long as she could, Ainsley restrained herself as Nathan had told her she must. By Friday the strain was too much. She gathered up some bottles of fruit and preserves and fresh loaves baked in the morning's oven.

"I am off to neighbor Huck's for a friendly visit," she told Mrs. Seeley, ignoring that woman's look of warning. "Please see to the guests until I return."

Ainsley saddled up the gig and wore her most sedate dress, with her hair smoothed under a simple, dark bonnet and a cloak covering her shoulders. She hoped she looked serious and mature—old, even, if it would help the matter.

It was early afternoon as she drove up the neglected track to the Huck homestead. No smoke rose from the chimney, but in one of the far, stone-fenced fields she could see Enos and three of his young sons scything the sparse crop of hay.

One bedraggled chicken pecked listlessly in the weed-clogged yard. The house was silent. Ainsley rapped on the front door and, after a long wait, the door opened a crack and Alice's youngest sister, a child of three or four years, peeked out.

"Hello," Ainsley said quietly, bending toward the child. "I have come to see Alice. Is she home?"

The child was silent, but her eyes opened wider and she backed away from the door. Ainsley reached out and pushed gently on the door, which swung open widely enough to reveal Alice's mother sitting in a rocking chair, working a drop spindle and spinning a thread of coarse flax.

Mistress Huck looked at Ainsley and there was no escaping the fear in her eyes. "You mustn't come here, Mistress," she whispered. "You'd best leave before Master Huck comes from the fields. He will be most fiercely angry to know you are here."

"I have just come as a neighbor," Ainsley said softly. "I have brought some preserves and bread for your evening meal, and hope to visit Alice. Is she well?"

The woman's eyes darted back and forth as though looking for escape. "You can't leave food here. My husband will not allow it. He wants us to have nothing to do with you—or anyone else. We are shamed, and it would be a kindness to let us alone."

"No," Ainsley responded. "Alice is but a child. A child who is going to have a child. It is sad, but it is not a thing of shame to her or you. And the baby should be given a chance—it has done no wrong either. Let me be Alice's friend. Let me be your friend. I can help."

By now the woman was frantic. "You must not talk to me!" she said, leaving her work and coming to Ainsley. "I must close the door and you must leave."

"Just let me see her. Let me speak to her, and I'll be gone," Ainsley promised.

The woman, obviously terrified, looked out toward the hay field. Apparently Enos Huck, so involved in the labor of haying, had not as yet observed the carriage in the dooryard.

"Go now before he comes!" Mrs. Huck exclaimed.

"Only after I see Alice," Ainsley stubbornly insisted.

The woman hung her head in sorrow. "She has been banished to the barn. She is not allowed in the house."

Horrified, Ainsley looked over at the ramshackle, two-story structure at the back of the property. The building was

surrounded by the muck and mud of the tramping farm animals, and the stench of their refuse was carried on the air.

The timbers of the barn were ill fitted and gaps of daylight showed between the planks. The roof was thinly shin-
gled, and she could see where several shingles were missing.
Any shelter to be found in such a building would be cold
and inadequate at best, to say nothing of the demeaning sur-
roundings and the awful isolation.

With quick steps, Ainsley picked up her simple gifts and
hurried toward the structure. It was hard going to walk
through the barnyard, and her skirts and boots were thoroughly muddied before she entered the gaping opening that
served as a door and walked into the cold, foul-smelling in-
terior.

In the shadows the only light were the streaks of thin sunlight that strained through the cracks in the walls.

"Alice!" she called. In one of the stalls in the dirt and hay,
she saw a nest of torn blankets and a small raggedy doll
made from corncob and quilting scraps. The sight of the doll
wrung her heart.

"Alice," she called again, and then, not caring about the
consequences, she added, "I have come to take you home."

Still there was no answer, and the barn seemed brooding,
filled with the rustling sounds of the mice in the hay and the
cooing of doves in the rafters. A dove fluttered down, and
Ainsley, startled by the sound and the fan of the feathers,
glanced upward and saw Alice.

She screamed, and then screamed again and again, until it
was somebody else's voice screaming. Until all the world
was screaming. Until the doves fluttered and wheeled and
whirled, terrified in the cool, dark air, and the smell of the
stables, the pigs, the cows, and the madness of the whole
wide world was caught in the awful sight and sound of the
barn.

Alice was hanging from the center rafter. She had fashioned a rope from her homespun cloak, and her small, young
body, with its tragic burden heavy in her belly, swung silently in the mote-spangled, dusty streaks of light, while the
birds winged about her like small angels trying to lift her to
paradise.

Not knowing how she got there, Ainsley returned to the
inn and brought back a crew of men from her fields. They

cut down Alice's body in front of the Huck family, who were standing as though turned to salt. Enos Huck was silent as they gently wrapped Alice in the beautiful shawl that Ainsley had brought and placed her carefully in the back of the wagon.

Without a word to anyone, Ainsley drove the wagon away from the farm. Watching them go, Enos took five strides toward the barn door, preparing to shout at the woman whom he hated beyond reason. His face was purple with rage, hate, and madness, but as he opened his mouth, he felt as though a blast of lightning struck his forehead. A searing pain ripped down the side of his face, his right arm and leg, and he fell, like an axed tree, into the mud of the barnyard.

Alice, unconvenanted and excommunicated, could not be buried in the New Parrish graveyard, and so she was buried in a plot of land which Nathan had fenced as the burying plot for those of the Marshfield household. It was a beautiful spot at the very brow of the ridge, under the spreading arms of a vast maple tree that hung like a green canopy over the white gravestones in the summer, and like a cloak of crimson in the autumn. In the winter, the spot, bathed in the whiteness of the snow, commanded a distant view of the sparkling waters of the winter sound.

Here rested Daniel Cothran and John Windsor, and now, with sorrow, the body of Alice Huck and her unborn child of incest. On the gravestone Ainsley had carved the words, "She has laid down her burdens."

When Nathan arrived home and heard the tragic news, he was grim-faced. Without a word he went out of the house, and within hours had returned.

"The Hucks are leaving New Parrish," he told Ainsley. "Enos has had a stroke and is bed-ridden. He cannot speak and his right side is paralyzed. I have bought their farm, and given the oldest boy enough money to help them get established somewhere else. I think the boy plans to take the family up to Vermont. There is still land to be had up there, although it is as rocky as the soil they had here. Some folk seem doomed to live their lives on rocky soil."

"A whole family destroyed by such a father." Ainsley sighed. "I wish we could have done more to help the other children."

Nathan's face expressed a deep and inexhaustible sadness. "Perhaps things will go better for them. Enos will not last long, and the oldest boy seems to have a good head on his shoulders. Besides, they have no wish to stay here. Too many memories to overcome."

It seemed to Ainsley as she snuffed out the candles that night, that she had aged a decade in the past month.

Chapter Thirty-five

During the following year Talmadge found his voyages to the West Indies fraught with tension. The waters of the Atlantic were teeming with ships, and it was impossible to tell friend from enemy. Privateers roamed the seas—French, Acadian, British, and Colonials.

If he were honest, Talmadge supposed he might be considered a privateer. Although he carried cargo as an agent from Connecticut producers and took them to fair harbor, nonetheless, whenever possible, he evaded the customs ships and tariff agents. Now, more than ever, he was thankful for the hidden harbor of Windsor Point. Few seamen used it anymore, and it remained a safe haven tucked away in the mouth of the river, hidden from view of the trading ships and government caravels that plied the waters of Long Island Sound.

That summer he tried a run to Boston, and when he returned he was filled with news.

"Secret societies are springing up everywhere," he told Nathan. "The city is a hotbed of insurrection. Samuel Adams has bearded the king in the courts, and has, as some say, lighted a conflagration that will not be put out."

Nathan listened soberly as Talmadge spoke of riots and documents of protest. "There are plays, poems, essays, and all kinds of entertainments, some poking fun at British rule, but others filled with inflammatory ideas. Who can say what will be the straw that breaks the British back, but they are foolishly piling them on. It is as though England has never comprehended that we colonists are mostly English as well—and every bit as proud and independent as they.

"'Struth, Father, they have not taken the measure of their colonists very well, or they would be wise to find some way of placating us instead of continuing to heap upon us indignity and taxes."

Nathan smiled. "Especially the taxes. I have learned in my years that we colonists do take our pocketbooks most seriously. Our honor and our wealth—we prize them both—and the opportunity to exercise the right to gain both. Anyone who meddles with those things will find themselves our enemy. Particularly"— Nathan raised his eyebrows— "most particularly—with our pocketbooks."

Talmadge laughed. "But we would not march under such a banner."

"No," Nathan acceded, "We shall march under the banner of our honor."

Just before the hurricane season, Talmadge set sail for the West Indies again. Connecticut was glutted with goods that needed to be exported, and desperate for reasonably priced trade goods. The troubles in Boston had become so acute that only British trade was going to the harbor, so, in spite of the hazards, Talmadge undertook a return to Kingston.

The Ainsley was a swift and noble craft, small and maneuverable enough that she could outrun most of the heavy, less agile ships that plied the ocean. Talmadge knew the seas and read the winds and currents, and he was a hard man to catch. Once again, he arrived safely in the bustling harbor of Kingston.

It was to be his last trip to that harbor.

After seeing to the unloading of his cargo and checking with the harbor agent, Talmadge made his way swiftly through the roistering market place, picking up a plump melon and a bottle of wine from his favorite merchant, and then hurried on down the narrow, winding street to the walled entrance of Clothilde's house. When he knocked on the door, he learned that she had married and moved away.

In truth, the information was something of a relief to him. The relationship had given him much sensual pleasure, but had done nothing to satisfy the need in him. Now that Clothilde was gone, he felt both guilty and ashamed of having used any woman in such a way.

That night, the news of a terrible storm at sea was brought into the harbor. Clouds scudded across the sky, and by afternoon a green-black darkness had fallen over the island. Talmadge had his crew load as swiftly as possible. The heavy barrels of molasses and the precious kegs of refined sugar made excellent ballast, and, by the evening light *The*

Ainsley slipped the confinement of the crowded harbor and moved out to sea, ready to ride out the storm on the open waves.

Battering and slamming, the wind smashed against the ocean, and hammered its fist of water and raging air into the wharves and anchorages of Kingston.

Out in the open sea, *The Ainsley* shuddered and climbed the mountainous waves, only to plunge into the troughs beneath. Time and again the trim ship was slammed through the angry seas. Her sails battened against the wind, her banners tattered to ribbons, and the rigging flying and whacking against the spars, it seemed a miracle that the sturdy craft yet managed to right herself and bear the pitch.

The ships in Kingston harbor were smashed like playthings. They sank, or were thrown up, whole, onto the crumbling docks. Tiles, roofs, whole houses flew through the air, and the market stalls of Kingston blew away like feathers on the wind.

When the storm had blown itself out, *The Ainsley* was far out to sea. Talmadge set a course for Baltimore, since Boston was no longer feasible. It was a wretched passage, wintery and storm-plagued, and when the ship landed in Maryland, Talmadge discovered to his dismay that the British presence in Baltimore was as authoritarian and unreasonable as in Boston. By the time the tariffs and customs taxes were paid, the profit from the voyage was a pittance, and the cruel trip had damaged *The Ainsley* so that extensive repairs would be necessary.

It was almost Christmas, and wounded in heart, exhausted in body, and with a battered ship, Talmadge beat his way up the coast to make harbor in Windsor Point. Ebenezer and Brosian greeted him like the prodigal son, and seeing the condition of the boat and crew, immediately took charge, arranging for dry-docking, and for the crew to receive hospitality at the inn until they were ready to continue their various journeys.

Talmadge paid his seamen, and then, with heavy heart, borrowed a mount from Ebenezer and made his way up the White Oak Trace to Marshfield.

By the time Talmadge entered the yard of Marshfield hours later, a light snow had begun to fall. He hated snow sometimes. It reminded him of the long-ago trek, of his captors, and of Mercy—thoughts which brought him no joy on this cold and frosty night.

Nathan, glancing out the window at the sound of an approaching horse, recognized Talmadge and ran, coatless, out of the house.

"My boy!," he shouted with pleasure. "Talmadge! We had not expected to see you until the warm months. How have you traveled home in such weather? How wonderful that we shall have you for Christmas after all these years!"

Talmadge was embraced by his father, and his horse was taken to be groomed and fed. "Into the inn, and warm yourself at the fire!"

Nathan's joy was warmer than any fire, and Talmadge felt some easing in the tension and weariness that he wore like a cloak.

The public part of the inn was full of men talking and shouting. Voices were raised, and Talmadge heard reference to Boston and the damned British.

"What is it?" Talmadge asked, nodding toward the common room where the gathered men were engaged in spirited conversation.

Nathan steered Talmadge into the family parlor and closed the door, shutting the loud voices out. "Stand by the fire, and rest, my boy. We may well need all the strength we can get. It seems that three days ago the Bostonians had their fill of the British tyranny; they attacked a British ship and dumped the cargo of tea into the harbor. Dressed as Indians, mind you."

Talmadge laughed.

"The British, unfortunately, have missed the humor of it," Nathan said soberly. "They have retaliated by closing Boston harbor. It is literally a city at siege. I fear the British have underestimated the mettle of the Colonies. They have stirred a buzzing swarm, and they will feel its sting."

The two men looked into one another's eyes gravely. Then Talmadge said quietly, "I do not fight other men's battles."

Chapter Thirty-six

In the winter of 1774, Boston groaned under the boot of British repression. No ships but British moved in or out of Boston harbor, which, half-deserted, bristled with British armed militia.

Under a load of heavy taxes, curfews, midnight raids, billeting of soldiers, homes requisitioned without the owners' permission, and no legal redress for the citizenry for the many wrongs they endured, a great smoldering anger seethed in the hearts of the people of Boston, and a vast secret organization began to build with but one desire—"Liberty!"

The cruelest development of the terrible situation was that the city became divided. Men and women who still were loyal to Britain and the crown saw the Insurrectionists as traitors, and the movement as a viper of rebellion that must be rooted out.

Old friends became mortal enemies, neighbor turned upon neighbor, brother against brother. Both sides were certain that they were on the side of right, and the pitch of emotion and political feeling was of such intensity that no compromise or forgiveness was possible.

Those loyal to the crown, the Tories, became the sworn enemies of their fellow citizens who were demanding the rights and freedom of a self-governing nation. In such a battle of wills, informing, vandalism, betrayal, suspicion, and suffering became the emotional currency of the city of Boston and its inhabitants, and the city reeled under the pain and deprivation.

Supplies were low as the winter progressed, and word of the suffering of the people of Boston reached the ears of the colonists in Connecticut. Incensed by the viciousness of the British restraints imposed on Bostonians for simply having the courage to act upon the feelings that many colo-

nists avidly shared, the surrounding colonies became eager
to aid the suffering city. Relief supplies were gathered in
towns and villages up and down the New England countryside, and shipments were smuggled overland, carried by
pack, saddlebag, wagon, and coach.

The secret traffic of relief goods to Boston slipped across
the roads and traces and through the woods of New England.
There were rendezvous points whispered through the villages, sentries who were bribable, safe houses established,
and forged documents supplied. An entire network of relief
supply, secret and efficient, spread through Connecticut, and
carried goods to the cold and starving people of Boston.

Talmadge had told his father he would not fight other
men's wars, and his father respected his son's hatred for war,
knowing the terrible price Talmadge had paid as a youth for
other men's battles. Nonetheless, Nathan could not comprehend Talmadge's behavior now that he was home at
Marshfield, with his ship dry-docked and under repair from
her hurricane damage.

During the months after Christmas, although he spent
some time examining the books and familiarizing himself
with the workings of the Marshfield estate, Talmadge spent
much of his time in the shops and taverns of Norwalk.
There, he explained to his father, he could stay in touch with
all the news—news of the British militia and of shipping.
Talmadge was such a good and quiet listener that he could
get men to talk—often to say more than they had expected
or wanted to say.

The months passed. Nathan was busy with the formation
of a Safety Committee, whose purpose was to stay apprised
of the explosive political situation and keep a vigorous
correspondence with other such committees throughout New
England. Constantly traveling to Hartford and the General
Court meetings, he was in residence at Marshfield for only
a few nights each month.

One evening, arriving home, he realized with some dismay that it had been weeks since he had seen Talmadge.
Ainsley informed him that Talmadge was away from the estate for weeks at a time but she was not sure what he was
doing.

All Nathan heard about Talmadge's activities made him
both disappointed and alarmed. Talmadge had bought a new

riding horse for himself, a powerful gelding with muscled haunches and withers of steel. The horse was as black as midnight, and when Talmadge rode him, he, too, dressed in black.

At the spring picnic on the village green, Nathan watched as Talmadge and the massive horse thundered to a win by three lengths in the two-mile run. He looked at his son's triumphant face and laughing eyes as he sat atop the massive steed, and for a moment this proud, self-reliant rakehell was a total stranger to Nathan. He did not like the feeling.

More and more Nathan heard rumors of Talmadge in taverns and roadhouses, drinking, carousing, and engaging in games of chance. Often days would go by and there would be no word of Talmadge's whereabouts, and then, suddenly he would appear in the dooryard, stained with sweat, his horse, Midnight, flecked with spray. Without a word of explanation, Talmadge would fall into bed, often staying in his room for several days, out of sight, taking his meals in his room. It seemed to Nathan that his only son had become a rake and a wastrel—and this in a time of peril and pending war.

Through the summer and into the days of autumn, Talmadge's behavior grew more mysterious, and his absences longer. Often Talmadge returned to Marshfield with companions who seemed to be as stained with debauchery and merrymaking as he. Laughing and leaning on one another, they would pound on the tables demanding rooms and drink.

Ainsley, too, felt Talmadge was changing into a different man before her very eyes. He never spoke of where he had been or what he was doing. Neither Nathan nor Ainsley asked—fearing what they might hear in reply, or that they might offend this mysterious man whom they both loved.

Ainsley wondered if perhaps she might be the cause of Talmadge's behavior. Even though it seemed more than impossible, she could not escape the uneasy feeling that some vestige of Talmadge's love and desire for her still remained. The thought made her uncomfortable.

One evening, after the carousing group had made their way up the inn stairs, Ainsley tapped softly on Talmadge's door. "Come in," he called. She entered swiftly, hoping to be unseen in the corridor. As she entered the room she was alarmed to see the room appeared empty. Whirling around, she saw Talmadge flattened against the wall behind the door, his pistol drawn and his every muscle alert. His face had lost all vestiges of its slack, drunken humor. He looked terrifyingly sober.

"Talmadge!" she gasped, startled and off-guard. "What are you doing?"

He was immediately at ease, tossing the pistol onto a chair and throwing up his hands in self-mockery. "When you keep the kind of company I do, you can't be too careful!" he answered with casual indifference.

"And what brings you to my lair, my pretty one? I am amazed that you do not fear to be seen in my somewhat questionable company."

She shook her head. "Talmadge! I don't know what has come over you. I—I thought perhaps you might want to talk. Ever since you returned to Marshfield, and to such perilous times, it is as though you are not yourself."

Talmadge laughed and flung himself on the bed, his hands propped behind his head. "It must be the week for serious talks. Father cornered me yesterday."

"What did he say?" Ainsley asked.

"Something to the effect that I was a disgrace to the name of Fairchild. In these times when every man should be preparing to answer the call, he feels I am a coward and a reprobate. 'It is one thing to sow a few wild oats.'" Talmadge mimicked his father's intonations perfectly. "'It is quite another to fly in the face of propriety when there are women and children starving for the cause in Boston, and men whose lives and estates have been put in jeopardy. When will you have had your fill of wine and revelry? Take your place as a man!'"

Ainsley sat quietly, thinking how painful the confrontation must have been for both men. "And you," she said softly, "what did you say?"

"I said to him, 'Remember my Indian name. It is Man With No Fist.'" Talmadge laughed, but there was no mirth in the laugh. "I do not fight other men's battles."

"Then what happened?" Ainsley asked, fighting an inexplicable desire to cry.

"We parted company—Father back to Hartford through the autumn splendor of the trees, and me, back to the gaming tables of New England. It is a grand time to be free, Ainsley. There is a sense of desperation abroad, it makes men wondrously mad, and money and wine and words flow like the river Styx."

"Then," said Ainsley, blushing deeply, "this has nothing to do with me? You are not avoiding Marshfield because I am here?" She was humiliated that she had verbalized her concerns, and wished, as soon as she had spoken them, that the words had remained unuttered.

Talmadge swung his legs around on the bed and stared at her. Ainsley stood rooted to the spot just inside the door where she had first stepped. How could she not know that she had never been more lovely? It was as though all the years before had been the unfolding of the bud, but now she stood before him a rose in the peak of its blooming, as rich, full-blooded, colorful, and warm as all the fruits of the Garden of Eden.

"Everything I do has something to do with you, Ainsley," he said calmly. "You know I love you, but the years of loving have made it a comfortable, accustomed thing, and now I am as comfortable with you as without. It is nice to have come to such a stage."

Talmadge saw her wince and knew he had hurt her, but it had also quieted her fears.

"Very well," she replied, her voice cold and formal. "You are a grown man, and know your own path."

She turned on her heel and left the room.

Winter came early, and Talmadge was seldom in residence. Ainsley could not believe the madness of his carousing. Nearly every time he returned, he had Midnight reshod, as though the horseshoes were worn through.

"It must be New York you are visiting," Ainsley said one night, as she observed the worn condition of Talmadge's traveling cloak and boots. "Surely you can find what you seek a little closer to home. Your father could use some help. The General Court is wearing him out. He acts as courier between the villages of lower Fairfield."

Talmadge nodded. "He wears himself out at the behest of others." There was a little chuckle. "Not I. I travel where the wind takes me, not the winds of men."

Later that night Nathan came in, exhausted, and Ainsley removed his boots and sat beside him as he lighted a pipe and drank a hot toddy. "I am too tired to sleep, Ainsley," Nathan murmured. "We have received more word of the suffering in Boston. The coldest winter in years, and nothing to eat, nor fuel to keep warm. Many households are burning their furniture stick by stick."

"What will it come to?" Ainsley whispered.

"War," Nathan answered. "Terrible, inevitable war. A child and a parent fighting—one to break free, the other to dominate. Who is right? I don't know. But I do know there can be no neutrals. Sooner or later, no matter what Talmadge says, it will be every man's war."

The cruel months of winter continued. The fields and woods of New England were packed with heavy snows, and the cold lay across the land like a blanket. Without cleared roads, travel was difficult, and the supply couriers were finding it harder and harder to smuggle relief goods into Boston without being detected.

Britain had tightened the screws upon the angry city. Every day more fresh, red-coated troops disembarked and flooded the streets. Guards and lookouts were posted, and curfews enforced.

Talmadge was scarcely home through the winter. Occasionally a friend or drinking companion would drop off a note for him and the letter would remain unopened, sometimes for a week or two, until Talmadge returned for a few nights of rest.

At last the terrible hold of the winter storms abated, and, by early April, the first garden peas were sending soft tendrils up the lattices, and crocuses were pushing their heads up from the snow.

Nathan was suffering with a mild bout of pneumonia and was home for the week. Talmadge rode up one cool evening and, after greeting Ainsley and checking to see if he'd had any correspondence, entered the parlor, where his father was seated before the fire, and and greeted him with a delighted smile.

"What luck," Talmadge said. "The two of us home at the same time, and on a lovely April evening. How say you we have a bit of supper together and you tell me all the news you are not forbidden to repeat—and even some of the unrepeatable things, if you wish."

Nathan smiled in spite of himself. "It grows more serious by the day, my son. The Train Bands in every town and village are drilling weekly. Money is being raised for arms and uniforms, and there is a heavy sense of waiting, such as one feels before a monstrous storm is about to burst."

Laughing, Talmadge walked over to the sideboard and poured himself a small glass of elderberry wine. "Then let us eat, drink, and be merry, for tomorrow cometh the whirlwind."

"When will you weary of this merriment, Talmadge?" Nathan asked quietly.

"When it ceases to merry, Father dear," Nathan responded.

The two ate supper together, but it was an awkward meal, full of long silences and unspoken thoughts. The two men parted early.

"I hope you are up and fit very soon, Father," Talmadge said, his voice flooded with genuine concern. "I wish I could remain another day—perhaps we could play a lively game of whist. However, I found a missive waiting for me that says there is a house party in Danbury, one that I must not miss, and so I will be on my way in the morning."

With a heavy heart, Nathan watched unobserved as Talmadge rode from the stableyard shortly after dawn. Talmadge was hatless, but something in the somber set of his face struck Nathan and he thought, that is not the face of a man going to a revelry—it is the face of a man with a mission.

Suddenly Nathan hurried down the stairs and into the kitchen where Ainsley was supervising the preparation of the morning meal.

"Ainsley, may I see you a minute?" She came to him, and they walked together to the small, private office of the inn. "Do you know what Talmadge did with the letter he received last night?" Nathan asked urgently.

"No," Ainsley responded surprised. "He usually takes his letters off with him—but wait! The letter may still be around. When he heard you were home he placed the letter back on the desk and went to see you. If he did not return to the office before leaving, it will still be there."

With a barely concealed look of eagerness, Nathan walked to the corner desk and sorted through the papers until he found the envelope addressed to his son. Without hesitation he removed the contents.

Ainsley was shocked. "You are reading his private mail?" she asked, aghast.

"I must, for my sanity, and perhaps for his sake." Without another word Nathan perused the brief contents, then let out a quiet sigh, as though a great load had been lifted from his shoulders.

Turning to Ainsley, Nathan smiled. "I," he said, "am an idiot."

Before she could react, he took the paper and held it to the flame of the small candle burning on the desk. The creamy bond caught fire quickly, and burned true and well. When there was but one corner unburned, Nathan dropped the sheet into the metal waste basket and watched the entire contents turn to ash.

"He should have done that himself," Nathan observed wryly. "Careless of the boy."

"Well?" Ainsley hissed, "are you going to tell me what is going on, or are you going to let me go insane?"

"He has been running supplies to Boston," Nathan whispered, wonder and admiration filling his voice. "Risking his life, his freedom all for 'other men's battles.' He may call himself Man With No Fist—and he would probably wrestle me to the ground if I even implied that he was involved in the war—but he is surely Man With a Heart, and he will no more step away from the things he believes are right than the noblest warrior."

Ainsley's eyes were filled with tears. "He could have been shot or imprisoned. All these long months, hiding, living in the woods, riding through the night. We will never know. No wonder when he comes home he sleeps as though the bells of doomsday would not wake him."

Nathan nodded. "The carousing, the drinking, the wild companions—all a ruse. They must move from tavern to tavern, seemingly too drunk to have a serious thought. Those fine young men. They have helped preserve a great city."

"And the note?" Ainsley inquired.

"A rendezvous in Worcester." Nathan said soberly. "A shipment is to go through the third week of April."

Now that they knew the truth of Talmadge's absence, the waiting seemed unendurable and the days stretched out with the slow passage of watched time.

Finally, one warm afternoon in late April, Ainsley was out in the garden, picking the green spring onions, their stalks as slender as grass, their sweet, tart taste refreshing the winter-old root cellar vegetables that must last until the summer crop came to harvest, when Talmadge galloped into the yard.

Midnight danced on the cobblestones under the washyard lines and his hooves rang like fire. "Call my father!" Talmadge shouted. "It is war. The British and the Colonials have exchanged gunfire at Lexington and Concord. There is no turning back now."

Chapter Thirty-seven

In the calamitous months following the Lexington Alarm, the Connecticut legislature issued a call to arms, and all towns and communities were expected to form Train Bands for the Connecticut militia.

Nathan had called new officers but remained in command of the New Parrish Train Band. They drilled five days a week, and the grueling schedule, plus all of Nathan's other duties and responsibilities—as a deacon in the church, a deputy to the General Court, and member of the town's Safety Committee—began to take a toll on the man who had always seemed immune to time. For the first time, as Ainsley served him a late supper, or quickly went over accounts and problems at Marshfield, she saw a sag in his broad shoulders and deep lines at the corners of his mouth.

These were times of grave tension, and although New Parrish was far enough from the coastal Post Road, and from the large cities where troops were massing, nonetheless the evidence of the conflict struck at the very heart of the community.

Anyone bearing allegiance to the crown, anyone giving aid, information, or comfort to the enemy, by word, contact, or contribution of any kind, was considered by the newly formed Continental army to be a traitor. Such acts of treason were numerous, and in the town of New Parrish it was the duty of the Safety Committee to ferret out all those who remained Loyalists.

The penalties for treason were bitter. All weapons were confiscated from anyone suspected of Loyalist sympathy, and the law required that they be stripped of their property and expelled from their homes. Nathan, as chairman of the Safety Committee, could not bring himself to exact such harsh penalties on men and women whom he knew as friends and neighbors. He persuaded the New Parrish Safety

Committee to confiscate all weapons from known Tories, but for those who would covenant to remain within the confines of their own property, under virtual house arrest, until the conclusion of the hostilities, there was no expulsion.

However, any Tory who was caught sending information, money, or goods to the British army was immediately punished to the full extent of the law. Houses and lands that had been settled by some of the finest families of New Parrish were left vacant. The Loyalists, penniless and landless, were either killed or sent away as refugees or prisoners.

This tearing apart of the very fabric of the town mirrored the wrenching, confused, devastated feelings of the Colonies, as they ripped from their hearts the essence of who and what they had been. Men who had fought at the side of the British in the French and Indian Wars now faced them over trenches as their avowed enemies. Friend turned to friend and saw the chasm of politics and freedom versus loyalty rip between them, creating a black void which could never be recrossed.

America was a nation being born, and, in the birthing, she was fighting her mother. The birth would be long, bloody, and violent, and would leave scars on both mother and child that would never completely mend.

Talmadge had disappeared again. Sometimes weeks would pass before he was seen, and then, more often than not, he arrived in the dead of night, travel-stained and silent. Nathan and Ainsley knew better than to question him.

"I had thought to ask Talmadge to take a commission in the Train Band militia," Nathan told Ainsley one evening as they sat watching the snows of yet another winter. They had heard that the British were planning to evacuate Boston, which could only mean that they would concentrate their forces on an attack of New York.

"It's only a matter of time until General Washington issues a general call for all militia. We'll most likely be sent to help prepare for the defense of New York. I would have liked to have had my son at my side." Nathan sighed. "It seems our destiny to be parted at the crucial times of our lives."

Ainsley was silent, but her heart was reeling with emotion. The war had permeated everyone's thinking. There was no feeling of safety or security, and the thought of final partings, and of danger, filled the air like a miasma.

How could Nathan sit there so close to her and not feel the need to reach out, to touch her hand? Her own hand trembled at the sight of his strong fingers lying wearily on the arm of his chair. It was all she could do not to reach out and touch him, beg him to look at her, and to reclaim the years of lost love before it was too late.

She looked at his bent head, the strong, silver strands thick and curling, brushed back into a neat queue held by a strip of black velvet. It was such a noble head, each line of it known to her more surely than the lines of her own face. He seemed so tired and burdened that she knew she could not add to his concerns. With effort, she held her peace.

"Talmadge is his own man," she said. "He will serve in his own way. He is your son and he has never shrunk from duty—only he will keep his own counsel."

Nathan assented. "I have known that. Something happened to him in all those years he lived with the Indians. Surviving alone taught him things we can not even imagine.

"For Talmadge, it would be impossible to order men to fight and die—or to give another man the right to give him such orders. He himself will only fight when it is his own decision—and in his own way. Somehow he must find a way to serve where he can act on his own. I feel, perhaps, he has already done so—but I know nothing more than that."

"It is better that we ask him no questions," Ainsley agreed. "I have sensed that."

That spring the orders came from General George Washington and the New Parrish Train Band, led by Colonel Nathan Fairchild, marched down the White Oak Trace, resplendent in the uniforms and weaponry which Nathan and the other town fathers had provided.

The troop had been remanded to the 5th Continental Connecticut Regiment, and would join almost five thousand troops on the defensive barricades preparing for the anticipated invasion of British troops.

As militia went, the New Parrish men were far better outfitted than most. They marched with wagons of provisions, and arrangements had been made with local farms and merchants for regular replenishment of their supplies as long as the roads remained open between the city of New York and the inland communities in Connecticut.

The morning was sharply cold with the heavy frost that

sometimes blew up from the sound on cloudy days in May. The men shivered, knowing that by noon the sun would be high, and as cold as they were now, they would be sweating in their uniform coats and wishing for the chill wind to blow again.

By June it had become apparent that this was to be one of the hottest, most humid summers in memory. Night brought no relief from the heavy heat that hung over Long Island Sound. Mosquitoes and mildew thrived.

Ainsley, in Connecticut, found that it sometimes took two days for the linens to dry on the line.

The men of the Train Band were stationed below Harlem Heights in a wooded area with a small trickling stream and a half-stagnant pool of water. There was no refuge from the sodden heat. During the day, they stood watch, worked on earthenworks, drilled, or sat listlessly, staring at the city below them and the hump of Long Island in the distance. The days dragged.

One day Nathan was called to staff headquarters to meet with all the commanders of the volunteer militia.

Everyone knew that even as they sat idle in the stupefying heat of Harlem Heights, waiting for something to happen, delegates from the thirteen colonies were meeting in Philadelphia. The men in Philadelphia were considering the questions of independence and nationhood, and in so doing, had been formally branded as traitors by the British government. The lives of the delegates in Philadelphia, their property, families, and liberty—all were at jeopardy.

Each day the Continental army waited for news, but none was forthcoming.

All around him Nathan saw signs of exhaustion, disarray, and lack of preparedness. He was astonished at how badly equipped most of the militia units were, and even more astounded at the lack of equipment in the Continental regular army.

Morale and any sense of nobility of purpose were being driven out of the waiting army by the oppressive heat. It was no secret to the commanders of the militiamen that General Washington did not consider them a valuable asset. Several contingents of Train Bands, their initial period of enlistment over, packed up and went home for planting and harvest. Sometimes Nathan wondered if that would not be the wisest course for him and his men. They could go back to New

Parrish, plant crops, raise cattle, provide much needed prov-
ender for the Continental army, and perhaps do more good
than sitting on the ramparts of the city day after day like
beached grunions.

The meeting of the commanders was interminably long.
General Washington had been expected to speak to the
meeting, but after almost two hours the great commander
still had not arrived, and Nathan thought it was unlikely that
the general intended to attend. Finally the heat of the tent
and the pointlessness of the wrangling overcame Nathan and
he ducked outside, walking toward the water wagon to get a
drink.

"Father!" a voice called, and he looked up to see Talmadge breaking away from a group of officers who were
standing in front of a sentried tent several yards across the
camp.

The two men embraced and then stood apart to look at
one another. No one seeing them could have doubted they
were father and son.

"I had hoped against hope to see you," Talmadge exclaimed. "I am to catch the evening tide and so I have only
minutes, but it is good to see you looking so well."

"And you, too," Nathan answered. "May I inquire what
has brought you here?"

Talmadge shook his head. "It is better not, Father. As a
matter of fact, it would be better if you forgot that I was
here. You have not seen me."

Nathan understood. "Very well. But I am most happy to
have not seen you."

The two men laughed. "Have you news of Ainsley?"
Talmadge asked. "Is she safe and well?"

"I heard from her with the last supply wagon. She is managing, although the town is half deserted. We have lost so
many of our Loyalist neighbors. I have bought many of their
properties, hoping to give them some hope of beginning
anew. Perhaps in Canada." Nathan shook his head. "So
many fine friends lost to us."

Talmadge put his hand on his father's shoulder. "The face
of our nation will not be the same. But, lest you feel too
much pity for our Tory friends, let me tell you, many have
banded together on Long Island, and even now are conduct-
ing raids all up and down the Connecticut coast. They kill,
rob, and plunder and create havoc on the innocent and the

HARVEST OF DREAMS 339

unwary. It is a most vicious banditry, which they justify in the name of Loyalism." Talmadge shook his head sadly. "When will we learn there is no nobility in war—only death and injury to those who least deserve it?"

Nathan sighed. "Ainsley has taken one of the larger abandoned Loyalist homes near the center of town and is turning it into a shoe factory. She is organizing a tannery out on Larkhill Road, and plans to buy all the dried-out milk cattle and aging horses—stock that has no other use. She has reasoned that an army must march on its feet, and those feet must be shod. Already she has signed contracts with two regiments."

Just then a tall man with a broad chest and massive thighs stepped out of the tent between the sentries who stood at guard. The man was dressed in formal uniform, even though the day was hot. The buttons on his coat flashed in the sun and his boots gleamed like pools of dark, refreshing water.

The powerful figure spoke softly to one of the sentries, and the sentry pointed to where Talmadge stood. With a brisk nod, the tall, silver-haired officer strode toward Talmadge and Nathan. He was followed by several younger officers, who clustered behind the man and at his sides like a circle of living armor. Nathan had immediately recognized the great general, George Washington himself.

"Captain Fairchild," the general called, striding toward Talmadge, "one more word, if you please."

Nathan looked at his son with startled eyes, and Talmadge grinned and explained softly, "Irregular army. Courtesy title."

Saluting, Talmadge turned to face General Washington. "Sir, I would introduce you to my father, Colonel Fairchild, commander of the New Parrish Train Band now remanded to the 5th Connecticut."

"Of course," General Washington said, shaking Nathan's hand. "I have heard of the excellence of your corps, Colonel Fairchild. We are grateful."

"Thank you, sir," Nathan answered. "It is an honor to meet you. We are at your command."

The general smiled with irony. "No, my good colonel, it would appear we are all"— he glanced around at his other officers— "at the command of the heat, and the British failure to attack. I would give a great deal to know the timetable of when we shall be free of both those things."

"I am something of a farmer, sir," Nathan replied, "and, if my eye and my experience are worth anything, I would say that the end of the heat will not come until the end of August. Perhaps the British are mindful of that as well, and wait for the cooler weather to make their assault."

"Like father, like son." General Washington appraised the two men in front of him. "Men of independent mind and wisdom. Such men will be essential in our new nation."

After a brief word of farewell to Nathan, Talmadge moved off swiftly with General Washington and the other officers, and the men reentered the headquarters tent. Nathan understood he was dismissed and, although he yearned to see Talmadge and talk further, he knew if it were possible, Talmadge would find him.

Feeling tired and strangely melancholy, Nathan returned to his men. They ate their simple evening meal, and the long evening, hot and oppressive, stretched out into the long, hot night.

In July the first cases of dysentery and yellow fever began to occur in the ranks. The area was swampy and dank, and the water supplies had become more and more evil-looking as the summer progressed.

Suddenly men were lying croaking for water, their skin as yellow as marigolds. Other men strained over the latrines, their intestines spilling out their lives in wrenching spasms. The food supply could not be kept free of weevils, mice, and larvae, and meat spoiled before it touched the fire.

Nathan nursed his men as they sweated and raged out their delirium. He fought to move the camp to higher ground, to a spot where evening breezes could blow away the insects. He burned contaminated clothing and linens and buried the dead.

Each night, at his camp desk, he wrote letters to the parents of the dead—letters that were written with his own tears as he watched the lives of young men who had laughed and lifted huge forks of hay onto Marshfield haystacks, or who had leaped on wild horses and ridden them to the ground, now lying helpless on the grassless, filthy soil of an alien city, and dying in the meaningless heat.

Finally, the medical supplies were completely depleted, and Nathan could not beg, borrow, or steal another draught, another sheet, more lye for purification—nothing. Every camp in the city was raging with illness, and the damned heat hammered on.

The night raids of the Tories from Long Island along the Post Road on the Connecticut coast had made travel into the entrenchments of New York almost impossible. Few supply trains were getting through. Nathan, knowing that Ainsley had collected supplies for the Train Band but could find no one willing to make the hazardous journey, was desperate to bring his men relief, and to stem the tide of deaths.

With great persuasion he convinced his direct superior in the regiment to give him leave to return to New Parrish and bring the supplies through himself. Choosing two trusted lieutenants, he made the journey along inland roads, some of them barely more than tracks. After two days of hard riding, he arrived at Marshfield, approaching his house late at night, in the dark and in silence, as though he came as a thief.

It was known that there were spies everywhere. The British seemed to know of every move, every deployment. In this emerging nation, no one was certain who was a true and loyal American, and who, under the disguise of loyalty to the Continental army, was in reality still committed to the British cause. Betrayal had become a way of life—and fear and distrust were the natural consequence.

The two lieutenants took the mounts and bedded them in the back stalls of the stable. They themselves took their saddlebags and prepared to bed down in the hay above. "We shall watch the night," they assured Nathan.

On silent feet Nathan approached Ainsley's cottage, but a careful glance through the windows told him she was not in residence. He crossed the herb garden and let himself in through the kitchen door, pausing to make sure the room was deserted. He smelled, for the first time in weeks, the rich, familiar fragrance of the room—the drying herbs, the roses on the table, the hint of baking bread, and sweet-sharp scent of vinegar and cloves. Suddenly the delicious aroma became the embodiment of Marshfield, the absolute sense, even in the total darkness, of being home, and, without bidding the thought, his mind was filled with the sense of Ainsley, as though she stood in his presence.

Shaking himself, Nathan proceeded across the flagstone floor into the private living quarters, through the parlor, and to the door of his bedroom. He knew that often, when he was not in residence, Ainsley slept in the dayroom next to his bedroom so that she could be convenient to the needs of the guests of the inn.

His own bed lay in the pool of moonlight. The linens were white and fresh, and the mound of the feather tick seemed so inviting his bones literally ached to lie upon it, but he knew he must first speak to Ainsley.

Without a sound he moved toward the double doors which led to the small room where she slept on a narrow daybed. Opening the door with only the softest click, he slipped through the threshold, not wanting to startle her awake.

She was lying, uncovered, in the warm summer night. The casement window was open, and the silvered light of the moon dusted the dark mystery of the room with a gentle, glowing outline. Her skin was so white, and her shift so delicate, that the light seemed to gather into her and he could see her face and form as clearly as though it were day.

Her hair was unrestrained, like a cloud, and her dear, unsuspecting face was as unlined and perfect as a marble cast of some Grecian goddess. He had forgotten how lovely she was.

Hungry, tired, and sick, he walked to her side and gently wakened her. He explained the mission and told her that his two aides were sleeping in the stable, taking turns keeping watch. In the morning they would gather the supplies, and load the wagons after dark.

Then, exhausted, Nathan stumbled into his room and fell asleep.

Ainsley, awakened unexpectedly, could not get back to sleep. She lay still, looking out the window and thinking of the war and the dark uncertainty of the future. What if Nathan were killed? What if Talmadge never returned? What if they were both caught and hanged?

Could she really make a life out of an inn and a farm and acres of property? All of her life she had just wanted to feel loved and safe. She had fastened on Nathan because he seemed so strong that nothing in the world could shake or destroy him. For the dream of his love she had given away all her womanly hopes—children, family, even a home of her own. Now, as she thought of Nathan sleeping in the next room, indifferent to her presence, she felt an emptiness that nothing in her lonely childhood could touch.

Is my life to be over before it has been lived? she wondered bitterly. Will I never know how it feels to have my body touched and loved? Will I never have the warmth of a babe in my arms? Only the sad, stubborn wish of my girlhood heart—an empty wish that I have hugged to myself like a hollow jar all of these years? Oh, Nathan, why couldn't I have heard what you told me in loving kindness? Why couldn't I have known you meant what you said? Dear friend, what will I do if I lose you? You are all that I chose—and now you are all I have left. I have sent Talmadge away from me forever, and this hellish war may rob me even of you."

The next morning, when Ainsley went to rouse Nathan, she found him thrashing on the bed in his sleep. She touched his forehead, and he was burning with fever. The bedsheets were wringing wet. Shocked, she refused to wake him, but hurried out to the stable to talk to the men herself.

Quickly, she explained Nathan's condition and also the chaotic situation in the town. "There is much confusion and lawlessness. We are fighting not only Tory raiders, but bands of highwaymen as well.

"We know that someone is spying on us—has been for weeks," she warned the young officers. "Our last three shipments have been raided within hours of their departure, and the route is always known—no matter what route our drivers take. Marshfield is not safe."

The men frowned with worry. "How can we avoid the same fate?" asked the older one calmly.

"I believe the shipments have been observed leaving the inn, either by someone at the inn or by someone watching it. I hope your presence has remained undetected and you will not be watched. I will keep Nathan's presence a secret so no one will suspect that anyone has come or gone.

"I have secreted the remaining supplies at the old Huck farm in a cabin which is now lost to the memory of most. The track to the house is almost completely overgrown. You should be able to go after dark. The wagon is waiting down in the south field. Take it to the Huck farm, load it, and leave from there. I will write out instructions to the Huck farm, and also for a return route that avoids the Post Road, using side roads almost all the way. Then I must care for Colonel Fairchild."

Hurrying back to the inn, Ainsley wrote out the directions and gathered up food for the men. Then she returned to the stable to bid them farewell.

"Be safe. The lives of the men of your regiment are depending on these supplies. If no one knows you are here, and if no one sees you leave, you should be all right."

Ainsley handed the directions to the two men, along with a bundle of cloth-wrapped rations. "My the Lord go with you," she said, touching their hands with her own soft, white ones.

When Nathan finally awoke, he was in a restless daze. "I have overslept," he groaned. "Must get to the men. The Indians are coming over the wall . . ." His words were slurred and his eyes unfocused. "Abijnah, sound the alarm. Stop the fires. The women and children—get them to safety!" He sat up in bed, his eyes unseeing.

"Nathan," she cried, "it's Ainsley. You are sick. The fever. Your men have left without you."

"Chastity?" he whispered the word with a tender smile on his face. "Chastity? Did I dream . . . ?"

"No, my darling." She put her arms around him and kissed the hot brow. "No. It was not a dream. I love you. You are home."

She nursed him around the clock, and on the second day of his illness, when he was delirious and knew no one, she bathed his entire body with cold water and vinegar. The fever abated and he slept.

On the third day, when there was still no improvement in Nathan's condition, Ainsley sent for the doctor—even though, with the fear of spies, she wished to keep Nathan's presence a secret. The doctor examined Nathan and told her the fever was difficult to identify.

"We hear rumors that the men are dying like flies in the camps around New York. What we need is a cold, hard frost. This blasted summer has bred pestilence upon our land." The doctor shook his head, and handed her a bottle of medicine. "This bark syrup will fight the fever, but I have no idea what other ills are plaguing his poor body, and he is worn out. He shall have a hard time fighting off the illness. He needs something to give him will and strength—and a great desire to live."

Ainsley blazed. "He has enough fight for ten men!" she retorted. "He will get well. I will give him the strength."

Chapter Thirty-eight

For three agonizing days the fever ran unabated, and Nathan raved. Ainsley slept on a pallet next to his bed, attuned to his every motion and sound. She bathed him and pressed the cup of healing potions to his lips. With her knowledge of herbs and nursing, she made cooling poltices, and when the fever would break and massive chills wracked his frame, she placed her body on his and held him in her arms, wrapped in blankets like a loved child.

He never really became conscious enough to know where he was, or to recognize her, but it touched her to the quick when, in his greatest moments of suffering and delusion, he cried for Chastity over and over again, like someone lost in a cavern, crying for the sun.

On the fourth day, with Nathan's presence still a secret except to Mrs. Seeley, Ainsley found her strength and resolve waning. She had not slept for days, and had scarcely eaten. When he was delirious, she had had to forcibly hold him in bed, and the effort had exhausted her. Now, as the day drew to a close, she looked at his pale face against the pillow, and suddenly he seemed inexpressibly dear to her in a tender, natural way. The old infatuation was burned from her mind and heart. She saw her feelings for what they had been—and she looked at this mature, handsome weary man, and felt the deepest love and admiration of an eternal friend, nothing more.

"Oh, Nathan," she cried silently, "why couldn't I have known sooner?"

If he died, with Talmadge gone—hating her, as Ainsley supposed—she had nothing to live for. She was losing Nathan, she could feel it. Death seemed to her exhausted fancy to be lurking in every shadow and fold of the room.

As the evening darkened, he became very still. She sat on the edge of the bed beside him, holding his hot hand. Weariness engulfed her, and she lay back against the pillow near his head and slept.

It was dark when she awakened. Nathan had thrown off the covers and was tearing at his nightshirt. "Chastity!" he cried. "She needs me. She is in the snow. Have to go! Have to go!"

"No, Nathan," she cried, struggling to pull him back into the bed, fearful he would run from the room and be discovered. If there were spies, and they were alerted to Nathan's presence, they would suspect a supply train was traveling to New York. The secret must be kept.

"Nathan, Nathan. I'm here. Listen to me. I'm here!" she cried, pulling him toward her.

He turned, and in the dimness of the moonlight she could see a smile on his face like none she had ever seen in all the years she had known him.

"Chastity?" he whispered. "My dear one. I knew you would come. I knew you would return to me. Oh, my sweet. How I have longed for this moment."

Tears were running down Ainsley's face. So this was what the love of a man and a woman was like. It was just as Talmadge had said—something beyond anything she had ever imagined or conceived. Nathan's voice shimmered with it, and his body was transformed. He was no longer sick and dying, but powerful and confident.

His arms embraced her. He caressed her, and held her head cradled in his powerful hands. He kissed her and touched her with the hands of a worshiper, and she watched him healing before her very eyes. "Chastity," he whispered in the dark.

"Yes, Nathan," she whispered. "I have come home, my dear. It has been so long."

She scarcely knew, in her exhaustion, what was happening. Only that she was not giving herself to Nathan, for all the years of love—but giving herself as a healer and a benefactor, not as a woman. It was not even herself that he was loving—it was the memory of the woman he had always loved.

She did not even know when she fell asleep, so close were exhaustion, despair, fear, and compassion.

Early in the morning she wakened, still lying on the pillow next to him. He was sleeping calmly for the first time, but when she touched him she realized that the fever was unabated.

Rising from the bed with a hollow feeling, numb and discouraged, and in a rage of guilt and shame, Ainsley went to her room and quickly bathed and changed.

Returning to Nathan's sick bed, she began to sponge his body with cooling herbs. This time his fever would not decrease. Nathan opened his eyes once in the afternoon, but would eat nothing, and his skin looked strangely translucent. She saw a sweet look of acceptance on his face, and her heart was clutched with fear as she clasped his hand.

"I'm just going out to the fields to work today, Chastity," he said in a clear, normal voice. "Tonight I shall return before dark. Do not weary yourself, my love." He closed his eyes again, and she saw such a look of peace that she needed to turn away.

He had gone from this place—he did not even know there was a new Marshfield or a woman named Ainsley. His mind and his heart, weary from the years of trying, had departed for the home he had loved in the old Marshfield. Neither she, nor the new Marshfield, nor the grown Talmadge, nor anything else mattered. He was back in the place of his greatest happiness, and she had given him the means to arrive there—had given him herself as a surrogate Chastity.

She dreaded to think what might have happened had she not. He would have run from the bedroom; she would have been unable to restrain him by force, and the secret would have been out.

She remembered the joy she had seen on his face. It had been worth it for her to know that it was she who had given him the gift of that joy. She would need to remember that in the days of guilt and remorse that were bound to follow.

By nightfall she could not rouse him from his coma. He had not eaten or taken a drink for over twenty-four hours. Ebenezer was sent in secret for the doctor. They came in through the back garden. "His lungs are filled with fluid," the doctor said. "There is no hope."

She sat by his bedside through the long night, with Ebenezer sitting by the outer door. Just as the sun pinked the western sky, Nathan gave a shuddering breath and once more he smiled. "Chastity," he whispered. Just the one word, and it was over.

Ainsley knew Nathan was dead before she felt his wrist.

She had felt his splendid spirit rise from his body like the sweep of air from the wings of an eagle. It seemed to her that her own heart left the room upon those wings.

His departure from her life was as sudden, swift, and immutable as his coming had been. Nathan gone—it was as though the anchor of her life had slipped away. She'd thought she'd known him. She had built her life on her imagined love of him, and yet she now knew she had only seen the real Nathan once in her life—on the last night of his life, when he thought she was another woman.

She bowed her head, leaning against his dear, folded hands. "Oh Nathan, my precious, unknown friend. What will become of us now? Talmadge, Marshfield, me? You cannot be replaced." And she wept.

The news of Nathan's death, even in a world where death had become commonplace, was a tragic blow to the town of New Parrish and to the men of the Train Band.

His friends and neighbors had grown to accept Nathan Fairchild as a part of their lives, always with them, always caring and responsible, always ready to shoulder the pressures of their needs, and now, suddenly, he was gone. With surprise and sorrow, they realized how much he had meant to their lives, and how much they had come to depend upon him.

Because she was not his widow, Ainsley could not mourn for Nathan publicly, except as a friend. She would not wear black, or withdraw from the world. The church funeral was organized and the eulogy was pronounced by the Reverend Witherspoon, who, although he had considered Nathan a foe, nonetheless, in deference to the love and debt the community felt toward Nathan, gave him a noble and inspired tribute. After the funeral, all the neighbors—united in their grief, filed through the rooms of the great estate of Marshfield, paying their respects to Ainsley in memory of Nathan.

Ainsley had tried to send word to Talmadge. Having no idea how to reach him, she had simply written to General Washington's headquarters in New York, hoping that someone there would inform him of his father's passing.

Grief permeated Ainsley's entire being. Her guilty secret, and the awful awareness that she had spent her life imagining a love that had never existed, made the reality of Nathan's death even more painful. The only person whom she could have talked to about her terrible dilemma and confusion was gone. Nathan alone could have understood why she had done what she did—and why his death meant not just the loss of the man, but also the loss of her dreams.

And now, how was she to build a real life? A life in which she faced the world without the comfortable armor of her unfulfilled love. How hard to discover now, at the far end of her youth, that she had wasted so many precious years. It was an unworthy tribute to the real and noble man that Nathan had been. A greater man, a finer man, than she had ever realized because she had been so intent on the Nathan of her fantasy love.

Sometimes she could almost imagine to herself that it was all a dream. That Nathan had never come home. That his illness, and that fateful night, had never happened.

Her days were unchanged, and the heat of the summer gave a sense of sameness to the pattern of her life. The inn continued to be packed with wartime travelers; the fields were gleaming, ready for harvest; and the town seemed to doze under the summer sun as though time stood still.

With very little effort she could make herself think that Nathan was not dead, but only away with all of the other able-bodied men of New Parrish. She could imagine him bivouacked in New York with his men, and think that she was just biding time until he would be home again.

Then the memory of their secret night would flash across her mind, and she would feel the heat of it and the awful awareness she now carried of the passion which she would never know for herself. Oh, to be loved as Chastity had been loved! Having to bear that sorrow in the private recesses of her soul only made it more exquisitely painful.

The message sent to General Washington's camp informing Talmadge that Nathan Fairchild was dead went unanswered. There was no word from Talmadge, and no one seemed to know where he was.

Ainsley had learned that the men of the New Parrish Train Band all wore black bands on the arms of their uniforms in tribute to their late commander. How gratified Nathan would have been, she thought, to learn how his men had held him in their esteem.

Still, without Talmadge to mourn with her, Ainsley continued in a strange trance, going through the motions of normal living, suffering in silence, and yet, not really accepting the great change which had been wrought in her life and in the affairs of Marshfield.

Late every afternoon, in the heat of the day, Ainsley would make her way to the burial plot on the brow of the ridge. This was the spot on the estate that best caught the offshore breezes blowing up from the distant sound, and there, under the wide, shady branches of the trees, she would walk between the stones, each one like a stone in her heart. Her father, Daniel, Alice—and now her dear Nathan.

She would kneel by his grave, placing a nosegay of flowers that she'd brought from the garden on the warm tombstone, and, with bowed head she would talk softly to the man she had loved for twenty years.

"Dear Nathan, I am having a devil of a time getting men to work the harvest. They are either gone off to war, or too busy doing their own work, short-handed.

"I am doing as you would have wanted, saving the gold. I know there will come a time when we shall need it to save Marshfield. For now, if the crops rot in the ground, so be it. We women will do what we can.

"Talmadge still remains away. I do not know if he even knows you lie here, dearest one. It will break his heart, for he loves you so. As do I."

Tears would fall onto the soft, bare mound that covered Nathan's resting place. The grave was still too fresh for the grass to have grown to cover it.

Usually she was completely alone, since the graveyard was a good distance from the road. However, once or twice as she toiled up the hill, she thought she caught a glimpse of someone under the trees. Always, by the time she reached the crest of the hill, the person was gone, and she could see no trace of anyone's having been there. Only she could not shake the uncomfortable sense of being watched. The most peculiar thing about the apparition was that he, or she, always wore a high-collared cloak, even though the heat of the summer made such a garment seem absurd.

Ainsley inquired around the inn if any of the staff were perhaps making visits to the ridge, but everyone denied having walked in that direction. Since she'd seen no more than glimpses, she decided to assume it was merely different travelers, resting in the shade and moving on.

Finally, the first cool breath of September blew along the Atlantic seaboard, and the New England Colonies heaved a sigh of relief. Fever and dysentery in the camps began to diminish, and a sense of renewed energy pervaded the troops.

Within a week, news began to filter through that the British had finally launched their long-planned invasion of New York. Under the onslaught of the superior training, superior arms, and superior numbers of the British regulars, the Continental army was routed and began to beat a strategic retreat. General Washington removed his headquarters to White Plains, and New York City lay in the firm grip of the British.

When Fort Washington fell and the troops retreated further across the Hudson to Hudson Heights, a great sense of doom fell over New Parrish. Word reached Ainsley that nine men of the New Parrish militia had died in battle, seven were captured, and eleven wounded. The toll on the families of the small community was almost unendurable.

Adding to the suffering of the town was the behavior of Reverend Witherspoon. Ever since the tragedy of Alice Huck, the minister had become more and more vituperative. His sermons were filled with anger and scorn, and he heaped abuse upon the heads of the congregation until they felt numbed by his preaching of hell, damnation, and personal failure.

"This war is but the scourge of an angry God!" he would shout from his pulpit. "If you die, you die in your wickedness. You have brought upon you the curse of Armageddon because you are filled with lust, greed; you allow your neighbor to sin, and you turn a blind eye."

As Ainsley watched the bitter, angry churchman castigate his weary flock, she noted to herself the unnatural flush of his face, and that his nose seemed to become more bulbous and veined. Often she detected a slur in his speech, and more than once, the church members had seen him stumble as he walked to the pulpit.

There was no question in the minds of many of the members of the congregation that the minister was partaking freely of alcoholic spirits. His administrative and pastoral duties went untended, as family after family received the bitter news of the loss of a son or a father, buried in some unknown graveyard far from home. Hearts were aggrieved and angered by the failure of the Lord's representative, who should have been their staff and solace but instead was an added thorn in their misery.

Christmas that year was a most dreary and heart-wrenching affair. The church services, filled with the haranguing of a minister seemingly half-mad, were unterminable, and the house at Marshfield, closed to the public for the day, lay silent, undecorated, and chilly. Firewood was becoming a commodity to be rationed. There were few men to cut the trees and split the logs, and firewood, food, cattle, shoes, and warm clothes were desperately needed by the troops stationed on the far side of the Hudson, and freezing in the coldest winter in memory.

Connecticut had become known as the Provision State. Supply routes through Westchester were under constant threat of raid, and the Connecticut militiamen were now remanded to collecting supplies, forming supply trains, and guarding them through the journey to the Continental lines.

Ainsley felt, as did every patriotic citizen of the town, that she and her household should make do with as little as possible, and that everything else must be sent to the men who were fighting not only for their own lives, but also for the life of the new nation which had been declared in Philadelphia in July. The menu at the inn had become simple and sparse: bread, thin soup, and buttermilk. Cheese, grain, smoked meats, dried fruits, blankets, firewood, and cattle on the hoof, were all being stockpiled, organized, and routed to the Continental army in New Jersey and New York.

Two days after Christmas, the first travelers to the inn brought cheering news—rumors that the Continental army had won the battle of Trenton. In a winter of fear, death, and defeat, the news seemed like the first harbinger of hope.

However, Ainsley found it hard to feel either joy or satisfaction. For her, the concerns of the war had faded away in the face of her own personal concern. Toward the end of October, two months after Nathan's death, Ainsley had begun to feel ill. It was hard for her to get up in the morning, and even the simplest foods seemed to give her dsypepsia. She had become irritable, and tired—tired all the time, with a tiredness that would not go away.

By the first of November she had begun to accept the truth, but, with the concerns of running the inn, organizing supply trains, and dealing with her deep and secret mourning, she was able to ignore what she knew to be true. Somehow, she thought, if she just worked and went about life, it would go away, and all would be well again.

She lived in a profound limbo of denial for weeks, but as the Christmas season approached, and the silence of memories pressed down upon her, she took to her rooms—the rooms which had been Nathan's—and faced the awful realization.

She was carrying Nathan's child, a fact that filled her with both terror and elation. She was unmarried. Her innkeeper's license would be torn from her, and she would be unable to hire people to work for her. The Reverend Witherspoon would have her disgraced and excommunicated, and her child would be raised with the indelible epithet "bastard."

Was this a legacy for Nathan's son? She could not bear the thought. For herself she could face whatever had to be faced, although if the Church chose to prosecute her under Church law, she could be stripped of everything. She could not stand the thought of leaving Marshfield—it would be like losing Nathan all over again.

Her mind raced round and round with the dilemma, but there was no way out. No answers came to her, only the certainty of disaster. The more violent the Reverend Witherspoon became, the more she realized the vulnerability of her and her baby's position.

The day she heard of the triumph of the Battle of Trenton, was the day she felt the baby move inside of her for the first time. Just the gentlest of flutters, a motion as soft as a butterfly's wing, and yet it clanged in her mind and heart like the clap of a great bell—filled with both joy and terror.

That afternoon as she made her way through the snow up to the graveyard on the brow of the ridge, she was surprised and disturbed to see several heavy footprints along the track. But, as she glanced around uneasily, she was reassured that she was alone.

Nathan's gravestone was covered with snow, and she brushed it off with her gloved hand. "Dear, dear Nathan," she said, pacing beside the stone. "What am I to do?" She placed both of her hands on her abdomen, where the first hardening had formed a small mound. "What joy to carry the fruit of your love for Chastity—and yet, what shall I do to protect your child? I am so ashamed. I know that I did wrong to deceive you—and yet I did not mean to do so. It was just that your need was so great and my fear so strong.

I know this will be a son—strong, valiant, noble. I pray he, and you, will forgive me."

She bent then and kissed the cold, gray stone. "Oh, dear one, rest well. The news of the battle is hopeful, but it will be a long, hard fight. Perhaps our loving Father thought you had fought enough wars and took you home to take your ease. But think on me. Oh, dear Nathan, think on me and your unborn child. May God have mercy on us."

She turned with a sigh and a shiver, and made her way back down the path. The thin winter light was deepening into dusk and she knew the inn would be busy.

As Ainsley hurried back down the hill, a man stepped out from the wooded copse at the side of the graveyard. He was wearing a deep cocked hat and a high-collared cloak, and his shoulders were heaving with silent laughter. "So, that's the way of it, is it? Nathan, you hypocrite! You ungodly, lustful, double-hearted, foul-bellied, holier-than-thou hypocrite! If you believed I should bear the punishment of my sins, then why could you not have stayed alive to bear the punishment of your own?

"Well, if not, I shall see to it that this bright young miss and her bastard child shall suffer for you. Suffering that you have made easy by your whoring ways. Got the girl with child and then died! Well, she'll wish she and the child had died, too!"

In a mock salute to Nathan's grave, the man removed his cap, and the last rays of the winter sun revealed the ghastly, ruined countenance of Junius Comstock. Under his cloak he wore the green coat of a Tory Loyalist, and in his hand he carried the spyglass with which he watched the White Oak Trace, the supply lines traveling along the Post Road.

Comstock smiled—as much a smile as his bitter countenance was capable of—and turned back into the shadows of the woods.

Chapter Thirty-nine

The three horsemen had ridden through the night. The hoofbeats of their mounts were muffled by the packed snow on the highway as they rode through the striped moon shadows made by the barren trees. Silver-tipped clouds scudded across the darkness of the sky, hiding and revealing the stars in a mad game of peek-a-boo. All three were heavily cloaked against the howling cold of the wind and the approaching storm.

When they arrived at Marshfield, the leader of the three showed the others into the stables, and then, scarcely more than shadows of the night themselves, the men glided through the apple orchard, with the blowing snow howling around them. Pausing at the empty cottage in which Ainsley used to live, they looked swiftly to the left and right, then entered, by key, through the back door.

Minutes later the cottage curtains were drawn and a dim light could been seen in the main room. No fire was lit, and soon the lamp was extinguished and a single man slipped out of the front door and hurried across the kitchen gardens, through the grape arbor, and into the kitchen door of Marshfield.

It had taken Ainsley a long time to fall asleep. Her room was cold, and in spite of the heavy quilts she had pulled around herself, she felt chilled and restless. As the sounds of the gathering wind and the approaching storm mounted, she had felt the isolation of the large bedroom which had been Nathan's, and the lonely memories of his bed on which they had loved.

Sometime after midnight, she had finally fallen into a troubled slumber, but her dreams were frightening and incoherent. Talmadge, entering the room in silence, heard her moaning as she slept, and he hurried to the side of the bed.

Reaching out to rouse her, he put his hand gently on her shoulder. "Ainsley," he whispered.

She rose in her sleep with such suddenness that it took him completely off guard, and, in one joyous sweep of motion, she threw her arms around him, weeping and crying, "Nathan!"

Astonished, he held her closely, and then he realized her head had slumped against his arm, and her breathing, deep and rhythmic, was the breathing of total slumber. "Ainsley," he repeated, shaking her gently, not wanting to startle her. "It's Talmadge. Wake up."

He felt a long shudder go through her body, and she shook her head and pulled back from him. "No." she said. "No. No. No."

She felt so weak and fragile in his hands that he was afraid to let go of her, so he continued to hold her upright, but her head continued to sag, as though she did not want to waken, did not want to see.

"It's Talmadge, Ainsley," he repeated. "I've come home."

She nodded, still not completely awake, and said, as though she were reciting a catechism, "Talmadge. Nathan is dead. Dead. I am so sorry. So sorry . . ." and she began to cry. It was a hopeless, sound.

Talmadge pulled her against him, and she leaned on the heavy folds of his snow-cold traveling cloak and wept. Wept all the silent tears she had had to restrain in front of others, wept for the son who could not attend his father's funeral, wept for the unborn child who would never have a father, wept for herself and for the empty years of her life.

Talmadge sat on the side of the bed and held her, and his stillness was more sweet and healing than anything she had ever experienced. When she had cried herself out, he brought her a cup of water and a cool cloth. She drank and he wiped away the salt stains of the tears on her face with his gentle touch. Then she rose and put a soft, woolen shawl around her shoulders, while he stirred up the small fire banked in the fireplace, and they pulled two low stools near the flickering flame and talked.

"I can tell you nothing of my commission," Talmadge told her, "except that I have come home to manage Marshfield, by order of the commanding general of the Continental army, because of the great need for food, supplies, and equipment.

"He says I will be of more use to the war of independence by raising and purchasing supplies than in any other way. Therefore, I will be living at Marshfield as a civilian, although my duties in procurement may take me away frequently—and far afield." Talmadge's eyes were intent upon Ainsley.

"In reality, Ainsley, you will need to continue running Marshfield. I will do whatever I can to help, but I shall still need you to care for the day-by-day operations. Also, I will need you to be my ears and eyes. Any unusual customers at the inn, any whispered conversations, anything the least bit suspicious—the smallest scrap of news. Train the rest of the staff to listen and watch, and report to me each evening when I am in residence."

Ainsley nodded, understanding, in some small measure, the importance of the things Talmadge was telling her and the necessity for her discretion.

"I know you ask these things for a great cause, Talmadge," she whispered. "Your father would have been proud of you, and would have understood that you fight in your own way. Although you hate violence, you love truth, and you will stand for the one and avoid the other whenever possible—but, when the two are in conflict, you will never abandon truth, whatever it costs."

Talmadge laughed. "You make it sound more noble than it is, Ainsley." Suddenly sober, he added, "I will miss my father. We had so little time together. So many of our years were stolen from us. He was a great man, you know. I would give my life to have him back again."

With poignant sympathy, Ainsley rested her slender hand on Talmadge's. "I know, dear Talmadge. Nothing hurts more than the thought of all the might-have-beens. All the wasted years . . ."

Her voice trailed off. Then, with strength and conviction she added, "There was something in him that was so noble and fine—we were blessed to have as much of him as we did. In the end, I think he was glad to go. He had been alone so long."

Talmadge nodded, and there was a sweet, companionable silence between them.

"In the morning, I will take you to his grave," Ainsley said. "I will also remove my things from these rooms and move back into the cottage."

"No!" Talmadge responded. "I want you to remain here, in the inn. It is the most convenient location for you to run the place, and I wish to occupy the cottage. My comings and goings, and those of my visitors, will be more private there."

He felt a certain agitation in her, then, and she rose and began to pace back and forth in the freezing room. "What is it?" Talmadge asked, sensing she was struggling to tell him something. "Is something wrong?"

Her answer was muffled. "I will stay for a month and put the affairs of Marshfield in order, and then I will be leaving."

"What!" He sprang to his feet and dashed over to her. "What are you talking about? This is your home. You are a partner. There would not be a Marshfield without you! Where could you possibly go? What madness is this? Is it because I have come back? Are you afraid of my presence without my father here to protect you? I promise you, Ainsley, I will make no inappropriate overtures if that is what you are thinking . . ." His voice was outraged, filled with anger and hurt.

"No!" she cried, turning to him with anguish. "No. This has nothing to do with you, dear Talmadge. I would love nothing more than to remain at Marshfield. It is my world. Everything I love is here—was here. My heart is filled with joy at your return. You must know how dear you are to me, how completely I trust you. No, I am not leaving because I wish to. I am leaving because I must, and where I shall go I do not know."

"Madam!" he growled in confusion, "you make no sense, and you fill me with alarm."

"Oh, Talmadge, do not hate me!" she cried, and she turned from him, unable to face him in her shame. "But I must tell you. I must tell someone or I shall die, and you are the only one in the world whom I can trust—who will understand."

Trembling, she walked to the casement window. The snow had begun to fall, and the reflection of the falling flakes looked like falling tears on her pale cheeks. She leaned her heated forehead against the cold pane.

"I am no better than Alice Huck. I am a sinner, a woman who has broken the commandments of the Lord. I do not excuse myself because of wartime, or because of my years of waiting and loving, or because of momentary weakness. I do not excuse myself, and I am completely willing to bear whatever punishment is deserved, whatever penance, whatever disgrace is meted out. But I cannot, I will not, allow my innocent child to bear that punishment or disgrace. I must, must, must . . ." She pounded her fist gently on the sill, as though talking to herself or making a vow to the heavens. ". . . I must and I will find a way to protect Nathan's child."

The words hit Talmadge like a blow. He felt himself reeling from the knowledge that his father and Ainsley had lain together. How often in his own dreams had he held her in his arms, felt the smoothness of her skin against his own, the sweetness of her imagined lips?

Until this moment he had not realized that through the years he had supposed that her infatuation with his father would come to an end, and lived with the hope that she might be able to see him as he really was. In all these years he had never stopped loving her. Every woman that he had held had, in the darkness, been Ainsley.

"When?" His voice was surprisingly calm. "When was this child conceived? How long?"

He could feel the weight of her sense of shame like a heavy presence in the room and even under the cover of darkness he knew she could not raise her eyes to his. His heart flooded with pity for her and, in an instant, his anger and jealousy turned to love and sympathy.

This was his dear, dear Ainsley, and she was in desperate trouble, and finally, after all these years, she had turned to him. He was her only hope—her only solace—her only buttress against a world that would surely try to destroy her and the unborn child.

"The child will be born in May," she whispered. "There is little time before others will know."

He strode to her and, putting his arms about her, tenderly turned her toward him. The light of early morning was beginning to filter through the falling snow, and the room was gray, bled of color in the faint light of a winter dawn.

"Ainsley," he said, "you do not need to tell me anything. Not any more. I do not need to know. Why should you be condemned for doing what all men do? Besides, if you were not married to my father by the church, you were married to him by love, by devotion, by time, and by the mighty power of the heavens. This infant shall be a Fairchild, as noble and true as his father and mother. You must not go away. You belong at Marshfield. Both of you."

With a long sigh, Ainsley answered. "You are wrong, Talmadge. I did not do this out of the years of love I felt for your father. I had come to know that was only my youthful fancy. No. It was Chastity he made love to—it was only my body. He was sick, delirious, and I was exhausted and had to keep him hidden. He never knew it was I."

Her voice was toneless. "We may know that this infant is a true Fairchild, but it is only because we want it so, Talmadge. The world, even our own loving neighbors, the workers in the vineyards, the staff at the inn, the members of our congregation—no one will accept this child as a rightful Fairchild.

"No one can allow this pregnancy to go unpunished, unremarked, or unjudged. We will all suffer. The memory of your father will be destroyed, and the child will have a life of living hell. Even the beauties and riches of Marshfield cannot prevent that if I stay."

"There must be a way!" Talmadge whirled in frustration and strode across the room, too agitated to remain still.

With an attempt at a smile, Ainsley whispered, "Just a piece of paper and a ring would make all the difference. A piece of paper and a ring." She looked up quickly, defensively, at Talmadge. "Such little things."

Talmadge had stopped in his tracks. "A piece of paper and a ring," he muttered. Then he hurried over to Ainsley and grabbed her arms, his eyes lighted by an idea. "Tell me quickly, Ainsley, where have you told people I have been?"

Bewildered, she answered him, "We have said we have been trying to find you through General Washington's headquarters, but that your assignment makes your whereabouts difficult to trace."

"True!" Talmadge exalted. "That is absolutely true. Therefore, there is no way that anyone could possibly have known when I have and have not been in residence at Marshfield. People are used to seeing me coming and going. As a matter of fact, if you will recall, I was at home for a week just before my father made his last journey home to Marshfield."

"Yes," Ainsley said, still puzzled. "We both remarked how sad it was that you could not have remained a week longer so that your paths might have crossed. I wish so even more now, since you would have been able to see him before his death had you remained."

"It will work!" Talmadge exclaimed to himself. "It will work, and no one the wiser!"

"What?" Ainsley asked. "What are you talking about, Talmadge? There are no solutions—I must leave."

"No, Ainsley, you are wrong." Talmadge took Ainsley's hands and led her back to the meager warmth of the dying fire. "A piece of paper and a ring. That's what you said. Well, the piece of paper is the important part. What if we had married last summer in such haste that there was no time for a ring. And now that I am back at Marshfield, headquartered here for the duration as supply master to the Continental army, well, our secret can be told—and I have found time to buy the ring."

"Our secret?" Ainsley questioned. "Your being here will not make the knowledge of my condition any more palatable. Perhaps even less so, since you may be in suspicion of being the father yourself."

"Not if I am also the husband," Talmadge said softly. Ainsley gasped and drew back, but he held onto her hands firmly.

"Think on it, Ainsley. It is the only answer—for the love we both hold for my father, for Marshfield, and for one another. There is no other solution. You must marry me." Talmadge's voice was firm with conviction.

She shook her head and her voice was filled with agony. "How can you think such a thing? How could I ask such sacrifice of you? To live a lie? To marry me, knowing I carry your father's child? I would be so ashamed, so indebted. I could never face you—could never hold my head up. Would this not be the final betrayal of both you and Nathan? No. This is madness!"

"Not madness," Talmadge answered, "but the wisest, surest, coolest reason. My father left two things of value—two things for the future of this country. One of them was Marshfield, and his vision for the town of New Parrish, and the other was this child. If you will not marry me, Ainsley, I shall never marry, and the Fairchild line dies with me if your child is a bastard.

"No, Ainsley dear, this is not madness but some great divine comedy. So cosmic design that we with our human limitations cannot fathom. I know that it is you and I who are meant to secure my father's legacy, and God has decreed that the only way we can do that is together."

The fervor of his voice filled her mind and her heart, and for the first time in weeks, she felt as though the terrible load had lifted, and the tight band around her head eased.

Her hands were fluttering in his grasp like tiny imprisoned sparrows, and her breathing was shallow and agitated. He felt the thinness of her fingers and wrists, and, in the gathering light, he saw the slenderness of her face and neck and felt a shaft of alarm.

"You have grown so thin. Are you eating enough? Are you well?" His eyes raked over her, taking in the disheveled hair, the eyes grown larger in her pale face, and the smallness of her body. "My dearest Ainsley, you need me. We need each other. You must not die, or waste away. Don't you see? You are everything. You are our heart, our soul, even our body. Let me care for you."

She swayed toward him, almost as though she no longer had the strength to resist. "I could do it," she said resolutely, "for Nathan, for his child. But I cannot do this to you."

"That is for me to choose," Talmadge said, and his voice was like iron. "And I have chosen. Come of it what will, it is you and I who will bear the consequences, whatever they may be—but I pledge to you, the child shall never carry a mark of any kind. No secret of the past shall ever shadow him; I will guard him with my life and my honor."

"And I, too," Ainsley breathed. "But, oh, the cost to you, dear friend. I wonder if you know. I wonder if you will be able to bear it. I have been such a fool, made such a mess of all our lives."

Talmadge stood up, and his tall, slender frame blocked the light from the window. He had not removed his cape, and, as he stood with his arms crossed on his chest, his handsome head bowed in thought, he was outlined with light, and Ainsley, looking up, thought he looked like the angel Gabriel, as though he had come to bring her redemption and hope in her annunciation.

"I will bring at night, on the morrow, a chaplain of my acquaintance. He's a Virginian, but a man with a Continental army investiture, which gives him broad authority. We will be wed, the paper duly notarized, and the date besmudged. You will have your paper, and a ring." Talmadge was thinking out loud.

"But what shall we tell people?" Ainsley asked.

"That we have been secretly wed since early summer. My military assignment was one of such secrecy that it was better our marriage remained undisclosed, but now that I have been given duty as a quartermaster, the marriage can be in the open." Talmadge paused, thinking the matter through. "Keep the details vague. The more vague, the more people will respect the delicacy and patriotic obligations of my former duties."

Ainsley thought for a moment. "It might work," she whispered. "Oh, there will be whispering and speculation—but the war is so compelling it overwhelms everyone's thoughts, and I think we may get away with it."

Suddenly she brightened. "We could have a celebration. Something very simple, because of the war, but people are eager to laugh and be happy, and perhaps we could announce the making-public of our secret union, and invite friends and neighbors to a belated reception. We could meet the matter head on."

"Good idea," Talmadge concurred. "I shall leave and take care of all the marriage arrangements as soon as my couriers are on their way. Do you have any food which I can give them?"

"Of course," Ainsley said. "Let me dress, and I shall meet you in the kitchen with what provisions I can find. However, dear, dear Talmadge, you must not leave immediately. First, we shall go together to the cemetery plot on the ridge and tell Nathan of your great gift to him."

"I think perhaps he already knows," Talmadge replied softly.

As he let himself out of the inn, Talmadge thought he had never felt more weary. His legs were like lead, and a great heaviness had settled upon him. "What have I done?" he thought to himself.

He knew it was the right answer, the only hope for all three of them, and yet, he also knew that in his heart he had hoped someday that Ainsley would be his true wife. That she would come to him of her own free will from a full recognition of his undying love for her, and from a great blooming in her heart of love for him.

Crossing the kitchen garden, dead and brittle with frost, he felt as though the frost had penetrated his heart. "Now she will never see me as a separate man. Now she will be my wife, but only in name. Her heart, her child—I, who love them both, will have to find some way to make up for all the things which have been lost."

The wedding celebration was full of a wondrous gaiety, as though the ominous canopy of war and the limitations on food, decorations, and firewood were more than compensated for by the yearning in the hearts of the guests for a moment to forget the stresses and anxieties of daily life, and to remember the merriments of long ago.

The musical quartet was now a trio, since the second violinist was fighting somewhere in New Jersey. Mrs. Seeley had produced a buffet which gave a festive feeling, even though the ragout was made with boiled salt beef and the bread baked with coarse-ground wheat. For dessert she had concocted honeycakes, rich with raisins, and had collected the cream from five neighboring farms to create a wonderful, frosty iced cream—possible only in the coldest, snowiest winter—and the punch bowl was filled with the last of the homemade cider, spiced with bark of cinnamon and cloves, and the slightest touch of rum.

Because the house was still in mourning for Nathan, there was no dancing, but the air was full of conversation, kind words, and a feeling of happiness and serenity which had been missing for many months from the community of New Parrish.

"I hope your father knew of this match before he went to join his Maker," Mrs. Eversham said to the happy couple, "although, heaven knows, you are both adequately along in years to make such a decision on your own. I should think it would gave him great pleasure to know that you had finally done the thing he always wished—even if it was done in secret."

She was an outspoken woman, white-haired and imperious, who looked through a single eyeglass which she held on a long ivory stick, suspended from her ample bosom by a long velvet ribbon.

Talmadge smiled and replied with dignity, "You are right, Mistress Eversham. This is a match of which my father heartily approved. It was the exigencies of war which made us elope. It is a good to now be able to share the knowledge of that event with our friends."

With an overly bright smile set her face, Ainsley had

stood by Talmadge's side through the long evening, greeting guests graciously, her hand on his arm. He could feel her hand shaking, and she dug her fingers into the muscles of his forearm, but the expression on her face did not change.

"Yes, indeed, Mrs. Eversham," Ainsley said. "Thank you so much for your good wishes. We feel privileged to have you at Marshfield."

Brosian had come up from Windsor Point for the event, and had brought him a sleigh full of logs. "These are to light the celebration of your marriage to Master Talmadge," Brosian told Ainsley. "High time you married the man! Ebenezer and me have thought it was the thing you should have done years ago. Brought that young man home from gallivanting around the world on his boat, and gotten him to settle down in time to raise a house full of young ones."

It has not occurred to Ainsley how painful everything would be, how difficult each kind word of congratulations would be to hear. In the masquerade that she and Talmadge were living there were no corners in her own conscience and soul to hide. Each word of joy, each assumption of the truth of their summer elopement, each tender offering of friendship and satisfaction in the match, struck at her heart like a fiery dart.

How could she carry out the pretense? she asked herself. Deceiving even their closest and most trusted friends—and even deceiving one another, because they would have to live the lie. They would need to appear joyfully, happily married, or the thin charade would fall apart. And how could they do that knowing that they had married to hide a shameful secret? Knowing that theirs was a marriage of convenience— and the most concealed, despicable, and humiliating convenience.

Could anything good come from such connivance and deception? Or would the weight of it destroy their years of loving friendship, and then, having destroyed that, eventually succeed in destroying both of them?

She did not know. All she knew tonight was that the hours were full of endless humiliation and misery, and that she felt she could not look another neighbor or friend in the eye, knowing the enormity of the lie she was living.

Talmadge, standing beside her, felt her pain through the trembling current of her arm. He held her close beside him firmly, willing her to take from his strength.

"I must say," said Marnie Talbot, coming up on the arm

of her father, a deacon of the church and an old friend of Nathan's, "you do seem to get all the luck, Ainsley Windsor. I mean, first you flout convention and spend your life doing a man's work—and now you have married the best-looking man in all of Connecticut!"

The young woman's cheeks were as rosy as winter apples, and her eyes danced as she looked Talmadge up and down. "Captain Fairchild, the war almost seems to agree with you! I declare you are even handsomer than I remembered!"

Her father was embarrassed. "Marnie! Hold your tongue, daughter!" He looked over at Talmadge. "She speaks first and thinks second—always has."

Talmadge laughed. "Mistress Talbot is correct, something does agree with me—but it is not the war—it is marriage." He turned to the daring young woman with a smile. "You shall make the man you marry quite dazzled I should think."

Marnie gave a delighted laugh. "Wit and beauty, Captain! That's a very nice combination. You are the lucky one, Ainsley!"

The father and daughter walked away, and Talmadge heard Edward Talbot say to his daughter, "Marnie, you do not say that men have beauty."

The girl laughed and replied, "Literary license, Father! It's a figure of speech."

"Educated females!" Edward Talbot harumphed in disgust, and walked over to the punch bowl.

At last the evening was over and the guests departed. The inn had been closed for the rest of the week, and so an unusual quiet settled on the house.

Talmadge walked into the bedroom after snuffing the candles. There was a sweet peace to him in the silent rooms, and for the first time in many years, he felt the beauty and comfort of the great house settle around his shoulders like a familiar mantle.

"When the war is over," he said to Ainsley as he walked into the bedroom where she was sitting at a small escritoire by the fireplace, a single candle lighting the room, "we are going to close the inn. Marshfield will be our home. Nothing more."

"But it is so large . . ." Ainsley began to protest.

Talmadge smiled, "Perhaps by then we will fill it."

She said nothing, but continued to write.

He studied her carefully, but made no move toward her. She was still dressed in the deep purple dress of raw silk which she had worn for the celebration. Purple was a color acceptable for mourning, but it was also a color of warmth, and it suited her vivid coloring perfectly. In deference to the occasion, not wanting to appear less than a bride, Ainsley had worn décolleté. He had not seen her in such a youthful style for years. The dress had full, puffed sleeves and a bows tucked into the ruffles that framed her shoulders. The neckline traced the creamy curve of her bosom and showed the merest shadow, and the swell of each breast. Sweeping out behind her, the skirt, caught with bows at intervals, made her lovely torso seem like a jewel displayed in a sea of dark silk.

She seemed so lovely, dark, and unreachable. He glanced down at her left hand and there he saw the glint of the gold ring, square, set with one perfect emerald. When he had returned with the minister, in full Continental uniform, escorted by four other officers, all speaking with the soft accent of the South, she had wondered how he had found such a magnificent ring on such short notice.

It had been given to him by a young subaltern. The lad was only twenty years old, the son of wealthy Philadelphians. In an early skirmish of the war, Talmadge had saved the young man's life, and the young man had become a fast friend to Talmadge. When the young Philadelphian had come to bid farewell to Talmadge and heard the news of Talmadge's hasty preparations for marriage, the young officer took the ring from his little finger.

"This belonged to my grandmother," he said, handing it to Talmadge. "She was a woman of courage and good taste. If your bride is as beautiful and brave as you say she is, my grandmother and I would deem it an honor to have her wear it."

Ainsley was silent, and her pen scratched on the paper. "What are you writing?" Talmadge asked, sitting down at the opposite side of the hearth and struggling to remove his high, shining boots.

"Here," Ainsley said, "let me help you." She left the desk and walked over to him. Bending low, she grasped the boot heel and instep and pulled. Sitting in his chair he could see the glorious, deep wonder of her bosom as she leaned over him, and he gripped the arms of the chair.

"I can manage," he said, more gruffly than he had intended. She dropped his foot and returned to the desk, picking up her pen again without a word.

"Surely you are not doing accounts at this hour!" he exclaimed, feeling irritated with himself and not knowing why.

"No, of course not," Ainsley said quietly. "I am writing to Letty. I would so have liked her to have come with her children for the wedding party, but they are under house arrest, you know, in New Haven.

"I heard Martin was at Fort Ticonderoga last year but I doubt if even Letty knows where he is now. She has three children, Talmadge. They are surrounded by hate—and I don't know if she ever has enough to eat."

Talmadge leaped across the room and put his hand over Ainsley's. He grabbed the paper and flung it into the fire. "You can't take such risks!" he exclaimed. "If the town's Safety Committee heard of you writing to a Loyalist—the family of a British officer, Tories! What on earth are you thinking! They could confiscate Marshfield! It would be considered treason!"

Ainsley watched the letter burn. "Treason," she said sadly. "Treason to send love to my oldest, dearest friend. What kind of world are we living in, Talmadge?" She sighed, "Letty's property has been confiscated. She is destitute."

He came to her and laid his hand gently on her shoulder. "Forgive my anger," he said softly. "This is war and I feel such a need to protect you. I have never felt fear before—none for myself—but now, suddenly, I feel fear for you. You must be wise, dear Ainsley. Your impulses, true and precious though they are, could destroy us."

Tears shown in Ainsley's eyes, "And so my love for Letty and Martin is a victim of this brutal war as surely as your father was. Will the purchase be worth the price, I wonder?"

"Only this child and his generation will know the answer," Talmadge replied, and he reached down and laid his hands on the rounded swell beneath her slender waist. He could feel the heat of his body through the heavy silk, and she moved shyly under his touch.

With a passion that would brook no barriers, he swept her up into his arms and buried his face in her breast. The flickering light of the candle highlighted the boldness of his brilliant eyes and the stern, strong lines of his maskless face. He was the truest, most private person she had ever known.

In Talmadge was a vast integrity that made the inner and

outer man as one person, but which set him apart from his fellow beings because he could not be swayed or controlled by others. He was what he was. In some ways a man always alone, and yet a man whose fiercest needs were to serve the needs of others.

It was a face she knew as intimately as her own, and yet, now, staring down at her with an intensity and power of desire that she had never imagined could exist, she felt she saw a stranger, and her heart rocked like a pendulum between fear and some mad desire, that seemed to swell in her like an uncaged, taloned eagle.

So unexpected was her need for him that she felt it come as a desperate betrayal to all she believed she was—all she believed she felt.

He kissed her then, and she found herself craving his lips, wanting more and more to have their strong motions draw from her the very fibers of her heart. She felt herself holding him to her with a hunger that shamed her at the same moment it delighted her, and in sudden bitterness at her own wantonness, she whispered to herself, cruelly, I am a whore, and then, as though to prove her disdain for the insane woman who writhed in Talmadge's arms with a lust and need that was so great it could not be contained, she gave herself over to him with an abandon that was like a raging fire.

Unable to get enough of her, Talmadge kissed her body, drank her body, memorized her body, held her body, stroked it and blessed it until the exhaustion of repletion overcame them both, and they slept on the tumbled sheets as the fire died away and the chill of the next day crept into the room.

Early in the morning, Talmadge wakened shivering. He turned to Ainsley who lay, sound asleep, completely naked. She was on her back, and her arms were raised above her head as though waiting for another embrace.

He stared at the place where the child grew, nestled beneath the precious dent of her navel, and he bent and kissed the spot. "Dear child," he whispered, "in some magical way, you have become mine tonight. I will never forget."

Talmadge covered her warmly, and went into the kitchen in his dressing gown and prepared herb tea and collected some left-over biscuits from the party and a small pot of honey on a tray. He re-entered the bedroom expecting to waken Ainsley, but she was already up. She had dressed, throwing on a flannel nightgown and a heavy woolen wrapper, and her hair was pulled up under a white cap.

Surprised, he looked at her. "No need for you to get up," he said. "The inn is empty today, and we can treat ourselves to one day of courtship before the world intrudes."

She was sitting in a wing chair by the window, her face white and serious and her hands folded in her lap.

"Last night was neither necessary nor right," she said quietly, pressing her hands together tightly so that they would not shake. She could not look at him directly, for, even as he has walked into the room, she had felt her need for him. Such delight she experienced now just in looking at his intense face, the power of his eyes, the grace and slender strength of his horseman's body, and his nature—so full of hidden complexities a lifetime would not be long enough to know him.

Where had such thoughts come from? she asked herself angrily. If I loved Nathan at all, then how can I love Talmadge so suddenly and completely? This is not love I feel, but some wanton, animal thing born of grief, terror, and relief. This is wrong. Wrong.

"Ours is a marriage of convenience, Talmadge. A marriage dedicated to your father. What happened here last night . . ." Her skin flamed crimson as she spoke. ". . . it was a sacrilege. We are married in name only, and I will not be a wanton. I will not be the things which the world would call me if they knew I was carrying this child by another man." She was almost panting with the pain and the effort of fighting against herself. Confused, angry, ashamed, and desperate in her need for Talmadge, she forced herself to be unyielding.

"We will not share the same bed again, Talmadge. We have sworn to protect this child, and our lust should not be a reward for my shame and error.

"I will remain chaste so that I can know in my heart that this child was not conceived by simple animal desire."

Talmadge could not believe his ears. "You mean to tell me, Ainsley, that you are denying me my conjugal rights?"

"In a marriage such as ours," Ainsley said firmly, "there are no rights, only obligations."

The argument raged through the day, but Talmadge saw that Ainsley would not be budged from her position, and he finally accepted the fact that if he forced himself upon her he might damage her, and their relationship, in ways that could not be repaired.

At last, as the night descended, he acceded to her wishes. "I will not require you to share my bed," he said in rigid fury. "I will force no woman to accept my love. But if you think I am such a fool as to think that last night was a mistake, then you are more of a fool than I. You loved me, Ainsley. Loved me with everything within you—body, heart, and soul. I know it, and therefore I can wait."

Ainsley shuddered at the passion in his voice, but she kept her voice cool and calm. "What can we do so that the servants will not suspect?" she asked.

"Damn, woman," he shouted, exasperated. "I cannot share this bedroom with you and not touch you. That is more than mortal man can be asked!"

"Then I shall sleep in the dayroom. No one need know. I have made that my bedroom on many occasions. After we retire for the night, I shall simply slip through the sliding doors. Since this apartment is self-contained, no one will be the wiser. To all we will give the appearance of being Mr. and Mrs. Talmadge Fairchild, but in our hearts we shall be living the truth."

Frustrated beyond words, Talmadge grabbed up his cloak. "I must get out of this room or I shall go mad," he said. "You foolish, foolish girl. In our hearts we will not be living the truth—our hearts *are* the truth! But you, for pride and shame, refuse to listen."

Chapter Forty

In the weeks that followed, an uneasy truce was struck between Talmadge and Ainsley. Their old friendship, their shared secret, and the child growing heavier and more evident every day, bound them together. Though it was a pale shadow of love, still it was a source of comfort and companionship to them both.

In Ainsley's heart she knew there was a carefulness between them—a barrier—which she had built, and, although sometimes she longed to tear it down with her bare hands, she maintained, as did Talmadge, rigid self-control over the yearnings which would not be stilled.

Talmadge was gone frequently. Often he left in the dead of night, after the arrival of an unseen traveler. She would waken to the sound of hoofbeats in the courtyard, or, more often, to the whispering of men's voices in Talmadge's bedroom, and soon after she would hear the quiet click of the outer door. In the morning when she rose, Talmadge's bed would be empty, and when she checked the stables, his horse would be missing as well.

With the wisdom of a true patriot and friend, she never asked questions, knowing that he would tell her whatever he could.

When Talmadge was at home, he was busy securing provisions, organizing supply trains, and arranging for their protection. To his friends and neighbors he explained his absences by saying simply that he had to scour the countryside to find the supplies which the Continental army required.

Without being told, Ainsley surmised that Talmadge had refitted *The Ainsley* and trained a small crew. She did not even try to discover what the purposes of the ship and its clandestine voyages might be. However, occasionally

Talmadge brought her a small cone of sugar or some peppers. Such goods could only come from the smuggling trade which was once again thriving.

Confusion reigned on the waters of Long Island Sound, as British traders and troop ships, Continental army ships in disguise, maverick traders, Loyalists and Tories in refuge on Long Island, bitter at having been cast out of their New England homes and seeking for revenge, privateers and honest trade ships, all sailed swiftly, silently, by light of the moon. Few ships flew their true colors, and secret harbors and inlets were pocketed with private docks and daring ships playing hide-and-go-seek. Even the French, when they could slip in, still plundered and disrupted the sea commerce.

The most dreadful aspect of the war in New Parrish, and all along the Connecticut shore, was the anger of the night raiders—the dispossessed Tories. With the full cooperation and encouragement of the English, the irregular Loyalist bands ravaged the Connecticut coastline. The most disheartening thing was that somehow the Tory raiders always seemed to know where the supplies for the Continental army were being collected and hidden. It was obvious to the citizens of the coast that there were traitors among them, traitors who were able to send information and messages to the Tory pillagers who were camped on Long Island.

The night raiders would strike without warning, in the dead of the night, always seeming to know the most unguarded and vulnerable places on the coast to land. They sailed from Long Island to Connecticut in swift ships, armed to the teeth, under cover of dark.

When they landed, the Loyalists also seemed to know exactly the right places to target. They attacked swiftly and unerringly, time after time stealing or destroying a shipment collected for the Continental army before it even began its journey to the battlefront.

Attacking with surprise and ferocity, the Loyalist invaders would murder, plunder, and set fire to whatever they could not load onto their swift boats in a matter of minutes. Then with death behind them, their bounty secure, and the supplies for the army in flames, they would sail swiftly back across the sound, evading pursuers and soon returning to the safety of the British-held territory.

Their fury was white-hot because they felt they were not stealing but only taking what was legally their own. So many Loyalists had been hounded from their homes, their property taken, their former neighbors viewing them with envy and hatred. They thought of themselves as heavenly avengers, and they did not shrink from murdering men, women, and children, or from leaving whole communities stripped of food supplies, clothing, and livestock.

Fleeing to Canada, to Long Island, or to any refuge they could find, the dispossessed Loyalists who did not pass the war under house arrest—imprisoned in their own homes—or imprisoned in Continental army prisons wandered penniless, homeless, and without a country.

Such was the bitter price of loyalty to the British Crown in a country which had declared itself an independent nation. Small wonder the Loyalists were bitter. They had been, for generations, landowners, respected citizens, good neighbors, and friends, and now they had become beggars in the country they had helped establish—spit upon, called traitors, and stripped of home and country.

Still the revenge they were taking upon the New England coast was most harsh and it created fear and deprivation in every home in New Parrish.

The Connecticut militia, much of which had been sent home from active duty, now patrolled most of the shoreline, but the Tory raiders still seemed to find unprotected spots. The obvious leaks in security were demoralizing and devastating. Fear and suspicion hovered like a shadow over the people of Connecticut.

It frightened Ainsley to think her father's ship was once more in service, making what had to be most hazardous journeys. She also worried about Brosian and Ebenezer in the relative isolation of Windsor Point.

In the past decade, as Norwalk, Rowayton, and Southport had increased their harbor activities, Windsor Point had become a forgotten port. The marsh grasses had grown so thick and tall that it was almost impossible to find the dock that was hidden there. Although a small band of militiamen patrolled the section of coastline that included Windsor Point, the little harbor itself had seemed too obscure and unused a spot to warrant much protection and Ainsley could not help feeling the two men who had been such loyal friends were in some jeopardy.

Of course there was nothing at Windsor Point of value, and since it was almost invisible from the waters of the sound, Brosian and Ebenezer assured her they were as safe as birds in a nest. Time and again she encouraged the two men to come and spend the winter at Marshfield, but they refused, smiling at her notion that they were in grave danger.

"Doesn't seem that any ship in the world besides *The Ainsley* even knows we're here, Mistress Fairchild," said Ebenezer, smiling. He loved to call Ainsley by her married name. "Besides, even though we are getting on in years, we feel we're doing our part by keeping the inn open to warm the militiamen and give them a place to sleep on a wet and stormy night."

For some time Ainsley had been aware that Talmadge had been gathering together a stockpile of supplies. She had seen the wagons passing down the White Oak Trace, and she suspected, though she never asked, that Talmadge might be using Windsor Point as a staging area. It would make sense, since the establishment was off the beaten track, almost forgotten, and yet fairly close to the major supply roads.

Toward the end of March, even though the wretched cold continued, Talmadge came to her late one afternoon. A group of five militiamen were mounted in the yard, and Talmadge's horse pulled restlessly at his tether. "I am going to be gone for a week, maybe two."

Suddenly her sense of apprehension overcame her and she could not help but ask, "Are you going to Windsor Point? I feel it is dangerous. I have been uneasy about it for a long time."

He nodded. "Logic tells me it should be the safest spot on the New England coast. My intelligence tells me it is free of surveillance, and Ebenezer and Brosian—and the militia—assure me that there is no interest in Windsor Point. Still, I too have begun to feel uneasy. Somehow those damned Loyalists always know too much."

Talmadge frowned, and she saw the shadow of his months of worry and heavy burdens borne alone. "It's as though someone could almost read my mind, watches my every actions, knows all the details about my life. But who? How? Who even knows of my existence? I have done nothing to draw attention to myself. No one outside of our friends and neighbors in New Parrish—and I trust them with my life. But who else would think to watch me? I cannot understand the puzzle and so sometimes I think it must be my foolish imaginings."

He had never said so much to her, and she knew it must be a measure of his worry.

He gave a careless laugh and then walked over to her. She stood and he bent to kiss her gently. As she pressed lightly against him, he felt the child move within her, and he sprang back with a delighted, startled look. With tenderness he bent and kissed her abdomen. "You two take care of one another. I shall return and we will be together until the birth."

She caressed his head gently. "You take care of yourself, too," she replied. "We two will be waiting for you."

Talmadge mounted his horse and he and the men were gone in a whirl of snow.

Something was slowly changing in Ainsley. For the first time in many months she moved about her work with a smile on her face and a song on her lips. There was a special warmth in her voice, and, even though the days continued unseasonably cold, she began airing the rooms, opening shutters, and letting the clean, crisp sunlight bring a new freshness to the stale, dark memories of the winter.

Still, in spite of her feelings of anticipation and joy at the thought of the coming birth of her child and of Talmadge's return, she also felt a unreasoning sense of disaster, and the fear nipped at her heart through the long days.

On the fifth day after Talmadge's departure, Ainsley looked out to see riders approaching. Two of them were young militiamen who had ridden off with Talmadge earlier in the week. The third man was Brosian, and Ainsley's heart almost stopped beating when she saw he was riding Talmadge's horse.

Filled with foreboding she ran down the bricked path and under the winter-bare arbor, she reached out and clutched the plunging horse's bridle. "Brosian!" she cried. "Where's Talmadge? What has happened?"

For answer, Brosian looked at her, swaying in the saddle, and then fell unconscious at her feet. The militiamen, one of whom was wearing a bloody bandage under his hat, saluted her and rode off quickly back down the trace.

Ainsley shouted for help, and, shortly, she had Brosian in a bedroom with a cold cloth on his forehead. Slowly he pulled himself back to consciousness and stared around the room, getting his bearings. Then his eyes focused on Ainsley.

"He's not dead," Brosian whispered. "They took him prisoner."

Ainsley fainted.

Chapter Forty-one

Talmadge woke to the smell and sound of horses, and the unmistakable yawing of a boat under full sail. He had been thrown in the belly of a small frigate, where the raiders' horses were kept. Fortunately, he had been placed behind a small partition or the restless horses would have stomped him to death.

He tried to move but his hands and feet were encased in heavy chains. With stubborn will, he forced himself into a sitting position, although his entire body felt bruised and his head was splitting. He could feel blood oozing down the side of his face from the head wound, and he recalled, in a flash of vivid memory, the rifle butt coming toward him. It was the last thing he could remember.

Next to him he heard a groan, and the hay moved. It was Wilson, one of the Connecticut militiamen who had ridden with him. In the gloom Talmadge could barely make out the young man's face. He had a gash across his cheek where a bullet had grazed him. "There are two more. Both of them were roving militia. I don't know their names. They haven't woke up yet. I hope they're alive."

Talmadge shuddered, "Only four of us—out of twenty. They killed all the rest?"

"I'm not sure, sir. It looked like everyone else was dead, but they didn't take time to check. We killed a few of theirs, too, but we didn't have a chance. Taken by surprise like that!"

"The more fools we," Talmadge said bitterly. "We should have kept better watch. I had a feeling . . ."

"Don't blame yourself, sir. We had to finish loading the wagons. We couldn't both watch and work, and day was coming. Besides, you had set sentries. They must have killed them before they could give warning."

"No," Talmadge said bitterly, "I made the mistake of using the coastal militia for the sentries. They had been lulled into a sense of security about Windsor Point and so, when the temperature dropped so cold, they left their posts and went into the inn to get a drink. That's where I found them just minutes before the Tories attacked."

There was a moment of sickening silence as the implications of that knowledge hit the young man. "Nearly twenty lives lost for a drink?"

Talmadge dropped his aching head to his manacled hands. "Twenty lives lost for a fool of a commander," he said, his voice ragged with self-contempt. "I should have set Ebenezer and Brosian to the task of guarding us—but they are such strong workers I used them unloading the ship instead."

There was a long moment of silence, and then Talmadge groaned again in the pain of his thoughts. "How did the raiders know?" he asked some unseen presence. "How did the Tories know we would be there? Know the night? Know where our supplies were cached? They knew—it wasn't just a guess. They didn't find the harbor by chance. They knew!"

His thoughts were raging and he felt himself almost mad with the puzzle of it. There was an answer, but the answer was elusive and infuriatingly out of his reach.

"Yes indeed, my friend, they did know," a voice said out of the dark. It was a rich, cultivated voice, and Talmadge knew he had heard it before.

Just then the boat lurched, and there was a loud thump against the hull. On deck there was the scurrying of feet, and the sound of sails being lowered.

"What is it?" the young soldier, Wilson, asked apprehensively.

The voice in the darkness answered, "Ice floes. The sound is full of them this winter. It is rumored that the sound froze over so solidly in January that a raiding party walked across to Bridgeport from Long Island and back again on the ice."

Again the maddening familiarity of the voice clawed at Talmadge's memory.

"Who are you, sir?" he asked. "What do you know of this matter?"

Then the man laughed, and he stepped forward in the gloom and lighted a small flint wick. In the brief flare of light, Talmadge saw a face of such hideousness that he drew back. The man's nose and ears were missing, and great purple brands marked his cheeks. His face was wrinkled and deeply lined, and his hair was thin and white and straggled in a fringe from his nearly bald head.

"I believe you know me best as Smith, however, my real name, the one I would like you to remember, is Junius Comstock."

"*You!*" Talmadge exclaimed. "Of course I remember! What are you doing here?"

The man laughed, and in his voice and laughter the old aristocratic arrogance and charm were still as fresh and compelling as they had been when he had been whole and handsome.

"It seems, Captain Fairchild, that a man of my skills is vastly necessary in times of war. The British pardoned my crimes, and I have been their eyes and ears for lo! these many months.

"I promised your father he would pay for my suffering with all he held dear. And so he shall. Wherever he may be, in heaven or in hell, he knows that you—his only living son—and your charming wife are never far from my thoughts.

"And since last summer, never far from my person as well.

"You see, this hideous punishment—this mutilation which your father arranged—has made me a creature of the darkness, a creature of the night, but I have not minded, for the night serves my purposes well. I have learned to live in hiding like an animal. Gone to ground, as the fox would say.

"You would be amazed how many places there are at Marshfield to hide. What a fine vantage point your ridge offers, how easy it is to see the comings and goings of the whole county—and of you and your young warrior companions."

Junius laughed. "If you could think of Windsor Point as the perfect hidden harbor, do you not think I could as well? Perfect. I only had to wait until I saw you sending the provisions down the trace. I could read your thoughts."

"I knew it had to be someone at or near Marshfield, but I never suspected . . ." Talmadge exclaimed, his mind reeling with Comstock's revelations. "Who would think of a man living like a creature in the forest, creeping about at night, spying, peering through windows, becoming less than human, months on end—a living phantom? Who could imagine such hate and obsession?" Talmadge shuddered. "Have you gone mad, do you think?"

Suddenly Comstock drew himself up, the gracious veneer scraped from his voice. "Mad!" he snarled. "If I am, it is your father who is to blame. I danced on Nathan Fairchild's grave!"

"And that arrogant Brosian, that black man who dared to think himself my equal—that cur who informed on me—him, I beat with my own hands. Don't let anyone tell you revenge is not sweet! I beat him to death this very night in the front hall of the inn where he presumed to call himself master."

Talmadge felt the bile rise in his throat like metal. "You did what!" he shouted. "That is not honorable warfare, man—that is bestiality."

"Hah!" Junius sneered. "I thought we had already established that I am a beast—I live like a beast—and I revenge myself like a beast."

"And Ebenezer?" Talmadge asked.

"Unfortunately, he was one of the first ones shot in the raid, so I did not have the satisfaction of killing him. You, however, I instructed the men not to kill. That is why you were simply disabled by the blow of the rifle butt. You I wanted alive so that you could know that vengeance is mine. Your father died too soon for me to have the satisfaction of watching him suffer."

Talmadge was silent.

Junius came forward and placed his foot on Talmadge's chest, forcing him down to the floor. "I could grind my filthy boot into your face, and you could do nothing," Comstock growled.

Talmadge still remained silent. Comstock kicked him in the ribs, hard, but Talmadge remained stone-still.

"Speak to me!" Comstock shouted. "Have you heard what I have said? I have destroyed your enterprise, taken you prisoner, and I shall return to an unprotected Marshfield and do as I will."

Talmadge did not make a sound. No word passed his lips. It was as though Junius Comstock did not exist.

Infuriated, Junius reached down and pulled Talmadge to his feet. In the gloom of the reeking hold, he shoved the prisoner back against the wall of the compartment, which dripped with the condensed moisture from the cold sea outside and the bilge waters within.

With his arm, the older man pinned Talmadge's throat and he put his horribly scarred face so close that even in the darkness Talmadge could see the glittering eyes.

"And I know the truth," the man hissed, saliva running from his ruined mouth. "I know the truth about the baby. I shall tell your minister. You are lost, the mother is lost, the child is lost, and Marshfield will be lost. I know that it is Nathan's child, not yours. I know the chaplain who married you—and when. I know it all. I have seen it all. I have watched and listened. There will be no legal heir to Marshfield, the house of Nathan Fairchild will be in ruins. Ruins. Do you hear me? So suffer and be damned—for I am damned and I suffer."

Still Talmadge said nothing. Junius Comstock drew back with a great roar of hatred and anguish and smashed Talmadge across the face with all of his strength, and Talmadge slumped to the floor, unconscious.

As soon as Ainsley had turned Brosian's care over to Mrs. Seeley, she had her gig harnessed and drove with haste to the home of the chairman of the Safety Committee.

"Who is taking the post to General Washington's headquarters?" she asked. "I must send a message at once."

"A troop is passing through this evening," Mason Endgrove told her. "They will stop for dispatches."

She handed him the hastily written letter. "This is to be handed to General Washington himself," she insisted. "It is concerning Captain Talmadge Fairchild. The Tories have taken him prisoner. They have him somewhere on Long Island. He must be exchanged immediately! I will write to every person of position I know—I will pay anything. Whatever ransom . . ."

"There, there, Mistress Fairchild." Mason Endgrove was sympathetic and encouraging. "They are making exchanges quite readily. As long as the prisoners are of mutual rank. I shall see that your message is sent posthaste."

The waiting was desperately painful. No word came. And the days seemed endless to Ainsley. Brosian was slowly repairing, although his injuries were vicious and extensive.

"He beat me with an old cane of your father's," Brosian told her. "It was like seeing a ghost rise from the grave. He came at me, and he was the most ugly thing I have ever seen. Hardly a man, even—or like no man I've ever seen. His face is a ruin. But he is a ruin, too."

Brosian's eyes stared with the memory. "He had another two men hold me so I couldn't move, and then he beat me until I couldn't feel anything and his arm was too tired to raise it again."

For the first time, out of his swollen mouth, Brosian gave a little laugh. "I think both of us thought I was dead."

The militia had buried the dead—all except Ebenezer. They brought Ebenezer back to Marshfield and he was buried under the trees near Nathan and Daniel and John Windsor. The inn at Windsor Point was locked and closed, the buildings on the dock were padlocked, and the river reclaimed the secret harbor as its own. There was just enough room in the reeds for *The Ainsley* to slip into hidden harbor.

When morning came, the Tories came down to drag their prisoners up onto the deck and to unload the stolen cargo. As they pushed Talmadge onto the wharf, the freezing breeze from the water cleared his mind so that, while still appearing dazed and stumbling, he was able, in reality, to take the measure of the situation. The other three prisoners, also manacled, shuffled behind him. They were shoved into a small hut at the end of the dock and left there with a guard.

In a few minutes a small squad of British regulars marched up. The commander of the guard spoke to the captain of the Tory raiding ship. With a shock of surprise, Talmadge recognized the Tory raider; he was a ship's master Talmadge had known who had sailed out of Rowayton. The man had a lovely home on a hillside, and a beautiful wife and several children, as Talmadge remembered. The two of them had met on many occasions. It grieved Talmadge to see this fine man now an embittered raider without home or community.

The British soldiers walked to the hut and threw open the door, and the Tory captain prepared to return to his ship, but Talmadge called out, "Richard! Richard Blount!"

Turning in surprise the captain walked rapidly over to the hut and looked in. Talmadge nodded to him. "It is Talmadge Fairchild. We sailed from the same harbor many a time. It is sad that we meet in such a way, old friend."

Richard Blount stared at Talmadge. There was no warmth

or kindness in his rigid face. "Sad indeed. Sad for all who have brought this ghastliness upon us. Revolutionaries, insurrectionists. You have destroyed the lives of every good, decent, responsible citizen of these colonies. Do not think that we are old friends. Friendship was lost to me the day I lost my home and my ship to your hellish declaration of independence. What right did any of you have to steal a nation?"

Blount strode away, but Talmadge felt, in spite of his words, that the man had been moved to see him. Something told him that the war had not completely destroyed the humanity inside the man.

The soldiers lined up the prisoners and commanded them to march. They were led onto a second dock and there they were placed in a heavy longboat. Four powerful seamen began to row them toward a large ship anchored in the sound with British regulars standing guard at bow and stern. Across the water they could see the mouth of the mighty Hudson River and the harbor of the city of New York. The harbor bristled with British ships.

As they pushed away from the dock, Junius Comstock came striding toward them, shouting to the British soldiers, "Stop! Bring him back! He is my prisoner!"

The young officers did not even deign to look back at the grotesque figure on the wharf; they simply stood guard as the steady sweep of the oars carried the prisoners closer and closer to the anchored boat. On its prow Talmadge made out the name *HMS Jersey*, and he knew they were headed toward the notorious prison boat from which few ever returned.

Talmadge entered the ship, whose bowels were worse than the lowest circle of Hades in Dante's Inferno, resigned with realistic fatalism to the fate of those who rotted to death in that hold. He had, however, misjudged the determination of Ainsley, and the affection in which he was held by General Washington. Within days of his capture and imprisonment, messages had passed through the highest military authorities.

A prisoner exchange was immediately arranged, and the three young militia officers who had been captured with him were traded for three young and titled English officers. However, the British sensed, because of General Washington's particular interest, that Talmadge was a prisoner of a different sort. Even though his rank was not extremely prestigious, they were smart enough to realize that General Washington was determined to obtain this particular prisoner, for whatever price they might require, and so, they proposed that Talmadge be exchanged for the leading Tory commander who was currently in prison in Boston.

In order to affect the exchange, the Tory prisoner had to be brought from Boston by ship. Choppy seas and another cold spell delayed the voyage, so Talmadge found himself facing more days of prison in the hellish hold of the prison ship, surrounded by more human misery than he had ever seen.

Wounded men, men dying of the cold, men with blue lips and crippled hands, men who were starving, men with dysentery, men blinded by gunshot, and men who had lost hope and sanity—all thrown together in the filthy straw in the rocking hold. Talmadge, who had never been seasick in his life, fought back the nausea of the constant rocking of the ship at anchor.

Food rations were minimal, and Talmadge felt his strength and his will to live gradually fading. The only thing that kept the fire in his heart blazing was the thought of Ainsley, and the last hideous threats of Junius Comstock.

"I must live!" Talmadge whispered to himself day after endless day. "I must live. No one else can protect her and the child. I must live. As long as Comstock is alive, I must live!"

After almost a month, Talmadge was dragged up from the hold. He was filthy, and the blood had matted on his hair. His eyes blinked in the unaccustomed light.

The commander of the prison ship looked at him with disgust. "What value you can be to the Continental army I can scarcely imagine. However, it would seem they wish your return enormously. We have been informed that the exchange will take place this afternoon. I would recommend you try to make yourself presentable."

Talmadge fixed the man with cold eyes, and the officer felt himself draw back from the power and invincibility of his prisoner's face.

"In the meantime, you are a sought-after fellow. Someone else has requested the opportunity to visit with you." The commander waved him off, and Talmadge's two guards pushed him toward the doors of a small deck cabin. He en-

tered and discovered Junius Comstock sitting at at a tiny
portable desk. The two guards stood beside him, and, on the
desk, Talmadge saw a large sledge hammer and file.

"These are the tools with which the guards remove your
shackles," Junius explained. "It seems, against my will, you
are to be exchanged. We spies are necessary, but not very
highly regarded, *n'est pas?*"

Talmadge stood silently, watching and waiting.

"I see you will not rise to the bait," Junius continued. "I
said, 'we spies' because I have received absolute confirmation that it is you who runs the Continental army's information services out of Connecticut. It is not just supplies which
you are sending to the army, but military secrets smuggled
in from Long Island and New York City. Posing as an innocent quartermaster you are doing more damage to the British
cause than a regiment!

"My superiors do not believe me. He is too far from the
front lines, they say. He is known to be organizing the supply wagons. He has no contacts. Yes, they have all kinds of
reasons why I am mistaken—and they know my personal an-
imosity toward you. In final truth, they do not really trust
me. But I will have the truth from you, before you are
traded.

"I will make you speak the truth and have you hanged as
a traitor or spy, or I will destroy you. Either way I will win."

Talmadge did not move, and his face remained as still as
a mask.

"Damn you!" Junius cried. "Have you no blood in those
veins? You *will* admit to the truth! We have only minutes!
Admit that you are the instrument of the Continental army or
I swear you will wish you were dead!"

Talmadge smiled. He could not explain even to himself
why he smiled, but, in some odd way, it was a smile of triumph. What could Comstock do to him that could possibly
be worse than what Comstock had already done to himself?
As Talmadge looked at the raving, desperate man, he suddenly realized that the most awful things this man could do
could not make Talmadge the prisoner that Comstock himself was. By the failures of his own life, Comstock had made
himself a prisoner—a prisoner of his own imperfections,
lusts, hatred, and misery.

"You smile!" Comstock screamed. "You smile!" He
grabbed up the heavy iron mallet and raised it above his

head, aiming at Talmadge. The guards, astonished, pulled Talmadge away from the blow, but Talmadge, weakened by his weeks in prison, fell off balance and his right leg stretched in front of him. In a flash, Junius aimed the mallet and the punishing blow smashed into Talmadge's unprotected knee.

There was a sickening crunch and the sound of splintering bones, and the world went mercifully black.

Talmadge did not know how long he was unconscious. He woke in the back of a wagon, and the jolting was so painful he had to bite his cheeks in order not to scream. A man's voice spoke, but Talmadge could not focus his eyes or see. Staring wide he saw only a great red sea and, in the middle of it the crashing hammer and the sound of destruction.

"Here," the voice said, "take this. It will put you to sleep. We have five more hours to Marshfield."

"Marshfield," Talmadge murmured. He did not cry, but the medical aide who had been assigned to accompany Captain Fairchild to his home saw in astonishment a tear running from the captain's closed eyes.

Chapter Forty-two

When the baby was born in at the end of May, Talmadge was still bed-ridden. After the long, intense winter, spring had come like a debutante late to her own coming-out party. No one could remember a spring with such balmy air, such abundant flowers, such a promise of rich harvest. Only there were no men to break the ground or sow the seed.

Women put on dresses made of poplin, hiked up their skirts, and waded into the fields. Old men who had long since turned the duties of farming over to their sons hitched up the mules once more and walked the plow lines.

Ainsley was not able to go to the fields, but she did work in the kitchen garden. It was her great love, and she planted the rows of peas, carrots, cabbage, and potatoes as straight and abundantly as ever.

Surprisingly, Talmadge was proving to be a good patient. He took his medicine, and filled his day with reading and correspondence. However, there was a change in him since his imprisonment. Some essential characteristic of his nature—the light, vigor, the sureness—seemed to have been lost. He would sometimes be lost in thought for hours, and Ainsley, sitting by his bedside stitching clothing for the new baby, would feel he was far away in some secret world of his own to which she would never hold the key.

The doctor had stared at the ruined knee and had known there was no hope of setting the broken bones. They were smashed into a hundred pieces. Fortunately, none of the splinters had broken through the skin, and so the dreadful fear of gangrene and amputation was lessened.

With little hope the doctor put the leg in splints and bound it tightly. "Nature and God will have to determine what comes of it, my boy," the doctor said, shaking his head sympathetically. "At least you have the prettiest nurse in Connecticut."

Talmadge turned to look at Ainsley. Even though she was very thin, as everyone was, with the severely limited food rations, still, somehow, her pregnancy became her, and she seemed to bloom and glow before his eyes. How he loved her, and yet, as he lay on the bed, a crippled and permanently damaged man, he felt as though his heart had turned to ashes. There was no wanting left in him, only a sense of grayness.

Instinctively, Ainsley knew that Talmadge needed time, and that his strong body and spirit would mend. With patience and a tender love, she cared for his wounds, fed him, acted as his secretary, read to him, and bathed his thin, exhausted body.

As the warmth of May filled the world, she flung open the windows of Talmadge's bedroom, and had a chair made in which he could sit and be wheeled around. His leg no longer caused him excruciating pain at the slightest motion, and the frown of pain which had become a permanent part of his expression was eased.

Little by little she knew his body was healing itself, and as his strength grew, she felt her love for him growing as well. It was as though, in caring for his body it had become part of her own, and they had become one being. And she felt her life would never be sweeter than in these weeks when they sat silently together, the two of them secure and away from the world, wrapped in the healing, mending, intimate knitting together of his body and their spirits.

When she went into labor, he knew it before she did. He was watching her read by lamplight one evening toward the end of May. It was unnaturally warm, and she had taken off her lace shawl. Her neck and breast were moist with perspiration, and her upper lip was dewed.

"Don't read anymore, my dear," Talmadge said. "I think you may need all your strength this night."

She looked up at him, surprised. "Talmadge," she laughed, "whatever do you mean?" The child was enormous inside of her, and she sat uncomfortably, at a hard angle in the chair. "By my calculations I have a week or more to go."

Talmadge acknowledged, "I have no expertise in these

things, but there is something about you tonight, Ainsley,
some sense of waiting and listening, as though to a song you
alone can hear. I think you know it will be soon."

From the dayroom, which had been made into Talmadge's
recovery room, Talmadge heard her first cry. She was in Nathan's old bedroom, just through the doors from where he
lay.

"Talmadge!" she gasped, and he grabbed the bell by his
bed and rang it furiously. Mrs. Seeley came running in in her
nightgown and cap, and before long, the bedroom was filled.
The midwife had come quickly, and the chambermaid was
running to and from the kitchen with clean towels, sheets,
and hot water.

In a frenzy of concern, Talmadge lay helplessly on his
bed, listening to every sound, every nuance. He heard
Ainsley's frantic breathing and groans, the muted cries of
pain. He heard the commands of the midwife to push, and
the gasping and grunting of the unbelievable effort.

"Ainsley," he groaned in sympathetic agony. "Ainsley."
His sweat-drenched hands grabbed the sheets and matted
them into a ball in his fist. In the midst of her suffering, he
felt his own heart break open. It was as though, while
Ainsley struggled to give birth to the baby, she had somehow given new birth to Talmadge—to the old Talmadge. He
felt all the emotions of his passionate heart flood back into
his body, like the return of his lost soul, and he suddenly felt
whole, and real, and, for the first time in his life he understood that man is born of woman.

At that very moment the air was split with the sharp
sound of a slap, and then the robust wail of a lusty newborn
infant. Mrs. Seeley ran to the open doors, and cried to
Talmadge, "It's a boy, Mr. Fairchild. The finest, fairest child
you ever saw. As blond as your father. Won't that be nice!
It will be like having a bit of your father with you always.
You and Mistress Ainsley are a family now, for sure and for
true."

Talmadge smiled. "Yes, Mrs. Seeley, for sure and for true,
a family."

Ainsley's milk flowed abundantly, and when she put her
white breast, filled to the point of pain, to the child's mouth,

he drank with a lusty eagerness. His face grew rosy, and his limbs were firm and wiry.

In the second week, as they removed the bindings from Ainsley's breast and abdomen and allowed her out of bed for the first time, she laughed out loud. "Oh Mistress Hartley," she exclaimed to the midwife, "you are much too careful of me. Why, I feel as well as a girl. You must not keep me cooped up in this bedroom another day. I am not an invalid, and I do believe that having this beautiful child has strengthened rather than weakened me."

It was true. Ainsley had never looked more radiant or more beautiful. She hurried into the room where Talmadge lay, and she gasped to see him standing, dressed, with crutches under his arms.

Rushing to him she threw her arms about him. "Dear, dear Talmadge! Look at you! Up and about and on your own!" She laughed with delight. "We have both escaped our beds! Stand there and I shall bring your son to you." She turned to go, but he laid a hand on her arm.

"No, I shall bring myself to him." With those words he moved forward on his crutches. His motions were awkward and stiff, but he made slow progress across the room. With each step he seemed to understand the rhythm more precisely. The smashed leg, still in its splints, was stiff, straight, and useless. It still would not hold his weight, but he dragged it, leaning on the crutches, and his other leg proved strong and dependable.

"Talmadge, you are doing wonderfully!" Ainsley exclaimed.

Together they stood by the side of the little cradle and both wondered, for the hundredth time, at the perfection of the tiny infant. His hair was the color of sunshine, and his entire body seemed to be dusted with gold.

Leaning over the crib, Talmadge placed his lean, muscled hand, browned from the years of sun and labor, gently, with infinite care, upon the downy head of the beautiful boy. "Rest well, little Nathan Windsor Fairchild." He smiled, and turned to Ainsley. "I can't wait!" he said. "I can't wait until he is old enough, and I am well enough, to show him Marshfield."

The next day, as Ainsley was nursing the baby, she looked out her casement window and saw Talmadge. He was swinging methodically on his crutches up and down the hard-packed yard in front of the stables.

Watching him, the effort of his labor showing in the strain of his face, the perspiration causing his shirt to cling to his thin body, the heavy panting as he paused, his head down gasping for air, Ainsley felt tears spring to her eyes. She knew that his time on the prison ship and his wound had weakened him, and it would be many weeks before he would be able to rebuild his strength—if ever.

Feeling full of vitality, and eager to make Marshfield as productive as possible with the few field workers that were available to her, Ainsley threw herself into the summer needs of the estate. Talmadge, however, withdrew into himself, and, other than the child, whom they called Windsor in memory of Ainsley's father, and the necessities of helping Ainsley run Marshfield, he had only one focus, and that was to walk again.

Ainsley watched him from the time he rose in the morning until the last weary minutes of his long day, and every moment that he could, he was exercising his body.

After a month, he had thrown the crutches away, and had fashioned himself a stout cane. Each morning, in his room, he did exercises and lifted stones wrapped in leather until the muscles in his shoulders, arms, and back were powerful and rippling again. In the afternoons, he walked. His limp was pronounced, and often she saw the sweat pouring in rivulets down his face, but he walked up the steep hill that led to the cemetery on the brow of the ridge. Up the hill he walked and paced across the fields, never stopping. Awkward and uneven though his gait was, she saw his stride lengthen, saw the muscles of the thigh and calf of his good leg grow hard and flexible. His other leg, too, became rigid with muscle, but nothing he did could make the knee bend.

She watched, in silent sympathy, the first day he remounted his horse. Without flexibility in his wounded leg he could no longer post to trot, but rode high in the saddle, clenching his mount with his strong thigh muscles. He would be able to ride adequately, but he was a man who had ridden a horse with the joy of absolute skill, as though he and the steed were one wild, free creature—and now, forever, he would ride with awkward carefulness.

His resolution, his lack of self-pity, his quiet acceptance, only made her love him the more. He no longer required her nursing care and she missed the touch, the sight, the comfort of his body.

Somehow, in her heart, Ainsley had believed that once she had recovered from Windsor's birth and Talmadge was up and around, he would come to her bed. Would speak to her of love. Something in her had softened with the birth of her son. She understood that love is too precious a thing to ever waste. She would carry the burden of her past in silence—her mistakes, her foolishness, her sins—but she would not let it destroy her opportunity to build a better life. She would give love to Talmadge, who had waited for it so long. Finally, at last, she would give herself to be loved by him.

Oh, she loved her beautiful baby son with all of her heart, but she realized that this love was not enough. Having known the passion of loving Talmadge, she yearned to have him with her again, to feel their marriage was final and fulfilled. She could not, would not, believe that Talmadge had lost all such feelings for her, and yet the weeks went by and he made no gesture or move which would give her hope that he thought of her as a desirable woman.

Perhaps, she thought fearfully, when they imprisoned him, they damaged some deep and inward part beyond repair. Perhaps he has lost the ability to feel deeply. Perhaps his heart, his hope, his joy—perhaps these are the real casualty.

In late July the doctor came to Marshfield to see Talmadge and to check on his progress. The two men were in Talmadge's room for a long period of time, then, finally, the doctor walked out alone. His face was solemn.

Ainsley ran over to him. "Doctor Allen, tell me. What do you think? Hasn't he made splendid progress? He is riding his horse, he walks miles every day with only the help of a cane. Surely such recovery is remarkable!" She looked desperately into the man's eyes for reassurance.

"I believe Talmadge has recovered in an amazingly short period of time," the doctor assented. "He has worked himself back to the peak of health. As far as I can ascertain, the bones of his leg have knit together very firmly."

"Then why do you look so grim, Doctor Allen?" Ainsley challenged.

The doctor sighed. "Perhaps it would be better if he told you himself. However, since you have some medical knowledge, I will try to explain it. You see, when Talmadge's leg was smashed, the bones of the knee joint were shattered.

Those bones have knit together in one continuous mass. They have knit remarkably well, I might add, so that the leg can take considerable stress."

"But that is good news, isn't it doctor?" she cried, distressed at the doctor's sober face.

"Well, yes," replied the doctor, "good news in that the leg will be usable and sturdy. But you see, Ainsley, to all intents and purposes, Talmadge now has no knee. He will never be able to bend that leg. Not in the slightest."

She stared at him.

"You see, my dear, he is very, very fortunate that he did not lose the leg, but he will always walk with a pronounced limp, and there will always be limitations. The leg will never bend again."

Tears were streaming down Ainsley's face. "Is that all? Do you think such things matter to me? He is still with us— well, strong, and able. He can go about his daily life, and do everything that matters. What care I a fig for a straight leg? It will only match the man himself—for he is as straight and true as the mast of a tall ship."

The doctor patted her arm. "He will need to hear you say that, Ainsley. This is a great blow to a man who has strode across the sea. A greater blow than you can imagine."

"I will not let it be so!" she blazed. "How fortunate we are that we bear so small a scar from such a great conflagration as this terrible war."

"Well said," the doctor concurred. "And how is our young Master Windsor?"

Ainsley laughed, "Just as plump and happy as his mother."

She meant to go to Talmadge as soon as the doctor drove away, but the baby started crying, and a small fire broke out in the grease pot near the kitchen hearth.

Talmadge's door remained resolutely shut, but, as soon as she put Windsor down for his nap, she walked over and knocked on it firmly. There was no answer, and she saw that Talmadge had left the room—probably when she had been tending to the fire.

Calling to Mrs. Seeley to watch the baby, she ran outside and looked around, calling his name, then she saw his tall, determined figure, with its oddly appealing, uneven gait, climbing the hill toward the ridge.

It was a perfect summer's day, and the air was washed

with sunlight and the gardens humming with the sounds of bees. Butterflies danced in the gentle wind, and the sweet smell of clover hay hung on the branches of the trees.

With eagerness she gathered up her skirts. She was wearing an old dress of sky-blue poplin with a white polka-dotted swiss collar and matching apron. Her waist was even more slender than before she had borne Windsor. "The child drinks me away," she had laughed to Mrs. Seeley as she asked the woman to take in the waists of several of her gowns. "There shall be nothing left of me if he continues so!"

In her haste, Ainsley had not bound her hair, and it hung to her waist in a forest of auburn curls. With skirts, ribbons, and hair flying, she raced up the hill in the direction she had seen Talmadge taking. Even at her fastest she knew she was no match for Talmadge's powerful, limping stride; still, if she could get to the crest of the ridge, she could see which way he was heading—perhaps call to him and have him wait for her to catch up.

Almost at the end of her breath, she raced over the crest of the hill and, panting, ran toward the little cemetery where now Ebenezer rested with the others. Talmadge had had a gray stone fence erected around the burial plot. Flowers and vines had grown over the stones, giving the place a soft, loved look, as though it were a sweet bower bed.

Ainsley paused, gasping for breath, and, looking up, saw Talmadge standing on the far side of the cemetery next to a great oak tree. His hand was resting on the trunk of the tree, and he was looking out over the spreading fields and woods of Marshfield and on to the distant glint of the blue waters of the sound.

Suddenly, fear clutched her heart. Was he looking at Marshfield, at the land, at this place of his inheritance—the place that she loved so much that she could not imagine others might see it differently? Or was he looking at the ocean, at the freedom of the seas?

For the rest of his life, on the land, he would be a cripple, a man of limitations, but on the sea he would be free to move with the swiftness of the wind. Was the sea, perhaps, calling him away? Calling him from Marshfield, from her, even from young Windsor? Were there only harsh memories here, and harsh realities and a future that would carry the past like a heavy stone?

For the first time she felt a clutch at her heart. For so long, almost as long as she could remember, she had taken Talmadge's love for her for granted. She had assumed it was as much a natural part of her life as the air she breathed, but now she saw him as a man apart. A man with his own silently borne pain, a man who could no longer live in the shadow of his father, a man wounded by others but who would not let those wounds define him. And she, Ainsley, who had married him, had accepted his love and then turned from it, had she wounded him as well? Did he bear her wound like a scar upon his heart?

Fear overwhelmed her. She could not lose him—not now. Not when she saw him for the first time as he really was, a giant of a man. A man who had lived his life for others, and in doing so had somehow become greater than the sum of all of them.

"Talmadge!" she cried. "Oh, Talmadge! I didn't know where you had gone."

He turned to see her, standing in the steady breeze at the top of the ridge, and he felt as though she had been blown to him on the breath of heaven.

She ran toward him on unsteady legs, and he turned back to stare out across the vista. "I'm standing here trying to figure a reason why wheat refuses to grow in our best fields. There must be an explanation, but it will not present itself to me. Perhaps one of our grandchildren shall discover the cause."

A shudder of relief went through Ainsley, and, feeling weak, she leaned against him. He had been thinking about—planning for—Marshfield, carrying it in his mind just as she did all the time. He loved it just as she did. He would not leave! Her heart lifted.

Talmadge leaned on his cane and put his free arm around Ainsley. The two stood staring out across the estate. They were silent for a long moment.

"I am damaged goods," Talmadge said softly. "I so desperately wanted to come to you whole and strong. But you shall have to take me as I am." There was in his voice a touch of humor and quiet acceptance. "Will you reconsider our marriage of convenience, Ainsley? Will you have me thus?"

Without a word she turned to him, tears of relief and joy

streaming down her face. "Have you, Talmadge? Have you? Oh, the joy of it! How can I tell you?"

"This way," he said, and bent to kiss her trembling lips. They tasted of salt and summer and life and tomorrow.

"You understand, Ainsley," Talmadge explained to her, "it was important to me that when I came to you at last—when we would be man and wife in truth—I wanted more than anything in this world to be completely healed in body and in mind.

"I could feel that my mind had healed, but I had to find a way to make my body strong and well. I gave it everything I could, but there are some injuries that cannot be healed— that we must wear forever as badges of our past.

"When the doctor told me the truth about my leg today, I had to be alone. I needed to think. In truth, it was a grave disappointment. However, as I stand here looking over Marshfield, the wonder of just being alive has overwhelmed me.

"I see Marshfield not as it is today, still half-wilderness, but rather, I see it as it could be—all its possibilities. Suddenly, all the coming days of my life seem infinitely precious. All the disappointment and loss has been replaced with a simple desire not to lose one minute more.

"Ainsley, my precious wife, will you take me as I am, flawed and injured, but filled with hope and determination to love you, care for you, raise our son, and build something of worth here together?" He looked into her wide eyes, and he saw, shining in them, his own reflection. "Dear dear Talmadge," she replied, "I too do not want to lose a minute more. I wasted the whole first of my life on an unwatered love; I will not make the same mistake again.

"My dear husband, I tell you true—your wounds have only made you stronger. To me, your walk is the noblest, grandest sight in the world. I would not trade or change one thing of what you are today—not one hair of your head, not one scar on your body, not one furrow on your brow—you are so dear to me. Dearer than you can ever know. Dearer than I can ever express."

"And you to me," he whispered huskily, abandoning his cane and sweeping her into his arms. Even though he limped, his strong arms carried her in total security down through the meadow and into the shelter of the oak trees.

There, in the woods, where moss and fallen leaves formed

a bed as soft as down, he laid her before him. Then, removing his long vest, he rolled it up and placed it beneath her head. His white shirt with its full sleeves seemed brilliant against the dark backdrop of shade and trees. She lay as silent as a doe beneath him, and, with a cry of joy, he lay full length next to her and gently began to unlace her bodice.

Ainsley's heart leaped with the glory of his hands on her breasts. He stroked her gently, and she felt as though she had never known her body before, had never understood where it began and ended—what its possibilities were. He was discovering her—and in doing so was discovering her for herself.

Her body began and ended where his hand lay upon it. Oh, the wonder of his lean and tender face above her own, filling her eyes and her universe.

His dark hair mingled with her auburn hair, and the moss and leaves clung to their bodies as they made love to one another as though they were the first in the world to discover the delights of flesh and bone and the secret places of the hidden heart.

"Oh, my darling," Talmadge whispered, "I have waited since the Moon Maiden called forth the earth for this moment. You are mine. You have thrown away all of the walls and the fearful care. You have given yourself to me."

His hands traced her alabaster skin, the smooth long line of her torso and hips, the slender curves of her legs, and the delicate instep of her foot. He kissed the instep and held it against his cheek.

When he lowered his body toward her, the muscles on his shoulders and arms were like cords of steel—a place of haven and desperate joy. She rose and licked his fragrant skin.

In the great cataclysmic moment of their lovemaking, Ainsley reached out and grasped the thick tufts of grass at the base of the tree, her fingers interlaced in the coarse strands of green, and pressed into the rich, loamy soil. In some cosmic way she felt as though in this moment of true union, she and Talmadge and Marshfield became as one.

This was the moment of their marriage—the moment of their beginning. All the days of their past had only been preparation for this glorious, holy, eternal completion.

Talmadge gave a mighty shout of fulfillment, and then, with a smile of infinite gratitude and love, remained above her, looking into her eyes and feasting for one last pristine moment upon the beauty of her white, pink-blushed skin.

"I thought I heard the angels sing," he whispered wonderingly.

Ainsley laughed. "You did," she said merrily, "and you shall hear them often. Again and again."

He embraced her then. "Ainsley," he whispered, "for the first time in my life, I am a whole man."

Chapter Forty-three

At last, Marshfield had a loving master in residence. Talmadge, confined by his injury, remained at Marshfield during the last years of the war.

Unknown to his friends and neighbors, he continued to run the intelligence organization for the Continental army. His couriers and sources created a stream of information necessary to the defense and battle strategies of General Washington and his assault on the British in New York. Supplies wagons, cattle drives, and the increased productivity of the farms and manufacturing centers in the southeastern section of Connecticut were also his responsibility, as he continued to be a supply master as well as a secret intelligence agent.

Talmadge also took over much of the running of Marshfield so that Ainsley would have more time for Windsor, and together they managed to keep the estate productive and efficient. The inn remained open, but they agreed that as soon as the war was over they would close it and remodel the house so that the whole thing would be their residence.

In September of that year, with Talmadge well and the baby strong and healthy, Ainsley and Talmadge joyfully brought young Nathan Windsor Fairchild to church for the first time.

As they walked into the lovely meetinghouse at the edge of the green square—God's acre, set aside at the center of the community as a place where all could worship—the tall spire shone in the morning light and the open doors seemed to bid all welcome. Friends and neighbors flocked around to cluck over the handsome child, but the Reverend Witherspoon, who had not come to Marshfield to visit Talmadge during his long recuperation, or to pay respects to Ainsley on the birth of her child, made no move of welcome. He stood high and unbending on the second tier pulpit, looking down with fury and contempt at his flock.

Over the last three years he had ceased all of his ministerial visitations, claiming, from the pulpit, that those who were diseased, or who had lost a loved one in the war, had earned such sorrow through hidden sin and did not deserve visits of comfort from one ordained by the Lord. Sundays had become a day of misery for those who attended church, and yet, if anyone dared to criticize or to attempt to issue a formal complaint against the minister, the man himself would appear on their doorstep and threaten them with the loss of their covenant and expulsion from the congregation.

Such was the power of the Reverend Witherspoon's office and personality that with all the influential men of the community occupied with matters of the war and survival, the years went by and the churchman retained his pulpit. Not only did Witherspoon remain the minister, but he continued to receive his portion of New Parrish's annual taxes, all of which were paid to the Congregational Church. Selectmen of the town were suspicious that Witherspoon's accounting held some questionable aspects, but, again, the rigors of the war had distracted those in authority from focusing on such matters.

Talmadge and Ainsley sat in the Fairchild pew toward the front of the church. Ainsley looked around her. The hall was only half filled. It smote her like a blow that with exception of a few wounded veterans and some young officers home on leave, the congregation was made up almost entirely of women and older men. She reached over and touched Talmadge's hand in gratitude. He looked at her and smiled, and all the love of half his lifetime showed in that smile. She blushed and ducked her head, her mind filled with the images and intimacies of their lovemaking.

A motion in the aisle caught Ainsley's eye, and she saw Marnie Talbot approaching. Marnie had married a lieutenant of the Continental army. The officer had been placed in charge of a contingent of the New Parrish militia, although his home was Baltimore, and had fallen in love with Marnie when visiting New Parrish as a guest of the lively young girl's brother. The two had been married at a small wedding in early spring, and now, Ainsley noted as Marnie slid into her pew and smiled over at Ainsley and Talmadge, that Marnie was expecting her first child.

The girl's beautiful face and dark chestnut hair shone in the drab, coolness of the plain church. She was wearing a claret-colored shoulder cape against the chill, and it was tied with a wide satin bow at her throat. Her trim satin bonnet matched the bow, and her dress was a deep shade of burgundy, but even its full, rounded skirt could not mask her pregnancy.

As the opening hymn began, Marnie stood and sang with all her heart, "O Loving Father, We Come Unto Thee." Her clear, pure soprano voice soared to the tall spires of the church, a prayer that united all of them in their spirits as they worshiped with hearts full of fear and need. She was obviously extremely happy in her impending motherhood, and Ainsley felt a shared joy for her young friend. What a sweet mother Marnie would be!

For a moment, the chapel seemed filled with the presence of all those who were gone—the sons, brothers, fathers, husbands—and every voice, carried by Marnie's heartfelt plea, singing for the Lord and for those who were in peril.

Only Ainsley noted that Reverend Witherspoon's furious eyes was upon the girl, and her glorious spiritual communion with the Lord through her song seemed to rouse in him an anger that stained his already beet-red face with a mottled purple rage. Scarcely had the hymn been completed than the minister was on his feet. His voice issued like a boom of thunder into the hushed congregation.

"Defiled! We are defiled! How dare any woman wearing the mark of the sin of Eve show her face in the House of the Lord until she is delivered of her evil and cleansed!

"You women—you fruit of the Devil who first required of man that he should fall—you who, under the cloak of marriage, cause men to fall and fall again until they are prisoners of those devilish and satanic emotions which bar man from God—how dare you come into the House of the Lord wearing the great belly of such shame! Do you not know that all who look upon you know by your visual testimony that you have committed the sin of the flesh?

"How dare you wear the issue of the pleasures of the flesh as though it were a badge of honor. No woman who shows the visual signs of such sin—married or unmarried—is fit to walk in the meetinghouse of God. Nor should she be seen upon the streets, or in the daylight. Nor allow herself to parade in front of children, men, and other women.

"Shameless. Shameless and proud." Shouting, he pointed his finger at Marnie. The young woman's cheeks were flushed with embarrassment, and she seemed to shrink before the onslaught. Putting her hand over her eyes, she turned her face away, but the minister would not stop.

"Leave! Leave this place of worship, and return no more until you are cleansed." His voice rolled like a trumpet into the silence, and Marnie began to weep quietly. She picked up her pocketbook and hymnal and tried to slide quietly from the pew, but, as luck would have it, her skirt caught on the edge, and, weeping frantically, she stopped to tear it away.

Talmadge was immediately out of his seat. He bent and whispered to her, and gently unhooked her skirt. Ainsley rose, holding Windsor in her arms, and moved to the other side of the lovely young girl, and together the three walked slowly, with dignity, down the aisle.

Infuriated, Reverend Witherspoon forbade them to go. "If you stand with her, you stand against God!" he shouted.

Silently, they continued toward the door. Suddenly, Mrs. Eversham stood up and began to walk behind them, and then the school teacher stood, and the manager of the general store, the foreman of the shoe factory, the old tanner—one by one the members of the congregation stood and filed silently from the church. Behind them they could hear the voice of the Reverend Witherspoon roaring, threatening them with fire and brimstone and the wrath of heaven.

With sympathy and love the women of the congregation surrounded the young girl and eased the sting of her humiliation. At last the group began to break up and return to their homes. Talmadge saw Ainsley to their carriage and told her he would walk back to Marshfield later, or borrow a horse. She did not ask what he intended to do.

The Reverend Witherspoon was still standing in the pulpit, glowering at the empty church, when Talmadge walked back up the aisle. "You shall all be damned," he said with quiet venom. "All of you."

"Perhaps," Talmadge replied. "But not by you, Reverend Witherspoon. You have long since abandoned your calling. You have ceased to minister to others or to the Lord, and so now, I give you the opportunity to resign from this pulpit. If you do not do so, I shall see that you are dismissed in disgrace. You are no longer the minister of this parish—or any other. I will inform the Congregational committee of this and, if you choose to fight it, I will have every member of this congregation come and denounce you publicly."

The Reverend Witherspoon opened his mouth to protest with fury, but Talmadge raised a peremptory hand.

"Listen to me, and listen well, Reverend Witherspoon. If you fight this in any way you will be accused of drunkenness, of preaching false doctrine, of cruelty, of neglect of pastoral duties, of brutality, and perhaps even of contributing to suicide. If such charges are made, you will become an outcast." Talmadge's voice held an edge of pity.

"I do not know why you have become a man of such intemperate nature—a man who uses the word of God to flail the hearts of your parishioners—but I think it must come from some inner sickness that has grown greater with the years." Talmadge paused, and the Reverend Witherspoon, for the first time, seemed drained of anger. He looked like a kite which had lost the wind, and before Talmadge's eyes he seemed to shrink into a wizened, wretched old man.

"How you make your peace with God and with the citizens of this community is up to you. Whether you wish to continue to live here is up to you. But from this moment, you will never preach in this or any pulpit again. You will have no more jurisdiction or access to tax money, and you may make no call of authority of any kind upon any member of this congregation."

Talmadge's voice was quiet, but the strength of his authority overrode any argument or protest the minister could muster. He knew, after the congregation had filed out today, that he had lost all credibility. He knew that Talmadge's threat of complete disgrace and expulsion was not only possible but probable. In the disaster that yawned before him, his only hope was that Talmadge would let the matter rest, and would allow him to remain in the old parsonage. Still, he could not acknowledge Talmadge's kindness and generosity.

"I speak only for the Lord," Witherspoon insisted. "This congregation has been too weak to heed his word. You have spurned the sword of God."

Talmadge shook his head pityingly. "You have misread His message if you think it is of the sword. How could a man of God fall so far from His hand?"

With that Talmadge turned on his heel and prepared to leave the building. "And the parsonage?" the minister whined. "I suppose you will throw me from my home as well as from my church."

Pausing in thought for a moment, Talmadge did not even turn to face the minister again. "Keep it!" He flung the words over his shoulder. "No true minister would want to live in it for fear your spirit might remain in the walls."

Because of the war, no minister was available to replace the Reverend Witherspoon, and so for five long years, no permanent minister occupied the pulpit in the church at New Parrish. Itinerant ministers preached, and sometimes members of the congregation spoke, but the pulpit remained vacant.

When Witherspoon died the following year, Talmadge purchased the old parsonage. He gutted the house, remodeled and repainted it, and gave it to the family of a wounded veteran of the town's Train Band. The wife loved the house, and when the first summer of peace came, she painted a dainty sign and hung it on a tree by the roadside. "Apple Hill," she had named the place, and soon the town forgot that it had ever been a parsonage.

Chapter Forty-four

Windsor!" Ainsley called, "stop teasing Tricia!" The two children were rolling down the hill in the deep grass, laughing and spilling over one another like rambunctious puppies.

"My goodness, Letty . . ." Ainsley laughed, but her cheeks were flushed with embarrassment. ". . . I don't know what's come over the boy. He is usually better mannered than this, I promise you."

The two women were sitting on a blanket at the top of the hill. Below them spread the south pasture with the cows, black and white against the velvet green of the grass, and the wink of the river, blue and crystal beyond.

It was a perfect summer's day, made all the more perfect because of the visit of Ainsley's oldest and dearest friend, Letty. The war was finally over—all those long and bitter years of deprivation. Throughout the war, Letty had remained under house arrest. In the little town which her grandparents had founded, in the townhouse where she was born she had been allowed to remain with her little children because of old friendships and regard. However all of her estates and holdings had been confiscated. She lived in one bare room with her children. Destitute, isolated, dependent on charity, she had remained stoic, courageous, and sweet. Her oldest son had gone to Canada at the start of the war, and was married now. Martin had been killed toward the end of the fighting somewhere in upstate New York, but, in the confusion of the British pullout, Letty had never been able to find where he had been buried. He had visited her only once, during the war. In secret. That was when Tricia was conceived.

As soon as Talmadge was sure it was safe, he had sent two trusted men, who had worked with his intelligence organization during the war, to fetch Letty and her younger children to Marshfield as a surprise for Ainsley. It was one of the most beautiful presents Talmadge had ever given her. When she saw Letty, it was as though the years had fallen away, and the two women ran and embraced one another as long lost sisters.

Ainsley could only guess at the deprivations, humiliations, and loneliness which Letty had endured. Letty's hair was as white as snow and she was very thin, but her face was young and unlined, and her beautiful brown eyes had in them a serenity and inner strength which reminded Ainsley of Talmadge.

It was as though the terrible war had not destroyed the two people who were dearest to her, but rather deepened and enriched them until they seemed to know and understand the human heart more fully than could be expected in ordinary mortal experience.

How Ainsley loved them! And yet, how she wished her own impulsive and impassioned nature could have found such depth and wisdom. In some ways she felt she had remained unchanged, still running wherever her heart led her. And, in truth, it led her, always, straight to Talmadge and to Windsor.

Even now, sitting in the pleasant warmth of the afternoon, she could look up, beyond the house, to the copse of oak trees, and, even though she considered herself a prim middle-aged woman, she found herself blushing with the memory of Talmadge and their lovemaking in the trees. Her unruly heart yearned for the evening and the sight of Talmadge's dear face, and she found herself trembling with secret excitement at the thought of him beside her in their bed.

The thought of Letty's loneliness smote her with guilt. She turned to her friend with loving eyes. "Dear Letty, I still can't get over the wonder of having you here. It is the most happy thing I can imagine. Tell me you will stay as Talmadge is urging you to do. Surely you cannot wish to return to New Haven where your friends and neighbors were so cruel to you. I hate them, I really do. How could anyone ever imagine you as treasonous, you are so dear and kind and true."

Letty smiled gently. "My darling friend, in all these years you have changed so little. Still so driven by emotion. They were not hateful, dear Ainsley. Only frightened, and fighting for something they believed in—and I must confess, I have grown to believe in it as well."

With a look of delight, Ainsley reached over and grasped Letty's hand. "Then you will stay? You are not going to Canada? Oh, Letty, that would make me so happy. You and Tricia and young Martin—you belong here, in this new land. It is your country, Letty. Our English heritage will always be a part of us—only now, we can choose the kind of people we want to be, the kind of government we want to have. It will be a great place to raise your younger children, I promise you, Letty."

Her friend nodded. "I know. You see, as long as Martin was alive—and even after . . . after his death—I could not turn from the things he believed in. We thought that loyalty was the greater virtue, but I have come to feel and believe that perhaps our loyalty was misplaced."

Looking at Ainsley intently, Letty continued, "I don't want you to think I regret the stand we took. I will never do that. We believed it was the right thing to do, and we sacrificed everything to that belief. But some of my neighbors were kind—they ignored personal danger to be our friends. They smuggled in what food, papers, and comfort they could—and through their kindness I began to think."

Ainsley was listening with tears in her eyes, trying to imagine Letty with her two children, one a newborn baby, isolated and rejected in the community where she had been born and raised. The thought was almost too painful for Ainsley to contemplate.

"When I lost my freedom for all of those years, I began to understand how precious freedom was. There were times when I would have given everything—even my own life—to be free. Then I began to understand why our country had to fight, why we had to declare our independence. Without freedom the human spirit dies as surely as a plant dies without light."

Tears were streaming down Ainsley's face. "Oh, Letty, please stay with us. Let us help you forget all about those awful years. Let us help you raise these two youngest children, for love of you and them—and in memory of Martin."

Just then a scream came up from the hill and Ainsley jumped to her feet to see seven-year-old Patricia Brewerton racing, screaming and laughing at the same time, pell-mell down the hill. In her hand she held Windsor's kite, which he had brought to fly during their picnic. Windsor was roaring after her, reaching for the kite, but she was managing to hold it out of his reach.

At the last moment, he dived for the kite, tackling the little girl, and the two of them fell in a tangle.

Ainsley and Letty, forgetting all dignity, ran down the hill, skirts flying, and pulled the children apart and dusted them off.

"Tricia!" Letty scolded, "will you stop bedeviling Windsor! I wouldn't blame him if he forgot you were a girl altogether and pummeled you. If he doesn't, I think I shall!"

"No!" Ainsley apologized, "it is Windsor to blame. He has completely lost his sense of propriety. Windsor, you will apologize immediately. Look what you have done to Tricia's lovely dress. It is ruined."

"My kite is ruined, too," Windsor retorted. "She's a girl, and she doesn't know how to fly a kite. I told her I'd show her, but she said she could do it better than I, and she ran off with it. Girls are supposed to be quiet and pretty. She's always trying to show off."

"Oh, Letty," Ainsley said in dismay, "I don't know what's gotten into him!"

"I do," Letty said with grim humor. "Tricia. That's what's happened to him. I declare, Ainsley, she is the most strong-willed, determined, fearless child who ever lived. If I didn't know better, I would say she was your daughter instead of mine!"

Ainsley looked up in astonishment at her friend's teasing smile, and they both burst into laughter. "Well," Ainsley admitted reluctantly, "maybe I do understand her. I know it would have driven me wild to have a boy tell me he could do something that I couldn't do, or could do it better! I would just have to show him it wasn't so!"

They hauled the two children up the hill to the house, and took them to their rooms for baths and fresh clothes. Windsor glared in baleful silence at Tricia, and she pertly stuck her tongue out at him as they parted.

It had been like that from the moment Letty and her family had arrived. Windsor, who was a strong-willed, independent, self-confident child, had never had a brother or sister to challenge him. He was a handsome boy, strong and tall for his age, agile and competent. With golden-blond hair, and startling blue eyes, and his skin tanned to a dusky gold by long days spent with his father in the open air, he was the joy of Talmadge and Ainsley's lives.

Letty's son Martin was twelve years old, and Talmadge had arranged to have him sent to a local preparatory school. The boy was slender and small for his age from the years of confinement and low rations, but Letty had tutored him, and he was bright, intense, and knowledgeable.

"I want to be a lawyer," he had told Talmadge, when Talmadge had his first long conversation with the fatherless boy. "I want to understand about law and justice, and what is right and what is not right."

Never had a boy gone so eagerly to school. "It was like watching a hungry man walk into a room where the tables are set with a banquet," Talmadge told Letty and Ainsley when he returned from registering young Martin at the school.

"He will board at the school, and receive personal tutoring until he feels ready to join his form," Talmadge explained. "I know you will miss him, Letty, but he will be with you one weekend each month and on the holidays."

Letty nodded. "I shall miss him, but I know he is where he wants to be—where he must be. Thank you, Talmadge."

Young Patricia Brewerton—whom everyone called Tricia—was another matter altogether. She too was small for her age, but wiry. Her little feet were as swift as sparrow's wings and she ran everywhere. It was as though, after a lifetime of confinement, she could not see enough, do enough, hear enough, discover enough.

Marshfield to Tricia was a cornucopia of wonder and possibilities, and she was determined to explore them all. Unfortunately, she knew no boundaries, and Windsor, feeling extremely territorial and challenged by this bright, swift, delightful bird of prey, reacted with masculine assertiveness and superiority.

The two clashed constantly. Their favorite conversation was " 'Tis . . ." " 'Tis not . . ." " 'Tis . . ." " 'Tis not . . . !" until one attacked the other, and the struggle was enjoined.

Very quickly the mothers realized, however, that the worse punishment for such wild behavior was to separate the two children. When they were together they fought, but when they were apart they were bereft and seemed as though their hearts would break.

One thing Ainsley had discovered quite by accident was

that when there was no challenge of superiority or territory between them, they played together with such natural coordination and mutual understanding that it was almost as though they had one mind. She watched them once when they found a wounded rabbit, and they mended and bandaged the rabbit together, each taking a natural part in the process, almost as though they had a blueprint of what to do, and the look of pain, caring, and responsibility in their eyes was identical. One mind, one heart. Then, the next minute, they were fighting like cats and dogs over which one of them should have the rabbit in their room.

As the summer waned, Talmadge went to Letty with an idea. "Letty," he said, "Ainsley and I have been talking. With Patricia and Martin still to raise, we know you would be happier with a home of your own—as happy as we are to have you stay here at Marshfield forever."

Letty nodded.

"This is our thought. Windsor Inn has been closed for the duration of the war, but now, as peacetime has increased the traffic on the Post Road, Norwalk Trace, and White Oak Trace considerably, we feel it would be wise and feasible to reopen the inn.

"We both love that old house, and, with repainting and repairs, we think it could make a wonderful home for you and your family—and still keep you close to us."

"Talmadge!" Letty exclaimed. "I could not accept such charity!"

"Not charity," Talmadge answered swiftly. "It is you who would be doing us a favor. We have bought the property back from Brosian, who has grown far too old and weak to care for it. He will spend the remainder of his days here with us. This is an important commercial enterprise for us. We need a good innkeeper—the best. You are a gracious hostess, a wise and experienced homemaker—you could make the inn a success. We know it."

Letty paused, looking at her thin hands crossed in her lap. "But, but, how can you be sure?"

Talmadge came forward and put his hands over Letty's. "Anyone who can survive what you have suffered, can do anything, dear Letty. But you are more than a survivor. You are a builder. And that's what this country needs now—men and women who have the courage to build on the trials and triumphs of the past."

So it was that Letty Brewerton oversaw the restoration of Windsor Inn. With each day she grew to love the old building more, and, by the time the work was completed, and the gracious dining room reinstated, she was grown healthy and strong and ready for the steady stream of eager customers that crossed the threshold.

The dock was repaired and used as a pleasure wharf, and the old supply stores became a shop for imported goods. People came from Norwalk, Rowayton, New Parrish, and as far away as Southport to look at Letty's abundant merchandise and to spend a night in the beautiful inn by the waters of the sound.

True to his word, Talmadge had closed Marshfield as an inn. He took out the partitions in the public rooms and turned the east wing into a splendid salon. From Letty he had bought the last of her possessions—a warehouse full of English furniture, paintings, silver, and oriental rugs, which her parents had shipped from the Continent the year of her marriage to Martin.

The household goods had not been taken out of storage during the years of war and, although all the rest of the Brewerton properties had been confiscated, the stored goods had not been included in the confiscation order. The money which Talmadge paid to Letty for the furnishings was enough to keep her in comfort and to pay for young Martin's complete legal education, as well as a dowry for young Patricia when the time came.

For the first time since the war, Letty knew the feeling of peace and security once again.

When the English treasures were installed, the pictures hung, and the rest of the house furnished with the most beautiful furniture crafted in Connecticut, Marshfield was equal to the long-ago vision which Nathan had when he first stood on the ridge and knew this was to be the place where his family would flourish.

The shoe factory was flourishing. Talmadge expanded it by buying the next house and connecting it to the original factory building by an annex. He also continued Nathan's project of buying choice and abandoned property in New Parrish. When he found bright young veterans home from the war and eager to start a family and work, he installed them on his far-flung properties, helped them to begin farms or businesses, and gave them the opportunity to buy the land if they so chose.

Gradually, through his influence and wisdom, the town of New Parrish began to re-establish itself, and the little town center bustled with new shops and bright new carriages, and the church on the village green received a new white coat of paint.

Two years after the war was finished, the year that Windsor turned eight, New Parrish finally found a permanent minister for its pulpit. For six months, ministers were sent to audition for the assignment, and the consensus fell on a young man only ten years out of the divinity school at Yale, but brilliant and warmhearted.

The young Reverend Buckingham loved the New Testament. He listened to the words of John the Beloved, and he reached his hands out to the weary and heart-sore congregation and seemed to hold them symbolically in his young, strong arms. "Come unto Him all ye that labor and are heavy laden, and He will give you peace," this very modern minister declared. The message fell like rain on dusty hearts, and, for the first time, the congregation of New Parrish had in its ministry a man who was on an errand from God.

The young Reverend Buckingham brought his pretty new wife to the brand-new parsonage and acres which the town—or rather, Talmadge—had given to him as his covenant gift. In the next months, Reverend Buckingham began his lifetime of visitations, which he kept track of in a careful accounting book. Each day of his life he visited in the homes of his flock. He attended newborns and new mothers, he went to the houses of grief, illness, and sorrow, he attended weddings and engagements, he reached out for the sinner and the proud, he helped plant and reap, and he loved them all.

One evening, Ainsley and Talmadge sat in front of the roaring fire in the marble-manteled fireplace in the grand salon. Tricia was visiting and she and Windsor had had a wonderful time until after dinner when they had been playing cards in the salon while Talmadge and Ainsley sat quietly reading.

Suddenly an argument had arisen over whether or not

Windsor had cheated. The boy was outraged. "I never cheat!" he shouted. "Never! I am a man of honor!"

"That may be," Tricia countered, "but I still think you peeked at my cards."

The quarreling escalated until Windsor, tried beyond his patience, grabbed the cards and flung them into the fire. "There!" he shouted, "that is what I think of your cards!"

With good-humored exasperation, Talmadge had sent the two off to bed, and later on, Ainsley had gone up to check on them and had found the two, in their flannel nightclothes, sitting on the top step of the grand staircase, laughing and whispering as though there had never been a moment of unhappiness.

"I had to tell him I was sorry," Tricia explained to Ainsley as she tucked the darling child back into bed.

"Oh, Tricia," Ainsley said, brushing the little girl's smooth chestnut hair back from her pretty brow, "I do understand very well. I know when you see injustice, or feel threatened, you just have to speak out or you feel you will burst! But I have learned that sometimes it is wiser to be sweet and gentle, and then the desires of your heart are not pushed away. They come to you of their own accord, on quiet little feet."

Tricia smiled. "That sounds so pretty, Mistress Fairchild. And I have so many desires in my heart. I just find myself wanting and wanting. I want to do everything, to be everything—with Windsor. It's always more fun with Windsor."

Laughing, Ainsley bent and kissed the lovely child whose dark eyes, so like her mother's, seemed to have in them a hidden, glorious fire. "You are so beautiful, you will have everything. It will just come to you. You won't need to fight for it. You don't ever need to fight. Just open your hand."

With a sigh, as though a heavy load had been lifted, the little girl closed her eyes and was asleep before she took her next breath.

Now, husband and wife sat companionably alone in the great room. "I love this room so much," Ainsley whispered with a little sigh of contentment. "At moments like this, I am almost afraid. It is as though our lives are too perfect. Too happy. I fear some angry god of the demiworld will become jealous and wish us harm. Isn't that what the people of the Orient fear?"

Talmadge glanced up from his book. "Do not fear the gifts, Ainsley. Understand them. We were given this for a purpose. This new country, this place to belong, our preserved lives—family, friends—It all has purpose."

She went over to kiss him, and hand in hand they went to bed.

Chapter Forty-five

The next morning cold blasts of wind rattled the windows and wakened them. The sky was dark gray, and so heavy it seemed to touch the trees. Within an hour, the winds were lashing the heavy limbs and stripping the last of the leaves from the branches of the woods.

"It's going to be a heavy storm," Talmadge shouted, rousing the farmhands and servants. "The stock needs to be secured in the barns, and the cattle need to be herded to safety. The lower pastures may flood; we'd better get them to high ground." Assignments were handed out. The wind was cold and damp, and whipped the men and women as they rushed to their work. Horses, chickens, and milk cows were led to shelter.

Ainsley spent the morning securing the house. Shutters were pulled closed, the washing reeled in, loose baskets, buckets, and tools placed in the storage sheds, and extra food brought in from the root cellar.

The storm was heading in from the sound, and as the sky grew blacker, with a sickly greenish hue, they knew it was going to be a furious autumn hurricane, and the time for preparation was limited.

With a load of half-dried laundry in her arms, Ainsley hurried up the center staircase calling for Windsor to come help pick the corn in the kitchen garden before the wind stripped the heavy stalks. There was no answer in the playroom, and she checked both of the children's bedrooms. Running downstairs, she screamed to Mrs. Seeley, "Have you seen the children?"

"I thought they were in the front yard with you," Mrs. Seeley answered. "I saw them go out about half an hour ago."

"What were they doing?" Ainsley asked anxiously.

"Nothing." Mrs. Seeley answered. "I thought they were looking for you. They were carrying a kite."

"Oh no!" Ainsley screamed. "They must think this wind is a plaything!"

She dashed out of the door and nearly ran into Talmadge. "The children!" she gasped. "They've gone off somewhere to fly kites!"

The sky was more ominous than ever, and the wind lashed at her face. A streak of lightning clapped down, lighting the darkness fiercely for a brief instant.

Talmadge had been leading his horse toward the barn, but now, without a word, he wheeled himself up into the saddle. "Go alert everyone to search. They can't have gone far. I shall head up the ridge—they would go for the high ground."

Ainsley watched him gallop into the wind and gloom and she ran around the house, shouting their names. The servants spread in every direction, everyone calling.

Just as she began to fear the search was hopeless, she saw Mr. Seeley running toward her, the two children holding his hands. "They were heading over to the south pasture; I caught them in time. Foolish young ones!" His voice shook more with relief than anger.

Ainsley ordered the children into the house, then ran to inform the rest of the searchers and told everyone to seek cover. Her greatest concern now was for Talmadge, and she hurried, walking, up the path to the ridge, but the wind almost blew her down.

Struggling and fighting, her cloak and clothes a terrible hindrance as they beat around her limbs, she pushed her way up the path. As she entered the grove of oak trees there was some shelter from the wind and she leaned against a tree to get her breath.

Talmadge's strong, brave horse fought its way speedily to the top of the ridge. Talmadge looked as far as his eyes could see in the gathering darkness and shouted the children's names, but his voice was pulled from his mouth. He wheeled to return down the path, and his horse shied from a figure standing next to the stone fence of the little cemetery.

In the confusion of the wild wind, the first onslaught of the heavy rain, the drops like steel, and the swirling of the dark cloak of the unexpected stranger in its face, the stallion

reared back. Talmadge, with his stiff leg, struggling to keep
his seat, did not see what happened, but he heard a sickening
thud, and then, looking down as he tried to calm the frantic
horse, he saw the person lying on the ground.

Gently patting the horse, fighting for control, Talmadge
dismounted and approached the prone man. He rolled the
figure over and drew back. It was Junius Comstock, looking
old and wizened, with a blood-red gash on his forehead
where Talmadge's horse had struck him with a wild hoof.

The wind was shrieking, and the horse was shuddering
with panic. The rain hammered down. Without a moment to
think, Talmadge loaded the inert body of the man across the
saddle, and, holding the reins firmly, soaked to the skin and
buffeted by the wind, he hurried down the path toward the
safety of Marshfield.

Halfway home the wind tore a gigantic limb from an ancient tree and it crashed in front of him, grazing his shoulder. The horse tried to bolt, and by now the rain was coming
in sluices so thick that Talmadge could not see his own feet.
For one ghastly moment, he was tempted to let the horse
have its head, to let it run away with its gruesome cargo, but
some deeper, more profound instinct made him grasp the
reins more firmly and lead the horse carefully around the ob-
stacle in their path.

As he slid and fought his way onward, his feet stumbled
on another obstruction, and he reached to push it aside only
to feel it move under his hands.

"Talmadge!" Ainsley cried. "I thought you were lost. I
was trying to reach you. I couldn't stay on my feet—the
wind!"

He could only hear snatches of her voice, but he held her
arm firmly against him, and the two of them, sliding and
slamming into the wind, came down the ridge path. Within
a few yards they were met by helping arms. A crew of the
farmhands had come looking for them, and together, they
made their way back to Marshfield.

The horse was bedded in the barn, where, even though the
wind roared and battered at the walls, the shelter from the
power of the storm seemed like a peaceful haven.

The men carried Comstock into the house and he was
placed in a bedroom in the old inn wing. The farmhands
went to their quarters, thankful to know that everyone was

accounted for. Now all had done their best and the storm would have its way.

When Ainsley saw the dreadful burden Talmadge had brought home she only asked in fear and anger, "Here? You brought him here?"

"What else could I do?" Talmadge asked quietly. His leg was throbbing and he was chilled to the bone.

"You could have left him," Ainsley said through gritted teeth.

The storm raged for four days, and the patient raved. None of the women servants could bear to look at the man's ruined face, and so Talmadge appointed one of the farm-hands who was adept at veterinary medicine to tend to the needs of the injured man as best as he could.

Talmadge had examined Comstock and felt that his collapse was due to illness more than to the blow to his head. He was running a high fever, he was painfully thin and jaundiced, and his clothes were filthy and in tatters. Watching the wretched human as he twisted on the bed, starting from his fevered dreams with fear and screams and then falling back, exhausted, Talmadge saw a shattered man, a person stripped of every vestige of decency and comfort.

In spite of himself, Talmadge felt pity. Who knew, who would ever know, what demon had beset the life of Junius Comstock? Whatever it was, it had racked its own penalty and it was beyond the bearing of the human spirit.

The young farmhand proved to be a good nurse. He showed no qualms about Junius's scarred and mutilated face, but simply cleansed, washed, dressed, fed, and administered to the needs of the delirious patient.

Most of the time nothing Junius said made any sense, but over and over again he repeated three sentences: "He is Nathan's son. I know it. I have seen him."

When Talmadge came on the fourth night, as the storm was finally abating, to check to Junius's progress, the young man said, "He keeps talking about you, Master Fairchild. He keeps talking about 'Nathan's son.' " I guess he recognized you before the horse kicked him."

Talmadge frowned thoughtfully. "Is he getting better?" he asked. "Is he coming to himself?"

The young servant shrugged his shoulders. "Perhaps. He is sleeping peacefully for the first time. I was going in to wake him and give him some broth."

"You may take a rest," Talmadge said. "I will go in and feed him." Talmadge took the broth from the man's hand and stepped into the bedroom.

The room had the smell of illness. In one corner, soiled linen waited to be taken to the washhouse. It was only raining slightly, and so Talmadge opened the window a crack. The cool, damp air stirred the staleness.

Junius was still sleeping, so Talmadge added another log to the fire and then sat down in the Windsor chair next to the bed and stared at his family's old enemy. His mind and heart were full of jumbled emotions.

It was almost an hour before Junius awoke. When he opened his eyes, he was lucid for the first time. For a long steady moment he and Talmadge stared at one another.

"You should have killed me," Junius whispered hoarsely, "when you had the chance. I will tell. I have heard Ainsley speak it. I have seen the boy. I know he is not your son. I will tell. People will believe me. He looks just like Nathan. You should have killed me. You are a fool." Junius's head fell to the side, and he was asleep again.

"Perhaps," Talmadge answered. "Perhaps."

Ainsley would have nothing to do with Junius. She refused to go to the bedroom where he was slowly recovering a little of his strength. The man was obviously dying. "Some worm is eating me from inside," he told Palmer, the lad who nursed him. "But I have one more thing to do before I die, and I will live to do it—but I must get well enough to quit the charity of this house first."

Talmadge visited every day, but said little. He inquired after Junius's health and his needs, and then went his way. However, unknown to both Talmadge and Ainsley, young Tricia, impelled by curiosity at the comings and goings from the room in the side hall, had peeked inside and had seen the man lying in bed.

At first she was horrified at his face and could not wait to tell Windsor that his father had a monster hidden in a bedroom. Windsor, outraged at such a lie, followed her to the room to prove her wrong, and he, too, spied the unknown being lying sleeping under the Marshfield roof.

It was as though an irresistible fascination had enveloped both of the children. They spent hours in the corridor, listening, peeking through the door, and bedeviling young Palmer to tell them who the man was that he was taking care of.

"He's just a poor stranger, out of his mind, that your father rescued in the storm. Now begone, the two of you; the man is not well, and he has no time or energy for the likes of you."

Late one afternoon, when Palmer was away and the children were sure the stranger was sleeping, they managed to creep into the room and up to his bed to get a closer look.

By now they were quite used to his appearance and did not find it repulsive, just a matter of intense curiosity. As they stood, silently, staring at the sleeping man, they suddenly became aware of the fact that though he had not moved or made a sign, his eyes were open and he was looking back at them.

Windsor gave a startled gasp, and Tricia moved closer to her friend, trying to hide behind his taller shoulder.

"You, boy," the apparition hissed, "stand in the light. I want to look at you."

Windsor, moved by the sight of the helpless, ruined man, wanted somehow to make him feel happier, more cared about. Without fear or argument, he moved closer to the window, and Junius searched the young boy's open, handsome face.

"I knew it!" Junius gloated. "I knew it! I saw you from afar one day when you were picnicking, and I knew it. You look just like your father."

"Thank you, sir," Windsor said. "I think so too, although I do not know if I shall ever be so tall and strong. All except for the black hair, of course. I have my grandfather's hair."

The boy spoke with such a natural friendliness and guilelessness that Junius was taken aback. Tricia said nothing, only stood staring at him still.

"Well," Junius growled at her, "don't you want to run screaming to your mama? Aren't I the most ugly thing you have ever seen?"

"No, sir," Tricia answered. "You are the saddest. I think you must be very sick, and Windsor and I do so wish to help, but we do not know what to do."

Windsor walked forward. "The weather won't stay this awful. We shall get Palmer to take you out to the gardens as soon as you are feeling better."

"Do you like to play cards?" Tricia asked. "We adore to

play cards—although I don't like to play with Windsor for
he cheats."

In spite of himself Junius smiled, and murmured with
mild sarcasm, "Cheating is not in the Fairchild tradition, my
boy. You shall have to mend your ways or you shall live in
my world where cheating is common but leads to ruin and
death."

"Your world?" Tricia breathed, fascinated by the exotic
mystery that seemed to surround this ruin of a man.

Junius gave a dry chuckle. "The gaming world. A world
where cheating is a capital offense."

"There," Tricia said, putting her small fists on her hips
and turning to Windsor, "I told you it could get you into
trouble."

"I don't cheat!" Windsor roared. "You dropped the card
on the floor. I couldn't help but see it. And I told you I had
seen it!"

"Be quiet!" Junius's voice was raised. He had not even realized himself that he had that much strength left in him.
"This is a sickroom, and you will treat it with respect. No
more shouting."

Just then, Palmer entered the room. He could not believe
that the children were in the room, and he shooed them out,
afraid that he might get into trouble for allowing them there.

"We'll come back with the cards," Tricia called over her
shoulder as the door was firmly closed.

That evening, Junius sat up in bed for the first time, and
tried to choke down some food. His cheeks had a spot of
color, and his eyes looked clear and lucid. Palmer could not
believe the improvement.

Each afternoon, when Palmer went down to the kitchen to
prepare the invalid's supper and to visit with the chambermaid, Tricia and Windsor slipped into Junius Comstock's
sickroom and brought cards, or books, or treasures from
their pockets.

One evening they brought a toad that Windsor had found
in a puddle in the garden after the rains had ceased. The autumn air had turned warm again, although there was a crisp
edge to the wind and the trees were unnaturally bare for this
early in the year because of the devastation of the storm.

It had taken almost a week for the roads and pathways to
be cleared of fallen branches, and the gardens had been up-
rooted. However, most of the damage was quickly repaired,

and the harvest moved swiftly. Talmadge became so involved in the retting of the flax, so that the linen could be sent to the weavers, that he was not able to visit Junius for several days.

Toward the end of the second week, late in the evening, Talmadge wearily mounted the stairs and walked through the corridors to Junius's room. He wondered how Palmer was managing, and if Junius was ready to travel yet. Opening the door, he was astonished at the sight. A warm fire was blazing in the hearth, and Junius was sitting up in his bed propped by pillows. An earthen pitcher filled with late autumn asters was on the bed table, and Windsor was sitting at the foot of the bed. A chess board was on a small standing tray between them, and Windsor was preparing to make a move.

"Think carefully, my boy," Junius said hoarsely, his voice little more than a rasp. "Remember what I told you about the knight and the rook." Windsor's hand paused. He thought carefully, and then broke into a smile and confidently moved a piece. Junius nodded in satisfaction. "Now you are beginning to understand the game," he said.

Seated on a footstool on the floor, Tricia was watching the game steadily. "The two of you are getting better by the day," Junius said, smiling down at her. "Tomorrow you shall play one another, and I will help both of you. You can only learn by playing."

Not knowing what to think of the scene, Talmadge cleared his throat and the three looked up at him in surprise.

"Thought you'd been swallowed by the earth," Junius growled at Talmadge. "Maybe I just hoped you had."

Windsor leaped up. "Father! We have been keeping Master Comstock company while Palmer attends other chores."

With a smile, Tricia stood up too. "It has been ever so exciting to have something to do. Master Comstock is a very good patient. That's what Palmer says."

"I'll excuse the two of you now," Talmadge said mildly. Without arguing they left the room, and Talmadge stared at Junius for a long moment.

"You are not well enough to be moved, according to Palmer," Talmadge said coolly, "therefore you shall continue to be cared for in the house. We will see to your every need, until you, or we, can make other arrangements."

"Am I your prisoner then?" Junius sneered.

"No," Talmadge said calmly. "You are the prisoner of your illness, your dissolute life. But I promise you, I will do nothing to hasten the end of that life—and you, in turn, must promise me that while you are in this home you will not attempt to spread damaging lies or to reveal our past associations. What you do after you leave the protection of my roof is your own affair."

"You should have killed me," Junius repeated miserably. "Why couldn't you have been merciful and left me to die?"

Talmadge shook his head. "I don't know," he said, "I honestly don't know."

Two more weeks passed and Junius became weaker. The children continued their nightly visits, somehow knowing when he was able to listen to their chatter and stories or to play with them, and other times wise enough just to sit quietly.

Sometimes Tricia sang, sitting next to the winking fire, and young Windsor worked with his penknife on a wooden carving. The room was filled with a cozy quiet, and Junius often could fall into a restful sleep.

Palmer knew Comstock's days were numbered. The man was too weak to turn himself in bed, and one morning, Palmer saw a deep bronzing in Junius's skin. When Junius opened his eyes the whites were saffron-yellow. The man's liver had collapsed completely.

The children came running into the room and threw open the windows. "Today has got to be the day, Palmer!" Windsor exclaimed. "Look outside. The sun is as bright and warm as summer, and Master Comstock has never even seen our garden. Oh, please, do carry him down and let him sit in the sun."

Tricia had walked over to the bed to greet Junius. The glow of the jaundice gave the invalid a false appearance of health and she laughed with delight. "Oh, dear Master Comstock! We knew you would get better. See, we shall take you out into the sun, and you will be up and about in no time. You look ever so sprightly today."

Junius, filled with the irony of her words, took a perverse pleasure in the plan. "Yes, dear Palmer," he whispered, "I think I feel perfectly well enough for a visit to the garden if you would be so kind."

Against his better judgment, Palmer allowed the children

to convince him to carry Junius down to the gazebo. It was a warm, almost a sultry day, and perhaps the air might help.

When Junius was installed in the padded wicker chair, with blankets, pillows, and shawls to prop him and keep him warm, the two children ran hither and fro, bringing him flowers, butterflies, grapes, and pretty stones.

"Now," Windsor said, "we shall saddle our pony with her red leather saddle, and come show you all of her tricks."

"Just a moment," Junius whispered, beckoning them over. They came close to him, their wonderful faces shining with innocence and the freely given affection of the very young. Standing by his chair, they looked at him, waiting for his request.

"Why do you do these things?" Comstock asked. "Why do you spend time with me when you could be off playing? What am I to you?"

"Our friend," said Tricia promptly. Then she stood on her tiptoes and kissed him right where the great scar of the branding iron had welted his cheek.

While the children were in the barn, saddling the pony, Talmadge came out of the house. Palmer, concerned that he had overstepped his bounds, had gone to Talmadge to tell him he had taken the patient into the garden.

"I doubt he'll last the night," Palmer said. "The man's liver has stopped, and he is filling up with his own poisons."

Talmadge could not help but think of the bitter symbolism of such a death. Junius had lived his life filled up with his own poisons, and, in the end, that was how he would die.

Walking toward the gazebo, Talmadge looked at the still figure in its wrappings, and wondered if he was too late, but when he arrived, Junius opened his eyes and spoke.

"Talmadge, you limp because of my hatred," Junius's voice was so soft, Talmadge had to stoop to hear the words. "I do not apologize." There was the breath of old defiance and hate in the voice. "What I have done, I have done."

Talmadge nodded, understanding in some half-perceived way. There was no rewriting of the past.

A long shudder shook the sick man, and Talmadge listened to see if the breathing had stopped. Then the voice started again. "He is his father's son. But so are you." Another long pause, and then the voice came a little stronger.

"I could have told. I could have told Palmer. He's a gossip

and in love with rumor. I could have told him and the whole
house would have been a-buzz—and then the whole town.
Shock—that's what all these righteous do-gooders that you
think are your fine neighbors want. Shock. And they'd turn
on you. Right as the day turns to night, they'd turn on you."

A long shuddering coursed through Junius's body, and
Talmadge put out his hand

"Calm yourself, Junius. It is too late for such things."

"Not too late," Junius gasped. "I could have ruined you.
I could have ruined the boy . . ." Suddenly Junius's frame
began shaking and Talmadge thought he must be having a
fit, but then he saw Comstock's mouth, which was stretched
into a smile, and heard from his twisted lips the sound of
dry, wheezing laughter. "I could have ruined him, and you
and Ainsley, but you, you have the last laugh—because instead he ruined me. He ruined me with his friendship. All of
you did."

Junius's head fell, and the laughter turned to desperate
tears. "Everything I was, everything I vowed to do—the
things I have hated all my life—these things were my life,
and he ruined them with his friendship. It was all for nothing. A little boy's friendship—it checkmated my hate, and
everything else became nothing."

Talmadge reached out with his strong hand and took
Junius's yellow claw in his own. "It is over, Junius. The past
is gone and done. All we have is today. Let it heal, Junius.
Let it go. A boy's friendship is not a bad bridge on which to
cross over into tomorrow."

For one brief instant Junius returned the forgiving clasp of
Talmadge's hand, and then his hand fell limp.

Talmadge knew Junius's life was over, but he sat in the
gazebo beside the shadow of his family's old enemy and felt
the miracle of healing pull around him like a great shining
cloud.

In the rosy sunlight of the afternoon, Marshfield had never
looked more beautiful. The walls were covered with growing tendrils of loving ivy, and the garden pathways and
pruned grapevines lay ready for the fallow season of winter
and the promise of spring.

From the barn he saw Windsor and Tricia bringing the
pony. Windsor had lifted Tricia into the saddle, and he was
leading the pony across the lawn. The two children were
talking to one another, the one with his golden head, so like

Nathan's, shining in the light, and the other with her long, smooth chestnut hair and dancing eyes, like an elfin spirit captured in the wilds and brought to the gardens of man to delight and teach.

Ainsley stepped from the kitchen door. She was wearing a dress of autumn gold and her walk was as graceful and young as it had been when he had first seen her on the lawn of Marshfield those many years ago.

For one brief moment, in the blinding circle of the sun, he saw the past, the present, and the future, like some great and wondrous vision—and he knew that all was well.

Postlude

I tell you yesterday is a wind gone down,
a sun dropped in the west,
I tell you there is nothing in the world only
an ocean of tomorrows,
a sky of tomorrows.

—Carl Sandburg

The two Fairchild men, grandfather and grandson, stood at the edge of Marshfield's snowy hill overlooking the roofs of the growing town of New Parrish. Randall was being sent to officer training, and both men knew the gravity of the situation.

The year was 1861 and the American nation was slashing its way toward civil war. In President Lincoln's inaugural address he had said, "Though passion may have strained, it must not break our bonds of affection." The new President had hoped that time and reason would prevail—but the terrible conflict had moved inexorably toward war.

Windsor Fairchild was eighty-four years old. He had buried his mother and father, Ainsley and Talmadge, four decades earlier. His wife, Patricia Brewerton Fairchild, his only daughter, and her husband had also passed away, and Windsor had been left to raise his young grandson, Randall Fairchild, by himself.

He loved the boy with the great and undying love of a father and grandfather combined. Now it was his painful duty to watch as his grandson buttoned the tunic of his Union officer uniform and prepared to join the company of soldiers already mustering in loose formation on the green in front of New Parrish church.

Randall's young wife, Maria, could not come to say farewell. The weather was raw and she was expecting a child in a few weeks. Her health was precarious. So the two men stood alone, as they had so often through the years of Randall's youth.

Windsor Fairchild looked as frail as a paper kite, as though the slightest breeze would blow him away, but he was still upright and handsome, his golden hair now turned to silver but thick and flowing on his noble head. Randall's hair was as black as a raven, but the two men shared the same strong features—the Fairchild face.

"I am determined to remain upon this earth until I see my first great grandchild," Windsor said. "Don't you fret and worry about things at Marshfield. Maria and I will take care of everything for you until you return."

The two men looked down at the spreading fields, at the distant town and the church steeple, at the ocean where it glinted on the winter horizon and then turned to look at the noble house. Marshfield. More beautiful today than it had been over a century ago when it had been built.

"It's a fine place," Randall said. "I'm proud to have been born here."

"It will still be here when you return," Windsor assured him. "Something was started by your great grandfather on this white oak ridge—something built from the strength of the good earth; something that grew out of men who had to fight the rocks; something that grew out of hearts that had to heal from mortal wounds; something that had to believe in tomorrow to make it through today.

"I hate war, Randall, and yet the irony is that Marshfield was born out of war. It came to life out of wounds and pain, and when you return from this dread battle, where brother will destroy brother, you will come back to this earth, to this very place.

"This will be the way of our family—the Fairchilds—for generations to come. Your children and your childrens' children will come here to gain strength, to learn how to love and be loved—and then they will go out in the world. They will fight wars for liberty and great causes. They will defend those in need. They will struggle to earn a living—to win the prize—to build the nation.

"But something will always bring the Fairchilds back. Back to this place that we sprang from. Back to the source of our strength.

"It will still be here, Randall, if need be, it will help make you—and the country— well and whole once more.

"This place will rebuild what will be destroyed. Something here . . ." Windsor waved his hand and Randall looked out at the freshening sky over the spreading trees, the rooftops, the spires, and the woods and hills. "Something here, my dear, dear grandson, has the power to heal. You and Marshfield hold the future in your hands."